AF098245

B.STEFFENS
L.E.SELLS

Copyright © 2026 by B. Steffens & L.E. Sells

Survive: From the Ashes by B. Steffens & L.E. Sells

All rights reserved.

This book or any portion thereof may **not** be reproduced or used in any manner whatsoever without the express written permission of the authors except for the use of brief quotations in a book review. No part of this work may <u>**ever**</u> be used for training, prompting, feeding, or manipulating, artificial intelligence. Violations will be pursued as intellectual property infringement.

Printed in the United States of America

First Printing, 2026

ISBN : **978-1-968700-94-2**

This is a work of fiction. Names, characters, and events are products of the authors imagination. Any resemblance to real people, living or dead, is purely coincidental.

Front Cover and Formatting: Melissa Cunningham of booklovedesigns.com

Publisher of Record: Indie Author Revolution

B. Steffens + L.E. Sells

PO Box 216, Oakley CA, 94561

b.steffens.book@gmail.com | lesellsbooks@gmail.com

TRIGGER WARNING & TROPES

Fated mates
Trauma bonding
Shifters Fantasy meets cyberpunk
Dragon/phoenix
Revenge
Who did this to you?
Dub-con
Enemies to lovers
Angst
Forced proximity
Virgin
Forbidden love
Abducted/prisoner
Bully romance
Drug/alcohol use
Robots
Torture
Secret identity
Reference to suicide
Strong FMC's
Class differences
Body positivity
Opposites attract
Primal (biting, marking, licking, scenting, chasing)

GLOSSARY OF TERMS

ALTAS: After taking over, humans renamed the planet Altas to commemorate the human scientist and leader Altas Montgomery, who invented the first Mech. Humans refer to the world as Altas.

ASSASSIN BOTS/DROPPERS: Used for mercenary/murder for hire purposes; highly illegal.

ASTRALS: Beings with the ability to shift between human and animal form.

BREATHER: Derogatory term for dragon astrals used by both humans and astrals.

DEALER BOTS/DEALERS/PUSHERS: Robots that serve in gambling halls and illicit trades.

DRONES/FLYERS: Flying robots used for trade and surveillance.

ELYSIA: The home planet of the astrals.

THE GREAT CLASH: The centuries long war that was predominantly fought between Phoenix and Dragon astrals for control over the entirety of Elysia.

MECHS: Robots built by Altas Montgomery that were controlled by the humans for varying purposes.

MECH SUIT/SCABS: A fully mechanical suit operated and worn by human military personnel.

MEDIC BOTS/BIPS: Used in hospitals and science labs for assistance during procedures, calculations, medication administration, patient care, and analysis of data.

THE MERGE/MERGING: When an astral comes of age (roughly between 12-16 years old) they merge with their inner beast, allowing them to shift at will and communicate with them.

MILITARY BOTS/MECHS/GRUNTS: Initially built as a form of protection against hostile astrals but were quickly transformed into soldiers used to fight in the human/astral war.

MUSCLE BOTS/TANKS: Used for heavy lifting, construction and other difficult jobs.

MUTES: Derogatory term used by humans in reference to astrals.

PLEASURE BOTS/BANG-BOTS/BANGERS: Used for any type of sexual gratification.

POLICE BOTS/PATROL: Used to patrol the cities to instill a sense of security and order.

SERVICE BOTS/SERFS: Used for general services like cleaning, cooking, working class jobs. Boxy top, roller legs for stability in all environments.

THE SLIP: A time/space paradoxical event in which humans were dropped onto the planet of Elysia.

TWITCHER/TWITCH: Derogatory term for phoenix astrals used by both human and astrals.

VENOM (V): Illegal drug found within Elysia with glowing blue and silver appearance. Dissociative anesthetic that forces the body to shut down instantaneously causing immediate death.

PLAYLIST

Listen to the Survive playlist on Spotify

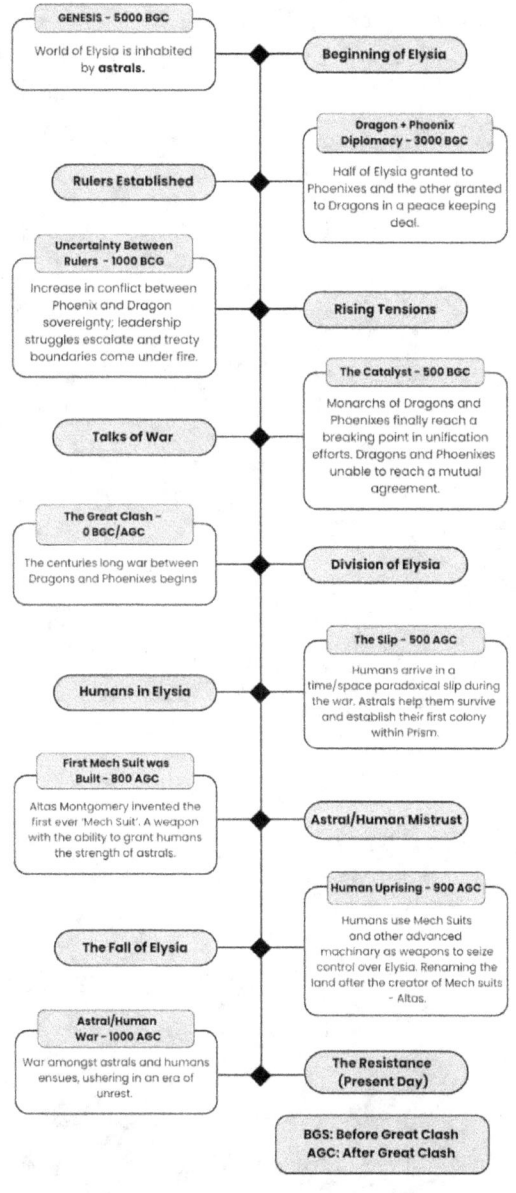

1
EILIDH

"**P**RISONER 2475, STEP FORWARD!"

A deafening buzzer sounds overhead, and I take a step into the dingy yellow stall. Fluorescent lights hum above me, and a single drain sits in the middle of the tiled floor. A hose perched within the wall shoots frigid water at my middle and it's all I can do to cover myself as I'm blasted with its ice-cold spray. The fresh brand on my wrist with my inmate number throbs with pain.

"STRIP DOWN," a voice echoes out over the intercom and with only a small beat of hesitation, I pull my soaked clothes from my body, one by one. "TURN AROUND AND BEND OVER."

Well, aren't they fucking thorough.

A guard holds me forward by the nape of my neck as another searches the depths of me with little humility. I expected it, but my cheeks still heat as their fingers linger longer than necessary, and a firm hand slaps my damp ass. My beast tattooed down my hip and thigh is on full display but the guards pay no mind to the fire bird etching my skin.

"Watch it," I growl.

"Shut your fucking mouth," the same large masculine hand grasps my hair, righting me. "No one here gives a shit about you. What are you going to do about it, huh?" he snaps, and I reel at the stench of his abhorrently bad breath.

Just get through this.

I clench my jaw and keep quiet as the male palms both of my breasts, kneading and playing with my nipples before he sticks his fingers deep in my mouth. He feels around beneath my tongue, working them as far back into my throat as he can manage, attempting to make me gag. His dirt-caked nails and calloused skin leave a bitter taste on my tongue. As a Phoenix, I have no gag reflex, which I'm not sure if this asshole realizes, since it seems me not gagging only encourages him to push his fingers back further.

"That's enough, Ryker," a feminine voice cuts through the silence.

Well at least someone has some tact around here.

"Yes, Sergeant." The male backs away from me and I'm handed a grey towel to dry off along with a pair of bleached, oversize underwear and a black jumpsuit that likely hides the stains from its previous owner. The words *IRONSGATE PENITENTIARY* are stamped in blocky white text on the back.

Once I finish dressing, I'm led to an elevator. The metal doors open and the male guard, Ryker, steps in first, leaving the female guard, Sergeant Nova Jackson according to her uniform, to guide me through. She places a hand on my arm and walks beside me into the tight space, pressing the button labeled 'Level 3' and we descend. I notice Level 1 is missing from the dial-pad.

"Is that on purpose or did the evil minions who built this lair forget how to count?" I motion to the buttons, and she glances at them but turns her hard stare on me. I'm finally able to get a good look at her. She has tightly coiled onyx hair that sticks out in all directions, casting a halo around her sharp ebony face. She's a head taller than me and she holds herself with sturdy confidence, like any of my best trained fighters.

Her dark eyes squint at the sides. Staring at me like I'm an idiot, I realize. "Don't ask questions, Inmate," her voice clear and direct.

Well, I suppose they are less inclined to share the layout of the prison with me, considering my circumstances. I need to remember my rank was left somewhere back in Pyrrh. Here, I'm nothing. I'm nobody other than the number now branded on my skin.

The elevator pitches as it reaches its destination, the doors slide open to a stout man with an oddly peppered mohawk that runs along his skull and a closely cropped beard to match. His left eye spins and whirs with a red light that sends a shiver down my spine.

"I'm assuming this is the inmate we've been waiting for. The one from the capitol?" His voice is like sandpaper along my skin, and I grimace as he looks over me with contempt.

"Yes, Warden. Inmate 2475 just finished with intake." Ryker salutes and the female nods.

The warden's lips curl into a hideous sneer as he looks at her, assessing her hand placement before saying, "Sergeant Jackson, I'd expect more respect from someone of yar rank."

Sergeant Jackson looks at me, and hesitation crosses her face before she removes her hand and salutes the warden. The male guard snickers beside me.

"Sergeant! Do not remove yar hands from a fresh inmate!" The warden booms.

I'm stunned.

He set her up to fail.

"Yes, Warden," she responds before taking hold of my arm again.

"Latrine duty on the sixth floor for the disrespect. As for yar reckless decision to take yar hands off the inmate, one week suspension. Unpaid."

"Yes, Warden," she repeats, this time, through gritted teeth.

The Warden shakes his head and steps around us towards the elevators without another word. Sergeant Jackson takes a deep breath before continuing forward and I'm finally able to take in the space.

Linoleum floors labeled *Block 3* lead to the first set of large ivory painted metal gates. Sergeant Jackson unlocks them by pressing her thumb on a blue keypad and we step through to a large corridor of cells stacked two high. I gasp as I take in the sheer size of it. There's got to be close to two hundred cells in this block. I school my features as we walk past cell after cell of leering dragons, noting a handful of other astral species within the sea of fiery eyes, all pining for a look at the new inmate.

Dear gods, this place is massive.

We near the end of the corridor when the male guard stops abruptly at a cell marked *33003*.

"This is you," he states gruffly before lifting a card to the padlock, sending a bolt flying outward to unlock the gate before he steps in to secure the door from the inside.

A female with rich, dark auburn hair and voluminous untamed curls stares back at me with piercing blue eyes. A red glow lingers in the depths of her gaze. Her face is lovely, despite the deep scars etched into her brow and cheeks; a beauty marred by war, and ancient fury; wounds that I understand deeply.

As she sizes me up, those pretty features darken and her lips curl into a sneer.

"You've got to be kidding," she looks between the guards. "Ryker? Nova? This is a joke."

"Shut your trap, Breather!" Ryker shouts.

He moves to unclasp my shackles but before he steps back out of the cell, he clamps a bulky, iron mask across the lower half of my face. A mockery of the beautifully intricate one I wear back home. The one I wore to give myself away to this wretched place.

Those are a badge of honor.

This is a muzzle.

"Inmate 2475, welcome to Level 3, Cellblock 3. The Breather Block. Or as some like to call it, Hell." With that, he slams the door closed and locks me in.

My new cellmate scoffs and I shift on my feet, unsure of how to proceed.

...A fucking Twitcher, just my luck...

"What the fuck did you just call me?" I ask. Her head tilts to the side and her glare turns hostile.

"I didn't say shit," she hisses, her teeth glinting in the fluorescent light.

I've never been referred to as a Twitcher before, a derogatory term for a phoenix known throughout Altas.

Elysia. Not Altas.

I've also never come face to face with a dragon either so I suppose I should get ready for an onslaught of hatred since I've been dropped into a cesspool of them.

In my frustration I almost miss that I've just heard her thoughts.

That's new.

I move towards the bed where fresh linens are stacked haphazardly on the plastic waterproof mat on the top bunk. Grabbing hold of one sheet, I toss it over one side and begin making my bed, tiptoeing around the glare I can feel digging into the side of my head as I work. Fluffing the hopeless pillow and placing it at the head of the bunk, furthest from the cell door, I turn to step over to the metal ladder but instead I find myself staring directly at the chest of my cellmate.

"Excuse me," I try, readying myself for the possibility of her taking a swing at me.

"Look at me, Twitcher," I can smell the sulfur on her breath and can feel her fighting back the beast inside, her skin but a thin veil leashing her snarling dragon just beneath the surface. "Stay the fuck away from me."

"Ah, just when I thought we would start braiding each other's hair and swapping stories of our youth," I spit with a saccharine smile and shove my chest into her. She's got several inches on me but that's never intimidated me. Damn near everyone is taller than I am.

Her nostrils flare and the red glow behind the ice in her eyes burns a bit brighter before she reigns it in and smiles back at me. "Unless you have a fucking death wish. Stay. The fuck. Out of my way."

"You don't have to swing your dick around. I don't want to be near you any more than you want to be near me. Let's call this a draw and move the fuck on." I push past her and climb the steps of my bunk, dropping myself onto the thin scratchy sheets.

She stands there for a few moments and I think she may continue, but she lets out a final huff and climbs into the bunk beneath me.

Get in, get out.

I close my eyes, the events of the day weighing heavily on me. The lights above us shudder out as a buzzer sounds for lights out and I reach into my braid to retrieve my locket. It was far easier to smuggle in than I had anticipated. Thankfully that guard was more focused on my nakedness and my lack of gag reflex than my hair. The cavity search didn't include much hair pulling.

Pity.

Running a finger over the etched flames and holding the locket to my heart, I think through what all I've seen and know of this place already. I'll need to keep that fresh in my mind as I plan my escape and report back to my mother. She will want to know every corner of the facility and I can't fail again.

Thoughts of Amell's rough hands grasping my face and kissing me softly play through my mind. He was always so good at calming my nerves.

I can feel hot tears well in my eyes and I blink them back, pushing away thoughts of him as I place the locket back between the knots of my braid. Shifting uncomfortably, I close my eyes and will myself to sleep when a soft moan echoes from the cell beside us. I roll my eyes and turn onto my shoulder, wondering where the guards are while two astrals go at it in the next cell over. Masculine grunts and a shrill scream echo throughout the corridor. Now more moans can be heard from cells surrounding us in an erotic cacophony of sound. It seems others are enjoying the performance these two are putting on and my stomach roils. I fist my pillow and slam it over my head in a futile attempt to drown out the noise.

The bed next door screeches as the pair shift positions and rhythmic squeaking rings through the corridor. Metal scrapes against the linoleum as, whoever the male is, pounds into the female. Her cries grow louder, and the bed begins knocking against our shared wall. If I weren't certain there was no one else in this minuscule cell with us, I'd wonder if the pair were in here too.

"XAN! I don't need to hear you and your latest whore rutting!" The Breather below me shouts.

Seems we agree on one thing.

A deep, velvety laugh sounds from the cell beside us and the male, Xan, picks up his pace, sending the female with him careening over the edge of her orgasm. He doesn't stop as she cries out her release while a few other astrals follow. Instead, he slams his body into her even harder, causing some of the dust from the brick wall between us to fall onto the floor for another few minutes before he finally roars his finish.

"Ugh, stupid fucking prick," the Breather below growls as the female next-door whimpers and moans. I can hear Xan as he pumps a few more times, groans and the distinct scent of cum from at least a dozen others wafts through the air of the corridor.

I've never hated my superior sense of smell more than I do at this moment.

A guard appears and unlocks the cell next to ours and I can hear the clinking of coins falling into a gloved hand.

Fantastic.

A curvy deer shifter with long chestnut hair strolls from the cell, her face flushed and beaming.

"A pleasure as always, Blue," the female drolls, and I watch from a small hole beneath my pillow as she blows him a kiss and is led by the arm back to her cell.

The corridor goes silent, and quieter hours pass as I toss and turn but sleep never finds me.

2
RHIANNON

The buzzer sounds and my eyes pop open. It's morning and I wake up feeling sorry for Xanth, because I am on a level of bitch mode that is lethally toxic. However, I'm already in prison so what the fuck do I care?

The Twitch bitch in the bed above me stirs and I groan, cursing the gods that she didn't die in her sleep last night. I should have prayed for it before I fell asleep, so maybe that's why they're punishing me. Then again, my torment is hers as well, so you know…silver linings and all that.

"Up, Breather whores. Shower in five," one of the guards bellows through the cell door and I run my hands over my face.

"Of course, in Hell I'd be mistaken for a Breather," the Phoenix mutters from the top bunk, and I kick the bottom of her mattress for the hell of it.

"No one asked for your input," I say and she hops down off the bed, her golden eyes flaring like two tiny suns as she glares daggers at me over her iron mask. It stunts the fire that I know licks the back of her throat and I roll my eyes. "Touchy this morning."

She inhales slowly, clearly trying to quell the rage marring her face.

She looks like shit.

Her stark white hair is matted, and her eyes are red rimmed from lack of sleep. A shadow of the pretty little snowbird who was locked in a cage yesterday.

"I have a name," she growls, making me chuckle.

"Not anymore you don't," I scoff.

"Where's your mask?" She asks, looking down at my bare face and her cheek spasms with pain I know all too well.

I lace my fingers behind my head. "Be a good girl and in a few days, maybe you'll find out." I cross my legs as the cell door swings open and Ryker, one of the burly guards, yells at us to get out. Curiously, he's one of the few guards in here that goes by his first name instead of his last.

Twitchy stalks out first and Ryker follows her with his eyes. I lazily make my way out of bed, contrarily taking my time and he sneers at me.

"Don't make me fucking come in there, Breather."

"Why is everyone so grouchy this morning?" I ask, holding up my hands in surrender. "Couldn't shoot your load off this morning, Ryker?" I flutter my lashes at him, and his jaw tightens. "Or maybe you just couldn't get it up. Perhaps the new girl will help you out."

"Shut the fuck up and go," he yells and I giggle as he pushes me forward. I walk slowly behind my roommate and another guard along the long sterile corridor to the showers. The harsh fluorescent lights flicker as we walk over the eye sore eggshell pique flooring to the open door of the collective showers. A scratchy gray towel is shoved into my arms along with generic bar soap that smells like chemicals, a clean jumpsuit, and a fresh pair of underwear. The guards watch us as we strip while more inmates file in. Maverick, Lune and Sabeer saunter in holding their towels, soap, and clothing. They each make their way to a shower head…far away from me.

Good. I smirk as I relish the open space around me and turn the knob. Tepid water shoots forth and my skin constricts, pebbling at the cool spray.

A tall dark figure with shocks of bright blue lacing his long onyx hair lazily strolls in. His entire body is a mural of tattoos and muscles. His towel is hung over his shoulder like a jacket as he leisurely tosses his soap in the air and catches it again.

"Mornin' Sunshine," he quips, hanging the towel next to the hook on the wall between his and my shower head. The water finally warms up, and I dip my head into the stream.

"No talking," Ryker shouts next to Jo Miller, the other female guard standing watch at the entrance.

Xanth Vulcan, a fellow dragon and my only friend in this place, glances back at him briefly and continues our conversation within the confines of our minds.

...He's in a mood... The sound of Xanth's voice brushes across my brain as I wet my long dark auburn hair.

He's always in a mood. I reply in kind. *And I'm inclined to poke the proverbial bear.*

...What did he do this time?... Xanth chuckles as he floods his long strip of dark hair at the top of his head under the stream of water. He scratches the closely shaved sides as the water streams through his fingers.

He's just a prick. He isn't what's pissing me off.

He's quiet for a minute and I see him smile under the waterfall of his black hair as he volleys the thought. *...Who got under yer scales this time?...*

Really Xan? Were you that far deep in Meadow's pussy last night that you didn't hear what landed in my cell last night? Seriously, it couldn't have been so good that he didn't notice *at all.*

Xanth scans the room, his stormy blue eyes darting between the multitude of naked bodies when they finally land on the Phoenix quietly showering in the corner, farthest away from everyone else.

I watch him take in her short petite frame, decent tits and, when she turns, the globes of her ass shine with water droplets before a low growl rumbles from his chest. The tattoo of a phoenix stretches down her right hip and thigh, her beast's mark on full display. I hate to admit that it's...kind of beautiful. I suppose it could be "objectively" pretty even though she "actually" sucks. My own beast mark tingles on my back and ribs as I linger on the phoenix tattoo for a moment longer than I'd like. I notice Xanth's dark gaze is *still* fixed on her and his muscles tense.

...How the fuck did ye get paired off with a Twitcher?...

Glad to see you've caught on.

His shadowy eyes meet mine and he gives me a withering look. I shrug and lather the soap, passing it over my hair and body. As I rinse, I look over to see Xanth watching me and I scoff.

Don't.

...Don't what?...

You know what. We've been through this.

...Come on, Doll. I'd make ye feel good...

I turn off the shower and wrap my steaming skin in the abrasive gray towel.

I'm not your Doll. *I'm not one of those sluts you bang and toss aside. I'm not ruining our friendship because you're horny, Xan. Let it go.*

...Ye can't lie te me, lass. Ye'r horny too. I can smell the-...

Stop.

His eyes follow me as I dry off and slide into my black jumpsuit. For the briefest moment, I let myself watch Xanth standing naked in the water. I would be lying if I didn't admit to being curious. Xanth is stunning. His body is sculpted and muscular, his tattoos only accentuate his masculine allure along with the myriad of body piercings on his ears, lip, and nipples. I'm sure I've even caught a glimpse of a few on the underside of his cock. He exudes dragon arrogance, casual grace, and unbridled anarchy that pulls me into his orbit and when I look long enough, it gives me chills.

We would be good.

We *would* be so fucking good, but there is just...something that doesn't fit and it feels too much like hooking up with a blood relative for me to consider messing around with him. He clearly doesn't have the same reservations, but I can't ignore it.

Not to mention his inability to sleep with anyone more than once. I need commitment and that male doesn't have a committed bone in his body.

I blink as I turn and snatch the clothing the Twitch bitch hung up on the wall and toss them in the center of the bath hall over the drain where all the used water is collecting. I smile as I hear her growl from the corner.

"None of that," shouts the female guard from the entrance.

"I knew you were on my side, Jolene," I say to the guard, and she glares at me as I walk to the wall and lean. "Or not." I laugh as she curls her lip.

"Don't fucking start, Breather. You know damn well to either call me Jo, or Miller. Don't give me a reason to send you to solitary confinement," she barks and I smile sweetly at her as I cross my legs at my ankles.

We make our way to the chow hall for breakfast, and I walk to the front of the line where I shove a massive bear astral named Torben out of the way and he growls. I face him and hiss; my eyes flash a warning flare of red, and he backs off.

"Good boy," I croon, and he huffs before lumbering back so that I can grab a slice of toast and an overripe banana.

I try not to think about coffee. The smell and ritual of it is something I crave every single morning. It has been the most difficult to let go of since arriving in this shit hole. Not to mention when the buttery rich scent wafts in the air, taunting me as the guards sip their cups in front of us. It's with Herculean level strength that I don't throw my mushy brown banana at their stupid faces.

I take a seat at a nearly empty table where I see Xanth picking at a bowl of watered-down porridge, his mouth arced in disgust as he lets the mixture plop from his spoon back into the bowl. His eyes flit to mine and they brighten from a cloudy night sky to a lighter shade of deep ocean blue that sends the females around here to their knees. His mouth ticks up as I sit down in front of him. Xanth launches into recounting the recent brawl he had with a gorilla astral in the rec hall. A tall blonde male with stacks of muscles named Zane. He's easily riled, which happens to be one of Xanth's favorite past times: pissing others off.

Xanth flashes a wide crooked smile, and it eases some of the tension in my shoulders as I nibble some of the stale toast. He stops talking and I look up to see him glaring at the astrals lined up with their yellow trays ready to be filled with food and notice my new cellmate standing several arm lengths behind a python astral, Vasuki.

"What I don't understand," Xanth begins, his burr more pronounced. "Is how the fuck those pricks at the top thought paring a Twitcher with a dragon would be a good fucking idea."

"They don't care," I say, folding back the skin of the banana and scrunching my nose, noticing the dark bruises along the white flesh. "She's wearing a halter anyway."

"Not for long," Xanth booms, his frustration and anger surprising even me. "If she goes after ye, I'll fuckin' pummel 'er."

I set down my banana as I look at him with a mixture of humor and incredulity. "Really, Blue?"

"She's a fuckin Twitcher, Rhi. Ye can't let yer guard down around the cunt," he says with certainty, his eyes darkening like storm clouds filled with the threat of rain.

"Okay, thank you for the vote of confidence, but I'm a big girl and I can handle myself," I scoff as I bite into the banana, instantly regretting it. I chew and swallow, wincing as I grab Xanth's cup of water and gulp it down. We both look over at the Phoenix who's grabbing a cup of water, a slice of toast, and an under-ripe banana. Turning, she finds her way to the very back of the chow hall, again placing herself furthest away from the rest of the astrals eating and conversing.

"Pathetic little thing, eh?" Xanth scoffs as he places his spoon in his mouth and makes a face, but I notice his eyes lingering on her. Before he can stop me, I stand up and walk over to where she is sitting. Her eerie glowing eyes flit up to me for a fraction of a second before they fall back to her food, dismissing me. She must wait for the guards to disengage her halter so she can eat, so I take the opportunity that's presented itself to me.

"Let's trade," I say, tossing my half eaten and bruised banana to her while taking the fresh one from her tray. Her hand juts out and claps over my wrist. I feel Nina stir to life beneath my skin. My eyes blaze crimson as the fire licks its way up my neck making the back of my throat glow a deep sun-fire orange. "I. Fucking. Dare you," I hiss, and her eyes shine bright like golden fire. Her grip tightens painfully before she releases me and I stare at her for a moment longer, her fists ball as she continues to hold my gaze, refusing to back down, our beasts circling and snapping at one another. Nina growls low and my teeth sharpen and then I blink, feigning nonchalance as a guard approaches.

"You got a problem, Breather?" Jo asks as I hold my new piece of fruit.

"Not at all," I say, watching as Jo holds up her key card to the back of the halter and it clicks before falling with a thunk onto the table. My eyes flick back up to the bitch's face, and I hate to admit that she's decent looking, even for a shit eating phoenix.

She has full, dusty pink lips and a gently sloped jawline. A pert nose that most would envy and high cheekbones with a slight rose tinge. Despite the shock of braided white hair, her skin is sun kissed and judging by the scarring on her hands and arms, she's either worked the land or the battlefield. Judging by her attitude, my money is on the latter.

Her eyes are what really tell a story though. They're brilliant and bright with ferocious intent, lined with dark purplish arcs swiped below her eyes that sing of sleepless nights and long days being worn too thin. Marks I know all too well, and I find myself actually *empathizing* with her for a moment. I blink hard, noticing Jo is watching me closely. "Just making sure my roomie feels welcome." I stretch my lips into a saccharine smile.

"Sure," Jo says, giving me a withering look. I shrug and start walking back to my spot beside Xanth when I notice another guard walk into the chow hall to join a group at the entrance and it's one I haven't seen before. He's putting a cup of coffee to his lips as he adjusts the rifle slung over his thick vest.

He's as tall as Xanth but burlier, his shoulders broad and commanding and his face wears a ruddy looking five o'clock shadow that I imagine scratches like sandpaper over soft skin. His hair is a mess of copper waves, and he smiles as he speaks to one of the other guards. A scar gleams in the light that slashes severely from his mid brow and ends under his left eye that gentles when he relaxes his face. They are a mirror of my own disfigurement, and my fingers swipe over my cheek, gently prodding the taut raised skin.

He swallows his coffee when his eyes meet mine and it's like the air is sucked from the room. His eyes are a rare mixture of clover green and bright ocean blue, like warm tropical waters. His strong square jaw tenses as he surveys me and I audibly swallow, trying to remember how to move and breathe as I stand arrested in his gaze.

Fuck, he's beautiful. He turns to look at me fully and Nina sighs inside, like she was admiring him too.

That was...new.

Admittedly, I'm having a hard time with the fact that I'm lusting surprisingly hard after a stupid human male. *A guard* no less. I clear my throat and tear my eyes from the guard before making my way back to the table. Xanth sits beside me, smirking as I peel back my banana and take a bite.

"The fuck was that all about?" He laughs as he looks back at the guard I was having a staring contest with. I shrug, chewing the far superior banana and pretending like my entire foundation didn't just shift seconds before.

"New guard. Just sizing him up," I lie, stuffing every part of my emotional turmoil down as far as I can so that Xanth doesn't get a whiff of it.

"You sure about that, Princess? Could've fooled me with those hearts dancing 'round yer eyes."

"*Don't* fucking call me that," I snap at him, and he holds up his hands in surrender, mirth playing in his eyes.

"Sorry, just making sure ye'r paying attention," he laughs and I roll my eyes.

"I'm always paying attention, dickhead," I say as I finish the last bite of my fruit and toss the peel on the floor. I stand to leave when a shadow looms over me from behind.

"Pick it up."

I look up to Xanth's face, his silver labret lip ring gleams with his pursed mouth, fighting a smile as his eyes fix on the figure behind me. My stomach drops and flutters at the same time as I turn and find the beautiful copper headed guard towering over me like an amber mountain.

I straighten and roll back my shoulders. "Pick what up?"

His mouth twitches with the ghost of a smile. "Pick it up," he says again in a low threatening voice and *fuck* I like it. I like it too much. I'm gonna get my ass kicked and it's going to be so worth it to hear this man yell at me.

"Pick. What. Up?" I say, throwing back every ounce of malice he threw at me.

Before I can register what happens, I'm on my hands and knees with a large, calloused hand at the back of my neck holding me down like a dog to the banana peel. "I won't repeat myself again." He utters in a near growl beside my ear and I inhale.

Fuck he smells good. Like whiskey, leather, sweat, and smoke. I hate that I want to lave my tongue over his neck and see if he tastes as good as he smells. His thumb presses into my neck, swiping along my skin and I strain against his impossible strength. I've never felt this type of tension with a human male. What the fuck is this guy on?

I move to pick up the banana but then he squeezes my neck painfully tight, and I grunt, inhaling him again and it's so good. Another, more faint scent lingers in the essential mix of him. Like the cloying sweet of opium but...grassy? The fuck is that? Nina purrs as his fingers squeeze my neck.

"With your teeth," He orders into my ear, and I am practically panting at this point. I absolutely love and hate what this guy is doing to me right now. I adjust my face to reflect what I *should* be feeling: angry, demoralized, frustrated, and ashamed. Not fiercely turned on.

I grasp the banana between my teeth, and he loosens his grip so I can stand. I straighten and the banana peel dangles from my mouth in front of the entire chow hall. The silence is palpable as every astral and human eye watches. I hold his achingly beautiful stare as I cross my arms in front of my chest and let the peel fall from my mouth, it topples onto the floor with a gentle wet splat. The guard's mouth quirks again as I keep my gaze locked on him and stretch my lips into a paltry grin.

"Let's go, Inmate," he grinds through his teeth before he shoves me forward. "Hands behind your back."

"Don't need to threaten me with a good time," I say with the same smug smile as I canter forward, clasping my hands behind my back.

He doesn't say anything as he walks me out of the chow hall and down the block 3 corridor. He shoves me in the direction of my cell which is odd and gives me another push that causes me to jostle forward. He opens my cell door, thrusting me in and I catch myself on the frame of the metal bunk. I turn to see him filling the open cell door, his head slightly ducked from his impressive height.

"Be grateful you aren't in SolCon, 2460," he gruffs as he steps back and closes the door to the cell. The iron lock clacks shut and the metallic sound rings through the empty corridor.

"Rhiannon," I say, reaching my arms through the bars as he steps back from me and I reach for him, but he evades my touch.

"I don't care," he says but he's still standing there, looking back at me with those bewitching teal eyes.

"Sure you don't, handsome." I smile and wink, resting my forehead against the bars.

That damn mouth of his twitches again and it makes Nina growl in time with my audible sigh, before he finally turns and walks away.

3
XANTH

A *fuckin Twitcher. As if the Gods haven't tested me enough lately.*

My biceps curl in on themselves, straining to lift the dumbbells from the ground between my knees. Beads of sweat trickle down my face and neck, expelling the tidal wave of anger roiling in my chest.

Forty-three, forty-four, forty-five. FUCK!

The loud clang of metal connecting with concrete rings out through the rec hall and I begin pacing, my head tilted back towards the fake sky panels in the ceiling. I puff out steam and work to subdue the beast writhing in my chest. Azure has been a raging asshole since we first saw the Twitcher.

"What's got you all bent out of shape today, Blue?" Cadmyr asks beside me. His chest muscles flex with each pull of his arms, lifting his squared jaw up over the bar above his head.

He's not a bad kid, all things considered. Cadmyr arrived shortly after I did, hells bent on burning this place to the ground. He reminds me a lot of my younger self. His dragon often takes over and he's been muzzled more than once because of it. Hot-headed little prick.

I like him.

When he minds his own business.

"Don't fuckin worry about it, ay?" I snap back.

He drops to the floor and raises his hands in surrender. "Alright, alright. Just asking. No need to get your panties in a bunch," he laughs and ducks away before I can take a swing at him.

My mind is reeling as I stack a few plates on a barbell in the center of the gym and towel my face dry. I'm going to need another shower at this rate.

Throwing back my bottle of water my eyes wander through the rec hall, bouncing off the different dragons scattered throughout the space. It's hard to believe these round ups only started a few years ago. There are so many of us here, it makes my skin feel tight.

A few of the other high-risk inmates that aren't dragons linger near the walls, the primates sit at a table with a couple of bear astrals, while a python astral makes his rounds between the throngs. The unlucky fucks ended up planted in the 'Breather Block' for bad behavior.

The deer shifter females whisper and giggle to each other while making it wildly obvious that they are staring in my direction. I've had each of them and don't intend to go there again. Even in prison my rules remain the same. Willow was a fun ride, but I can't be bothered to give a shit if she wants more. It just won't happen. I'm not into sloppy seconds, not even my own.

Another set of dragons walk by and a tall, leggy blonde dragon waves at me. There are so many astrals that I have yet to *need* to go back on my second rule. It's sickening. All of us are here for no reason other than that we exist in a world with human vermin that seek to subdue us. If it weren't for their tech, they would never have been able to imprison us.

It all started with Altas. That fucker built the first mech suit about a hundred years ago and his ego grew tenfold. He started spewing bullshit about astrals having ruled the lands for long enough. How it was 'Time to put the power back in the hands of the people'. Elysia fell quickly under the mech attacks, they amped up their ability to take us down after finding some sort of bio warfare bullshit that limits our ability to shift when we come into contact with it and we all went into hiding. Astrals have, for the most part, always been peaceful.

Outside of the Twitchers, of course. As soon as the dragons tried unifying the lands and they lost their thrones, the war between our kinds started and they haven't stopped, even after we took their throne. I think that's another reason why it was so easy for the humans to take over.

We were divided.

We still are.

Prism fell first during their takeover, marking it as the human's home base, which is still the case. Next thing we knew, Elysia became *Altas*. I think they built the prison alongside the mech suits with full intentions of using us. For what, I have no idea. The power-hungry fucks haven't stopped since the first attacks on the avians that lived in Prism before them.

The shittiest part of it all? We *gave* them this land. Three thousand years ago, humans first entered our world through The Slip, some crazy wormhole or time space paradox that formed when our world collided with theirs and they were forced to inhabit our lands.

So, we willingly gave them Prism as a place to take refuge, and they shit all over our generosity. My father oversaw their transition and the astrals did all they could to make these ungrateful fuckin' leaches happy. Apparently, the houses and food we supplied them with wasn't enough.

They got greedy.

They wanted it all.

Now they can all burn alongside those fuckin' phoenixes.

My Paps never liked to talk much about what happened with my Mum, but I knew what happened. I understood more than I should have and as I got older, the more mead I pumped into my Paps belly, the looser his lips got. When the dragon and phoenix wars were at their peak, a phoenix strike team landed in Mum's camp and all the dragons there were eviscerated.

We were notified via a letter in the mail. A cold piece of paper was all that we got in return for her giving her life during that raid. They couldn't be fuckin' bothered to knock on our door to see the pain etched into my Pap's face or to look a young babe in the eye and tell them their Mum wouldn't be coming home.

Spineless fucks.

Paps was silent for an entire week after we got that letter. I'll never forget the rage I felt. I was nay more than a boy when I swore to seek vengeance on my mother's behalf. I'd kill every phoenix that ever crossed my path. I was lucky enough that I'd never met one.

Until now, that is.

Speak of the fuckin' devil and she will rise.

The platinum haired bane of my existence moves across the floor with graceful, fluid steps. She walks past the tables filled with dragons snarling and shooting daggers in her direction with their eyes, not paying attention to a single one of them. I watch as she gathers her hair at the back of her head and pulls it into a thick ponytail, easy for grabbing and my cock twitches involuntarily at the intrusive thought.

Fucking prick needs to get it under control. He may not have a brain but I sure as fuck do and there is no way in all the nine hells I'll sleep with a Twitcher.

She approaches the punching bag on the opposite side of the gym and unzips the top half of her jumpsuit, pulling the sleeves off her arms and tying them around her waist to reveal her fitted sports bra beneath.

I clench my jaw. *That should* not *be sexy.*

A low whistle sounds beside me. "Nice rack for a Twitch, eh Blue?"

My blood boils to the point I can feel the heat rise beneath my skin.

Does she have any idea how many fuckin males are in here starin' at 'er tits?

Cadmyr is unable to dodge the hit this time and I smack him upside the head. He laughs, a loud barking sound, and the phoenix turns in our direction, her eyes colliding with mine. Golden embers burn within her gaze, and I'm rooted in place under her scrutiny. She scans me with those molten irises, starting at my feet, and slowly making their way up the length of me. Nothing in her expression changes other than a single eyebrow ticking upward, seemingly disappointed with what she sees.

I can't explain why that angers me even more.

...I'm well aware of every pair of eyes on me, Dragon... A sultry, feminine voice fills my head, causing it to spin.

How in the hells?

She turns her lithe body back around and begins her reps in quick succession.

One, two, three, kick.

One, two, she steps back with her left foot, plants it firmly and twists, driving her right heel into the bag with such force the chains holding the bag rattle.

"Gods," Cadmyr lets out a breathless huff and I whirl on him, readying to send my fist through his face this time. He backs up a step, "Okay, man, I get it. She's all yours. I won't touch her."

"She's nay mine," I growl deep in my chest. "I wouldn't touch 'er if there was a fuckin gun to my skull." My fists ball, unable to hold in the rage that's been building since I heard a phoenix had entered our block. Cadmyr is a friend but for some reason this Twitcher has me seeing red.

"Well, in that case," his eyes dart behind me and my chest rattles, Azure rising closer to the surface. It takes genuine effort for me to push my dragon back. "Don't mind if I do."

Cadmyr steps around me, making his way over to the phoenix and I track his movements. Everything in me says to get over there. To prevent anyone from being near her.

She's dangerous.

My hatred for her kind is seated so deeply in my soul that I can think of no other reason as to why I'm having such a visceral response to Cad stepping into her and leaning down to speak directly into her ear.

He's close to 'er. Too fuckin' close.

I march over and press myself between them. The scent of rain and wind fills my nose, and it takes immense effort not to close my eyes and breathe in the smell that reminds me of flying. Droplets of sweat slide down between her breasts and an unbidden image of licking the wet lines left behind rises to the forefront of my mind.

...In your dreams, Breather...

There it is again. That fucking voice.

How are ye doing that?

She stares back at me but says nothing more. From this vantage, I have to look down to see her, my chin almost grazing my chest. She cranes her head back, the ponytail now slightly messy and her eyes still filled with gilded fire as she stares up at me. I could bend and snap this female in half should I choose, yet she looks at me as if *I* could be split in two.

"Yer nay wanted here, Twitch. Ye'd be wise te keep te yerself."

The gods damned female steps into me, her chest colliding with my lower abdomen and my traitorous cock chooses that exact moment to stand at full attention. Mindless fuckin' prick.

Her eyebrow hitches in that infuriating way again and a growl rumbles through me, vibrating the blood in my veins.

"It would seem that Junior here disagrees with you." Her voice sounds from beneath the iron mask, and I swear it shoots straight through my groin. It's warm and velvety with a slight rasp that turns my already hardened dick to steel. She needs to stop talking or I'm going to rip this thing from her face and do it for her.

Fuck, get a hold of yourself ye bastard.

I grab the bottom of her muzzle and lift her chin higher than I know is comfortable and lower my face to hers, so we are sharing the same breath. I hear her let out a nearly silent whimper and I bite back a groan. "Ye're the last thing on this entire godsforsaken rock I'd fuck. Don't flatter yerself…Little Dove."

"I'm not a bird, you hateful prick."

I'm taken to my knees with one blow as her fist connects with my balls. "Next time you decide to threaten me, leave your hard-on in your cell with your whore." She turns back around and slams her knuckles into the bag one last time, splitting it directly down the center and sending sand spilling out onto the floor in front of me.

I take a moment to catch my breath and let the shooting pain up my stomach wane as Cad attempts to help me up. Baring my teeth, I push him off. He's the reason I ended up on the floor to begin with. I brush the sand from my knees and look in the direction the phoenix went only to find she's already gone.

My mind replays the conversation, and I keep getting stuck on her insinuating that I have a specific whore.

Who is she talking about? Rhi?

After a few more moments of mulling it over in my brain I realize that Rhi mentioned she arrived last night. She must have heard me and Meadow.

A smirk lifts the corners of my mouth and a laugh bubbles in my throat.

The little dove is jealous.

4
EILIDH

After my certifiably insane encounter with Xanth, I rush to the latrines to splash some water on my face. I haven't seen the sun in over twenty-four hours now and I think it's fucking with my head.

He talked to me in my head.

I talked back.

Splashing more cold water over my face, I scrub at my eyes and will away the feel of his erection pressed against me. I've heard that happens when males are worked up and of men popping one in the heat of battle, but I've never *actually* experienced it first-hand.

And I've experienced quite a lot in the last three hundred or so years of my fucked-up life.

The sight of his tattoos cloud my mind, traveling up his arms and around his chest, nearly covering him entirely. His dragon's maw tattooed on the front of his neck, as though he were consuming me, flashes before me and I groan.

Shaking myself from my Xanth induced stupor, I towel dry and head out. A buzzer goes off, signaling another rotation of the inmates and I find a guard with reddish hair standing against the wall just outside the door, His face drawn up in a smirk. Glancing around, I wonder who in the hells he could be smiling at because it surely isn't me.

"'Afternoon, Inmate…" He pauses, long enough to grab my wrist and look at my brand that's now scabbed over. "2475. I'm Major Haley and *you* have laundry duty. Let's go."

"Laundry duty?" I ask dumbly, still unsure as to why he's not dragging me away without a word or threatening me.

"The one and only." The kelly green in his eyes shifts to a bluish tone that reminds me of the coves around Pyrrh. It's almost heartbreaking.

The scarring on his face slices right down his eye and I wonder what caused it. I've always loved discussing battle wounds with other warriors. Their stories make me feel better about my own, and more importantly, understood.

"Let's get going, it's shift change, and I've got somewhere to be. I figure you'd need a moment after that scene out in the yard, so let's get you to the washroom," he chuckles to himself and my cheeks blaze.

Of course, the cute guard saw me lose my shit on that infuriating asshole.

Major Haley leads me down a series of halls, all of which have a gate both in and out of them. The keypads range from fingerprint codes to badge accessibility. None of them are standard lock and key.

Because why in the hells would anything be that easy?

We approach a set of swinging doors, and I'm led into a large open room filled with long tables in the center. Washing machines line the walls on one side, dryers on the other and twenty or so inmates flit through the space, all performing their duties and working efficiently. Three dragons are pulling large sacks filled with linens towards the washers, another two are stuffing a staggering number of jumpsuits into a machine and turning it on before moving to the next. Around ten astrals are seated at the tables, folding and sorting out the clean laundry and on the other side, Xan and two other dragon inmates are filling the dryers.

Just my fucking luck.

...Miss me?... His voice fills my head, and I roll my eyes. Refusing to meet his weighty stare.

"You'll start on the folding line," Major Haley says. "Lumara will show you around." He tips his chin in the direction of a beautiful female astral with long black hair and somehow even darker eyes.

I nod in response, and he turns on his heels to retreat out the swinging doors. Lumara gestures towards the spot beside her and I sit. Her spindly hands work through a large pile of socks as she folds and tucks them away into clear labeled bags.

A spider astral.

I've only ever known one and she gave me nightmares when I was a girl. Her eyes were solid black, much like Lumara's eyes and my child-brain conjured all sorts of terrifying stories, starring her as the eight-limbed monster.

Unsure of what to say, I offer her my name. "Eilidh."

A smile creeps across her pale skin and her pitch-black eyes shift to me in a way that has the hairs on the nape of my neck standing on end.

"I heard they put a phoenix in the Breather Block, but I had to see it with my own eyes to believe it." She tucks a lock of her onyx hair behind her ear and lifts a stack of cellophane bags, handing them to me. "We will start with labeling." She hands me a list. "Inmate numbers are here. All our clothing has our inmate number stamped on it, so you'll just need to find the number on the clothing item, fold it and place it in the corresponding bag." She turns to a large rolling cart with a massive, lined basin sitting atop it. "Just place the bags in there once you've filled them and another astral will deliver them this evening."

"Simple enough," I say and start on the undergarments before me.

From the corner of my eye, I watch as Xan loads another stack of wet clothes into a dryer. His back muscles flex beneath his jumpsuit and I have to close my eyes for a moment to catch my breath.

"Something the matter?" Lumara asks quietly, and I'm almost certain I hear a click of her tongue. "Do you need to go to the infirmary?"

I shake my head furiously. "No, no. Just feeling a bit tired. I didn't sleep well last night. First night and all that." I say, dismissively.

"Ah, I see," she hesitates for a moment before continuing. "I don't suppose the sound of Xanth fucking Meadow last night helped you get much sleep either." Her creepy smile returns, and I feel heat creep up to my cheeks.

"No, no it didn't help." No use in denying what the entire corridor heard. I can only hope that Lumara wasn't one of the astrals pleasuring themselves to the sounds.

...Did ye touch yerself when she came fer meh last night, Little Dove?...

I did no such thing. I spit back to him in my mind.

I can hear the rumble of his gravelly laughter in my head, and it makes me want to scream. I'm not even safe in my own thoughts anymore.

In an attempt to change the subject, I ask, "So do we have the same job every day?"

Thank the gods she pivots easily and doesn't bring up Xan or last night again.

"No, each day we rotate jobs. They say it's to keep us from going insane from the monotony of doing the same thing over, and over, and over… and over…" Her voice trails off and I wonder how long she's been here and if she's lost her mind already.

Despite all of her misgivings, she's a beautiful female. Long, inky black hair and eyes that upturn at the corners. She's thin, almost frail but beneath her sunken eyes and vacant expression I can see her beauty peeking through the cobwebs. I wonder what brought her here and then reel in the thought before it takes hold.

I have no desire to make friends in this place.

"Wait until they put you in the parts hall," Lumara starts. "Thousands upon thousands of tiny pieces to be put together like building a puzzle. Yet no one tells you what you're actually building." The empty look in her eyes turns cold. "But I know. They think I don't. No one thinks I do, but I know."

Another chill spreads down my spine and I stiffen.

It's clear they're using us for slave labor. But what are they building?

I repeat that in my head a few times. I'll need to get the information to my mother when I have the chance and I'm not yet sure how to do that. The thought of sending a letter crosses my mind but I immediately squash that idea. I'm sure they would read any incoming or outgoing mail. That is if they even *allow* mail in this godsforsaken place. I'll need to come up with another way.

Following that train of thought, I recall the hallways I was just taken through, working out a map of sorts in my head so that I can recall as many details as possible once I'm out of here. I didn't see any elevators, which leads me to believe that the one I entered on may be the only one.

At least for prisoners.

A few hours pass when a small, wiry male with beady eyes and sandy brown hair walks in. He looks around, catches sight of Lumara and cringes.

I guess he doesn't like her much.

All the same, he steps over to our cart, peeks in and begins to pull it away, likely for delivery.

I notice his ears twitching imperceptibly as he slowly rolls the cart towards the double doors. He's listening for something, but for what, I can't be sure.

After mind-mapping the places, I've been already, I think through different ways of getting out. There are no elevators besides the one I came down in. No windows to be seen and even the ceiling in the rec hall is only plastered with fake looking clouds and blue sky to give the illusion of the real thing.

They're fucking mocking us.

And I'm trapped here.

I begin to spiral. My thoughts bouncing around my head in a flurry of panic and I notice my hands trembling. Amell used to pull me out of my panic attacks, so I think of him and his honeyed eyes. I think of his hands running circles over my back as he recites our favorite story to settle my mind. I think of his windswept brown hair and the smile he reserved for only me. My heart rate slows, and I take a few deep breaths before the tremors begin to fade.

After a few more moments, I'm back to normal and begin working through escape plans in my mind again. One thought snags in the back of my brain that I save to dissect later, when prying minds aren't lurking nearby.

I lose myself in the rhythm of folding and packing. Allowing my thoughts to quiet and the rolling tumble of the machines to lull me into a state of calm.

5
RHIANNON

There are very few things that I enjoy about being in this hellhole, try as I might to find the glass half full in such empty circumstances. Alone time is certainly one of the things that I deem a positive. I mark myself as fortunate to have had my own cell for so long. I relish in the solace and relative peace.

Now, however, the addition of my Twitcher roommate has taken that half full glass and shattered it against the unyielding cement walls. I'm convinced it's part of the reason I'm even more irritated than necessary. Rationally, I know she didn't ask to be put in the cell with me but it's easier to direct my ire at my sworn enemy.

Also, I'm not perfect. Plus, she sucks.

But currently, I am completely alone.

And it's *fantastic*.

All the shifters on the block are either in the chow hall or off at their assigned "jobs". Xanth isn't even here to poke around my brain, and I find myself feeling completely free…despite the bars caging me. The irony of it is almost comical.

The red-headed guard is the first to occupy my mind for obvious reasons, mostly because I just watched his spectacularly shaped ass walk away from my cell. I sigh, falling back against my bunk while the specter of him crowds my head. But here, in my brain, I imagine him shutting himself in the cell with me.

"Up against the wall. Hands above your head," he orders and I comply, pressing my forehead to the cold cement as he moves closer. He runs his big, calloused hands along my body over my black jumpsuit with slow deft pressure, travelling over my back to the narrow dip of my waist and then over my abdomen. I bite my lower lip as he moves up my ribs stopping right before he touches my breasts.

"Turn," he demands, and I do. His tropical sea eyes are hooded as he continues to run his hands over my arms, my stomach, my hips, down the length of my thighs and legs. I drop my head with a thud against the wall as he kicks my legs apart and slowly drags his hands up my inner thighs, hesitating at the apex.

"Tease," I whisper, arcing my hips towards him and he pushes me back into the wall with the hard expanse of his body.

"You do not have permission to speak, 2460," he says in a low threatening voice.

"Say it," I reply, my gaze unwavering as I stare back into those bewitching turquoise eyes. His hands are instruments of torture as they skate up my abdomen, the tips of his fingers lightly grazing my breasts and I whimper.

"Say what?" He asks as his forehead presses into mine, his hips pressing against the mound of my sex and I ache with desperation.

"M-my name," I say as every part of me begins to unravel. He catches my lower lip between his teeth, and I wrap my leg around his waist, damning the consequences, I need him closer. He presses against me, and I sigh, only satiating part of the bonfire that begins to ravage the lower half of my body.

"Rhiannon," he whispers, his lips brushing feather light over mine before he presses them to my mouth and I'm overcome with his taste, surrounded by the whiskey and leather scent of him. He unbuttons my jumpsuit tantalizingly slow and slides his rough hands over the soft skin on my stomach, reaching around to grasp my ass with a firm grip. His tongue glides into my mouth and I'm already at a tipping point as his fingers press bruises into my skin, his powerful body fusing to mine.

"Oh gods," I breathe as his hips begin to thrust against my aching clit, the pressure building with the heat in my body. Nina flares to life and roars as my climax barrels forward and just before I topple over the edge he whispers in my ear.

"Ciara."

I open my eyes as my climax rips through my body. I bite my lip to suppress a cry, arching my back as my fingers continue to work me through the high. The pleasure sparkles through my veins as I pant, the sweat beading on my forehead and chest as I relax my fingers from clasping my breasts.

"Fuck," I whisper into the still quiet air. I don't really know if it's a good or bad thing that I'm lusting so hard after that stupid guard. I can't really help it. I suppose it was bound to happen at some point. It's just shitty that it's a guard.

My brain sucks.

Nina licks her teeth as she settles back into my body, the black scales that emerged slide back beneath my skin, as the ache in my back recedes from where opalescent black wings tried to spring free.

I stand up, button my jumpsuit and wash my hands at the rusted steel sink, noticing in the cloudy metal mirror that the crimson halo around my irises is beginning to wane. I feel Nina sigh, reposed and sated. I'm glad one of us is unphased by my clear ineptitude for selecting objects of my affection. Unlike Xanth, my lust does not come empty handed. It's intrinsically connected to the other parts of me that I'm too terrified to share with anyone. Which is why I typically stifle my desire with brute force at every opportunity that presents itself in this place. The temptation has always been there, especially with some of the other dragons, but they all fell short for one reason or another. I'd messed around with some, just to feel a little less lonely or just to satisfy some of that need, but it was never more than messing around. And I couldn't bring myself to fuck any of them. Maybe I'm just a picky bitch. But this time it's…inexplicably different and the challenge is almost painful to resist.

So, as I dry my hands on my jumpsuit, I conclude that I need to stay as far away from that guard as I can, because I don't know if I can trust myself not to give him the parts of me that he doesn't deserve. As far as I'm concerned, he will never earn that prize seeing as he is one of my captors, and despite how deliciously handsome he is, he's a human. That alone is enough reason to keep my distance.

I rest my back up against the wall, letting my head knock against the cement as I stare at the springs beneath the top bunk, noticing that the Twitcher had tidied her bed before we left. I scoff and then laugh to myself.

Definitely a military bitch. I chuckle as I note the perfectly tucked sheet corners and fluffed pillow. It looks like she staged her bed for a magazine ad. *Better Cells and Shackles: Ironsgate Penitentiary Edition.*

So, I decide to fuck it up. Spectacularly.

I rip the sheets in half and shred the pillow, eviscerate the mattress and then collect all the tufts, strips, and pieces back onto her bed... neatly. Staged. So, it looks just like her bed, only in bits.

She is going to be so pissed. I laugh as I admire my work.

Too far.

The intrusive thought pierces me as I settle on the lower bunk.

Where did that come from? I start to wonder if the solitude is fucking with me a little more than I'd like.

She doesn't deserve this. She didn't deserve that.

Okay maybe I'm coming down with something. I close my eyes again and take a deep breath, settling myself into the calm silence when the last thing the guard says to me from my fantasy whispers in my mind.

"Ciara."

My birth name. My *real* name. One that I gave up when I arrived at this shit hole to protect my family. To protect the girl that should be here instead of me.

Fianna.

My baby sister.

She had just gone through her merging with her dragon. Had called out her dragon's name for the first time as she struggled to join with her in a charred field full of burned tents, supplies and bodies.

Oriane is her dragon. The Golden One.

I spared her from this life, making her swear to keep it a secret to save the fragile peace between the dragons and humans. One that threatens to fracture with any small misstep. One that will destroy our family because I see what is really happening: the humans have the upper hand. Their engineering, robots, and mechanical military are far too strong for us to defeat now and if war breaks out...

The dragons will die.

My family will die.

So, I accept this life of confinement because to me there is no other option. Fianna will step into my role as the dragon heir, and she will live. She and my parents will move on without me, even if my heart breaks to see them again. Even if I would do anything just to see them one more time. To laugh and hunt with my sister. To be held by my father. Hells, even seeing my cold and distant Mother again would be considered a grace and a mercy. My eyes begin to sting as I think of Fianna's face when I told her to run, to save herself. What I would give to just tell her I love her one more...

ENOUGH.

Just...stop.

I inhale a shuddering breath. I am *not* Ciara anymore. That version of myself is gone. Far away from prodding minds and eyes. Far away from me.

The thoughts of that former life, the family that is no longer mine is a dagger between my ribs and every thought of them thrusts it deeper between the soft tissues, threatening to pierce through the walls keeping me whole.

I swallow and let it all sink again, down beneath the personae of who I am now.

Rhiannon.

I am Rhiannon.

Lawless, boundless, bloodthirsty, murderer, arsonist, rebel, dragon, bitch, insufferable menace.

Rhiannon.

I am Rhiannon.

I fall asleep chanting my own name and as my consciousness fades, I swear I hear the handsome guard's voice as my thoughts dissipate into the dark.

6
KIERAN

"So apparently, President Montgomery signed a new executive order that says all humans with known whereabouts of astrals within the territories of Altas will receive a monetary reward for reporting their location to the local authorities. Which probably means an influx in prisoners. And here I was, thinking the arrests were going to slow down! But I think…"

It's like she never stops. Like…words never *actually* stop flowing out of Rhetta's mouth. They are like a waterfall cascading from her head through her hot pink painted mouth and there's no escape.

I nod, pretending I'm interested because really, I'm trying to be a gentleman. Rhetta got me a coffee again. It's mixed with some kind of weird Italian Sweet Cream bullshit that I don't really like, but it's coffee, and I'm not one to complain…openly. So, I feel like I owe due diligence here to let her talk.

And talk.

And talk some more.

My thoughts begin to drift as she starts going on about what her sister thinks of the President's new executive order and they land on the thing that's been on my mind for days: long rich auburn hair and light blue summer sky eyes, high cheekbones, soft delicate looking skin with freckles like sun-kissed constellations over the bridge of her nose. Those same gentle feminine features are marked with scars that mirror mine, only softer and lighter, like a violent story told in a whisper.

My mind's eye hovers on her full hips, and that mouth. That *fucking* smart ass mouth. Every wise crack and snarky retort from those luscious lips had me biting back a laugh and a hard on.

I think of the way her hair smelled when I had to make that stupid show of power in the chow hall and how, by some magic, it smelled of honey and vanilla. Like warm comforting nostalgia only in long thick curly chestnut tresses. I wanted to run my fingers through it, to revel in its softness and its ability to overpower the synthetic smell of the bullshit soap the prison provides.

Gods, she is the most beautiful thing I've ever seen, and it is concerning how often I think about her. She's bulldozed all my focus with the number of times I have had to redirect my thoughts from the swell of her ass and the sway of her hips while she walked down the corridor to her cell. The way she reached for me. Fuck I nearly let her touch me. I wanted to let her. I could have.

But I didn't and I won't.

Ever.

Not because she's a dragon or because she's an astral, or even because she's an inmate, but because I have a fucking job to do and I'm better than those other dickhead guards who can't keep it in their pants. What's worse is that I don't think only one time with her will ever be enough for me and the thought triggers a more primal part of me that is getting harder to suppress each time she crosses my mind.

"So, what do you think?"

Oh fuck.

"Oh um." *Shit, what was she saying?* "About which part?"

She tilts her head and bunches her brows. "About the incentive program!"

Oh, that. "I guess we'll just have to see how it goes." *I fucking hate the idea.*

"I think it's a *great* idea!"

Of course you do, Rhetta. "Yeah, maybe," I mutter as I glance down at my watch and rise with my coffee in hand and say, "well, I should get back."

"Already? We've only been sitting here for ten minutes. I thought you got at least an hour break."

Dear fuck, I can't take another 50 minutes of her prattling on. "Yes, I just have a lot of important emails to catch up on. Thank you for the coffee, Rhetts." *Why? Why the fuck did I call her that?*

"Oh! Rhetts! That's so cute! I'll be your Rhetts and you'll be my Major Hot Stuff."

No. No. Absolutely not. "Okay." I smile weakly over my shoulder as I walk back to my office.

"I look forward to tomorrow, Major Hot Stuff! I love our coffee dates!" She calls after me. I wave at her and continue walking away.

I like Rhetta and I like that I have a friend in this place. But I'm beginning to worry that maybe she thinks there's something more between us. She tends to go out of her way to bring me coffee and schedules her breaks at the same time as mine, calling them "dates." And now the cutesy nicknames.

That, however, was all my fucking fault and I kick myself silently as I walk through the elevator doors for not telling her outright that me being anything other than a friend is never going to happen. Not to mention, under no circumstances, in any lifetime, will I ever submit to being referred to as Major fucking Hot Stuff.

I knock on the door of Cain's office, and hear him rummaging around before he grunts, "Come on then."

I open the door to him sitting at his desk watching the television. He runs his hand over the long mohawk strip of salt and pepper hair running down the center of his head. The faint sound of his whirring red mechanical eye is unmistakable despite the volume of the TV. His broad shoulders curl over as he leans on his knees watching an interview with Vice President Arden. I salute him and he doesn't even look at me. I expect it, but he's still a fucking prick because of it.

"Afternoon sir, I have those reports you requested about,"-

"Ah fuck off, Halsey. Not while she's talkin'." He jabs the remote at the television as he speaks, and I want to backhand him with the paperwork that he adamantly demanded several times.

71, 89, 8, 90, 82, I recite in my mind as my shoulders relax, and I exhale slowly. I dip my chin and stand at ease, holding the files in my flexing fingers at my back as we both watch Annalise Arden talk about the new incentive program.

"...It's a genius idea, really. President Montgomery has worked tirelessly to ensure that the incentive program not only protects the sovereignty of the human citizens of Altas but gives back so that they can live richer and more satisfying lives," she says in that smooth rasp of a voice.

"Yeah, right," I mutter under my breath to no one and Cain's head snaps to me. Shit, I didn't realize he could hear me over the television.

"The fuck you say?" He snarls, his cheeks quickly gaining color.

"Nothing, Sir," I reply, and I hate it, but I don't rise with him. I don't meet him at his cresting rage where he burns.

"You calling me a liar, Halsey?" He growls.

Man, he is big mad. It's almost comical. "No, Sir." I say, fixing my gaze ahead as he stands.

"If I ain't a liar, then tell me what ya said. Or are ya too much of a coward to say it?" His face is red as he spits his overreaction through his tight lips.

Normally I would resort to blows, but as I look at him, I see right through his plastic friable baiting rhetoric and fix my face to resist smirking.

I gaze up to the sharp yet lovely visage of Vice President Arden and then back at Cain and wonder. My eyes narrow as a thought crosses my mind. I inhale and try my fleeting hypothesis on for size.

"What I said was that I agree. In fact, I think the administration would do well to have *her* address these new incentives to the public more frequently."

Cain's face cools, his lips soften along with his shoulders and as if that wasn't enough confirmation, he then responds with a new lightness to his tone, "Yeah. Yeah, they should. It's bullshit she ain't out more often."

My eyes flick back to Annalise Arden; her signature fire red lips stretch in a wide perfect smile as she laughs with her interviewer. I double my efforts, sweetening the pot as I say, "She certainly makes the administration much more attractive."

"What d'you mean?" Cain says as he looks back at me, his face beginning to flush again. Gods it's like trying to feed a rabid animal as it snaps, snarls and foams at the mouth.

"All I'm saying," I begin, trying to quell some of the anger Cain is impetuously stoking for the sake of his infatuation, "-is that she seems as wise as she is beautiful."

Cain purses his lips as he surveys me, weighing my words between his pride and punishment. Honestly, I don't give a shit either way.

"You have no idea, Halsey. No idea," Cain says as he sits back in his chair. His hand brushes over his neatly manicured beard as he reclines back, his gaze lingering on Annalise Arden's face while she concludes her interview. "-and you know why?"

"No, Sir."

"Because she called me personally to tell me how good of a job I'm doing in this establishment. Not one government official has bestowed that kind of honor. Not one."

Really? He's getting all twitterpated over an overhyped 'atta-boy'? "That is truly an honor, sir. One of a kind." Ugh, I nearly gag on the words as they come out.

"That's how I know she's different. She's not like the rest of 'em." He doesn't even look at me as he watches her shake hands with the interviewer and walks off frame. He clicks the TV off and turns to me. "You'd do well to show some respect for her, especially around me. Understand, Halsey?"

It's Haley, you fucking dipshit.

71, 89, 8, 90, 82.

Neutral.

"Yes, Sir," I say as I set down the documents he requested on the edge of his desk.

"Okay, fuck off," he says and I reluctantly salute him, before I turn to go. He flourishes his hand in a dismissive gesture, and I will my face to remain passive as I pivot towards the door and leave.

As I walk through the open corridor back to my office, I wonder how deep his obvious infatuation goes for Vice President Arden and what level of servitude he would steep to gain even a glimmer of her attention? Fuck, what would he do to win a modicum of her praise or even her affection?

I close my door behind me and sit down at my desk, continuing to measure the magnitude of his affinity for Annalise Arden and question what lengths Balor Cain would go if he thought the Vice President actually *desired* him. How easily that could be exploited if she only knew.

But she wouldn't know. Because why would she? I would be surprised if she even remembers talking to him or much less, remembers his name. No one important or worthwhile is paying attention to a shriveled sack of shit like Balor Cain and I will enjoy seeing how his infatuation will inevitably fuck him over.

And if I'm patient, if I'm lucky enough, maybe even his destruction.

7
RHIANNON

"But why the mattress?" Xanth laughs as we walk over to the planter boxes. I hand him a set of worn and filthy gloves to begin mixing the soil and compost.

"Why not? I think it was a nice touch." I shrug, picking up a trowel as Xanth rolls up the sleeves of his jumpsuit and pitches a large bag of compost over his shoulder.

"Oh, believe me, I wish I could have seen the bitch's face. It just seems-" he stands there for a moment, thinking of the word before he rips the bag open and dumps the contents over the hardened soil. "-a bit petty."

I scrunch my brows, my face pinching incredulously as he waves away the dust and debris of compost that wafts into the air. "What's your point?"

His brow scrunches, looking like he's stumbling over his thoughts briefly before he responds. "Mah point is, maybe next time ye just pummel 'er somewhere I can watch ye hand 'er 'er ass."

"There he is," I chuckle, digging into the hardpan surface and mixing the compost in. "You had me worried for a minute there. Thought you might be sweet on the Twitch queen."

Xanth's smile pulls tight as he swallows and forces a laugh. "I have this thing called 'standards,' Rhi." He drops the first bag and spills the contents into a planter. "And she's nay a queen. The phoenixes lost that title long ago."

"Oh yeah, right. Pretty sure she fulfills most of those standards, dude."

"She's a damned phoenix, Rhi. The fuckin' enemy. I dinnae care if she has a third tit and a cunt made of candy, it's not gonna happen. Rule number three, ye don't fuck a phoenix."

My brows arc up as I look back at the work in front of me. "Okie dokie, then."

He huffs loudly and practically stomps back to retrieve a shovel.

...Enough, Rhi...

I suppress a giggle. *Sorry,* I chuckle back into his brain and his growl practically vibrates the hair down my neck as he lumbers back like a raging bull.

You are way too easy bud.

...Too far...

Fine, I won't insinuate that you're sweet on your mortal enemy anymore.

...Good, because I'm nay sweet on 'er and it's fuckin' insulting...

She is pretty though.

...Can ye please shut the fuck up already?...

But you'd miss me!

...Right now, ye'd be hard pressed te see me shed a tear if ye shut yer trap...

Fair enough.

"What's the deal with you, 2459?" A heavyset guard named Bruce says as he loops his thumbs into the belt that's currently hiding behind his rotund gut. His cheeks gleam with taut color, while the rest of him is perpetually in some kind of state of overexertion or sweating profusely. It's a wonder he hasn't had a stroke or some kind of cardiac event at this point.

"Ye a'right there Brucey?" Xanth asks as he leans on the long handle of the shovel after pressing the blade into the dirt.

Bruce squints at Xanth, jutting his big belly out a bit more. "Why?"

"Ye look like yer in a right state. Did ye have te take the stairs this mornin'? Och, no wonder yer face is like a ruddy tomato," Xanth continues and I suck in my lips trying not to laugh.

Bruce narrows his eyes, gripping his baton in his swollen pink fingers. Bruce is kind of low-hanging fruit for Xanth for obvious reasons, so he usually leaves Bruce alone and sticks to the real competition. But I suppose I must have really set him off today.

"Latrine duty for the next week," Bruce spits through his teeth, his cheeks flushing an even deeper shade of crimson.

"Is that all then, Sergeant Cream Puff? Ye think I'm scared of cleaning a few dirty toilets?"

Bruce grabs his stun gun and I'm up before he can reach Xanth. I knock his hand away but not before Bruce hits me with swift blunt force twice on the side with his baton. I yell out as I crumple, my ribs snapping as I scream in pain.

"Come to save your little boyfriend, 2460?" Bruce yells as he hits me with the baton again on the same spot on my side and I yell out just as Xanth lunges, but Bruce points his taser in Xanth's face, halting his momentum. Bruce stomps my side with the heel of his boot, and Xanth's dragon rumbles a low growl in his chest, blue-black scales clack on his forearms as cobalt flames wisp from his mouth while he licks his lower lip.

"Burton!" Another deep voice bellows from the entry of the greenhouse. I pant and sputter on the ground as my ribs shoot lightning bolts of pain up and down my sides. "Stand the fuck down!"

"They were insubordinate and disrespectful, and this one," Bruce says as he kicks dirt in my face. I squeeze my eyes shut, resisting the urge to cough as my ribs pulse in agony.

"She was protectin' me, ye lousy bastard!" Xanth yells, his dragon making his voice boom like the clap of thunder.

"Take them to SolCon next time," the handsome copper-haired guard snarls as he comes into view, and I groan. "Now we're down a healthy worker because you can't get your temper under control."

"He was being an asshole, Kieran. I couldn't just-"

"It's Major Haley, Sergeant Burton!" He roars back at Bruce. There's a pause that is thick with tension between the three seething males before I'm picked up and cradled in unfamiliar arms. I bite my cheek to keep from shrieking in pain. What comes out is a hiss between my teeth that sounds like a pathetic whimper. "Report off to Corporal Elliot. He'll sub in for you in the greenhouse today."

Bruce scrunches his purpling face, making him look like an oversized, pissed off toddler with sparse facial hair.

"Fine," Bruce gruffs as he shoves Xanth forward, leading him in the direction of the Breather Block. Xanth turns to look back at me, but Major Haley turns down a different hallway and I'm being carried away from the blue UV lights of the greenhouse.

Kieran.

His name is Kieran.

And he's holding me, although I can hardly focus on the way his hands feel on my body. Yet I still feel the press of his fingers on my legs despite my screaming rib cage. He carries me past the greenhouse all the way to the infirmary. The scenery changes to one of cleaner white tile floors and walls. The smell of astringent stings my nose.

"Hang in there, we'll get you fixed up," Kieran says as he places me on an empty gurney. A little round bot comes rolling up and elevates itself until its black screen face is right over me.

"Welcome to the infirmary, please present your identification tag."

Kieran holds up my wrist with the scarred numbers. The robot scans the brand and then says, "Welcome inmate 2460. I will perform a brief diagnostic scan to generate a personalized treatment plan. This will not be painful. Please hold still for the duration of the scan to ensure its accuracy. Thank you for your cooperation."

The shooting pain radiates through my spine, and I squeeze back tears.

"In order to begin the scan, I require your consent, inmate 2460. You can provide consent by simply saying, 'I consent,' or by saying-"

"I consent," I interrupt the robot's spiel as the pain begins to climb up to my shoulder blades. Fuck it hurts so bad.

A warm calloused hand presses onto the upper plane of my chest and a gentle deep voice whispers against the shell of my ear, "Don't take deep breaths. Keep them short and shallow."

I dip my chin, as a hot tear runs down my cheek. I don't care at this point. A rough thumb caresses the expanse between my breasts, and it isn't sensual or sexual, but a calming nurturing intimacy that reminds me of home. Of the ones I left behind and I sob gently, trying to shorten my erratic breathing.

"That's it, Rhiannon," Kieran says softly, and I wish I could marvel at the way he says my name. I wish I could imagine it in different circumstances while his warmth presses into the top of my chest. His hand, his voice, his presence is like a salve against the growing panic that spreads its spindly limbs along my body.

A mechanical whir sounds as the Med-bot begins its scan. A few seconds later, its cheerful artificial voice states, "Inmate 2460, your 7th, 8th, 9th, and 10th ribs have complete fractures, along with a slight pneumothorax in the lower lobe of your left lung from a dislodged bone fragment from the 10th vertebrochondral rib fracture. This is a serious injury requiring immediate medical attention. Would you like me to proceed with the necessary treatment?"

"No," I say but I'm interrupted by Kieran.

"Yes," he says at the same time. I open my eyes to his aquamarine irises staring wildly at me. "Why?"

"Treatments cost money. I can't-" the pain stabs hard and I gasp.

He blinks and looks at the robot. "Perform the necessary treatment with override code 1170KH5."

The familiar prickle of panic begins to creep its way up my neck and chest. If I can't pay for the treatment with money, it could mean that I will have to pay in other ways. Others who couldn't pay have been forced to sell limbs, organs, tissues, skin grafts that left permanent disfigurement among other things to fulfill their debts here at Ironsgate.

"Please," I say looking up at Kieran, "I can't-"

"Keep quiet," he hushes me.

"Authorization granted for treatment. I have reviewed your chart, Inmate 2460, and will now administer the appropriate sedation and pain management suitable for your species. Please remain still as the sedative and pain medicine is being administered."

Kieran takes my hand and squeezes gently as he meets my eyes. "Just keep looking at me."

More Med-bots appear with bags of fluids and vials of medicine. There's a sharp pinch on my arm as one bot inserts an IV and connects a tube. "Side effects from the sedation and pain medicine are drowsiness, lethargy, impaired memory…"

My eyes begin to lull, and the sounds of beeps and electronic whirs begin to dampen, the pain in my side dulling. My lids droop heavily as I focus on teal eyes that seem to glow under the iridescent lights as he stares back at me, and I fall asleep feeling Kieran's warm hand on my chest.

I don't know how much time has passed when I finally wake up. My side aches. The pain is dull and deep. I creak open my eyes, blinking into the bright fluorescent ceiling with pretend blue skies, fluffy clouds and cheesy palm trees. As if that should comfort me, knowing that paradise is out there, but I get to look at a plastic comparison and that's probably all I'll ever see again.

I try to sit up and the pain is like an electric shock down my back. A rough hand covers my shoulder, and I look to the side to see Kieran sitting there.

He's still here.

Why is he still here?

"Don't move just yet," he says, his thumb swiping over my skin and my head thuds back onto the plastic-coated pillow.

"How long was I out?" My voice is hoarse.

"Not long. Maybe three or so hours," he says, running a hand through his hair and scratching the back of his head.

I groan. My hand runs over the bandages that encase my upper body and tightly bind my breasts. I look down and peek under my blanket to find pale ceil blue hospital pants and only the bandage to cover my top.

"What did they-"

"Your dragon DNA was healing your ribs, but they weren't set right, so the Bips had to re-break your ribs and set them correctly. They had to place a tube in your lung to fix the pneumothorax but that healed quickly after your ribs were reset. It should only be another hour or so before you feel like yourself again."

"Oh," I say and clear my throat. "How am I going to pay for-"

"Don't worry about it. It's taken care of."

"By whom?"

"By the facility."

Bullshit. I look up into his turquoise eyes and purse my mouth. "So, *you* paid for it?"

He prods his cheek with his tongue as his eyes flick to his folded hands in his lap. "Can you just let it go?"

"No. How much did the treatment cost?" I inch up and flinch as an electric pain shoots up my back.

"Stop trying to move," Kieran chastises as he presses a button on the side of the bed that inclines my head. "And you don't owe me anything. Burton should not have reacted the way he did."

"Why do you care about how he treated me? None of the other officers give a shit."

"I'm not the other guards or officers," he says as he crosses his leg over his knee. "I tend to give a shit."

"You didn't answer my question," I say, my voice still rasping. "*Why* do you give a shit?"

He drops his foot back down and leans his elbows onto his knees as he gets closer to my face. "I don't need to answer anything if I don't want to, Inmate."

I roll my eyes. "Whatever," I say, chuckling and then wince.

"It's like your hellbent on making it worse," he says while he presses a button on my side rail and a Bip rolls in.

"How can I help you, Major Haley?"

"She needs more pain medicine," he tells the bot.

"No, I don't," I say quickly at the smooth white pill shaped bot with its blank black screen.

The bot is quiet for a few seconds as its screen faces Kieran and then me. "I do not understand."

"As the proprietor of Inmate 2460's care currently, I'm requesting that you give her more pain medicine."

I shoot Kieran a withering look as the Bip says, "Of course, Major Haley." The little white robot produces a syringe and pushes the medicine through the IV connected to my arm. It starts working in seconds.

He's smirking at me as my head lolls back onto my pillow. My brain is beginning to feel like mushy Jello. Wobbly and losing its form the more I try to think. It's as close to being drunk as I have ever been.

"You know," I start, feeling like talking might be a bad idea but doing it anyway. "I have never been with a guard before. Like seggsually." Ooof that is a hard word to say right now. Also, I don't think I should have said that word to him.

"Okay," he laughs and leans back into his chair. "Nor have I."

"You could though. You could have any guard or inmate you want. You know why, K-keernan?" Oh boy, his name is even worse.

His smile makes the warmth from the drug feel like it sparkles in my veins as it works its way down to my fingers and toes.

"I have a feeling you're gonna tell me whether I want you to or not," he says flashing perfect white teeth and I feel my lower half ache.

"Be-because you are so pretty. Like, the prettiest boy in all the world, I think."

His smile grows wider and if I didn't currently feel like a bowl of pudding, I'd probably melt into the floor. "Okay, I'm glad the drugs are working."

"No, I'm super serious. I would let you do very bad things to me. Because I like you more than I'm allowed to."

"Allowed to?" He says as his brows furrow, his smile still wide and glorious.

"I heard you, you know," I say and I think at this point I'm just letting my brain run through the gamut of whatever the fuck it wants without a filter.

His smile wanes a bit as he asks, "You heard me?"

"Mmhmm. You said my name," I sigh and turn a little to face him, the pain a dull ache this time. "It sounds just like how I imagined it would."

"Y-you've imagined me saying your name?"

Stop. You have to stop. But here comes more words that I don't want to say out loud. "Over and over. With your mouth on mine and your hands on-"

"Okay, you don't need to say anymore," he says chuckling. But apparently that doesn't deter me.

"-On my ass underneath my jumpsuit, squeezing my tits, running your rough fingers over my nipples. I imagine you whispering into my mouth right before you slide your tongue inside and-"

"Stop," Kieran says softly but I'm not looking at him at my bedside,

I'm staring at the version of him in my mind, and I'm getting lost in it as I continue talking.

"-And it feels so good I wonder what it will feel like between my legs and it's then, right as I imagine your tongue swiping over my clit that I co-"

"Rhiannon," he says more forcibly, and I open my eyes. He's hovering over me, his eyes bright in that otherworldly teal glow that ceases my train of thought.

"Yeah, like that," I whisper as he exhales and I smell the mint from his gum, the leather, the smoke, and that…odd cloying sweetness that I can't quite figure out. I reach up and touch his hair and for the briefest moment he leans into it, he turns his face to my palm, and I feel the softness of his lips on the mound of my thumb. My breath hitches but he backs away. He stands a few arm lengths away from me and there's a part of me that's glad, because it isn't right. He and I…we aren't right. But I feel Nina purr in my belly, the warmth dances in my veins from his nearness. "What's that cologne you're wearing? It smells sweet like…like opium or syrup or-"

"I'm glad to see you are feeling better, Inmate," he says and steps back.

"Rhiannon."

Ciara.

NO. Not that.

His mouth quirks with a shadow of a smile as he says, "Rhiannon." He turns to walk out the door.

"Major Haley," I call back and he turns in profile. "I will pay you back."

His eyes glitter as he chuckles, shaking his head as he walks out the door.

8
EILIDH

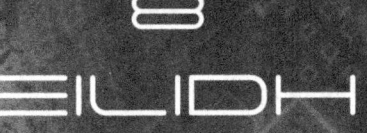

It's been three days.

Seventy-two hours in this hellhole and I haven't had an ounce of luck with any of my attempts to get out of here. I've made a few valiant attempts, but they've all failed and left me feeling more and more discouraged.

Every time I try to slip past one of the guards, another sees me and redirects me back to where I'm 'supposed' to be.

I tried fidgeting with one of the card readers the other day to see if I could get a lock open. No fucking way in hells I'm getting past the coding. Not without my team and equipment to help me shut down the security system. The wires are all hidden behind welded metal tubing so I can't cut the power either.

I even began scraping a small hole in the floor with a spoon I smuggled from the chow hall like a fucking mole astral, as if that's going to somehow get me out of here.

Nothing has worked.

Nothing is working.

My patience is wearing thin and the fact that I'm stuck on the Breather Block with a bunch of astrals who hate my guts for what I am isn't helping my mental state. My second night here, I came back from laundry duty to a completely decimated bed and had to sleep on the linoleum like an animal while my *roomie* slept peacefully.

She snores.

Not loud, but enough that I want to kick her every time she falls asleep.

It's midday, we're currently in our cells and I can hear her. A soft sawing sound coming from her nostrils. The agitation whirling within me has me seething and my beast slams against the cage of my body, desperate to escape. Three days without sun for a phoenix feels like what I imagine a fish out of water must feel like. Hollow and gasping for the life source I desperately need. The faux sky ceilings mock me, a ludicrous farce reminding all of us of what we no longer have access to.

Another quiet snore slips from my roommates gaping mouth and I send my heel back into the bed, rattling the metal frame.

She sits up with a start, rubbing her head and looking around, likely searching for the commotion that woke her up. When she finds nothing, she stands and faces me at the top of the bed. "What the *fuck*?"

"Can I help you?" I feign ignorance and pick at my nails. Happy to see that I've pissed her off. I need to offload my misery right now and I know I can rile her easily.

"Bold move to wake a sleeping dragon. You got a death wish, Twitcher? Didn't your parents teach you anything?" Her cool blue eyes pierce through me as her head tilts in an almost serpentine way.

Got her.

"My mother didn't tell me much of anything, I learned it all on my own. And my dad? Who knows where that fucker is. So no, I can't say I've received much training on how...*delicately* I need to handle your kind." The condescension comes off in waves.

I can feel her hackles raise as the tension in the room doubles. "Delicate? We'll see who's really fucking delicate." She launches herself at me, claws and teeth bared. I flip myself over so she can't pin me to the bed and slice my eyes out, but her knee still catches me in the side, knocking the wind out of me.

I twist at the waist, bringing my elbow back on her shoulder and she roars in both pain and frustration. My anger ignites my blood and we both start swinging, slicing, kicking and snarling in a flurry of limbs and hair.

She gets another good hit on my face and blood bursts from my cheek. I growl and dip low, swiping my leg and dropping her to the floor before straddling her and driving my fists into her face. She wiggles her arms out from under my thighs and pushes me off after a few solid blows.

We both sit on the floor, clothes ripped, bruised and bloodied while we pant in each other's faces.

"Who's Fianna?" I ask, breathless.

Her features twist with what looks like a mixture of rage, pain, and shocked surprise.

"How do you know that name?" She speaks low and in what I assume is a tone reserved for her worst enemies. So…me I suppose.

"If you won't answer my question, I won't answer yours," I say, matching her malice.

Good.

"Don't *ever* speak that name again." Her arms shake and as much as I want to continue to fight her, the fire within me is receding and sadness begins creeping in its place. "If I hear you say her name again, I'll tear your fucking throat out with my teeth."

I have no more fury to give her. I feel like an empty shell of myself.

My mother would be disappointed in me.

Without another word, I stand and make my way to the sink so I can wash some of the cuts on my face. Even with daily showers, this place is filthy. I inspect my clothes in the small mirror above the sink.

Great, they're fucking ruined.

Instead of getting back into bed I stand beside the open bars of our cell.

Xanth hasn't had another female over in a few days and I've relished the quieter nights. Even now, all I can hear from his cell is the scrape of a pencil against paper. It's almost peaceful.

I'm a bit surprised he didn't intervene with the fight my cellmate and I just had. They seem to be close and usually when we argue, he has something colorful to say to me about it. Today, however, there is nothing but silence and pencil scratches.

I wonder what he's writing, or rather, who he's writing to.

I shake the unwelcome thought from my mind. I don't give two shits who he's writing to. The only thing on my mind concerning him is getting out of here and being as far away from him as possible.

This is a fool's mission, and my mother knows it. No one, and I truly mean *no one*, has been able to get in or out of Ironsgate. It's the single most guarded post outside of the President's personal quarters and every known escape attempt has ended horribly for the astrals involved. Knowing my mother, she likely sent me here to die because she couldn't kill me herself without raising a few brows in Pyrrh.

She may hate me, but our people do not.

They care for me, almost as much as I care for them.

They are the reason I keep going. The reason that I accepted this mission and want my rank back. I know the types of folk vying for my mother's position, and I'd rather die than see Pyrrh handed over to one of those sniveling sycophantic narcissists.

My heart clenches and I will myself to shift my train of thought. This emotional spiral I've been working through since I got here is draining me.

Looking around the block, I notice a few newly occupied cells. Men in white coats escorted by two guards came down the other day and stood by as the guards opened a cell and pulled a female dragon from her bed. Everyone watched as she was ushered away in uneasy silence but as soon as they were past the cellblock three gate, everyone resumed what they'd been doing before, as if nothing happened.

It was eerie.

My gaze travels from the cells to the guards milling about. Some walk along the corridor, looking into cells and poking at the inmates. Others look bored, like they'd rather be anywhere but here. There's a small group of guards standing a good distance away but I'm able to catch some of what they are saying so I tune out the sounds around me and listen in.

"Rookie, I'm telling you, you may not want it now, but the time will come where you're gonna need to get your dick wet," one of the guards, the male who brought me down here I realize, says to a young, decent looking blond male.

A female beside him pushes his shoulder and rolls her eyes. "You're disgusting Ryker. Leave the kid alone."

Ryker looks at her and smirks, "You can't tell me you haven't ridden at least one of the cocks in this place, Jo." He pauses and squints his eyes at her. "Unless you prefer the company of females."

Jo flushes and looks away.

"Ha! I didn't realize we had so much in common, Jo!" He nudges her. "You'll have to tell me more about which one you bagged later." He turns his attention back to the younger guard. "Now, Gunnar, my boy. In here, favors are everything." His smile turns wicked. "Offer one of them a favor and they'll let you do damn near anything you want to them."

Gunnar looks nervously around him before whispering, "what sort of favors?"

"Some are easy. They want chocolate or a cigarette, some want information on other inmates, and for the ones that are particularly hard to crack, those you just offer a chance to see the upstairs rec hall. The fifth floor has an open ceiling that is open to the sky. There's not a single Mute in here that wouldn't give you anything you want just to catch a glimpse of the sun again."

My ears perk up and my back straightens.

Shit.

That's it.

9
EILIDH

Later that evening, I find myself setting my tray down beside Lumara in the chow hall. Her thick black mane shifts to the side, revealing her ear and I know she's already listening. A guard stops by to remove my iron mask.

"We're relieving you of the mask for the time being, Inmate 2475," The guard says to me. "After chow you can return to your quarters without the halter." A large hand waves the hideous muzzle in front of my face, and I nod my acknowledgement.

My face feels lighter already. Once the guard is out of range, I settle in with Lumara.

"Tell me about the guard favors." I waste no time getting directly to the point. I've been eager to have this conversation for hours now. Lumara may be a bit odd, but all things considered, she's the only one around here that's been willing to talk to me.

Her lips spread into a wide grin, and I take a bite to keep from looking like we're scheming. The last thing I need is another guard poking around in our conversation and getting suspicious.

"Interesting," she hisses. "What sort of things motivates a phoenix to fuck the humans they so despise, hm?"

My fingers tighten around my fork, but I remain calm. "The sun. I overheard some guards talking about the rec hall upstairs having access to the sun." I toss her a pleading look so that she doesn't see through my act.

It's true, I *do* want to see the sun again. It's been killing me since the moment I arrived, but once I'm free I'll have as much access as I need. My goal remains the same.

Get in, get out.

Out of the corner of my eye, I see my cellmate and Xanth entering the chow hall together and they begin filling their trays. I track their movements, the two of them are lost in conversation but I can feel Xanth's attention on me like a weight against my skin, pressing and suffocating.

"Ah yes, the sun," Lumara starts, "my knowledge of phoenixes is limited so I apologize for my ignorance. Of course, birds of fire would require heat's greatest source." She scrapes her fork through her mashed vegetables before continuing. "It seems the price to sleep with one of the guards isn't too steep for you," she finishes just as the two dragons pass our table.

Xanth stops in his tracks, and his head turns slowly towards me. His eyes, now burning blue flames, envelop me and the temperature around me rises. I catch a hint of scotch wafting from him and wonder if he's managed to pay the guards for alcohol as well as sex. That can't be right though. Oak and moss follow the whiskey scent, and I lean into it.

Gods, he smells good.

My cellmate pauses when she realizes that Xan is no longer following her. She looks between us and her eyes narrow on me.

"Eilidh." She nods and my mouth drops open slightly.

I didn't even realize she knew my name. It's usually *Twitch Bitch* or some variant of the two words.

"Xan, what are you waiting for? Let's go." She gestures with her head in the direction of their usual seats before she turns around and continues.

…What did Lumara just say?.. His voice rumbles through my head and I bare my teeth.

I believe your master just told you to hurry along, dog. I quip. Decidedly glad that my internal voice is stronger than my actual one when he's staring at me in that all-consuming way and the smell of him is turning my brain to mush.

He visibly seethes.

…Ye'd think that by now ye'd know I serve only myself. Others get on their knees fer me, nay the other way around. It's a shame that'll never be an option for ye… His expression changes to one of pity before resuming

his earlier ire. *...Now, what did Lumara just say about ye and the guards?...*

"None of your business. I've had about enough of this."

...I've just made it mah business, Little Dove. Now tell me. What. Did. She. Say?..

A ripple, so small I would have missed it had my eyes not been trained on him, passes over his skin. Scales, as black as night with a blue, iridescent shine, reflect off his skin and are gone again.

Instead of answering, I drop my eyes from his and say to Lumara, "So it seems," I say vaguely. "I'm wondering if it's all of the guards, or only a select few who...partake."

...This conversation isn't over... He growls.

Xanth blows hot air at me that ruffles the loose strands that have escaped my braid, but he doesn't linger. He stomps off in the direction of his friend and I watch as the two of them begin a heated conversation that includes huffing, rolling eyes and several points in my direction.

Fantastic.

"There are a few that are easier to seduce," Lumara speaks as though she's missed the entire interaction with the dragons. "Ryker is the easiest of them."

No surprise there.

"However, every guard is privy to the favors and when they are in the mood, they'll come."

I don't miss her innuendo.

"So, do I just have to wait? Or can I approach them and work out a deal without them blowing my brains across the hall?" I ask.

"Ryker will be your best bet if you plan on approaching a guard. He's eternally horny and isn't bad to look at. The others, you'll have to rely more heavily on seduction to get one of them to agree. It's easiest to let them come to you." With that, she picks up her tray and heads for the garbage can, leaving me to hash out the rest of my plan in relative silence.

I spend much of my dinner watching the guards and their behaviors, trying to decide which would be the least repulsive or difficult.

Two of the older guards, Harvey and Bruce, sit together at a table with similar expressions of irritation and boredom. Bruce has a belly that sticks out from beneath his oil-stained shirt, and I gag a bit at the thought of his smell. I'm almost certain the man hasn't showered in at least a week.

Harvey is a short, bald man with a permanent scowl etched into his mouth and brow. He's the shortest of all the guards I've met so far and has the quickest temper. I cringe and continue my perusal of the guards.

Ryker sits at a table with Jo and Gunnar. His dark brown hair cut close to his head on the sides and styled perfectly at the top. Lumara is right, he's not bad to look at. He's got a thick muscular build with a jawline that reminds me of Amell's, but his positive attributes end there. The man is full of himself. I think he only hangs out with Jo because she's quiet and Gunnar because he's new and doesn't know any better. I watch him prattle on about how he took down a bear astral the other day with one arm and I roll my eyes.

Highly unlikely.

Looking at Jo, I marvel at her beautiful face and large brown eyes that often turn down during Ryker's rants. Her dark hair is always pulled back in a low bun showcasing her lovely long neck. I don't know much about her, but she seems safe enough.

I add her to my list.

Next, I look at Gunnar. Young, blonde, pale and nervous. All the other guards call him Rookie, and I can see why. His confidence is practically zero and I worry that he would get us caught before I ever would. Good looking guy but…

Pass.

Skimming the rest of the guards, my eyes land on a table towards the front where Major Haley sits with two other guards. One, a broad-shouldered man with dimples in his cheeks. His ebony beard is full and cut short with tightly curled hair that's cut square atop his head. His eyes are kind, and he laughs at something the Major says. I've never seen him before but something about him seems… Warm.

He makes the list.

The female beside them smiles and shakes her head. Her tightly wound locks sway as she moves, and the natural rosy color of her full lips has me burning with envy.

Another good option.

Major Haley looks out at the crowd, seeming to search for someone before he returns to the conversation with the other two guards.

I think back to our previous interaction and while I was more than a little embarrassed that he had seen my fight with Xan, he's hot and he didn't seem like a complete asshole like many of the guards in this place.

His teal eyes kick up again and latch onto something across the room. I look to where his attention has gone and am more than a little curious when I notice it's my cellmate that he's watching. He sits completely still while she laughs loudly at something a dragon beside her says and then her glacial stare finds his and…whoa. Talk about sexual tension.

Well, Major Haley is off the list.

When I notice that most of the astrals have left the room, I stand and grab my tray, readying to head out.

The smell of spiced whiskey and oak forests descends like fog, just as a large, tattoo covered hand slams down on my plate and I look up to Xanth's furious face. The only other time we've been this close I had an iron mask preventing me from picking up his scent. Now, it digs its claws into my chest and has my head spinning.

Well, that was rude, even for you. I say in my mind, attempting to move the tray out from under his arm again but he presses down more firmly, and I can't move it an inch.

Bastard.

"Indeed I am, Little Dove," he answers my inner thoughts, and I bristle. "I told ye our conversation wasn't over. Now tell me, what were ye and the spider whisperin' about?" His voice is calm and cool, but I can sense the danger within his words, and it sends a shiver down my spine. I shouldn't like this as much as I do.

"As I told *you* before, it's none of your godsdamn business what I talked to her about."

His eyes linger on my mouth, and I realize this is the first time he's heard me speak without a mask on. He's transfixed by my lips, and I use that to my advantage. I lick them slowly and his body tenses. A tick in his jaw turns his gaze hungry and that weight from earlier returns to my chest.

"As I said before," he mocks me. "I'm making it mah business, now tell me why she mentioned ye fuckin' a guard?" He looks back up at my eyes.

"Because I want to fuck one," I say with more certainty than I feel.

Xanth's head tilts to the side and something rattles within him. In my head, I hear his velvety tenor.

…Ye want te fuck a guard? Like a right whore?..

His words enrage me. My fists clench and I can feel my beast pressing against my skin, trying everything to claw her way out. Bolstered by Solara's fury, I press into him with my teeth bared.

"You've called me every terrible name there is, and you think *whore* is the worst opinion you could have of me?" I scoff at him and continue. "*Fuck you* Xanth. Fuck your names, your hatred of me, and your infuriating voice in my mind." I'm seething now, my emotions flowing from me in a flurry of words that I'm unable to stop. "Yes, I want to sleep with a guard, and it's none of your godsdamn business. Also, whether you believe it or not, I'm a fucking *catch* and I enjoy getting railed just as much as the next female. Just because you have some stupid misplaced resentment of me doesn't mean everyone else does. You may not want me, but I can guarantee you there is someone in here who *does*."

I stand there, intimately aware of how close our lips are now while he is leaning against the edge of the table with me pressed against him.

"Maybe, if you're lucky, you'll hear the echoes of *my* pleasure so you can jerk off to it on the nights Meadow isn't there to warm your bed. Maybe hearing the *phoenix whore* scream another male's name will make you hate me more, and that is just fine with me."

Before I can step away, he reaches out and grasps my hip tightly, holding me to him.

"Say it again," he whispers. His lips only a breath away from mine.

"Wh-what?" My earlier boldness has plummeted right out of my ass as my heart punches my sternum.

"Say my name again." His eyes dart between mine and warmth floods my insides.

Xanth. I say in my mind.

"No, I want te hear ye say it." The rumble of his chest vibrates against me and my breath catches. He lifts his other hand to my face and brushes the pad of this thumb against my lower lip, parting them.

I've clearly lost all sense of logic as I breathe, "Xanth."

A low sound that's part growl, part groan, rumbles through his chest and he drops his head back towards the ceiling, exposing the bulging veins in his ink covered neck.

...Ye won't like what happens if ye go through with this. That is the only warning I'll give ye, Little Dove...

Or what? You'll kill me? Sorry if that doesn't scare me the way you want it to. That threat is getting old, and since when do you care what I do? I can't will the words past my lips but my mind hurls them at him in quick succession.

...If ye think I've only just started concerning mahself with what y'er doin', y'er wrong. I've had mah eyes on ye since the moment ye came through that fuckin' gate...

He leans in to the hallow of my neck and inhales deeply, right over the surface of my skin causing chills to rush down my spine.

I step back from him and this time, he lets me. Picking up the forgotten tray, I all but run to the trash and out the doors to my cell.

10
RHIANNON

I turn on the water from the rusted tap in the cell, cup my hands and splash the icy cold over my face. The ache in my side from my healing ribs is a dull throb now and I prod the pale thin scar that's left in the wake of Bruce's temper tantrum.

As I gently press, a diminished pang runs through the tissues where Kieran's hands were as he carried me to the infirmary. It's hard to focus on the specifics due to the pain, but if I close my eyes and focus hard enough, I can remember his wide calloused fingers, gentle and warm, the tight cords of his neck against my brow, his breath displacing my hair as he briskly ran with me in his arms.

Gods, I am *pathetic*.

I don't need to be thinking about this…about *him*. It's ridiculous and nothing is ever going to happen between us. *Ever*.

What I *should* be concerned about is the conversation with Xanth in the chow hall and the way he responded to Eilidh talking with Lumara. Honestly, I don't understand why he lost his shit. Yes, she's a phoenix, but despite that, he still…*cares*. Even if he won't admit it to himself.

I've felt from the moment that shifty Twitcher arrived that she was up to something. She's not some quiet, demure, scared little thing… she's cunning and careful. She observes everything, like she's taking mental notes of what happens in here. And it seems like she misses nothing.

She's calculating. Devising.

So maybe Xanth has good reason to be invested in whatever the hell she's doing. Even if his interest seems wholly selfish. I can't tell if he wants to kill her or fuck her, though. Perhaps both and in no particular order. But she *is* planning something and maybe talking to Lumara is just a way for her to scope out more of the facility. Find its markers of vulnerability and blind spots for better surveillance.

Which is smart...

But why Lumara? She's literally the *last* person I'd trust in this shitcan with *anything*. Lumara reeks of betrayal by self-preservation and narcissism. She would sell out all of us to save herself and I can practically *smell* it on her. So why would Eilidh want anything from her?

Unless she was desperate.

I'm leaning into my hands on the rim of the sink when the door to the cell opens and Eilidh steps through. Jo locks the gate and Eilidh stands at the doorway. I look up at the dinghy clouded steel mirror and see her silhouette staring back at me. The first thing I notice is that the thick blocky halter mask is gone.

"Evening, Twitch," I say as I turn towards her. Her face is lovely, even though it's twisted in a scowl.

"Evening, Breather." She smirks and the corner of my mouth ticks up. I like that she mirrors my attitude. It's like a permission slip to continue being an asshole.

Too far. She doesn't deserve this. She didn't deserve that. My thoughts from the day I shredded her bed cycle back to the forefront and for some reason they stifle my desire to lean in and continue being a dick.

"I saw you talking to Lumara," I say, walking forward and leaning against the metal bed frame.

She huffs and rolls her eyes. "Yeah, and?" She replies dryly.

"How much do you know about her?" I ask, trying to be more genuine.

Her brows arc and her lips pucker a bit as her eyes narrow. "First Xanth and now you? Why do you care?"

"I don't speak for Xanth and whatever bullshit he has going on. I only speak for myself. You can do what you want, but Lumara is-" I run my tongue along my teeth as I try to place my words a little more carefully. "-She has her interests. They usually don't align with anyone else's but her own."

Eilidh scoffs as she crosses her arms over her chest. "And I suppose *you* align with my interests?"

One for the phoenix. "Fair point," I say bobbing my head to the side. "But you also haven't really shared your interests with me, so…"

"Hang on. Are you *actually* insinuating that after the warm welcome and treatment I've gotten from you thus far that I should *trust* you?"

Two for the phoenix. "Okay yeah, I suppose I could have been nicer but it's prison, Eilidh. There's a hierarchy and I have a fucking reputation to uphold, one that keeps me alive and fucking unbothered for the most part. Not to mention that you are a *phoenix,* and I am a *dragon.*"

Eilidh? Man… Am *I* growing soft on the Twitcher now?

She stares at me and blinks a few times. Her lips part gently as her golden eyes remain wide.

"You know my name," She says softly. It's strange because it feels like vulnerability. Like she's peeking over the stone fortress around her to see who's there.

"I have my sources," I say with a wink.

She stares at me with that mild bewilderment until I decide to continue.

"Anyway, whatever it is you're planning, there are other, more reliable, allies you can choose who are far better than the spider. Allies that will have your back and not immediately throw you under the bus the minute they catch a whiff of danger. There's a reason Lumara operates alone."

"Noted," she says as she climbs up to the top bunk. She stands at the top rung of the ladder and stares at the replaced mattress, sheets, blanket, and pillow. "Wait."

"I had a favor to call in. You're welcome."

She stands there for a few more seconds before climbing onto the bed. "I would say thank you, but you're also the reason I needed new things in the first place."

"Yeah, don't." *Because you didn't deserve that.*

Her eyes soften as she tucks her hands under her head. I climb onto my own bed as the lights suddenly shut off and the buzzer sounds. I turn onto my side that aches and I hate that I start thinking of him again.

"Rhiannon."

I exhale as I remember his voice, deep and dangerous and I turn onto my back while I squeeze my eyes shut.

"Good-night, Eilidh," I say, gently nudging her from the bottom of her mattress.

She huffs quietly, "Hardly fair I don't know your name."

I smirk as I reply, "It's Rhiannon."

"Ciara."

I press my fingers to my temples, trying to push the thought away, burying it underneath where it cannot be seen or heard.

She shifts above me, making the metal groan and it's quiet for several seconds. The sounds of scurrying rodents, dripping water, and the gentle snores of inmate's echo in the dark before she says so soft I almost miss it. Almost.

"Goodnight, Rhiannon."

I wake to the buzzer but no guard. My eyes flit open and after the shriek dies down, I hear soft cries over the speaker. Whimpers mixed with sobs. My brows pull together as I sit up and the bunk above me squeaks as Eilidh does the same.

"Ironsgate Inmates," a deep voice bent in a round cockney accent drawls over the intercom. I hop off my bed just as Eilidh climbs down from her bunk and we stare side by side at an average sized, muscular officer, with a brown beard and mohawk and the most unsettling glowing red mechanical eye standing in the middle of the Breather Block. There are camera drones hovering around him along with Ryker, Bruce, Jo, Axel, Harvey, and Nova standing guard beside him. Behind them, a quivering male astral I have never seen before sits on his knees. He has shaggy auburn hair, bright brown eyes, alabaster skin and he looked like he must be in his early twenties. From the scent of it, he smells like a fox shifter, but it's hard to tell. Right next to the cruel looking man with the accent, is Kieran, heavily armed with a sullen look on his face.

"What is this?" Eilidh whispers under her breath and I shake my head softly, trying to make sense of it also.

"For those of ya that don't know my name, I'm yar esteemed Warden, and today, I've decided to bring back an old tradition. One that sadly has been replaced by bureaucratic diplomatic bullshit that I find…rather fucking tedious."

"I saw him on my first day here and he was an absolute prick. What's he doing with that astral?" Eilidh whispers again, her eyes flitting to my face briefly.

"No idea," I respond under my breath.

"Another inmate informed me that this Mute 'ere tried his luck at escaping last night," the man with the mohawk bellows over the mic clipped onto his chest and it's deafening as it vibrates in my ears. "So, I have decided that I need to address this issue personally and send all of ya Mutes a very clear message."

He snaps his sidearm from his holster and fires it at the astral's temple. Blood sprays onto the laminate block floor and onto Harvey's pants. Harvey doesn't blink as brain matter sticks to his boots and the astral slumps before falling dead on the floor. Cries and gasps echo throughout the block. Eilidh and I stand stunned in disbelief. Shock, confusion, fury…an amalgamation of collective horror at what just happened radiates into the cool morning air.

Kieran's face is stoney. He doesn't move as the blood pools from the astrals temple and collects at the soles of his boots.

"I think we all understand the message, eh? Starting today, if any of ya astral *FUCKS* try to escape my prison…I will personally put a bullet through yar *fuckin' skull!*" His face is red with rage, and he holsters his firearm before he kicks the dead astral away from his path. As he walks to the elevators, Kieran's face remains impassive and cold, following closely behind the warden.

No one collects the body. No one cleans up the blood that is pooled in a macabre lake or the scattered bits of brain on the floor. The dead astral just lays there, mouth slightly agape, lightless eyes staring at nothing as his limbs lay splayed out in odd angles.

"Holy shit," Eilidh whispers.

...*You two alright?*...

Xanth's voice is raspy even in my mind.

No. You? I reply, but he doesn't respond.

I turn and walk back to the sink, unsure if I would throw up or not. I swallow back the bile and turn as Eilidh presses her back against the bars, her face is paler than normal as her golden eyes flit up to meet mine.

"Please, don't trust her," I say, so soft that I'm unsure whether or not she hears me.

She nods, acknowledging what she heard, just like the gunshot that took that boy's life.

Her eyes turn down, and she dips her chin ever so slightly as the locks click open and we file out to the showers.

11
EILIDH

I'm still rattled by the time I enter the rec hall that afternoon.

The air in the block is thick with tension and uncertainty. No one here can be trusted. Rhiannon told me as much before this morning's performance. I suppose in a place like this, many adopt the attitude that it's them against the world. Everyone is out for themselves and that scares me more than the ones who have formed small groups.

They have no allegiance and therefore are wildly unpredictable.

The punching bag that I ruined sits untouched in the gym area. Instead, I head over and begin my reps after removing my top. A large line of duct tape was used to patch the bag where it busted open, and I stare at it with pride as I recall sending Xanth to his knees and shocking the shit out of Cadmyr just before splitting it.

Something about Xanth drives me insane.

Besides the fact that he is hells bent on hating me.

I make my way through the first round of reps and then move over to the pullup bar. My arm muscles strain and I lift myself over one, two, three times before my thoughts start to wander again.

I wonder what Amell would do if he were here.

The thought has my arms trembling and I'm only able to get a few more good pulls in before I drop to my feet.

The sanctimonious bastard would have run up to that astral and tried to save them. I'd then have needed to jump in to save *him*, and we would have blown the whole place down in our efforts to take out the warden and his guards. We played that same tune a thousand times before and I still can't believe he's gone.

It's been over three years, yet I still see him when I dream. Feel the warmth of his hands on my naked body before I wake up and my reality comes crashing down around me.

My heart aches and I feel the hot sting of tears well in my eyes. Grabbing my water bottle, I drink until they've passed and I'm able to wipe my face without looking like I was about to cry.

A few dragons are using the weight racks, so I start stretching my calves and quads, prepping for a short jog around the complex. Now that the mask is off, I've been itching to stretch my legs and run again, even if I'm confined to this mediocre track.

I prop my toes up against a wooden block and bend over, working out any tightness. My hair drapes down over my face but I still when the air around me shifts.

Xanth.

I hear him before I see him.

His laugh bounces off the walls of the hallway and he steps through the doors to the rec hall with the grace of a cerulean god with two twin dragon males on either side of him. He's the tallest, most gorgeous male I've ever seen. His broad shoulders pull his jumpsuit tight over his chest and his muscles strain against the material. The veins in his hands run up the length of his forearms and I have to wipe the drool from my mouth.

Today he has his long hair pulled into a bun at the top of his head and I can more clearly see the tattoos peeking out beneath the short fuzz on the lower half of his head

I wonder which one of them his dragon gave him.

His eyes dart in my direction and pierce through me. I haven't tested the strength or range of this strange mental link he and I share. I don't *think* he can hear me from across this massive room but I'm unsure.

He slowly peruses my body, and I feel stripped bare. My chest heaves and I realize I'm still bent over with my ass up in the air. I stand and turn away, unable to hold his stare any longer.

My feet hit the outlined laminate track, and I round the first corner of the rec hall. I try to tune him out, but it's pointless.

He's all consuming.

I can feel his attention on my skin like a physical touch. Sweat breaks out across my chest and forehead. I'm panting by the time I make it halfway around the track like an amateur, as if I haven't spent my entire life running.

His eyes are no longer on me, but I can still feel the prickle of his awareness. It follows me with every stride.

It takes all my willpower to avoid looking back at him when I near him. His spiced earth scent pulls me in like a drug, but I make it past him without succumbing to the temptation to stare.

I continue running, still keenly aware of him but doing my best to shake my thoughts from straying to how his jumpsuit is unbuttoned at the top, revealing more of his chiseled chest.

Keep moving.

I push my legs to continue, even as they strain and scream for me to stop. It's been over a week since I last ran and with the lack of natural sunlight to strengthen me, my body is so much weaker. However, I continue to put one foot in front of the other. Over and over until my chest feels like it's about to burst.

From the corner of my eye, I see four deer shifter females approach Xanth. They all have varying colors of long, wavy brown and blonde hair hanging down their slender bodies. I recognize Meadow from the first night I was here. Her jumpsuit clings to her generous curves, and I'm hit with a sharp pang of envy. She's soft in all the right places. Her body is free from scars, and the light catches her eyes, making them sparkle.

She's gorgeous.

Quintessentially perfect in every way.

She's the type of female I can see Xanth being with and it's no wonder they're together.

His mirthful laughter invades my mind, and I finally cave and look at him. Curiously, he isn't looking at Meadow or the other deer astrals. He's staring over their heads at me, and I slow to a walk.

All four of them surround him, the two males he'd been walking with long gone. One of the females looks up at him from beneath her lashes and a small smile plays on her thin, feminine lips.

"What's yer name, Doll?" Xanth asks her. His hand comes up to play with a strand of her hair and I wonder to myself what their reaction would be if I set the strand on fire. Apparently, his affection for Meadow isn't as exclusive as I thought. She stands near them, her hands roaming the plane of his chest as he gives the other astral his full attention.

"Fawn," she breathes.

"Mmmm," a deep rumble sounds from his chest, and I can physically feel it squeezing me. "The pleasure is mine, Doll."

He grabs her hand and lifts it to his lips where he kisses her knuckles, and her cheeks turn an attractive shade of pink.

I think I'm going to be sick.

Unable to watch anymore, I jog back to the water fountain and take a sip before I make for the door. Xanth looks up and our eyes meet again before I dart behind a group of dragons, evading their intimate little party.

I can still hear Fawn giggling over something he whispers in her ear as I run away from the unwelcome feelings burrowing in my chest.

"What are you doing here?" I ask as I'm escorted back into my cell by the rookie guard, Gunnar. He was the first guard I could find after fleeing from the rec hall. Returning to my cell felt better than bearing witness to whatever shitshow is happening between Xanth and Fawn right now.

I wasn't expecting to find my cellmate sitting in her bed.

"I live here, too dummy," she shoots back, more playful than normal.

"Touché." I hop up onto my bunk and quietly pull the locket from my braid. Rubbing circles over the face of it, my breathing begins to steady.

"You seem out of sorts," she says from below. Her tone seems... softer. Less malefic than normal.

I think for a moment. Unsure of how to proceed. Between her giving me advice, last night and now this, I'm still on unsteady ground with her. Something has shifted between us.

"I miss home," I reply.

Saying home feels vague, but accurate. I'm not sure if it's the place, my people, or an idea that I'll never have again that I miss. I just know that my heart is aching for something unreachable.

She takes a while to respond as well, and I wonder if she's battling with similar notions. Finally, she says, "I miss home, too."

Equally as vague.

Equally as understandable.

I swipe my thumb over the locket once more before I tuck it back away in the safety of my hair and jump down from my bunk.

She's staring at me with wary eyes, but I brush off her unease and seat myself on her bed, opposite where she's sitting with crossed legs.

"We've been cellmates for almost two weeks now-" I start. Testing the unsure ground we've found ourselves on. I swallow thickly and extend my arm, offering her the inside of my wrist in the Elysian traditional way of respectfully greeting a new astral. "-and I've never introduced myself properly. I'm Eilidh."

Our introduction last night wasn't acceptable. It certainly wasn't one my mother would have been okay with. She'd have my head if she knew that I was speaking to a dragon, but our traditions run deep. Even our enemies are met with noble customs, if they meet peacefully.

She stares at my wrist for a long moment. The lights out buzzer shrieks through the corridor and I start to think she won't return the gesture, but I hold up my arm for just a while longer. Finally, she lifts her arm and rests her wrist over mine.

"Rhiannon."

I nod my head, sighing at the weight of what's changing between us. It doesn't feel heavy. Or bad.

"Goodnight, Rhiannon," I say quietly.

"Goodnight, Eilidh," she returns.

Slipping back into my sheets, I listen as the inmates all file into their cells. Chatter and laughter echo throughout our chamber for several minutes before the noise begins to die down as everyone tucks in for the evening.

A familiar moan sounds from the cell next door.

I suppose this is how he copes with death...and everything else.

I close my eyes tightly and take two deep breaths. Their groans grow louder, my chest tightens and my efforts to sleep are thwarted by Xanth's intoxicating scent, now mixed with the sickening smell of rose petals and musk.

Suddenly, I'm ripped wide open.

Silent sobs wrack my body as every painful memory from my past blurs before my eyes.

The day my mother left me on that damned island to rot when I was just a child.

Finding the locket my father gave to my mother that she had thrown out the window in anger. Feeling it call to me, my mother slapping my face and throwing the locket in the trash where I later retrieved it and hid it away.

My first bully throwing me into a freezing lake and laughing at me as I crawled from the water gasping for air.

The sound of the shot and spray of the astral that only wished to get out of this hell. His face morphs with Amell's on the day Amell died and the empty look on his face before he withered to ash in my arms, disappearing from my life forever.

My shoulders shake and tears stream down my face as Fawn's pitch increases and she's pounded into the thin mattress. My aching heart drums in time with each thrust.

The last thing I see before darkness consumes me is Xanth's face, twisted with rage and pain that mirrors my own.

12
KIERAN

I close the book on the desk, rubbing my temple as I take a swig of water. My fingers run through my hair for the hundredth time, scratching the sides of my head as I stare down at the book as if it owes me an explanation. Concentrating on any of the information is futile at this point. I thought studying for my advancement test would preoccupy my mind but it's useless.

Every time I close my eyes, I see the face of that astral boy with his bewildered pleading eyes staring up at me, as if I could change anything that was about to happen. As if I could have prevented Cain from putting that bullet through his head. It makes me nauseous.

And then came the shot.

One that, in many ways, was more significant than any I've heard in my long career as a soldier in the Human Mech Army.

It was a marker in time. An ear-note for all who witnessed it. This was one of those moments when everything changed. When the foundation cracked, and all conscious thought is pulled to the forefront for all to see.

That boy didn't try to escape, and no one told Cain shit. But his sentiment was heard loud and clear: Every astral will die here. The most potently ominous part of it is that no one is safe from him, not even the human guards.

However, Balor Cain's time is coming. Not in a poetic justice sort of way, which would be him being torn apart by all the astrals and humans that he's tortured and killed throughout his career. An end that would warm my cold insides. Instead, I'm sure his time here in Ironsgate is close to being up. I keep thinking this must be the year he's going to finally retire but like the cockroach he is, he persists.

I stand and find the remote to the oversized television that I rarely watch, needing a distraction. Without lifting it from the side table in the living room, I press the power button, and the TV blinks on to a newscast. A man with a square jaw and far too much make-up reports on another murder. One of several that have taken place on the streets of Prism over the last few years, and I turn up the volume.

"Prism authorities state that the victim was a veteran of the Human Mech Military making this the second soldier to be slain within the last year. Police are working to determine if this was the work of the Resistance, or an unrelated attack, though it has been suggested that this may be an individual attacker and not a group. Crime investigative teams have yet to find any trace of DNA, fingerprints, video footage or even a shoe size for the attacker."

Another woman in a lab coat appears on the screen with light gray eyes and skin so pale, it's a wonder if she's ever seen sunlight. "It's remarkable really, whoever this is leaves absolutely no trace of themself. At this point, it seems as if we're chasing a ghost."

The corner of my mouth ticks up and for some reason, I find myself wondering what it would be like to be a ghost.

"Local police continue to investigate this dangerous individual, and citizens of Prism are being warned to stay alert, especially at night. Soldiers of the Mech Army are to be particularly vigilant, since it seems they are the primary targets of this Ghost of Prism, so far."

"Ghost of Prism," I mutter and chuckle as the reporter shifts to another segment. "What a name."

Heroes deserve to be remembered, not ghost assassins with a vendetta, but I suppose villains get names too.

Turning off the TV, I'm still unable to work up the motivation to open my books and study.

Ugh, okay I'm just going to work out.

I slip into my running shorts, T-shirt and trainers, pop in my ear buds and turn on the loudest death metal I can stand. I head out of my apartment towards the gym. The elevator door slides open to a woman with perfectly quaffed blonde hair and blindingly pink lipstick.

She says something to me, her whole body practically quivering with excitement and I pull out an earbud.

"Evening, Rhetta," I say as she glances at my fingers holding the earbud with music blaring through the tiny Bluetooth speakers.

"Oh! I was just saying you are just the man I wanted to see!" Rhetta says with a wide smile.

I smile back at her as I walk past the elevator, and she hurries to catch up with me. Rhetta hands me a piece of paper colorfully decorated for a birthday party. I blink as I look over all the bright letters and banners and find that it's a party for LTC Balor Cain.

Fuck that.

"He doesn't usually do staff parties for his birthday but for some reason I was able to convince him this year, along with a decent budget to make it really fun."

Double fuck that.

"I know it would mean so much to him if you came."

"I seriously doubt that," I say with a smirk. She's quiet as I look at her. *Ugh, she wasn't talking about Cain.* "I'll check my schedule, though." I say, trying to backpedal a little.

"Great!" Rhetta says brightly as we approach the gym, and I head towards the door.

"See you later," I say as I jog through the wide windowed doors, and she waves at me. I pop my earbud still screaming death metal back into my ear and make my way to the track.

Stepping into the open-air gym, the wind feels cold and briny as it sweeps over the ocean beyond. The stadium lights illuminate the red polyurethane granules and the synthetic green grass field with gleaming light, the thick white lines create a perfect oval and a boundary to follow. It's empty and I stand at the perimeter, pulling out my earbuds for a moment to listen. The thundering whoosh and spray of water is faint from the coast and the wind gusts with a high pitch whine that ruffles my unkempt hair. I slide my earbuds in the pocket of my shorts and start running. The cold bites against my ears and cheeks as I round the first corner. Another bluster of wind pushes against my body and creates a vacuum of sound that sighs like a voice. One that rasps and lilts with seductive femininity, lingering in my brain with quiet punctuation.

I increase my speed as the sound begins to arrange itself into words, the tempo of my heart increasing as it whispers across my mind.

"...never been with a guard before."

My breathing picks up with my pace as I concentrate on picking up my heels and elongating my stride on my third round of the track.

"I would let you do very bad things to me…"

Her face appears in my mind and it's different from when I saw her lying there in the hospital bed. The swelling and cuts are gone and what remains is smooth, perfect skin, with a smattering of light brown freckles across her nose. She leans up on her elbows on the gurney, so her face is closer to mine.

"…Because I like you more than I'm allowed to."

She was drugged. People say shit like that when they're intoxicated. She didn't mean it. But *fuck* I can't help it. I can't help the wash of blinding frustration and desire as I picture her dark lashes fluttering up to meet my gaze, her full lips parting to say more.

"With your mouth on mine and your hands on my ass underneath my jumpsuit…"

I pop my earbuds back into my ears, the screaming and discordant music drowning out her etheric whispers from my mind.

I complete my thirtieth lap, and my chest and sides feel as if they're ripping to pieces as I pant thick plumes of steam into the chilled air. Sweat pours in thick rivulets down my brow, neck and back, saturating my T-shirt. I keep my earbuds in my ears, letting the drums, guitars and guttural roars of the lead singer preoccupy my brain as I walk back to my apartment. I keep them in as I turn on the shower and drop my sweat-stained clothes on the floor. I reluctantly remove them when I step under the hot spray. My mind quiets as the heat hits my skin like a thousand tiny knives. I wash my body and hair and step back under the water, bracing my hands against the tile as her voice ripples across my brain again.

"...squeezing my tits, running your rough fingers over my nipples."

I groan as she picks up right where she left off. Right at the part that gets me off the most and instead of fighting it, I let her continue, let myself see it as the words spill from her lips in my imagination and I grip myself, stroking as I picture my hands on her tits, passing my thumbs over her beaded pink nipples.

"*...I imagine you whispering into my mouth right before you slide your tongue inside...*"

"Rhiannon," I say aloud as I stroke harder and I catch her smile as she kisses me back, her fingers threading through my hair and fisting it tight. I groan as I stroke harder, imagining myself pressing between her thighs.

"*...it feels so good I wonder what it would feel like between my legs...*"

Fuck, that part. That was the part that made me wild. My hips snap forward as the pressure builds in my hips, my balls tighten as I picture fucking her mercilessly, her legs are a vice around my waist and her head arches back as she moans, revealing the long soft plane of her throat. In my mind, I run my canines along the most vulnerable part of it, as her fingernails dig into the skin of my back and she screams, pulling me into her as she comes.

I roar out my climax, continuing to stroke out thick jets of cum on the shower stall and I open my eyes, my vision blurred by the water running down my brow. Her face is still a misty specter in my mind, bright and beautiful.

Godsdammit.

This is bad.

I have to be careful. The fact that I know her name. The fact that she knows mine. That she has *this* kind of effect on me...I need to stay away from her. She's a humongous fucking liability when I shouldn't have any.

I need to let whatever attraction I have for her go before it becomes something it shouldn't be. What it can't be.

I dry myself off and finish getting ready for bed. I climb into my sheets and stretch out one of my legs to the open air and grab my phone.

Distraction, I need a distraction, I think to myself as I pull up a number I know I probably shouldn't be texting, but I do anyway because I'm desperate.

> Me: Coffee tomorrow morning?

I send off the text with an audible whoosh and begin to put my phone back when it pings. I look at the reply and groan.

> Rhetta: Of course, Major Hot Stuff!

Ugh. I am an idiot.

13

XANTH

Scraping plates and dropped silverware mix with a cacophony of talking, chewing and banter that makes my skin crawl.

It smells like the cooks made fried rice for lunch again and they burnt the shit out of it in the process.

I grab a plate filled with scorched eggs, undercooked rice mixed with freeze dried vegetables, along with a glass of water and a protein bar. Looking around, I spot the twins, Tatsu and Ryu, sitting in the far back table of the chow hall and head in their direction. Both males have their straight black hair hung down over their shoulders and their eyes find me at the same time. Tatsu puts down the sticks he was using to shovel rice into his mouth and waves me over.

I'm late to lunch so I don't expect to see Rhi anywhere and I refuse to humor myself with looking for that fucking phoenix.

Rhi's gone all soft on me. I overheard her and that cunt talking the other night and I just about keeled over.

I never thought I'd see the day where Rhi would *befriend* a Twitcher. I thought we hated them with equal fervor.

I suppose she doesn't have as much reason, what with my Mum dying at the hands of them and all, but she didn't strike me as one to let the well-known vendetta between our kinds go so quickly.

I haven't thought about my Mum in a while, but with the phoenix in the cell right beside me, driving me fuckin' insane, I can't help but pull out my charcoal at night and sketch like Mum and I used to. She loved to use a wide range of Elysian colors and paints while I preferred the blacks and greys from charcoal. It mirrored our personalities and Mum used to always tell me that I could be a famous artist one day if I wanted to.

I chuckle. Me, an artist.

If only she could see me now.

"Where'd you go, Blue?" Ryu asks. I hadn't even realized they were talking to me.

"What do ye mean?" I reply, only half listening as thoughts of my Mum begin to fade back into the recesses of my mind. "I'm right here ye bastard."

"We've been talking to you for like, five minutes now and you've just been staring at your plate," Tatsu says.

Tatsu likes to say he's older because he was born two minutes and thirteen seconds before Ryu. It's an endless argument that I've heard a hundred times over and there are moments, such as this, where I can agree that Tatsu acts more like the older brother. He's always ready to defend his brother and for the most part, it's endearing.

"Is this about the Twitcher?" He edges.

Today, however, I'm in no mood for what he's insinuating.

"Why in the fuck would I be thinkin' about that *thing*? Eh? Don't ye two have anything better te do than meddle in mah business?" I point my fork between them and take a bite.

"We're not meddling, Blue. We're just worried about you is all." Ryu. Ever the fucking martyr.

"Well quit worryin' about me and worry about how yer goin' to hit yer next PR on deadlifts will ye? It's fuckin' pathetic watchin' yer flimsy arms lift the way ye do." I know I'm being a dick, but I've been feeling sour ever since the Warden put a bullet in that astrals head. I thought fucking that little deer would take the edge off, but it didn't. I could feel the Twitcher next door having a nervous fucking breakdown the entire time and I had to fake my orgasm so I could get the female out of my bed.

Ridiculous.

"Hey," Tatsu puffs up in defense. "Shut your fucking mouth. I don't care how pissed you are that you haven't been able to bag that phoenix, don't make that shit our problem."

My beast rises to the challenge, and I watch as his inner dragon cowers.

"I don't have a fuckin' problem getting any cunt I want in this place and I sure as hells don't give a rat's ass about that fuckin' Twitch. I'd have to give a shit for 'er to be affectin' me." I end my rant with another bite into my food.

Ryu raises his hands in surrender. "All right, all right. We're just worried about you is all. The Warden shooting that astral has everyone on edge and maybe we misread some of the things we've seen between you and her, but you've seemed pretty out of it."

"There's nay a damn thing between 'er and I beside the knife I plan te put in 'er chest the first opportunity I get." My stomach turns, but I refuse to believe it's anything more than this terrible food.

After that, the twins stop talking and we fall into an uncomfortable silence while we finish our meal and head out to the rec hall to start our lifts.

We make it through an hour of reps and a jog before both males finish their workouts and decide to catch up on local news on the other side of the rec room. They both like to keep up with all the chaos happening between the humans and the Rebellion. Very rarely does the news cover any astral-human fighting, but the Rebellion does an excellent job of making their attacks publicly known, primarily by attacking Prism directly, so they're often featured in news stories.

Thankfully Paps set up the bar in a smaller neighborhood within the Plains that's far enough away from the capital for him to not be affected by much. When we moved away from the dragon lands of Ignis, I thought we would never find another place worth calling home, but now, I miss that bar more than anything.

I'm alone, pulling the weights off a rack when the hair on the back of my neck raises.

Ye've got te be kiddin' me.

Zane, the gorilla astral I knocked on his ass a few weeks ago circles around my front. Without taking my eyes off him, I straighten and use my periphery to note who he's brought with him in this sad attempt at rebuilding his reputation.

Joining us in rec hall are two other gorilla astrals that look like steroid junkies with muscles bulging from their arms, stand alongside an ox with spiked black hair and a thick silver ring between his nostrils. They circle strategically around me, blocking escape routes.

They even have a female astral distracting the guard on duty. She leads him off to a dark corner making it crystal clear what's about to happen.

However, I'm not alone. Dragons outnumber these assholes and with one word, they'd step in if I ask. Yet they'll hold off until I ask. An honor code amongst dragons. Most of us prefer to fight our own battles instead of losing our standing amongst our own ranks.

This is more than I typically handle on my own. I've also just spent the last two hours wearing myself down but I'm certain that was Zane's plan all along: to catch me when he thinks I'm the weakest.

Fucking coward.

The blond-haired bastard smirks at me before he charges, barreling his broad shoulder into my sternum and I wrap my arms around him to throw off his balance. I'm significantly taller than he is, but gorillas are fucking strong.

I'm able to wrestle him to the ground but just as I do, one of his friends comes up behind us and drives a foot directly into my spine, and I yell as I rear back. The other two males each grab an arm and pull me from Zane, opening me up for him to strike.

I lift my chin, readying for the first hit with a smile on my face and Zane swallows hard. His nostrils flare and he rears back, his fist aiming for my jaw when something, no, *someone*, grabs Zane in a headlock from behind and pulls him backwards. Unable to breathe, he fights and scratches for purchase but only meets air. All three of his buddies watch in shock as a five-foot two female with hair the color of freshly fallen snow tightens her arm around Zanes neck, and he passes out.

Little Dove.

One beat passes.

Then another, before all hell breaks loose.

The two males holding me drop my arms and head for her but I'm able to grab hold of their wrists and yank before they can take more than a single step in her direction. They collide and fall to the ground where I grab the backs of their heads and bash them together. I look up to see the infuriating phoenix blocking and dodging heavy blows from the last standing gorilla and I lunge for him. Some asshole that hadn't even been part of the fight fists my jumpsuit, hauling me backwards but my attention stays firmly planted on the tiny bane of my existence.

She swings with practiced punches and every time she dips to avoid another strike from the gorilla my beast roars and claws with rage to be released. The male with no business getting involved pulls me back again and I twist to hammer my split knuckles into his teeth. All around me, inmates are now fighting, ripping and tearing at each other. It's a fucking madhouse.

I look back in the direction of the phoenix and can't find her or that fuckin' gorilla anywhere. Panic rises, drumming wildly in my chest as I fight my way through the growing crowd, guards now piling in to break up the brawling inmates and I finally see her. Her back is pressed flat to the ground between the male's thighs and wiggling to get out about thirty feet in front of me.

I run for them.

As I approach, she sends a knee into his lower back, and he arches in agony just enough for her to slide out from under him. He twists from his seated position, but not soon enough. She's spun in that all too familiar way with her right leg poised to strike. He raises his arms to block her hit, protecting his face, but the momentum of her twist sends her heel tearing through his arms and knocks him backwards so hard his head bounces off the linoleum with a resounding *crack*.

She scrambles to her feet and I leap, reaching her before she can slip away. I pull her back down to the ground with me where she struggles for a moment before realizing it's me pinning her with the full weight of my body atop hers.

"Why the *fuck* did you do that?!" I yell. I know I should calm down but Azure's fury has taken over all rational thought and he is ready to raze this entire prison.

Confusion twists her features and her nose scrunches as she stares back at me in a way that has the useless organ in my chest beating faster.

"You're fucking *welcome* for helping you!" She shouts back. The chaos around me continues to rage, but it feels as if she and I are the only ones in the room.

"I didn't need yer help! I had it under control!" I roar back at her.

"CLEARLY!" She lifts her head off the ground, baring her teeth and I swear to the gods the gold in her eyes flares brighter than any light

I've ever seen. I want to bottle it up and steal it for myself. "Had I known it was going to hurt your fucking feelings, I wouldn't have bothered."

I'm a breath away from her mouth, I'm unsure when my hand came up to grasp her jaw, but my thumb grazes something sticky and wet on the side of her face. My eyes dart down her face and I see a gash slicing across her porcelain skin. Azure barrels through my chest, scraping and clawing, demanding he be released.

"Did he do this to ye?" My whisper is quiet but deadly.

It takes her a moment to catch up.

"Did what to me?" She attempts to push me off, but I refuse to remove my body from hers.

"Who cut yer face, Little Dove?" I ask again.

Her lips tremble and my jaw aches to bite into them. To lick them raw and watch her squirm beneath me.

"He got one good hit." Shame has her eyes drifting from mine and I nudge her to look back up at me.

"He's lucky ye kicked his ass before I could get te him," I say honestly. My thumb strokes her face, and I rest my forehead against hers.

I can feel her anger rising and it makes me smile. I like it when she's heated.

"No, no you don't get to do this," She says, shaking her head.

It's then that I realize the noise in the hall has died down and a few guards are escorting some of the inmates away. I look over my shoulder to see Tatsu, Ryu and Rhiannon standing beside each other, watching me pin the phoenix to the ground and caress her face.

It's then that I remember who the fuck I am.

My eyes grow cold, as my lips curl in a hard sneer. "It's a good thing I couldn't give a fuck about ye, even if ye were screaming mah name fer help." I release her, and she pushes me again. This time, I move off her and climb to my feet.

She tucks her feet beneath her and rocks up to stand, brushing invisible dust from her and spits back, "Wouldn't you like to know what I sound like screaming your name." A statement, not a question.

She scoffs at me. "That will *never* happen. You are *infuriating*! I can't keep up with your ridiculous mood swings."

I grasp her neck, and a soft sound escapes her that muddies my brain, but I continue. "If I wanted ye te scream, I know *exactly* how te do it. Let me make this simple fer ye, Twitch whore," I look back to my friends and Rhi shakes her head at me. I set my jaw and double down. "Ye could be bleeding out and I'd just push the knife in further." My gut twists again and I release her throat.

She lets out an incredulous huff. "You're unbelievable."

I shrug. "Yer kind don't deserve te walk this earth with the rest of us. Next time, do me the favor of not getting in mah way, or at least die so I don't have te dirty mah own hands with it."

Her lips tremble again, and her body begins to rattle with rage. She looks off to the side at nothing in particular and takes a deep breath before meeting my eyes again.

"You know what? Fine. I won't get in your way again. I'll leave you to your *actual* whores. Or are they prey? I've really lost track of dragon mating rituals. I didn't realize they were so sexually attracted to their food." She tucks a lock of ivory hair that's escaped her braid behind her ear. The urge to mess it up again is unbearable. "I suppose this means you won't mind me hooking up with a guard now. Unless they're on your feeding list too?" She taps her chin with a slender finger, and I growl. "Ah well. As I said, don't worry about me. You'll never have to see me again after tomorrow."

My blood boils as I watch her turn and saunter out of the rec hall.

...*You're an idiot, Xanth. You have no idea how badly you've fucked up this time. She's going to hate you for this...*

Rhiannon's voice rips through my head like a shot to the mouth, but what she doesn't know is that no one hates me more than myself.

14
EILIDH

I'm still fuming as I wake up the next morning.

What a fucking asshole. I think to myself as I drag myself from my bed and rub the sleep from my eyes.

Using my index finger, I scrub my teeth in the dinghy sink and then splash my face with ice cold water to rinse away the last of my exhaustion. I tense as I rinse the injury on the side of my face, the sting causing my teeth to clench. Looking in the cracked mirror, I notice a bruise beneath my left eye and a long, angry-looking cut stretching down the right side of my face, just below my ear. I pat it dry with the inside of my sleeve and pull the tie from my braid.

I'm working through pulling each knot apart when my locket falls from my hair with a loud clunk, and I scramble to retrieve it before anyone sees.

Rhiannon casts me a quizzical look and tilts her head to the side.

"It's nothing," I say, but she doesn't buy it.

"Hiding something in your hair isn't *nothing*." She stands up and pads over to me. I can hear the shuffle of guards opening inmate gates for showers and my heart thunders in my chest as they near ours. She comes closer and a quizzical look pinches her features. "I recognize this from somewhere." Her finger strokes the flame on the locket's face, and I hold my breath.

"This symbol is…so familiar."

"Please, don't say anything," I beg. She's quiet for a few fleeting seconds and then she blinks and nods back at me. I tuck the locket away behind the loose piece of wall that I created with a spoon back when I was desperate to find a way out.

I finish pulling the last of my braid down when Gunnar approaches with a kind smile and asks if we're ready for showers.

Before we can answer, a shout comes from a few feet away. "Don't be so fucking *nice*, Rookie!" Ryker chides.

Gunnar looks back at us apologetically and unlocks the gate, motioning us through.

Ryker stands in front of Xanth's cell and waits for him to emerge. The dragon's eyes slide to mine when he finally steps out of the cell and I quickly turn away, walking towards the showers.

I can feel Xanth staring after me and a petty part of my brain wants to irritate him. The altercation I had with him last night left me reeling and the weight of his stare has me prickling with irritation. It's been weeks and I haven't gotten nearly as far with my escape plan as I'd like to. Being told that the inmates around me would rather see me dead was nothing more than a cold reminder that I need to get out of here. His words stung but I don't want him to know he's affecting me.

A wicked idea floods my brain that has me laughing under my breath.

I look up at Gunnar and bat my lashes.

"Good morning, Gunnar." I flash a dazzling smile and bite my bottom lip. There's an audible growl from behind us, but I ignore it as I move closer to Gunnar so that our arms are touching as we walk, Xanth and Ryker trailing behind.

He leans in, voice quiet to keep Ryker from hearing. Quiet enough to fool a human, but a dragon?

"Good morning." His smile is just as bright, and a slight flush touches his cheeks. "I hope you slept well last night."

"I did but," A devilish smile dances on my lips as I whisper, "I would have slept much better had you been with me."

The rumbling behind us grows in volume and Ryker shouts, "Shut the fuck up, Breather!"

Gunnar hardly notices, but I smile a bit brighter knowing I'm getting under Xanth's skin. He moves so that he's pressed more firmly against me, and I lean into him as we continue walking.

Gunnar may have been marked off my list but I'm going to seize the opportunity that's presented itself.

Gunnar is a cute male. His blond hair stands a few inches longer on the top and is shorn short on the sides. His baby blue eyes sparkle with innocence that almost makes me feel bad for using him.

He folds like putty in my hands.

"You know," he starts, "there are ways that we could make that happen."

"Really?" My eyes light up with feigned excitement and a dash of ignorance. "How?"

"Some of the guards give special treatment to the inmates that are open to spending some… quality time with them," He says slowly, like he's trying not to scare me away.

"Quality time?" It's incredible how easily I'm able to slip into this naive maiden act.

"Yes," he hesitates. "That is, if you'd be interested. I could even do something for you. A favor of sorts."

"A favor?" I tap my chin. "Like what?" I see Rhiannon's head shift slightly in our direction, listening to every word we say.

He dips his head to look at the ground, a nervous but attractive smirk playing on his face.

Here it is. The exact thing I've been waiting for.

"There's really incredible food in the guards' quarters. I could bring you something significantly better than the slop they serve at the chow hall?" He says hopefully.

I tap a finger to my chin, pretending to deliberate and shake my head slightly. "To be honest, I don't care much about the food around here. What does intrigue me, is the sun."

"I could take you upstairs to the second floor. They have a rec room with an open ceiling. It allows the sun to shine through." He pauses, gauging my reaction and I school my features to avoid giving away too much. "I've heard that is something that your kind-" He clears his throat, "-dragons, that is, enjoy."

I don't even correct his assumption of me being a dragon. I smile fully and nod.

"I'd love that, Gunnar," I say his name breathlessly, laying the flirtation on thick and he returns my smile with one of his own. We reach the showers, and Gunnar places a hand on the wall above my head.

Xanth pushes between us then. His body shoves Gunnar back a step as he stomps towards the wall hooks and begins pulling off his clothes.

I look back at Gunnar, avoiding Xanth as Gunnar brushes a finger under my chin sweetly.

A stab of guilt pierces through me but I brush it off as I head in to remove my clothes. I only make it a step before Gunnar captures my arm.

"Consider this an extra favor."

He leads me to a small alcove where a private shower sits and I'm able to shower alone, in relative peace, for the first time in weeks.

Even though the water is still tepid, not having to cover myself feels like a luxury. I take my time washing the grime from my body and dress in privacy that I haven't gotten since before I walked through the doors to this hellhole.

Breakfast is a blur as I sit by myself again. I'm just finishing my bowl of mushy porridge when Xanth walks by and bumps into my table, intentionally spilling my meal all over me and the floor.

I glare up at him but hold my tongue. He's trying to get under my skin, but I won't let him. I'm coming to terms with the fact that he hates me, especially after yesterday's outburst, but I refuse to buckle under his passive aggressive attacks. I expected this after I baited him with Gunnar earlier.

I wipe myself down with a napkin and pick up my plate to leave. I watch him round the corner heading in the direction of the rec hall.

We've moved on to petty games, I see.

Once I've cleared my tray, I'm led off to my job for the day by Nova.

Enormous machines with black smoke billowing out the tops that whir and creak as they work grab my attention when I enter the room. Sewing tables line the walls around the roaring machines. A female with greying hair and age lines etched into her face, sits with a stack of fabric at the entrance.

"Inmate 2475, this is Inmate 968. She'll be your mentor today." Nova gives me a slight shove forward and I look into the white veiled eyes of a dragon elder.

"Right this way," the old dragon astral says. She stands and hobbles around the corner of her desk and leads me off to one of the machines. "Sit." She gestures in front of her after pulling out a wooden chair that's seen better days.

"I've never sewn before," I admit, unsure if she'll show me the same hatred the other dragons have.

Her eyes soften and her trembling hands grasp mine after she places a bolt of fabric on the table in front of me.

"I've been sewing since I came to this place." Her voice sounds frail, and I wonder how old she is. "Teaching you would be my honor."

Interesting word choice.

"Thank you," I say and look away, unable to hold her watery gaze.

"My name is Sahaar," she says after Nova leaves.

"I'm Eilidh." I lift the scissors and cut along the lines that Sahaar marks for me on the fabric.

"I know who you are, child," she says, and for some reason, this comforts me more than it should. As a dragon, she likely hates my kind but the way she looks at me and the kindness in her eyes and her tone eases some of my worry.

We're quiet for a long time. I cut out the patterns she outlines while she sews them together. It seems as though we are the only two in the room as the sounds of the machines fade into the background.

When she speaks again, she doesn't take her eyes from the sewing machine before her.

"How much do you know about dragons, girl?" Sahaar asks quietly.

I continue to snip the fabric as I respond. "Not much," I admit. "But I'm learning."

"I'm sure you are," Sahaar chuckles. "We aren't all just one type you see. Fire dragons are known for their volatility, Earth dragons for their strength," she explains, and I pause my cutting, unsure where she's going with this. "Ice dragons are known for their mercilessness. Air," she gestures to herself, "for their wisdom, and carefree nature." She looks at me then and her face softens into what looks like concern. "Water dragons, they're much like the sea." Her fingers move in wave-like motions as she continues. "Their emotions run high, and they change like the ebb and flow of the tide. Sometimes the water is low and calm, while other times, their anger crests, wiping out an entire village and leaving no trace." Her movements slow and she grasps my chin. "Sometimes, pain can be hidden within the deepest depths where it seems impossible to reach and yet it still shifts the tide. Find the depths, child. Find them and you'll move the beast within."

I'm completely confused as the buzzer sounds overhead, and she starts to tidy up the area before guards enter to escort us back to the rec hall.

Why in the hells did she tell me that? What tide am I supposed to shift?

I'm dazed as I walk into the rec hall, so I find a seat off to the side instead of going to work out like usual. Watching and observing seems like a better option after the fight that broke out yesterday.

...Where's yer baby-faced guard, Little Dove?... His voice threads through my mind and I inhale, not ready to deal with him just yet. I sigh. I haven't even been sitting here for more than a few minutes.

I'm not one to turn away from a fight though, plus I'm still pissed at him after yesterday

Hmm. I think. *Perhaps he's waiting in my cell for me.*

I look around the room. Sensing Xanth but not able to see him.

...Is that so?... His inner voice is rough with a deadly edge that makes me shiver. *...Do ye think his cock is as small as his personality?...*

I stifle a laugh. I won't give him that satisfaction.

Do I hear a lick of jealousy in your tone, Breather? I know pushing him after all that's happened is not a wise decision, but it is effective. Also, I simply don't give a fuck.

I see him rise from a small table across the way. His eyes search the crowd before landing on me and he storms over. His tattoos ripple with his flexing muscles and his hair flows behind him in messy abandon that makes me want to thread my fingers through it.

I shake that thought from my mind.

...What makes ye think I'd be jealous of a fuckin thing ye do, Twitch Bitch?... He's still speaking in my mind. I'm not even sure he realizes he's still doing it, but I meet him there anyway.

Oh, I don't know. Maybe it's that you can't seem to stay away from me

when you know I've got a date with a hot guard. You were wondering about the size of his cock, perhaps I'll let you know once I've fucked him. I place my hands on my hips, and he tracks the movement, his eyes lingering.

His face turns red as I see him struggling to come up with more vitriol to spew at me.

He smirks, his face stoney and arrogant.

…Nay, Little Dove, I can't wait te see Gunnar fuck ye and leave ye. Yer poor little heart will be broken. Yer knight in shining armor will drop ye like a sack of shite after he's used yer cunt and soiled ye first. Then, the other guards will come. Perhaps ye'll fuck Ryker next. I've heard he likes te take yer ass. Ye seem like an ass kind of girl…

My mouth drops open.

I feel heat burning my cheeks as fury sweeps me away.

Me? You think I am the used-up whore here? My eyes trace his body, as I scoff out loud. *You're so fucking pathetic you can't even admit when you have feelings and would rather fuck them away into another nameless female's used up cunt. Don't think I haven't noticed you call them all "Doll." That's all they are to you. Toys for you to work out your temper tantrums and run away from your problems.*

His eyes turn fiery and his fists ball at his sides.

But I'm not done yet.

As a matter of fact, I'll bet my freedom that you'll turn away from this conversation and go find one of those slutty little deer females you can't get enough of. You'll go get your little prick off inside of them to remind yourself that, though you may not be able to control me, you can *control them. So, excuse me if I don't give a damn about your opinions of me. I'll fuck whoever the hells I want and while Gunnar's DNA is running down my legs, I'll sit in my cell and laugh at the miserable sounds of you and your next "Doll."*

A resounding crack comes from over my head as Xanth's fist connects with the wall above me. He's caged me in, but I don't move, staring up at him in defiance.

Ye'll regret that, Little Dove. I can promise ye'll regret that.

Removing his hand from above me, he backs away, step by step.

Fawn approaches him from behind, wrapping her thin arms around his waist and he turns to leave, just as I said he would.

15
RHIANNON

I dip my head back, letting the water from the shower saturate my hair. I'm stalling more than I usually do as my gaze shifts over to Eilidh in the far corner. Her back faces me but I can feel her anger undulating off her like heat from a flame.

Xanth is on the other side, and he's equally as pissed, only he pulls no quarter in hiding it. Eilidh clearly has the upper hand on her emotions, even if I can feel them rolling off her like smoke.

I chuckle to myself and Xanth shoots me a caustic look.

"What has ye in such a good mood then?" Xanth hisses, water spraying from his lips with each syllable.

"No talking!" Jo shouts from the entryway and I suck in my lips to suppress another laugh as steam begins to billow off Xanth's boiling skin.

Xan…chill.

…I am chill. Ye're pissing me off…

Why? Because I'm laughing?

…Ye're laughing at me…

How do you know that?

Xanth shoots me a look that would probably kill if I wasn't already a dragon. *…Ye really think I'm that much of an idiot, Rhi?…*

Do I have to answer that?

His chest rattles, low and threatening as his dragon slithers along the surface of his skin, black-blue scales clack over his forearms.

"Cool it, 2459," Jo hollers at him again. Xanth places his hands on the tile and steadies his breathing.

I feel the constant prickle of Eilidh's attention like a looming gaze on the back of my neck.

...Forget it... Xanth growls, as he flicks off the shower head, snatches his towel and wraps it around his lower half, stalking towards the exit where Ryker and Jo let him pass.

That prickling begins to grow, and I peek over the walls that I put up the moment I knew Eilidh could mind-speak. She can't penetrate my mind and I'm grateful for that. Some mind-speaks cause irreversible damage if they aren't trained well. Mind-speaks like that are the Blades of the dragons. Blades are brilliant and brutal in their interrogation methods, an effective instrument of torture under certain circumstances.

I've never known a Phoenix with the ability to mind-speak, but it was a relief all the same that she couldn't penetrate my mind. At least that I know of.

Shields are like the fortress that keeps everything out from a Blade's penetrative abilities. With my Aetherion blood, I have both. It's what's given my ancestors the edge to keep their place as rulers. I can tell that Eilidh didn't really know how to do either very well, but I had a sneaking suspicion that she could be pretty damn good at either one.

I turn and see her rinsing her hair. Her eyes flit to mine and practically glow like two bright yellow suns in the dim corner.

Why are you always over there by yourself?

I watch her as I volley the thought and her mouth twitches. Her hands still as she rings the water out from her long moonlight colored hair. That prickle grows along my skin and then it's like a gentle breeze along the corridors of my mind, brushing up against the steel of my walls like a gentle knock, a request for entry. I cautiously lower my defenses to let her pass through.

...I didn't think I was welcome...

I smile as I pick up the soap and begin washing my hair for the second time.

"Really 2460? A second time?" Jo says wearily and I look at her and shrug.

"I got extra sweaty yesterday, sorry." Jo rolls her eyes, and I continue to lather the chemical smelling soap into my hair.

Don't be such a loner and come shower next to me.

Eilidh scoffs a laugh and grabs her towel. *...Maybe next time...*

Shit I have stuff I need to talk to her about. *Wait, Eilidh.*

She halts in front of me as she makes her way to the exit.

"Keep moving, 2475. We don't have all day." Ryker says as he steps to the side so Eilidh can pass. His eyes graze her naked form, and I repress the urge to gag.

Meet me back in our cell. I say as I switch off the faucet.

...How?...

Make something up.

She scrunches her brows as she continues to stand there.

"Let's *go,* Mute." Ryker yells from the doorway.

Eilidh walks forward, peeking back as she passes through the exit. As she retreats, those steel walls rise, shutting the rest of the world out once more.

"What took you so long?" I ask from my bed as Eilidh finally steps into the cell at the end of the day.

"I tried. No one would let me leave," she says leaning back against the cement wall, crossing her arms across her chest. "How did *you* get out of work duty?"

"Menstrual pain," I say with air quotes.

"That works?"

"Depends on who you talk to."

"Huh," she says, chewing her bottom lip. "Female guards?"

I flash her a fiendish smile. "Male guards. They don't want to hear anything about it and will escort you to your cell or the infirmary to get out of that conversation. It works occasionally. Speaking of things that work on guards..."

Eilidh crosses her ankles over one another as she tilts her chin up.

"Are you planning on seducing the guards for favors?"

She shushes me and walks forward. "Seriously? They will hear you."

"Isn't that the point?"

Eilidh rolls her eyes. "Well, I'd like to try and keep it *somewhat* quiet." Her eyes dart to Xanth's cell beside us and awareness dawns on me. She doesn't want him to hear.

I lower my walls, letting the thoughts begin to flow like water through the spaces beyond my fortress. *How about this then?*

A gentle prickle flutters across my skin and flicks its featherlight touch against the steel. I lower it further, granting her access.

...Yes...

Is this an attempt to escape?

...Jesus, right to the point then Rhiannon?...

Always.

She sighs as she sits down on the bed next to me, facing me. Her golden eyes steady on mine as we stare in silence while our conversation increases its fervor in our minds.

...Perhaps...

And you are trying to accomplish this by sleeping with a guard?

...Perhaps... She repeats. *...I need to get to the sun. Once I do, then I can escape...*

Ah. I forgot how much phoenixes derive their power from natural sunlight. I imagine being locked up like this with nothing but artificial light is pretty draining. I suppose the UV light from the greenhouses wouldn't suffice either. *I want to help you.*

Even in her mind I can sense the hesitance in her tone *...Help how?...*

I want to help you seduce a guard to escape.

Eilidh sits up straighter, her eyes blink in disbelief. *...Why?...*

I want out too. If we are working together, we can get the job done faster.

...What's the catch, Rhiannon?...

I shift uncomfortably on the bed. Her question catches me off guard because...well, what is the catch? Why do I want to help her? I hated her last week. I wouldn't have given a shit if she got her ass handed to her or if she fell off a building. So...what is it now? I pick at my nails as I think, prodding my teeth with my tongue as I consider doing the one thing I swore I would never *ever* do with my mortal enemy.

I clear my throat as I say, "You asked me a while back who Fianna is."

Eilidh is silent and I don't look up at her as I grapple with reluctance to continue.

"She's my little sister," I provide, my voice sounding worn even though I don't feel that way.

Eilidh nods and I see her hands twitch and flex on her lap. "I-is she...alive?"

"As far as I know."

Another dip of her chin and her lips purse. She's quiet and patient, waiting for me to continue, but I'm caught in a moment of surreal clarity.

I have worked so hard to shove down my past, bury my memories in boxes hidden behind solid walls in my mind. Yet the memories rise as easily as if they just happened. I was resigned to staying in Ironsgate, ripped away from everything I love in order to keep them safe, allowing my baby sister to step into the role that I was meant to fulfill so our line would continue. So that the Aetherion name would persevere and continue to rule over the dragons.

But Eilidh...something about her gently prods at those notions like a devil's advocate, challenging each of my plans without a word by simply being who she is. I haven't decided if it's a threat or the unsung redemption I thought was forever lost to me.

When you asked about her is when I realized you can mind-speak. She looks up at me and I smile. *Gotta work on being a little more covert, Phoenix.*

Eilidh laughs and it's like an entirely different person. She is lovely but I never realized how beautiful she is until she laughs. It's lilting and soft and it's no wonder Xanth is so unbelievably beside himself over her. She is a godsdamn knock-out.

...I didn't know I could until I met you and-...

We don't need to talk about him.

Eilidh swallows hard as she picks at her jumpsuit.

...Right, thanks...

I don't push her further and instead, I change the subject.

Anyways, that is my motivation. My sister. My family. They're important to me and if I can get home...

She hesitates for a moment. I can see her working through possible reservations, the same way I was hesitant to share information about my sister with her.

...I was thinking about starting with Gunnar...

Shock and amusement eddy in my chest as I realize what this means.

She's trusting me.

So much is yet to be determined but it is enough for me to feel like I have a responsibility now and it bolsters something in me that I haven't felt in a long time. Something that when I became Rhiannon, I didn't realize I would ever be afforded again. That ember smolders low and warm in my ribcage. Like a promise when the odds are not in your favor. A lighthouse during the darkest of storms.

I face her more squarely. *Why Gunnar?*

Her expression changes to one that reminds me of the generals in my father's army. It's calculating, cunning and determined...war imbedded in her bones as she proceeds with the resoluteness of a leader.

He's new and young, so he will be easy to convince. Initially I had written him off, but he practically folded in my hands earlier. I can't give up this opportunity.

I bob my head and consider. *True. He's easy on the eyes too, so that helps.*

I think of Gunnar and imagine Eilidh making him sweat with her hands gripping his light blond hair, showing him where he can place his trembling inexperienced hands. Boy, that was going to be a quick tryst for her.

"Rhiannon," Kieran's voice is like a phantom wind through my mind, and it sends a shiver down my back. It knocks me off kilter as I try to navigate if that was a memory or...

I have another idea.

Eilidh tilts her head as she waits for me to continue.

I have a guard in mind...for me.

Eilidh is quiet for a minute as she looks around at nothing in particular. Yet her mind is a tapestry of thought, weaving and shaping threads of different colors into place.

...The red-head?...

I smile tightly at her as she nods her head.

"Maybe we go over it all in the morning?" I say as I stand and head to the sink to wash my face.

"Yeah," she agrees passively, her lips press together as she works through something in her mind. "Can you...never mind."

I turn around with the water still cupped in my hands. "Oh, do go on. I'll figure it out one way or another," I say with a wicked grin.

She rolls her eyes. "Yeah, um. Could you show me how to do that steel wall thing?"

I arc my eyebrows, impressed that she was able to sense it, but also *see* it in her mind. I finish washing my face and use my jumpsuit as a towel.

I tell her about Dragon Shields and Blades as I settle onto my mattress, resting a hand under my head. She listens quietly as I walk her through the differences between the offenders and defenders of the mind.

Imagine the hardest surface you can think of. Something impenetrable. Something you use with no doubt in its strength and durability.

She remains silent for several seconds and then she whispers. "Do you want me to do that right now?"

"No time like the present, Phoenix," I laugh and she exhales a breathy chuckle. I close my eyes and follow that thread that leads my mental connection to hers. It glimmers like a string of gold, and I glimpse at the wall she begins to build. She starts with different materials, trying them as they appear in front of her, changing her mind from brick, to steel, to granite, to concrete. She shakes her head and squeezes her eyes shut. Balling her fists and her body quivers as a white-hot flame bursts out in front of her. It's a towering fortress of searing fire that is blinding to look at and boils my skin from the proximity. I canter back, shielding my eyes as I retreat from the confines of her mind.

"Whew," I pant as I open my eyes, my skin flushes from the heat that scorched my flesh moments ago. "Perfect."

"You saw it?"

"Uh, yeah. Clever, using fire." I nudge her with an arm, easily falling into camaraderie with her.

"I didn't think of it," she says. "It just…came out."

"Even better," I reply, wiping some of the sweat beading on my brow. "In addition to your impressive wall, you will want to hide away any particularly important thoughts. Powerful Blades can break through even the most impenetrable of walls. You will need to find and fortify all the memories and information that you want to keep secret. Think of it as an insurance policy for your insurance policy."

She's quiet and pensive, taking everything in. In those moments of stillness, I attempt to slide back along that glimmering thread, into the confines of her mind and feel the radiant heat of that white flame wall still erected and glowing bright.

Good, I think to myself. I knew she would be good at this.

We are both quiet for a long while as the buzzer sounds and the lights flick out. She hops up to her bed as the dim fluorescents from the ground floor gently illuminate our cell, but the dark is enough to encourage the lull of sleep.

"Rhiannon," Eilidh whispers softly into the increasing stillness.

"Hm?" I hum back quietly. That gentle sweep along the steel ushers another quiet request, and I let her in.

…I hope you get to see your family again…

My body locks as the room contracts a bit, the air thinner than it was moments ago.

That hurt.

The pressure builds in my eyes and it's a pain that doesn't smart like the words we've hurled at each other in the past. Ones meant to wound, harm, and maim. These words hurt due to something else entirely. It is a pain that is born of something stronger than steel and white-hot flame. One that connects me to the people that I left behind.

I wipe a hot tear as it streaks down my face, and I send my last thought before we both fall asleep.

I hope so too, Eilidh.

16
EILIDH

The morning buzzer rings out and everyone shuffles to rise from their beds.

It's been five days since Rhiannon and I decided to work together on our plan to get out of here and we haven't wasted a moment of it. We've been planning every last detail down to the hour.

I hop off the top bunk and cast a knowing glance at Rhiannon. She nods in acknowledgement and that's all we give away as we brush our teeth in silence and get ready to be released for showers.

She's been incredible. Her ideas and problem-solving skills are something to be admired and yet I still have my reservations about her help.

What if her hatred for my kind outweighs her desire to leave this place?

I remember the look on her face, soft and delicately dusted with freckles but unyielding as she told me about her sister. She opened a door for us to come together, now I just need to trust that it will prevent her from selling me out.

I still can't help but wonder if I'm expendable.

I wouldn't be able to tell anyone about her sister if I die.

Shaking the negative thoughts from my mind, I push my hair out of my face and prepare for the cell door to open.

I'm led down the hall and over to the showers by Ryker. He's always been heavier handed with me but today, he's extra pushy. I look around, hoping to see Gunnar in the crowd but can't find him anywhere. Ryker shoves my shoulder past the shower entrance, and I look up at him, confused and more than a little bit irritated.

"Trash duty today, Breather," he says, "You'll shower after breakfast so you don't smell like shit all day long."

I huff out my frustration but move along, collecting the trash left behind on the chow hall tables and tying up bags before dumping them in a large rolling cart. Each cell block trickles through for food, and I work until they've all passed through. Once the hall has cleared, I walk through the swinging doors and Bruce, a guard I rarely deal with, stands from his slouch and points towards the shower, his eyes never leaving the small phone screen he has crushed between his sausage-like fingers.

I breathe a sigh of relief when he doesn't follow me in, hopeful that I'll get another shower all to myself.

That dream is shattered when I walk in and see Xanth's perfectly muscular back flexing as he removes his pants, folding and placing them neatly on a bench just outside the showers.

Gods he has a nice ass. Even if he is one.

The last few days I haven't seen much of him outside of leaving our cells at the same time each day. I've felt him nearby, knowing that his attention is never far from me, but a silent truce was struck after our last argument and neither of us have dared to push the other again.

He doesn't turn around to face me, but I know he can sense me. Our scents mingle in the humid air, and I stand back, giving him a wide berth. If I'm being honest, I also don't trust myself to see him naked. Not when the water drips down his muscles in rivulets between his thickly corded muscles like that.

"Don't stare," he says and I shift my body away from him.

"I wasn't staring," I grit through clenched teeth. Unbuttoning my jumpsuit, I hold the fabric to my chest and wrap a towel around my body so I can shimmy out of them without him seeing me.

He huffs out a laugh. "Yer kidding, right?"

I realize I'm being childish by shielding myself. We shower in the same space every damn morning, but this feels more intimate somehow. There are always hundreds of other bodies around us and I've always been good about covering myself for the most part.

In here, alone, there's no hiding from the dark blue depths of his eyes.

I raise my chin and turn back to stare at him with my towel wrapped tightly around my body. His hair is slicked back, wet from the shower and his arms are lifted, pushing the water from his face and back over the length of black hair behind him.

His piercings glint in the yellow light. One at the center of his nose, several lining his ears and two on one side of his lower lip. The last is a pointed stud through his eyebrow but as I take in more of him, I notice that they don't stop there.

My eyes travel lower, marveling at the tattoos covering nearly every inch of him. His neck, his broad shoulders, his chest and arms are all wrapped in ink. He has piercings in each of his nipples that send lust careening through me. The ink travels down his stomach, over his muscular thighs and along his calves. Swirls, text, pictures and markings I don't understand lace his body but my gaze snags on one tattoo in particular.

On the left side of his chest, a phoenix with beautiful black and white feathers is overturned, plummeting from the sky. Panic and fear shine from its inky gaze and a spear runs right through its heart.

My beast screeches inside in imagination and my cheeks heat with anger but I don't allow it to take root in my chest.

"Ye like this one, ay?" He says, gesturing towards the dying phoenix on his skin. "She was inked by mah best mate a few years ago. Impeccable detail, if I do say so mahself."

I shake my head in disgust.

"No," I say quietly enough that I'm not even sure he hears me, but I continue all the same. "It's inaccurate." I walk to him then, unbothered by the streams now soaking my towel as I approach his hulking form. I rest my finger on the phoenix's claws grasped tight around the hilt of the spear and his skin flinches at the contact. "We would never fall like this." I look up into his eyes then, my finger never leaving his chest. "We burn and rise again. You would know that had you ever fought one of us before."

His breaths come out in harsh gusts, and I slowly pull my towel from my chest, allowing it to fall into the water swirling at our feet.

I stare at him as his eyes narrow yet begin a slow descent down the planes of my body, lingering on my most intimate places, taking in the curves of my breasts and dips in my waist. His hands flex at his sides, but he doesn't remove my hand from his chest.

Our anger is palpable, making the air heavy, but as our breathing slows, it morphs into something far more dangerous.

I can hardly breathe.

My jaw relaxes, as my lips part and I inhale a breath that causes my chest to rise. My breasts lift and Xanth leans into them, pressing his naked form closer to mine. My nipples brush lightly against his skin, and I can see the exact moment something snaps within him.

One second, I'm staring up at him, readying for a fight.

The next, I'm being lifted by the backs of my thighs and spun around. I'm slammed hard against the wall and my brain hasn't had time to catch up before his full lips are on mine. Our tongues fight for dominance. Our teeth clash together, and my hands weave through his hair, tugging and pulling. We're a flurry of limbs, scratching and grabbing for purchase.

Something within me flares, a blinding bright light that has my body moving without thought. I can feel it building inside my chest, growing and consuming me whole. Water dances with white fire and steam billows out around us. I'm too far gone to stop whatever has taken hold.

My core clenches as I feel him grind against my center and his cock jerks when I throw my head back and let out a moan.

That's when I feel the piercings.

Nine barbells stacked in a ladder on the underside of his massive cock, each one rubbing against my clit slowly and making my head spin.

I rise, pressing into him further and he bites at my lower lip, sucking it into his mouth while he uses his hands to guide my ass up over his length, positioning himself at my entrance.

Someone shouts in the hall. I all but jump from Xanth's arms, tumbling away from him as if he'd burned me.

He pushes away from the wall in one quick motion and stands several feet away, panting and gripping the tile behind him as he stares at me with bewildered eyes.

"Don't ye ever fuckin' touch me again," he seethes between gasping breaths.

My insides drop at his words. The blow, though not physical, takes my breath away all the same.

I rush from the shower, grabbing my clean clothes and hauling them onto my still dripping body.

Fuck the shower. I don't need one.

I run out the doors and Bruce looks up from his phone just long enough to jerk his head towards the rec hall.

"My cell." I'm still panting and so I take a deep breath to steady my breathing. "Please, I'd like to go to my cell. Period cramps." I hold my lower abdomen to sell the lie.

A gruff sound comes from him, clearly uncomfortable with the idea that females bleed each month, as he stands and leads me back towards the gates of cell block 3.

Once the door of my cell slams closed, I scramble into my bed and pull the blankets over my head.

Tears stream down my face as all that just happened plays on repeat in my mind. Shame, guilt, embarrassment and pain barrel through me in powerful waves.

What the fuck did I just do?

17
RHIANNON

I prod my gloopy oatmeal with my spoon, pushing the raisins to the side because I hate them. I'm convinced raisins were created as a form of punishment. Which makes sense that there would be bastardized grapes in my oatmeal, because this is prison. And the usual punishments of being in prison include degradation, slave labor, objectification, barely passable living conditions, chemical smelling soap…and raisins.

I set down my spoon and watch as Eilidh grabs her food. Clearly the cooks felt that today's breakfast would suffice for lunch also.

Lazy fucks.

Eilidh locks eyes with me as she walks to the far end of the hall before I retract the steel encasing my mind to catapult a thought her way, the golden thread pulsating with electricity as it travels to the white wall of flame that crackles with vibrant light.

Sit with me.

She passes me but I feel her eyes on me as she stops, the thought quietly passing through her defenses.

In my mind, a gentle hand presses against the cool unyielding metal and as it passes through, I can feel her turmoil roiling. I don't have an opportunity to ask what's wrong before I hear her say softly:

…Here? Everyone can see…

I turn and look at her. Her face is set in calm trepidation.

Yes, dummy.

She smirks and then walks back to take a seat next to me. I continue to poke at my oatmeal.

"You think if you poke it long enough it'll turn into steak?" Eilidh asks as she picks up her spoon.

"I haven't decided yet," I say, shoveling out the little black blasphemies from their pool of tepid mush.

She watches me as she takes a bite, raisins and all. I make a face at her as she chews.

"What? I like 'em," She chuckles and takes another bite.

"Of course you do," I retort with a scoff, and she elbows my side. The TV is on in the chow hall so that people can watch the news during breakfast. Some think it's a luxury we are afforded. I think they do it so that we can all watch our home burn to ash from within the prison walls; destroying any hope of rebuilding what the world of Altas is dismantling. Sometimes, it's hard to believe some of the stories the news reports on. They make astrals out to be criminals and hateful beasts which is fucking ridiculous, but I suppose if they are selling us as the villains, telling the truth wouldn't work in their favor.

The human government has gotten more and more radicalized since Altas Montgomery created the first Mech suit and gave them a fighting chance against the superior strength of an astral. They grew an overinflated Gods complex and decided that they were entitled to the land of Elysia. They even renamed it to suit their religion, systems, and agendas. Since then, it's been us versus them.

And we aren't winning.

At least that's how it seems.

That's why I hate watching the fucking news. It's just more fear mongering propaganda to keep human hatred burning bright and astrals afraid. It provides them with some modicum of control.

As I look at the flickering screen, I see a sketch artist's rendering of a masked cloaked man with a black hood. Under the sketch in red block letters reads the title "The Ghost of Prism," and I tune in momentarily to hear that this "Ghost" has brutally murdered two human soldiers involved in the public maiming of astrals several years prior and that the Rebellion seems to have cropped up shortly after, inciting riots, increasing protests and influencing attacks on humans. They conveniently leave out that the humans being attacked are all military members. No civilians have been attacked.

...I smell smoke... Eilidh gently prods.

I look up to see Eilidh's golden eyes watching me inquisitively. I chew on my cheek and put my spoon down. Eilidh looks back at the TV and then at me.

...Something about that Ghost guy bothers you?...

I exhale and tent my fingers over my nose as I notice Kieran walk into the chow hall. He looks fucking perfect.

Ugh. The exasperation hums across our line and Eilidh sits up a little straighter as she looks over at the red-headed guard.

...Ah, I see... She murmurs quietly back.

No, that's not...

Fucking liar.

Eilidh arches a brow at me in equal disbelief, and I rub my temples.

I hate the news, that's all. I'm also a tad jealous and in awe of the vigilante justice. This Ghost guy is going around killing fascist soldiers to bolster the Rebellion and it's fucking inspirational.

...Damn. I didn't realize you were such an anarchist. I like it...

I'm not. I'm just...pissed off. And... I look back up to Kieran who is already looking at me with those beautiful teal eyes and I squeeze mine shut to stop the visions of his tongue sliding into my mouth.

...Ah, yeah. Understood... She nods and takes another bite of her oatmeal.

Godsdamnit.

...You know you could just fuck him for fun too. Perhaps get it out of your system... Another phantom pang of pain from Eilidh rushes across our mental connection and I wonder if Xan has anything to do with it.

No. No, I agreed to do this with you, and I will.

Even if I don't really know what I'm doing. I'm strapped with the knowledge that this endeavor is probably going to hurt like hell, but I am going to go through with it anyway. My knowledge of sex includes plenty of messing around with other dragons and astrals. I feel like I have grown rather proficient in kissing and found I'm particularly good at using my mouth for pleasure. However, it's everything *but* what Eilidh and I have agreed to, and Kieran is fucking *massive*. I can only imagine that his dick is going to reflect his size.

I feel my palms start to sweat and a familiar prickling brushes against my skin. Eilidh's stare is like a wave of static as it caresses me.

...Rhiannon...

I look over at her and she looks…concerned.

"Wh-why are you looking at me like that?" I whisper aloud.

…You… She pauses a moment, weighing her words before she continues. *…You have had sex before, right?…*

Shit. Shit shit shit. My cheeks flush red.

Um, yeah. Lots of times. I don't even believe my own lie.

"Fucking hells…" Eilidh breathes out, her eyes pinched closed and she lets her spoon drop into her bowl.

Eilidh gets up, snatching her tray up as she walks to the trash to throw away the rest of her food.

…Deal's off… Her tone has shifted back into that commander's voice she used before. She's walking away faster than my thoughts can catch up.

Stop, Eilidh, wait. Wait!

She turns around just before she reaches the trash, and I quickly dodge tables to stand beside her again.

Look, you're the only one that knows, okay? It was something that I- I don't know. I guess I chose it. But it's fine. It's not a big deal.

…Rhiannon, you're not doing this. You aren't losing your maidenhead to a fucking guard. I refuse to ask that of you…

It's mine to give, Eilidh. I want to get out of here more than I want to keep my virginity.

Her eyes blaze with sun-fire, golden and dangerous. Her pursuit to protect me is kind of nice but also a little frustrating. She's fighting for something that is personal to me, and I don't really know how to process that.

She hesitates again, her eyes darting between mine.

…You're right. It's yours to give. All I ask is that you think about this more. Don't give it to someone who doesn't deserve it, Rhiannon. We can always figure out a different plan. I'm not leaving you here. You will see Fianna and your family again….

Something rises within me. An unfamiliar watery feeling presses into my eyes. I wipe away a stray tear and stare down at where I flicked it with as much anger as I can muster but it falls flat.

I fucking hate crying.

"Major Hot Stuff!" A shrill voice calls out and Eilidh and I both turn towards an obnoxiously dressed woman with gleaming blonde hair. She's in lime green pumps, a pair of matching lime green rimmed cat-eyeglasses, and an all-white skirt and blouse. She is practically hanging on Kieran, and I feel my stomach drop as Nina begins to growl low in my gut.

"Hi Rhetta," Kieran says as he smiles tightly at her. She hands him a coffee and brushes a kiss to his cheek and the fire in my blood ignites.

...*Down girl*... Eilidh slides into my head space as the wildfire roars through my ears. ...*Don't let him get to you*...

"What time will you be picking me up for the party on Saturday? Don't forget to wear a blazer and a red tie to match my dress." Rhetta smiles wide, flashing her white crooked teeth. She waggles her brows, and I think I'm going to either scream or throw up.

Kieran's eyes flick to meet mine and I see his throat bob as he swallows. His smile is shallow as he looks at Rhetta and says, "I'll be there at six."

"Fuck this," I growl and before I charge at the blonde Barbie bitch, Eilidh grabs my arm and pulls me back firmly.

"Rhiannon, stop," she says low and gravely, like she understood that anger and hurt. Like she knew how it felt beneath that fury. The ache and tearing of flesh that you don't realize is there until it's too late. Tender and new, now torn to pieces.

...*He doesn't deserve you. We'll find another way*...

The pressure and prickling start behind my eyes again and I nod my head as I walk calmly forward, willing myself to tip up my chin and shove back the emotions that fought to break free.

I walk past Kieran and his blonde whore without a glance. I can feel his eyes following me.

"Good morning, 2460," Kieran gruffs as I near the exit.

I look back at him glancing briefly at his little arm-piece. I paint a phony smile on my face and meet him with all the cheer I can muster.

"Morning, Major Haley. Or should I say, *Major Hot Stuff*." I bark out a laugh that's false and derisive. "Hope you two have fun on your date."

I walk out of the chow hall feeling Kieran's gaze bore into the back of my head the entire way. Once I turn to the hallway back towards the

Breather Block, I press my back against the wall, lean over and place my hands on my knees, willing the bile back down my throat.

Eilidh stands in front of me, concern lining her face. I swipe away the last tear I will ever cry for Kieran Haley from my cheek, take a deep breath, and head out to formation for my daily job. Shoving back the sound of his voice as it echoes in my brain.

18
KIERAN

"Well, that was weird," Rhetta says as she wipes the hot pink lipstick from my cheek, and I resist the urge to pull away. "Do you know her, Kieran?"

Rhiannon disappeared through the exit a few seconds ago and I can still see an outline of her in the light as if she left an imprint of herself there to taunt me.

"Uh, yeah," I say, as gnawing, snapping panic begins to crawl its way up my gut the farther Rhiannon moves away from me.

I need to explain. I need to tell her this isn't what it looks like.

The unwelcome thoughts barrel through my head as I continue to move away.

This was my intention. This is the distraction. I try to remind myself. *This is what's going to keep her and I away from one another and it's working. It's working.*

And yet.

That clawing within me turns into wet slithering dread that makes my gut turn on itself as I pull back from Rhetta and she juts out her lip in a pout. It's childish and doesn't have the effect on me that she's hoping for.

She tries to grab me as I back up further, ready to run after Rhiannon.

"Where are you going? I came all the way down here to bring you coffee and spend time with you on your break."

"I know and I appreciate it, Rhetta. But I need to take care of something," I say as I begin walking towards the front of the chow hall where Rhiannon's outline still mocks me in the sterile light.

"Okay well, I'll see you around!" She yells back at me, waving. I force a smile and round the corner outside of the chow hall, adjusting my tactical vest as I go. The corridor to the Breather Block is empty so I turn and look down the hall leading to the laundry and the greenhouses.

Nothing.

I don't know her job schedule, I don't know where she would have gone. Maybe the bathroom?

Stop. You shouldn't.

I really shouldn't. I stand in the cross-section between corridors and sigh as I begin walking down the hallway to the laundry facilities. I don't really know why I resign myself to this particular direction apart from feeling like it's the better choice. But the more I open my senses, the more I'm pulled this way. The smell draws me in. It's cookies and…

"Oof," someone says as they round the corner and run right into me. They rebound off me and all I see is a flurry of long auburn hair. She looks up at me with watery eyes and a solemn expression and I stare back at the source of the scent…vanilla and honey.

"Rhiannon."

Her lips quiver and she tucks them between her teeth for a moment as she straightens up, her eyes turn to ice. "I'm late for my job. Excuse me."

She dips her shoulder and pushes past me.

Fuck. *Fuck.* "Wait." *No, don't do that. Don't fucking stop her. This wasn't the plan.*

"I'll get put in SolCon if I'm not there in the next five minutes," she says as I catch her arm.

What the fuck are you doing? My mind yells as I hold her, swiping my thumb over her bicep. Her skin is soft, supple, yet taut over the toned muscle.

71, 89, 8, 90, 82. Calm. Calm the fuck down. "Let me explain." I say softly, but she pulls her arm away.

"No need. Seems pretty clear what's going on," she says, and her tone is biting but lacks venom. There's pain and weariness laced through her words, and it feels like she's trying her damndest to be anything but vulnerable.

"Rhiannon," I mutter and her fingers tighten into fists.

"Stop that," she whispers, looking up at me and *fuck*. She's like a strong force of gravity, pulling and pressing me apart as her lips part on an exhale, her brow pinches together and her eyes soften. "Stop saying my name like that. I can't…just stop."

She doesn't move though and neither do I. I look down and see that her hand is so close. I could reach out and touch it, feel her skin against mine for just a second. Just once. My index finger flexes as it creeps closer to her.

You have to stop. This is wrong.

She straightens up and clears her throat. "Goodbye, Major Haley," she says more clearly, and my limbs become idle to the rest of my body. They move without my permission as if something inside of me decides all on its own. I catch her hand and grip it, halting her progression as I pull her into me. She collides with my chest and my fingers thread through her hair, the warm sugary smell of her is thick and heady as it wafts into my face. She presses her hands against all the tactical equipment on my vest, pushing me away and I let her.

Wrong. Wrong. Leave. Let her go.

Her eyes are wide as she looks at me. The clear blue of her irises unwavering as her gaze pierces through my resolve. Fuck, I want her so bad it hurts.

Not right. Not right. 71, 89, 8.

I don't care though.

She inhales as her eyes flick to a door on her right. She twists the handle, and it opens to a small closet of brooms, mops, rags, and cleaning solutions. The door opens wide, and she takes my hand to pull me in. We barely fit as she closes the door with us inside. I can't see anything.

But I feel her.

Her fingertips swipe along my jaw, her thumb presses against my chin so that my mouth opens and then I see two glowing red eyes staring at me through the dark. It should terrify me, but my blood is raging in my ears as I unzip my tactical vest, and her hands splay out over my chest. I want them on my skin. I want to feel her skin on mine so damn bad.

"Is she yours?" She whispers.

"No," I reply quickly. "A distraction."

She clicks her tongue softly. "From what?"

From you. "Rhiannon," I plead like a supplicant, begging for mercy.

"Say it out loud," she says, her voice barely audible, but it's a roar in my ears, a sonic boom to the very fabric of my being. "I need to hear you say it."

"From you. She's a distraction from you," I admit and a strange weight lifts from my chest as the words are set free.

Not right. Not right. My rational mind echoes over and over until whatever is driving me begins to take over with a new chant. It whispers like a prayer as she grabs my shirt in her fists and pulls me into her. I feel her warmth against my body, feel her breasts press against my ribs, feel her eager fingers skate up around my neck and pull me closer. I feel the tingling warmth of her exhale, barely a breath away from my mouth.

"At least you have a distraction," She mutters and I feel the movement of her lips, the heat of her breath.

Right…right…not…right…8, 90, 82. Take it, you idiot.

Fuck.

She exhales a gentle shuddering breath. It brushes hot against my skin, and I can't take it anymore.

I press my lips to hers and it's as if I'm breathing for the first time. Like I've been holding my breath my entire life and I'm finally inhaling fresh air.

It's not what I imagined. Not what I've pictured probably hundreds of times, as I fisted my cock in the shower, dreaming of what she would taste like, what her lips would feel like.

It's better.

So much fucking better.

I'm lost and found. Complete and undone as she opens and slips her tongue into my mouth. I feast on her lips. Hungry and unraveling as my tongue swipes along hers.

Godsdamnit the way she tastes.

There's no way to describe it other than fucking irresistible. Like finding your favorite thing and knowing you'll never be able to get enough. She's a drug. My black tar heroin and nicotine hellbent on me taking it until I shrivel and die. I keep pressing, pushing, tasting, touching more of her. I pull her into my body, molding her shape into mine, wanting to feel every curve, every strand of thick auburn hair on her head, memorize the flavor of her skin, hear every sound that she makes when I touch her and taste her.

"Ah," she whimpers as I press my hips against hers and realize all the bulky shit on my belt is digging into her. I unbuckle my belt and let it drop to the floor with a clang, and she wraps a leg around my waist. I feel that wet warmth between her legs. That home that I need so desperately to return to, even though I've never been.

I want it.

I want her.

Fuck, I want *her*.

"Kieran," she whispers and, gods, it's kerosine on a spark. It flashes hot in my body as my hands rove over her ass and my hips press into that heat with the throbbing length of my erection. She sighs and it's a symphony that I could listen to forever.

My mouth presses into hers again and her taste is all I know, along with the curves of her body and the soft velvet of her lips.

Her fingers weave into my hair as I wrap her other leg around my waist, slotting my hips firmly against her apex and she moans into my mouth. I thrust my cock against her clothed sex and it's almost too good. I run my teeth down the side of her neck, as her hands scramble and flex along my neck, landing on my shoulders as she grabs hold of me. Her head lolls back onto the wall as my tongue laves over the area where my teeth dragged across her skin.

"Oh gods," she whines. My hips drive into her again as the pressure builds. "K-Kieran." She groans softly and I grip her ass hard in my palms, the feeling now overtaking me as her body tenses.

"I want to hear you," I rasp into her ear. "Say my name as you come, Rhiannon."

"Oh fuck," she whimpers, "fuck."

I can't stop. I won't.

Right…right…so right…not…right.

I barrel my rock-hard cock against her once…twice…three more times and she grips the back of my shirt as she yelps and moans.

"Kieran, I'm gonna-"

"That's it, Rhiannon, that's so good. You're doing so good."

Her entire body contracts as she presses her lips to mine and chants my name against my mouth as she climaxes, squeezing my waist between her powerful thighs.

I am so close. My balls begin to tighten as I push against her two more times and her legs pull me into her as she pants, still saying my name against my lips.

"Wait," she says and my hips immediately still, despite the orgasm that is a breath away from spilling out of me. She unwraps her legs, but keeps me close to her as she unbuttons my pants and reaches her fingers in. She sighs as she gently pulls my rock-hard leaking dick from my pants.

Oh gods. Oh fuck.

Her palm grips my shaft, and she begins stroking. I lean forward and press my hands against the wall as she pumps my cock.

"Rhiannon," I say hoarsely, my body starts to tremble as my climax barrels ahead. "Shit, I'm-"

"Kiss me," she says, and I look at those crimson eyes, burning like a forest fire in the dark. I oblige as I take her mouth, feeling her slick tongue dive in and I moan at the invasion of her taste. I'm bucking into her delicate hand as her fist tightens. I'm panting as the pressure climbs once again. My balls pull in tight as I grunt and spill out into the space between us. She's still pulling on my length as my hips continue to jerk forward, milking me of every drop as I rest my forehead against hers.

We're both gasping and sweating, still, apart from our lungs expanding erratically.

"I-" she whispers. "I'm so fucked," she says and she sounds like she's smiling.

"Not yet," I reply playfully, and she chuckles.

"I mean I'm gonna be in trouble," she says softly. Her hand is still gripping my dick.

I've never realized how much I love utility closets.

"No, you won't be," I mutter back, pressing my mouth to hers softly and I feel her teeth as she stretches her lips into a smile.

"You gonna give me a hall pass or something?"

"Something like that," I say and kiss along her jaw, letting my teeth scrape against the skin of her neck and her hand tightens on my cock. The pressure starts to build again.

"Can I ask you something without you freaking out?" She asks as her lips trace my jaw. She could ask me anything she wanted right now.

I hum my response as I find the spot on her neck that is soft and smells like baked goods and *her*. I press my mouth to it, and she leans in.

"Wh-what are the-" She takes a breath and says quietly, "the numbers?"

I keep kissing her neck, letting my tongue lave over her soft skin and she sighs. "What numbers?"

She pants and says, "71, 89, 8,"-

I straighten and take a step back. It's cold and I don't like it but…

"H-how do you know that?"

I see her blood red eyes glowing in the dark, peering up at me. "I heard you say them."

I never say them. Never out loud. Never out loud.

"I know you didn't say them out loud."

Fuck. FUCK. What?!

I pick up my belt and vest, buckling and shrugging back into my gear.

"You didn't know." She realizes quietly, almost to herself as I open the door to the caustic light. I squint into the brightness of the hallway.

I shake my head, affirming her as I run my fingers through my hair and gesture for her to follow. She adjusts her jumpsuit and hair as she walks beside me to the laundry. I will my dick to settle the fuck down, still burning alive with want, her proximity still a magnet and a force that beckons me, constantly pulling me in.

But I can't. We can't.

Not right. Not right. The numbers flash through my mind like a salve to my resolve that I try to revive from ash. *71, 89, 8, 90, 82.*

My eyes flit over to her and she's chewing her kiss swollen bottom lip as we head into the laundry. Nova looks at me from across the room and she straightens as she salutes me.

"You're late again, 2460." Nova says to Rhiannon. "We talked about this."

"She's excused," I say to Nova, and she arches her brow. Curious or not, Nova knows better than to question me.

Rhiannon doesn't look up as the corner of her mouth twitches. I watch her walk to the line of astrals folding laundry, then pull out my phone and pretend to be doing something important as I try to process what just happened.

How could I have been so careless?

I didn't realize she could mind-speak. I couldn't have known that. I knew some dragons could, I just wasn't aware it was *her* ability. She also could have kept it from me. She could have kept it a secret...but she didn't.

They're just numbers. I think, as my eyes flick up to her and she blinks a few times. *Rhiannon.*

I nod to Nova and head for the exit.

I just need some time.

She dips her chin and continues folding as I make my way out of the laundry room.

The numbers flood my brain now. *71, 89, 8, 90, 82.* Calming my thundering heart, neutralizing my over firing nerve-endings. Reminding me that I'm in control.

I'm in control.

The numbers march through my mind in perfect rhythm. Forcing everything into its steady beat. I walk down the corridor and pass the closet where we just were and her voice whispers across my mind.

"Kiss me."

I did. I kissed her with all I had.

It's then that I realize repeating numbers and calming breaths would not keep me from doing it again.

I would. I would do it again.

19
EILIDH

"I need a different option." The words spill from Rhiannon's lips. There is something lighter about her, but I don't pry. Not after our conversation during lunch and the revelation that she's a godsdamn virgin, one that was ready to hop on the *seduction train* just to get out of here. I'm not going to push her for more information. I don't want her to give that up in our attempt to escape.

We are getting out of here though. *Together*. Somehow.

Her eyes shine a bit brighter, and her face is flush. The freckles dotting her cheeks are more prominent with the added color to her skin and I decide that I like seeing her this way. I could almost be convinced that she's happy.

A stab of pain slices through me and I dip my chin as I remember what Xanth said.

"Don't ye ever fucking touch me again"

I school my features before raising my head to meet her eyes again.

"I'm glad you came to your senses." I raise an eyebrow at her, deflecting as I cross my arms.

When you're used to disappointment, focusing on someone else's problems helps to soothe the dull ache left behind when you're let down again. My mother sliced through the thin layers of my heart long ago and since then I've prided myself on the scar tissue that has strengthened my resolve. I won't allow some mercurial fucking dragon who can't decide if he wants to kill me or fuck me cloud my mind for long.

It's unfortunate that of all days, today was the day he kissed me.

He shook me to my core. I can still feel his teeth on my tongue and the wild way he gripped my hair. It was as though a dark beast had been set loose, and it was determined to destroy anything in its path.

My sick mind wants him to destroy me.

I pull myself from thoughts of Xanth and focus on my roommate. She's sitting upright on her bed, her hand clasped on her lap staring at the ground with a faint smile on her lips.

Interesting.

I let my mind wander to hers, brushing the tendrils of my white-hot flame against her steel shields and she opens for me.

Anything you'd like to share? I ask.

Her cheeks flush a deep shade of pink, and a stiff nod is all I get in return.

...I-I won't be able to. I will not seduce Kieran. I won't. I understand if this means you'll be leaving without me... She stares back at me, and a genuine smile stretches across her face, softening the scars and making her eyes glitter. *...But I'm glad to have met you. I hope you make it out of here...*

I rear back.

Bitch, you're coming with me whether you get stuffed by a hot redhead or not. I step towards her, and she laughs out loud. *I'll find a way for us both to escape. Just be ready when the time comes.*

Her eyes skirt to the cell door and back to me. Resolve washes over her and she nods again in affirmation.

...We're getting out of here tonight...

I've just finished dinner. The cold stew and stale bread sitting at the top of my stomach turns when I enter the evening rec hall and see Xanth working on deadlifts in the corner.

I swear to Gods he never stops working out.

A small shelf with a handful of used and torn books sits beside a threadbare couch and I skim the titles, selecting one at random.

I sit down on the couch and pretend to read as my eyes glance over the top of the pages at the people around me. Searching but not seeing.

Fuck.

Rhiannon sits with a few other dragons, the twins, I recognize, and her gaze finds mine. She looks around the room, then back to me and shakes her head.

He's not here. Gunnar isn't here.

My heart sinks but only momentarily. I need to get out of here and I refuse to wait another day. Who knows what other terrible decisions I'll make if I have to face Xanth alone again.

I assess the guards present. One of them will have to do.

Bruce leans against the door, face buried in his phone. Nova sips from a travel mug and sighs. The clean-cut guard I saw a few weeks ago with Major Haley stands near the door and I set my sights on him.

I casually stand, brush off my jumpsuit and saunter over to the bookshelf to replace the novel I'd picked up. Walking towards him, I roll through lines in my head, thinking of ways to approach a new guard and seduce him.

Gods I hope he's easy.

I'm still several feet away when Ryker enters through the door and approaches the other guard. They share a few words, Ryker smiles and taps the other male's shoulder, who glares back at him before turning on his heel and exiting the room.

Fuck!

My feet don't slow. They propel me forward until I'm standing directly in front of Ryker and he's looking down at me like I've lost my mind.

Perhaps I have.

His short dark hair reflects the light, and his stubble has grown out to give him a slight shadow on his squared jaw. He's an attractive male, all things considered.

Swallowing hard, I look over my shoulder, back towards Rhiannon who encourages me with a nudge of her head. Turning back to Ryker, I plaster on a blinding smile and bat my lashes a few times.

He gets the hint quickly. I didn't take him for much of a foreplay kind of guy.

"Well, well, well," he says as he adjusts his heavy belt on his hips, "took you long enough, Breather." His eyes rove my body, and I repress a repulsed shudder.

I'm well acquainted with Ryker's type. He's the kind of male who likes an easy catch. Someone who will submit to him without question and that he can leave without another word the next day.

Act dumb. Play the game. I recite to myself.

"I-I don't know what you could possibly mean?" I croon, feigning innocence.

His hands grip my cheeks painfully. His dark brown eyes turn sultry, and he lowers his head closer to mine. "I've wanted to work these pretty lips since the moment you stepped foot through that door."

I'm taken aback by his forwardness but not a single guard stops him from touching me.

This is normal for him.

I can feel a familiar pair of deep blue eyes on my skin like a hot iron, branding themselves onto my skin but I don't turn out of Rykers grip.

"What would you do to get between them?" I ask him in a hushed voice. I nibble my bottom lip to sell the appeal and Ryker bites.

A straight-tooth, white smile slowly creeps up his face and his other hand reaches out to pull my waist in closer. My breasts graze his lower chest.

He's much shorter than Xanth.

My nipples harden involuntarily at the thought of them, naked and dripping wet as they danced across Xanth's abdomen before he took me in his arms in the shower.

While my musing may not have been about Ryker, my visible arousal excites him all the same. His eyes narrow on the peaks poking through my jumpsuit and he hisses through his teeth. The sound is drowned out by a familiar snarl rumbling through my mind.

"Name your price," Ryker moves a thumb closer to my lips.

Yes.

The victory steadies me.

"One hour in the fifth-floor rec hall with my cellmate. She and I have some unfinished business." I lean into him and bare my teeth.

Insinuating that Rhiannon and I are going to fight is the only way to keep him from questioning why I'd want her in there too. Now I wait, holding my breath and hoping that Ryker hasn't noticed us getting closer recently.

He chuckles and I relax a bit.

"Fiery little thing, aren't you?" His thumb brushes my lower lip, and I can feel Xanth approaching from behind me. He's tense, the air following him hard enough to crack.

I bat my lashes a few more times and look down at my feet before returning my eyes to his. A move that turns most males to putty.

He looks up over my shoulder and I'm sure he sees Xanth standing only a few feet away, staring at us.

Ryker looks back down at me and his face lowers so that he's only a breath away from me. "You've got yourself a deal, Breather."

I sigh with relief that I had hoped would ease some of the tension in my chest but as Ryker straightens and turns to walk away, the storm that's been brewing approaches.

...So, y'er going te do it, ey?...

I let my forehead drop against the cold wall where Ryker had been standing.

I don't have time for this.

Even in my mind's voice, I'm tired.

...I'll kill him...

The heady scent of aged whiskey and burnt oak wraps around me as he steps forward to stand directly behind me. I can feel the phantom touch of his body surrounding my back and I know he's only a few inches away, bent over me like a beautiful dark angel.

No. I shake my head softly, rubbing it against the concrete wall. *You won't, because if you did, that would mean you care about me. You would never admit that.*

His hands cage me in, each one planted on either side of my head.

...Don't do this, Little Dove. I won't repeat mahself again. I will kill him, and his blood will be on yer hands...

I close my eyes tightly, balling my fists at my sides but when I turn, Xanth is already gone.

The nighttime buzzer sounds.

All the inmates begin to wind down for the night while my thoughts are caught in a spiral of logic and emotion warring within me. I hold tight to my locket, pressing it to my chest in hopes that it will guide me through this. That I'll have enough willpower to walk away from the prison and not think about the faces I've come to know here.

The overhead lights tick off, one by one, and the corridor falls into a deafening silence. My ears roar and I drop my locket in its hiding place as I roll off the mattress to rinse my face.

Booted footsteps echo down the hall and I turn to meet Rhiannon's blue gaze. I drop my shields, allowing her in as the boots grow closer, ticking away the moments before I cross a line I can never return from.

...*You are brave*...

I don't feel brave. My hands begin to tremble, but I clasp them together in a meager attempt to stop the shaking.

...*You don't have to go through with-*...

I do. I stop her train of thought. *I must do this, and I will. I'll be ok and soon enough, we will both be out of here.*

She sits up and lets her blanket fall to the ground. I'm looking down at it, trying to avoid her stare when her arms wrap around my shoulders, and she pulls me in tightly.

... *I'll never be able to repay you for this*...

I take a shuddering breath and ease her from the confines of my mind, replacing the wall and stepping back after squeezing her one last time.

She sits back in bed and covers up just as Ryker reaches our cell door.

The lock clicks and the sound reverberates, through my entire body. I step forward, taking Ryker's outstretched hand in mine and moving out from within the safety of my cell. Whiskey and oak billow from the gate beside mine and I cast a glance over my shoulder, expecting to see darkness but instead I'm met with Xanth's intense stare. His arms slung out from between the bars, and he leans against it with smoke billowing around him.

...Don't...

It's the only word he says to me.

Ryker leads me away from our cell, his hand now firmly planted on my ass as he walks eagerly towards the block gate. Once we are past the cells, he turns to face me, his eyes hooded with lust, nearly black in the darkened corridor and I shift a bit uncomfortably. He looks deranged.

...Eilidh...

Xanth speaks my name in my mind for the first time, and it sounds...pleading. A tear slips down my cheek as Ryker takes my mouth with his. He's rough and brutal, shoving his tongue between my teeth and gripping my ass with so much pressure it hurts.

It's nothing like my kiss with Xanth. Nothing like the passion I felt exploding from inside of me. When fire and water danced between us. Nothing like home.

A quiet whimper escapes me when his hand grabs hold of my breast and twists painfully. There's a loud creaking sound that descends down the hall, but I don't think Ryker notices. thereHe continues his fervent groping of my body and begins rubbing his hardening length against my clothed hips.

Another loud creak sounds and a booming crack resounds through the corridor. Finally, Ryker lifts his mouth from mine, looking down the hall but not releasing me. Fear and disbelief mingle on his shadowed features.

My eyes follow his and I stare slack jawed at the sight down the corridor.

I can't believe what I'm seeing.

A cell at the very end of the hall is rattling. Smoke billows out in an endless stream and two clawed hands wrapped in blue-black scales are visibly pulling each of the bars off the cell door. Every piece of iron that's yanked from the gate hits the linoleum with an earsplitting clang before the beast within reaches for the next.

"What the fuck? Hey! HEY! STOP!" Ryker sounds frantic.

Another bar hits the ground and the astral crawls from the cell and turns towards us, cloaked in smoke.

Dark, storm blue eyes meet mine and my heart stutters.

Xanth, no.

...Mine... A growl unlike any I've ever heard sounds throughout my mind. It's Xanth's voice but it's laced with something darker, more sinister.

I don't have an opportunity to react. One minute I'm standing there with Ryker's hand wound tightly around my breast and the other white knuckling my ass. The next, Ryker is ripped from me, face ashen and the smell of fear trickling down his leg.

Xanth roars, shaking the entire hall and sending the other astrals into a frenzy. Screeching, hooping, hollering and snarls reverberate throughout the block from all around. He rips Ryker's arm that twisted my breast clean from his body and tosses it aside just like the bars from his cell. An earsplitting howl rends the air and blood gushes from the wound, soaking the ground beneath them.

Ryker scrambles for his gun with the arm still attached but his head starts to loll backwards. He's losing too much blood, too fast.

The two males slide, the slick floors quickly sending them to their knees. A struggle happens but Ryker is too far gone to put up much of a fight.

Xanth pins him to the ground with his hulking weight and begins to wail on him. Punch after punch lands on Ryker's face, leaving behind a bloodied and bruised mess. I can hear the gurgled screams over the cacophony of sound around us, but I'm stunned in place.

Paralyzed.

Xanth's arm lifts to send another blow to the guard's face when a gunshot rings through the hall. My heart stops for what feels like an eternity, dread seeping through my chest as flashbacks of Amell's dying face play behind my eyes.

Xanth turns to look at me, none of the blood coating him is his own and as fucked up as it is, I'm relieved as the roaring in my ears settles.

I take one step forward, ready to pull him from the carnage when a long, electric cattle prod rams into Xanth's back. He arcs and roars up towards the ceiling. His bellowing yells ring like a death knoll in my mind.

The fire in me ignites, my beast takes hold, frantic with the need to help him. I rush forward only to be hauled back by the nape of my neck by a cold metal hand.

A scab? I didn't think they used those here...

Balor Cain stands with his mechanical eye spinning, an eerie blue electric rod in hand as he shoots wave after wave of electricity through Xanth's body, and I cry out.

"What a surprise."

20
XANTH

Tingles like tiny fire ants run through every nerve of my body. Shocks cresting and receding in even intervals that tear through my body, causing convulsions and I feel like I'm being ripped apart. Every second is pure unbridled agony.

My beast keens in my chest and I work to focus my eyes on what's happening.

A tall, shining Scab holds Eilidh by the back of her neck and I will my body to move toward her. The desire to pull her from those cold, lifeless hands and hold her against me shrieks like a siren song in my head.

I blink away some of the blood splatter from my eyes. I can still see Eilidh, she's yelling something, but I hear nothing beyond the roaring in my ears. She blurs before me and then there are two of her. I can feel myself fading in and out of consciousness, any minute now I'll be no more than a heap on this bloodstained floor.

Another shock bolts through my limbs and my head falls back on another yell, but nothing comes out, my vocal cords worn and frayed from screaming. The ringing in my ears grows to an unbearable pitch and I claw at the sides of my head, willing it to stop.

Balor stands in front of me, blocking Eilidh from my view and I glare back at him.

I need to get to her. She's not safe. She's mine and she's not safe.

His mouth moves. He's speaking to me, but nothing is registering other than this incessant ringing in my ears. His head turns and he mouths something to someone else. His hair is slicked back but a stray strand moves about his sweat greased forehead, reminding me of the drunks my Pap and I would kick out of our bar nearly every night back home.

I'm hauled up by my shoulders and giant metal gauntlets are placed on my limp wrists, an ominous green glow pulsing in the center of the lock. My eyes close and my brain slows. I'm unable to keep my feet steady and my body slumps forward, dead weight resting in unfamiliar hands.

I can feel myself being dragged backwards, my feet gliding against the cool linoleum floors. I struggle to lift my heavy eyelids, only to see that they're taking me away from her.

I thrash in their hold. Azure rattling and raging in a panic, though he seems far away. Nothing feels right. It's as though I'm watching the world through a tin can.

The last thing I see before I'm pulled out of the cell block gates is Eilidh's screaming face. I lunge one final time and another shock courses through me before blackness sweeps me under.

I wake on a damp floor that reeks of piss and sweat. At first, I wonder if this is what death feels like, but a drop of liquid hits my face, and I figure that can't be right. I open my eyes to nothingness, panic settling in my chest when I see nothing as I work to move my arms and legs.

Did they blind me?

I'm face down on the floor and every movement feels like I'm stuck beneath a crushing weight. My body is bunched up and curled in on itself in an unnatural way. My fingers twitch, I brace my hands beneath my chest and push up to sit. I feel a wall at my back and stretch my legs out in front of me.

Or at least I try to.

My feet meet another wall only a few short feet away, forcing my legs to stay crumpled up against my chest. Shifting again, I try to find a direction that is longer so I can stretch out my limbs, but I'm met with close walls on all sides.

Fuck.

A faint buzz can be heard outside of the box I'm in and without notice, a bulb hung only by a single red wire flicks on overhead. The abrupt change of light has me squinting through my eyelashes and covering my face. When I've recovered slightly and blinked through the worst of the pain, I take in my new surroundings.

Four identical concrete walls encase me, none wide enough for me to stretch more than a single arm out at a time. A drain hole sits in the center of the floor beneath me but there is no sink, no toilet and no bed. Only me and this piss-stained cell.

A clear liquid trickles from the concrete ceiling and drips onto the floor. The pads of my fingers are pruned and tender. Everything is sore.

How long have I been out?

The buzzing continues outside my cell and the light flickers on and off erratically. I sit for Gods only knows how long before the variable blinking causes a migraine that pounds and thrums in my head.

A high-pitched beeping starts, and I groan. It beeps in a pattern of long and short notes, so shrill that it feels as if each beep is being drilled into my brain. The sound, coupled with the lights, causes the throbbing in my head to mount and I vomit. I try to aim for the drain hole but even that doesn't stop the putrid smell from filling the cell.

The light flickers off and I rest my head back against the wall, willing death to claim me.

My arms are stretched out above my head and my body swings from a chain attached to the ceiling. Pain lances through my spine as I'm struck with a multi-strand whip equipped with clawed tips. I bite my tongue and push my screams into the back of my throat that's still raw from the last beating.

A male wearing a black cloak that covers him from the top of his head down to his ankles walks over to a sterile medical table with all sorts of tools and gadgets laying out across it. He scans the tools and picks up a small syringe.

Eying the contents, he squeezes a small drop out and turns back to me. Only thin rectangular glasses separate his eyes from mine, but I see them all the same: small, beady grey eyes with white brows stare back at me from the thin cutout.

"This will sting," he says in an electronically altered voice before he stabs me with the clear liquid.

Lightning pain immediately flashes hot and sharp through my body. My veins bulge from my neck and arms as I fight to breathe through the convulsions. Foam fills my mouth and cascades down my chin as my body bucks and spasms involuntarily.

The male returns to the table, selects another tool, turns back to me and places stickers with wires attached to them along different parts of my chest.

"And this? This will really hurt," he says.

I can't hold back my screams any longer.

They never feed me meals at the same time. Water is dropped in occasionally but never soon enough. My lips are chapped, and my skin feels leathery.

This is the longest I've been in complete darkness, I think. It feels like the seconds stretch on into hours, but I can never be sure.

Time doesn't exist here.

I think of Eilidh and shake my head.

She doesn't belong in this place.

I push her from my mind and think of my Paps. I hope the bar is doing well. I hope he's been able to make ends meet with me being gone and unable to run the underground that oftentimes kept the doors open.

The drug peddling, the hired hit men, and the rampant gambling enthusiasts that helped line our pockets.

We built an empire.

I wonder what's become of it.

My mouth hurts from a metal claw clamp they used to rip out a tooth earlier. The blood has clotted and though the gum is swollen I can hardly feel it at the back of my mouth. My cheeks must have cracked and bled. I can feel the sting of my sweat in the wound.

The high-pitched beeping begins again from outside my cell, and I groan. Tucking my head between my knees and cradling my face and ears, I wait for the agonizing light show to pass.

"Get the fuck up 2459!" Ryker yells from the sidelines. The stump where his arm once was is bandaged and he walks with a limp. It pisses me off all the same.

He should be dead.

They kicked the shit out of me while I was strapped to a table today and threw me in this festering pit of feces and other dying animals. The rhino astral was a surprise. I wonder what he did to land himself in SolCon. Perhaps he attacked a guard like I did.

The thought makes me smile.

I wipe the blood coated spit from my dried and cracked lips, looking back at my opponent. The astral, who's at least three times the width of any male I've ever seen of solid muscle, rears back and charges me again, his shoulder slamming hard into my stomach, sending me flying back.

I may be no more than a broken male at the moment, but at least my chains are off.

I stand on wobbly feet, waiting for him to charge again.

He rears back, the same as the last four times and I ready myself for the hit. Just as he nears my stomach I kick back, flattening my body and sliding between his legs where I fist my hands together and punch hard, directly to his groin with all the strength I can muster.

He hollers and I stand, aiming my next hit for the base of his spine. My heel connects with the sensitive spot, and he cries out in pain, his face careening into the shit filled mud at our feet.

Before he can rise, I jump. Both of my feet land with all my weight on the back of his neck and a sickening crack rends the air.

A silent moment passes while blood trickles from the astrals nose.

"Get back in your fucking box, Breather." Ryker sounds disappointed as he chains my arms behind my back, one hand at a time.

I stare into the dead eyes of the rhino astral and wish it was me lying there instead.

The Warden came to visit me today. I thought I had already experienced the worst of it all.

I was wrong.

I've never known a hell like this.

21
RHIANNON

I'm angry for several reasons today. If I'm being perfectly honest, anger is the broad stroke over the myriad of other colorful emotions that I'd simply rather not pay attention to. Mostly because all of them hurt like hell.

Thankfully, Eilidh is silent for her own reasons this morning. I'm sure many of them mirror my own, but I'm choosing to lean heavily into my anger, because if I don't...

I'll collapse in on myself in despair after all that took place, and I just can't.

I fucking *can't* right now.

It has been an entire week. Seven days since Xanth had his cataclysmic episode and tore Ryker's arm off, which I have to say was poetic fucking justice because Ryker is the biggest sleazeball of this *entire* establishment.

Even more so than Xanth and that is saying something.

Seven days of having to talk Eilidh off a godsdamn ledge because she feels entirely responsible for Xanth's reckless, volatile behavior. Seven days of pent-up worry because each day he doesn't return causes another marble of hope to drop away from the small pile that I have been holding on to. That Xanth is actually okay in the hellacious depths of SolCon, and they haven't dragged him out in a body bag. Now I'm slowly beginning to feel the panic that Eilidh tries desperately to quell each morning and night. Seven days of realizing Eilidh and Xanth's contentious situation, with sexual tension that rivals a teenage dance party, is clearly more than it appears to be and I'm gearing up for *that* conversation.

Seven days since I've seen or talked to Kieran.

Not that I care.

It's completely fine, because we aren't compatible and Eilidh was *right*. I laugh to myself as I fold my laundry next to her and she peeks over at me as I burst into a random chuckle fit. Her eyes look like they did when she first arrived, and I don't like it. They're hollow. Everyone is worrying the hell out of me right now and *I don't like it*.

I feel Eilidh's familiar warm touch along the long cool steel wall of my mind and I exhale as I let her in.

...*What's so funny?*...

I scoff and say aloud, "Everything."

Her eyebrows bunch as she folds. I peek at her from the corner of my eye and decide to downshift my bitch-fit for her sake.

"You were right," I say plopping my freshly folded towels into a neat pile. "The irony is amusing."

She's looking at me with those eyes that now remind me of suns in winter: paler, cooler, and distant. "Do I need to guess the punchline or-?"

About Kieran. I shoot the thought off to her and it somehow glides through the white flame wall of her mind with ease.

...*You haven't heard from him?*...

"Nope," I say aloud pointedly, continuing to fold more towels.

The sound of the machines whirring fills the spaces between us as we continue to work, but I feel Eilidh's mind tumbling her thoughts in time with them.

...*I'm sorry, Rhi*...

"Don-" I start and hold my breath as I turn to face her because I'm trying to be mad. Angry. If I'm angry, I won't have time to feel the other things. The painful things.

...*Rhi it's okay*...

"It's not okay though." I whisper-shout back at her, trying my hardest to be mad, but the pressure behind my eyes is building, that familiar pin prick of despair begins creeping along my spine and threatens to show itself. In front of her. In front of everyone.

I squeeze my eyes shut and ball my fists.

Change. The topic. Rhiannon. I whisper to myself.

"I've been trying to connect to Xanth," I say to Eilidh, and she straightens.

"Y-you have?"

"I don't know if they have him collared or if they've drugged him or what, but I can't reach him."

Her brows knit together to form a small crease between her brows. "Is there anything else we can do?" she asks.

I think you will be able to reach him.

"What? Why me?"

I look at her and continue to parlay my thoughts into her skull. *Because I believe your connection is stronger.*

Eilidh's eyes grow wide, and she looks down at her hands.

...What makes you think that?...

I scoff again and prod her ribs, which are way too visible for my liking right now. She's starting to worry me as much as Xanth is at this point.

You may have to work harder to connect with him if they've got some kind of wards surrounding SolCon, but if you can get through to him-

...-I could communicate...

Exactly.

She looks back at me and asks, "How do I start?"

The corners of my mouth twitch up. "Start like you always do."

Close your eyes, I whisper into her mind, and she does, still cleverly folding the towels perfectly. *Find the connection thread you two share, follow it until-*

"Oh gods," Eilidh gasps aloud and her face crumples in agony, she doubles over while holding her head in her hands. "Oh gods!"

"Eilidh?" I ask as I follow her down to the floor.

She groans as she hits the floor and rolls into a fetal position, her body beginning to tremble.

"Eilidh, what's wrong? Are you okay?"

Do you see him?

...They're killing him Rhi! He's dying!...

"It hurts!" Eilidh screams and she arches her back at some invisible strike, her eyes wide and yet her awareness is wholly elsewhere. She chokes out a silent scream. "No! Stop!"

"Eilidh!" I yell at her.

Come back, Eili!

...I can't leave him Rhiannon! I can't leave him like this...

"Eilidh!" I scream again and Harvey peers over at us, finally having heard our shouts over the sound of the machines.

"What the fuck is her problem?" He gruffs as he touches his baton, ready to use it at the first sign of an altercation.

"For fucks sake, Harvey, get help!" I shriek, but instead of rushing to the door, or calling over the radio to dispatch a doctor, he straightens and points a weathered finger at me.

"Tell her to keep it down," he says as he adjusts his belt and walks back to the entrance.

"Ar-are you serious?! She needs a doctor!"

Eilidh continues to writhe and scream on the floor as more invisible lashes slap and seemingly tear at her flesh.

"When she's done you can take her back to her cell. We don't need to waste resources on her psychotic break," Harvey says finally.

Piece of shit.

"Rhiannon!" Eilidh screams, and I take her hand as other astrals begin to crowd around to see whatever the hells is happening.

"Everyone get back to work!" Harvey bellows from the entryway.

"Eili I'm here," I say, brushing the hair from her face as it clings to her sweaty forehead. Her breathing is ragged and pained.

"It hurts. It hurts so bad," she whimpers as tears run down her face.

...They're whipping him, the clawed ends are shredding his flesh. I can't leave him. I can't...

YOU MUST, EILIDH. Come back now.

I close my eyes and take hold of that golden thread that is between her and I and clasp it tight in my hands, yanking *hard*. Eilidh inhales sharply and sits straight up. Her face slack, slick with sweat and pale. She grabs my hand tight in her fingers as she turns to face me.

"They're killing him, Rhi." Her voice sounds distant. "H-how did you-,"

"It doesn't matter," I say and I help her stand up. I help her walk to the entrance where Harvey is still standing with a smug expression.

"All done with your little fit?" He says and Nina growls low in my chest, the sulfur creeps up my throat as my teeth sharpen.

"I'll just take her back to her cell," I say with a hiss and Harvey grins back.

"You do that, Breather."

I will enjoy peeling the skin from your bones, little man. Nina's deep rasping voice growls in my mind with a purr that I've missed as I walk with Eilidh's weight on my shoulder.

Harvey escorts us to our cell, unlocking the door for us to walk in.

"You have an hour, then you'll both return to work. Daily quota remains the same," Harvey says before he slams the door shut and I set Eilidh down on my bed. Her eyes are still wide as she reaches for something on her back.

"Rhi, I felt it like it was happening to me. Did they split my back too?" She asks as she unzips her jumpsuit pulling it down so I can see her back. Sure enough...

"Um," I say, swallowing as I run my fingers lightly over the raised marks and she recoils. "There are red welts, like someone hit you hard with something." But not a barbed whip like she was saying.

"What? I saw it though. I saw the whip and I felt it, I felt him!" Eilidh shrieks and a wild look steals her usually calm expression.

I put my hands on her arms and steady her. "I believe everything you told me. I'm just telling you what your back looks like," I say, smiling.

"Why are you smiling? This isn't funny!"

"You're right it isn't funny at all." I help her slide her jumpsuit back over her shoulders as she winces in pain.

"Then why are you laughing?" She asks and she looks like she's either going to hit me or cry, or maybe both.

"Because this is so fucked up, Eili," I say laughing a little louder now. "A-and you know what that stupid asshole would do if shit got bad?"

Her brows pinch and her eyes fill with more tears.

"He would fucking *laugh*. Xanth would laugh like the ridiculous asshole that he is!" Now I'm laughing hard. "That stupid son of a bitch would laugh!"

Eilidh's mouth ticks up as I continue to laugh and take deep, heaving breaths. It takes her a few minutes until finally she begins to smile and chuckles a bit with me as her own hysteria grows

"H-he would laugh so h-hard at the *worst* things a-and at the *worst* times!" I bellow as I guffaw into the quiet of the cell, now full with our laughter. I take Eilidh's hand and pull her up to stand and I do something I never thought I would ever do in my life.

I wrap my arms around her, and we laugh as we hold each other until the laughter turns into something else, and that broad stroke anger I tried to hide my pain behind is suddenly stripped away and all that is left is my pain.

I let myself feel it all against Eilidh's too frail shoulder.

I should feel ashamed and terrified of how this will be received.

But I'm not.

I just...let go.

The more I let myself feel the more I cry and the tighter she holds me.

I became a tidal wave of tears and anguish. For my friend that is being tortured and can do nothing about it, for the friend before me that experienced the same agony, and I was equally inept to help her, for my family that I miss desperately, and finally and most quietly, for a man I can never truly have.

Suddenly Eilidh is cupping my face, and her warm brow is pressed against mine.

"Look at me, Breather," she says sternly, "he...he's going to make it out. Do you hear me? He will be let out of there."

"But when?" I sniff, realizing my face has become a dumpster fire of tears and snot.

I don't care.

"I don't know, Rhi, but we're going to wait for him. As long as it takes. I'll reach him again. I can keep trying."

"No, I can't watch you go through that again," I hiccup and try to find those tendrils of shame and anger that I clung to earlier but nary a one can be found. So, I let the tears, snot, and hiccups continue.

Eilidh smiles softly as she looks at me, her eyes looking more like the suns that I'm used to seeing, bright and vivacious. "You're adorable when you cry."

"Oh gods, shut all the way up you asshole," I say as I sit back against the wall wishing Xanth was eavesdropping in the cell next to us. He'd have some snarky response that I would love to hear right now.

Eilidh laughs and sits next to me. "It's true! You know how some folks cry, and they just look ridiculous? You don't look ridiculous at all. Your nose scrunches and your eyes get all big and childlike. It's adorable." I roll my eyes, and she laughs but continues, "Does he really laugh during inappropriate situations like that?"

I chuckle as I wipe the snot and tears from my face. My sleeve is ruined. "Oh yeah. It is infuriating. I've been in here for five years with him and have never seen him shed a tear, and-" I hiccup again before I continue. "-I just know this would have been one of those times where he would just..." I gesture my hand and chuckle with a wet smile. "It felt like the only right thing to do for some reason."

Eilidh nods and tucks her knees close to her chest. "What do you usually do in moments like that?"

"Well, I usually don't laugh," I say, ironically laughing at the same time and she joins me. "I actually don't know. I've never really thought about it before," I finally answer.

"Me neither," Eilidh replies softly. "I don't laugh either. I just... deal."

"To be honest, I think it's a coping mechanism for him. When he's uncomfortable or sad, even when he's angry he laughs. It's kind of ridiculous."

Eilidh watches me as I talk, I feel those two golden orbs tracking my movement as I speak, staring ahead at our rusted metal bunk frame.

"I know he's made it really *really* fucking difficult, Eili, but I promise once he gets over being this prickly stubborn version of himself, Xanth is an amazing person."

Eilidh chews the inside of her cheek, then inhales. "I want to believe that. I really do, Rhi, but I have given him *several* second chances. I don't know how many more I can give."

"And he doesn't deserve any of those chances with how much of a jackass he's been." I nudge her with my shoulder. "He's going to be so pissed with how close we are once he's back."

I watch Eilidh's face fall, and she rests her head on her forearms.

She doesn't look up at me but wipes her eyes with her sleeve. "Xanth Vulcan is the most stubborn belligerent asshat I've ever met in my entire godsdamned life. He won't let torture in Solitary Confinement be how he exits this world. Not by a longshot."

And somehow, I know down to the very fabric of my bones and blood that that is the truth. Even if Eilidh is still learning about him, I think she knows it too.

We get through the rest of the day quietly. We finish our job and hit our quota with seconds to spare, eat dinner, go back to our cell and the buzzer sounds for lights out so we file into bed. The metal frame shifts and squeaks as she climbs on top.

I tuck my arm behind my head and close my eyes.

...*Rhiannon*... Kieran's voice whispers in my brain and my eyes pop open.

No.

But my brain isn't done yet. I feel his hands in my hair, his soft determined mouth, his leather and smoke scent pressing into my skin, the peppermint taste of his tongue that still tingles on mine, his large heavy cock that I could barely wrap my hands around as I stroked him to completion.

"Well then," Eilidh says from her bunk. I can hear the smirk in her voice.

Shit. I've been a gaping wound all day and haven't even thought to pull up the steel shields protecting my thoughts.

"I don't want to talk about it," I say and roll on my side.

She heaves a long and heavy sigh. ...*I'm here when you're ready, Rhi*...

Thanks. I volley back as I cover my head with my pillow. Finally allowing the steel armor around my mind to slide up before I fall asleep.

22
KIERAN

"Gods you look so good!" Rhetta sings as she claps her hands together and steps through the front door into my apartment.

"You look nice too," I reply truthfully. She really does look nice. Her hair is down in soft blond waves and pinned back at the front so I can see her face which is equally lovely. She wears muted toned makeup with coal-black liner, a sheer black dress with bright red pumps to match her red lips. She's a knock-out.

I shrug into my blazer and grab my apartment key card and wallet while she talks about our "agenda" for the evening.

"Warden Cain invited some of the Prism investors so that we can schmooze a bit. We're hoping to butter some of them up so they will invest in a flight pad. It would allow us to visit mainland Prism a little easier than that horrible boat ride."

The boat ride really was fucking terrible. My stomach lurches just thinking about it and I don't get motion sick. Ever.

"Yeah, that would be great," I add as I shut the door to my apartment feeling less and less social the farther away I get.

Rhetta weaves her fingers through mine and that feeling that I've been stuffing down all day rears up again.

Betrayal. Longing. Ache.

For her.

Rhiannon.

I clear my throat, and she looks up at me. "You okay?" She asks, and I smile tightly at her, unsure of how to answer.

It has been an unbelievable task trying to compartmentalize that day in the utility closet. Every time I think I've got one emotion handled, another one crops up somewhere else. It's like Rhiannon's a virus that won't leave my system. She's attached herself and invaded every part of me, moving her way through my body until I am nothing but a mess. I want to forget her. Because it would be easier, but the fucking wanting...it's too strong.

So, I'm putting all my eggs in the basket of Rhetta, praying to the gods that she will finally be the antiviral that leaches Rhiannon from my system.

To be the fucking distraction I need.

Rhetta looks great tonight, so I'm hopeful that things will go well.

"I was thinking we could start with the Altas United executive, Bernice Yim? She's the one that has all the cash and wants to expand her travel quotas. So, I was thinking-,"

Fuck she never shuts up.

"Rhetta," I say, turning her to face me. She's quiet as I look down at her.

Her eyes are soft and warm, like long auburn hair. Her red lips part gently as she smiles softly, and I wonder if Rhiannon would ever wear red lipstick. Gods, she would kill me with red lipstick on. I cup Rhetta's cheeks, and I lean in and gently press my mouth to hers.

Her lips are soft and yielding. She melts into me as soon as our lips touch and it's nice. She smells incredibly sweet. Like cotton candy and citrus which is also nice. A little cloying, but still nice.

She puts her hands over mine and parts her lips for me. Her tongue is tentative and gentle as it prods mine. She tastes like cinnamon and the spice is almost overwhelming, but again, it's...nice.

It isn't enough.

Keep trying, you idiot.

I pull her closer, her petite frame pressing against me and I feel her ample breasts on my chest. Her hands move to my waist, pulling me closer to her and I let her. Her tongue swipes against mine and I angle my head more, hoping to get past the assault of cinnamon. She sighs and the sound isn't right. It's too high pitched. Too dainty. She's too gentle and soft and...

Not her.

Fuck.

I pull away with my hands still on her face. Rhetta's eyes remain closed as I open mine to look at her.

Not her. Not her.

I tried. For nine days I stayed away. I occupied my time with exercise, death metal, work, and Rhetta. Pushing everything in front of those images and feelings so that I couldn't see it or feel it anymore. But that viral load…it's gotten out of control.

Rhetta finally opens her eyes and they're bright and inviting. But not enough.

"Rhetta I-"

Her brows pinch together as she looks at me. "What's wrong?" she whispers, her lipstick smudged outside of her lips.

"Kiss me," Rhiannon's voice wisps like a ribbon of velvet across my mind and the feeling is more electric than any of the kisses I could share with Rhetta.

"Rhetta I'm-I'm so sorry."

Her brows knit together more tightly, anger beginning to lace into her confusion. Her lips tighten as she steps back. "What do you mean, exactly?"

"I can't do this. I tried, I really did but I- I still am so messed up,"-

"What, over that inmate?"

Fuck.

"No," I say with finality. "Someone else."

"Who then?" She asks and her lips begin to quiver. "And if you're so hung up, what are you doing here, kissing me?"

"I don't know. I'm an idiot, Rhetta. I'm so sorry," I say squeezing the back of my neck as I try to take her hand, but she keeps her distance.

A tear streaks down her face, and I feel fucking terrible. I didn't want to hurt her like this. Fuck I'm such an asshole.

"Well then. I wish you all the best, Major Haley," she says formally as she straightens her dress and turns to walk down the hallway.

"Rhetta," I call after her, but she doesn't look back and it serves me right. I look down at my shoes and see my reflection on their shiny surface.

All dressed up and nowhere to go, you selfish prick.

I rub my face with my hands and then turn to walk back to my apartment.

...Kieran...

Nine days. It's only been nine days.

I can't fucking take it anymore.

I don't even bother changing into my guard uniform as I make my way back down to the blocks. Passing the guard station with mostly patrol bots and scabs so that our normal staff could attend Balor's party. I pass by some old guy named Dan or Don sitting at command on the Breather Block and he stands in salute. Ignoring him, I badge through the gates until I finally reach the inmate block and stop at her cell. She's lying on her side on the bottom bunk and her hair looks like a waterfall of rich autumn as it cascades over the side.

Rhiannon. My mind volleys out to her and even though, logically, I know she can mind-speak, it is still a thrill to watch her turn to me, the cerulean sky blue of her eyes practically glow in the low light of her bunk.

"Kier-I mean, Major Haley," she says as she sits up and walks to the door. I grip one of the bars of her cell, my hand barely fitting through the slots. All of the inmate cell doors were replaced after the inmate beside Rhiannon busted out and snapped Ryker's arm off like a twig. Now the bars sit so close together you can hardly pass a coin through sideways.

"Where's your cellmate?"

"In the rec-hall, I think," she says quietly. "Why?"

I press my badge to the reader at the door and the locks clack loudly as the door slowly swings open. She straightens and crosses her arms in front of her chest.

"Come with me," I say directly and she tucks her arms a little tighter across her chest.

"Why? Where are you taking me?"

I chew my bottom lip, and she watches the movement. "What did I say about you asking questions, Inmate?"

"No," she says squarely, her lip wobbling a bit as she takes a step back. "No games. You tell me, or I'm not coming."

"You don't get to make demands, 246-"

"Rhiannon," she interrupts and gods it's like the medicine I've been craving for the last several days. That fire, that tenacity, the defiant will that I'd like to bite into with my teeth.

I exhale slowly, trying to compose my raging heart.

"Rhiannon," I whisper softly and she loosens her arms, letting them drop to her side. She steps forward until she's right in my face and her vanilla and honey scent nearly knocks me on my ass. She scans me, starting at my shoes and working her way up to my hair before finally her eyes meet mine. They, too, nearly send me to my knees.

"I'll go anywhere you want, if you tell me where," she says quietly. The block is empty and it's only our soft voices that echo across the linoleum along with the occasional drops of water or skitters of rodents.

I smile deviously, running my tongue over my teeth and she tracks the movement. "I'm taking you to a movie."

She looks at me incredulously and quirks a brow. "A what?"

"You heard me. Now let's go," I say and stand aside so she can step out. I close the door behind her and lead her through the block to the elevators and up to the fourth-floor closed rec space where an old movie theater was previously used for inmates to enjoy replays of cinema classics. Balor closed it down shortly after becoming Warden and it never reopened as anything else.

It was an absolute mess when I stumbled upon it earlier. Almost like I knew even then that I would go to her tonight. There were no working cameras, and no one came by to check on the place while I fixed it up. Plus, I was able to get the projector to work and play at least one decent movie. Decent might be a bit of a stretch, but I got *a* movie to play.

I lead her into the dark open room, which is more of a meeting area than a traditional theater, with a white pull-down screen. Taking her to one of the two chairs in the center under the projector, she sits while I click on the projector, and it flickers to life. It's an old movie about a woman who falls in love with her dance instructor at some resort.

"I haven't seen this movie in years," Rhiannon gasps and tents her fingers over her nose as the opening credits begin.

"So, you like it?" I smile as I sit next to her.

"Fianna and I-," she stops mid-sentence and swallows hard, staring wide eyed at the screen.

"Fianna?" I ask softly and she looks back at me, her face riddled with surprise and shock.

"Yeah, um. My sister." Her fingers flex in her lap as she looks back at the screen and then back down into her hands.

I didn't realize she had a family. I mean, of course she had a family. I'd just never thought about her life outside of the prison, but now… now I'm wondering where her sister is, if she has any other siblings, if her parents are still alive…judging by her expression, however, this may not be the time to ask.

"You don't have to talk about her if you don't want to."

"I know," she says softly and her fingers relax in her lap along with her gaze. "I just didn't realize I wanted to tell you about her." She laughs quietly.

"You can tell me anything. I'll listen," I say. I yearn to reach out and take her hand. To touch her, feel her skin, her hair, her breath. She's my drug and my disease, the malignancy that threatens to take everything I am and raze it to nothing.

It scares me how much I want it.

Like walking into a burning building because you're enamored by the flame.

"Whatever I want, huh?" She rasps in that voice that has been haunting me since the moment I met her. Following me. Taunting me.

I look at her and she's staring at me, the glow of red now peeking behind the diameter of blue like the ocean caught fire and I welcome the burn.

My brows lift and I say with utmost certainty. "Anything."

"I think about you," she starts in a low voice. The movie continues in front of us, with the dialogue of the actors and music playing like static in the background, but her voice is all I hear right now. "It's a problem how often, really. I wake up thinking of you and then I think of you throughout the day, but at night," she hisses softly, "at night I think of you the most, do you know why?"

I didn't realize I had stopped breathing. I inhale a shaky breath and ask, "Why?"

"Because I can close my eyes and imagine it's you between my legs and not my fingers."

Oh, my fucking gods.

"At first, I imagine the way you kiss me, the way your hands feel on my body, how much I want them on my skin. Then, as I stroke myself harder, I imagine the way your tongue tastes and how nothing else has flavor anymore because all I want is your taste in my mouth."

My breathing is erratic and it's taking every ounce of control not to touch her, not to pin her to the floor, rip off her jumpsuit and fuck her hard into the filthy linoleum. My dick is straining in my pants, and I adjust myself. Her eyes flick down to my lap and then back to me, a kaleidoscope of molten crimson and blue. Two colors that don't belong but still exist like magic in her irises.

"I want to know what you feel like, Kieran Haley. It's all I've thought about since the moment I saw you. I want to know how it feels to be torn apart by your big hands and impaled by your even bigger cock."

The fortification cracks as my last bit of resilience dies spectacularly. I stand and pull her up with me, grabbing the front of her jumpsuit and ripping it down the center, sending the buttons flying and she gasps as I yank it down over her body.

Fuck. Fuck. Her bare breasts are perfect, her waist taut and her hips ample. Her skin glows in the light of the flickering projector, and I feel dizzy with how beautiful she is. Her scars extend down the planes of her body, marking her skin with memories of the life she's lived. She tentatively steps out of her clothes and is more careful with my shirt as she works each button loose. Her fingers tremble slightly as she finishes. She makes quick work of my belt and pants buttons, sliding her hands over my ass.

"Gods your ass, Kieran," she says, biting her lower lip. "Are you aware of how beautiful your ass is?"

"Not from you," I say huskily as I cup her face with my hands, swiping my thumb over her cheek bones. "My turn."

"Kiss me first," she whines and I do. I bite her lower lip and suck her into my mouth. She squeezes my ass as her tongue plunges into my mouth and that feeling of breathing fresh air...of taking a full breath for the first time comes rushing back. Only this time, I can touch her soft supple skin, feel it against mine as I shrug out of my shirt and pants.

"You've been haunting me, Rhiannon. I tried to stay away but you're...addictive. I can't stop wanting you, needing to touch you," I admit as I brush my fingers over her nipples, tracing her scars down her body, moving lower until I'm swiping into the wet folds of her sex.

Fuck, she's so wet, Godsdamnit.

"Say it...out loud," she whimpers as I find her clit. She threads her fingers into my hair and kisses me.

I pull away. "Are you this wet for me, Rhiannon?"

"Gods, yes. Only for you, Kieran."

I lift her and she wraps her legs around my waist as I lay her on the ground over my blazer.

"I wish I could hear what you're thinking." The words slip out before I can even consider it and her hooded eyes open to meet mine.

"I'm kinda glad you can't," she laughs.

"Oh? And why is that, Princess?" I say as I drag my teeth along her neck, and she stiffens a bit at the nickname but relaxes as I lave my tongue over her taut nipple.

"Because you'd never stop fisting yourself in the shower," she moans as I run my tongue down her ribcage.

"Who says I don't anyway?" I respond against the skin of her hip, peppering soft kisses above a star-shaped scar. She sighs and arches into me as I dip my mouth lower and finally run my tongue through the soaked petals of her core.

And I thought her mouth tasted good.

Fuck.

My eyes flick up and watch her as she bites her lip. I work her swollen bud, the pressure building in my hips as her eyes roll back and her hips rock into my face.

"Oh fuck, fuck," she groans through gritted teeth but it's not only her voice this time as her chest glows orange, and a purr erupts from her throat. "Make us come, Wild Man. I can smell you. *I* can smell *all* of you."

Her dragon.

Its voice is low and sensual, like a content rumbling hiss as it speaks through Rhiannon and their voices intertwine. She writhes as scales clack along her arms, but I don't hesitate even as her beast speaks to me. Instead of balking back in her dragon's magnificence, I place my hand on her lower abdomen holding her body in place as I close my mouth over her clit and suck. She screams as she arches her hips into me while her entire body contracts and her hands fist my hair painfully.

Then I hear her chanting my name, over and over, like a prayer spoken in the night and I think it may be the most beautiful sound I've ever heard. I crawl over her, and she peers up at me with sated summer sky eyes, that ring of red fire still blazes bright around the diameter.

"What's your dragon's name?" I ask, and the corners of her mouth tick up, revealing her beautiful teeth and making the scars on her face shine.

"Nina," she answers as she runs her thumb over my mouth, pulling my bottom lip down. "Why? Did she say something?"

"You didn't know?" I ask mildly bewildered.

"I was a little preoccupied," she laughs and I lift her leg to wrap around my waist. I laugh as I kiss her mouth, gliding my tongue along hers, relishing the taste of her.

I press my brief shielded cock against her throbbing wet core, and she moans into my mouth as she bites my lip.

"Kieran."

I meet her bright eyes as I inch off my boxer briefs and wipe her hair off her forehead.

"Rhiannon." I say back, placing a kiss gently on her lips as I line up to her entrance.

"Kieran, wait." I still my hips and my eyes flick back up to her.

"Is this not okay?" I pull away, feeling like I went too far. Stepped over a boundary I should have sensed, should have seen.

Gods, how could I have missed it?

"You didn't do anything wrong," she reassures me. "I just need you to know th-that..."

...I'm a virgin...

The words flick through my brain faintly, like a wisp of smoke before the lick of flame on tinder. But it's there.

And it is her.

Her voice. And then she says it aloud before I can dismiss it in my mind.

"I-I've never done this...before."

"Oh," I say and I sit up. "Oh Gods, Rhiannon."

Not like this. Not on the dirty ass floor of an old, retired rec-room of a prison.

"I don't think we have a lot of options Kieran. It's not like you can take me to a resort hotel and rail me there."

I sit up on my knees and ring my fingers through my hair. "It still isn't right, and I can...no I *will* do better than this dump," I say as I pull my briefs back up over my hips.

"Wait, no I still want to-"

"Not tonight, Rhiannon."

"You don't want me?"

I laugh. Hard. When I open my eyes, she looks a little hurt. I give her a bemused look and point down to my achingly hard dick still standing at attention in my briefs. "I guarantee you *that* is not the case."

You're all I want.

Fuck.

The thought just runs through my head before I can even shut it down. So, I try to make myself not sound so desperate as I help her up to her feet and help her dress. "When this finally happens, and it *will* happen, it'll be somewhere far nicer than this shithole."

"But I want to, right now with you," she says as she wraps her arms around my waist, her perfect little tits pressing against my lower ribs which doesn't help to quell my assuredly leaking dick in my pants.

"Not here. You deserve better than this for your first time, Princess."

"I don't like that nickname," she blurts out contrarily.

"Well, you know what that means."

"No."

"Yes."

"No, Kieran!" She says hitting my shoulder.

"You are henceforth-"

"Ugh, shut-up-"

"-and forevermore-"

"-stop you ass!"

"-known as Princess."

She buries her face in my chest and yells as I pat her head.

"There, there, my Princess," I say chuckling. "Let's get you back to your cell before your roommate catches wise."

We finish dressing and I escort her back to her cell just before rec-time is finished and the inmates are brought back. As soon as the door is closed, she reaches through the bars to grab my hand.

"You never told me what Nina said to you," she says as her thumb swipes over my wrist. I pick up her hand and kiss her palm, dragging my lower teeth along the mound of her thumb.

"Now...that is between Nina and me," I say in a low voice against her skin. My eyes flick up to her hooded fire and ice eyes. I wink at her and then turn around, walking back to exit the Breather Block, feeling her gaze follow me the entire way.

23
RHIANNON

When the buzzer sounds in the morning, I find myself less reluctant to crawl out of bed and start the day than I typically do. The lightness in my body feels surreal as I pull my blanket back to make my bed look a little less like a toddler slept in it last night. I walk over to the sink and brush my teeth when I feel the now too familiar prickle of Eilidh's thoughts swipe across the steel around my mind. I'm realizing I should just make her a side entrance or something.

…You feeling okay?…

I cup cold water in my hands and splash it over my face.

Fine. Why?

"Well," she says out loud as she finishes tucking in each corner of her blankets and fluffs her pillow until it looks immaculate. "Where do I start?" She says almost to herself. "First, and the most obvious, is that you're up before me. Second, is that." She points to my bed.

"What about it?" I ask, looking indifferent.

"You made it."

"Correction. I tidied it," I say as my eyes flit up to her bed that looks like it's staged for a magazine. "Comparatively speaking."

"It usually looks like a bomb went off in it."

"Well, I decided to do something different today."

She arches a brow at me. "What's gotten into you? Are you sick?" She reaches for my forehead and I bat her hand away.

"Quit fussing. I'm fine. Sue me for wanting to try and be a little tidier."

A single, perfectly sculpted brow arches. "Yeah, okay," she says skeptically as she bumps my hip away from the sink so she can brush her teeth.

"Five minutes until showers!" Nova yells into the block as Eilidh spits into the sink and then grabs my sleeve to wipe her mouth.

"Really?"

"My jumpsuit is one of the more black ones. I want to try and keep it looking decent."

Who are you trying to look nice for? I catapult the thought, and it's received as easily as it was sent. Maybe she already made a separate door for my thoughts. I need to catch up.

...Only you, Raisins...

"Raisins?" I laugh with my brows raised into my hairline. "Since when-"

"No idea, it just came out, but it kinda fits."

"Kinda doesn't."

"No shit," she chuckles as we lean against the wall waiting for the guards. Eilidh checks the hall for who's coming and stifles a laugh.

"What's so funny?" I ask.

...You'll see in three seconds...

Wait.

"Good morning, ladies." Kieran's deep voice is like a sensual slap in the face. My stomach drops directly to my ass while simultaneously doing somersaults.

...That's why...

I look up at Eilidh and the smirk on her face is so self-satisfied that I pinch the backside of her arm.

"Ow, bitch that hurt!" She says in false offense, rubbing her bruised skin.

You could have warned me!

...I DID!...

You could have done better.

"Where's the fun in that?" She says with a bob of her head as Kieran opens the cell door with his badge and Eilidh steps through first.

...Try not to swoon too hard, Raisins. You might fall over...

Okay seriously? Raisins? I try to say but she's already several steps ahead and then it's just me looking at Kieran and his bewitching teal eyes.

"You coming?" He asks and I straighten.

"Oh, she'll be coming alright..." Eilidh giggles and I swat at her.

"Yeah, sorry," I say with forced nonchalance as I walk out of the cell, and he shuts the door. "Not used to seeing you in the morning, Major Haley." I say walking a little more slowly than normal and he matches my stride as the rest of the inmates in our section of the block file into the showers along with Nova.

"Warden's orders," He says.

...He's been in a terrible mood, so he sent me here as punishment. Little does he know...

His thoughts slip through my steel barrier like it didn't exist and the revelation makes me swallow nervously. I nod to him in response, not really knowing how I could respond for the sake of appearances.

...Can I ask you something?...

I look up at him and he continues to communicate through the quiet solitude of his thoughts.

...How can I hear you?...

"You're human so you can't. It's impossible," I quickly say.

...But I can...

I stop walking. "Excuse me?"

...I heard you yesterday...

"You couldn't have," I repeat. "Humans can't mind-speak."

"Keep your voice down," He says louder and more direct. The show of power has a paradoxical effect on me however as I prod my cheek with my tongue as the corners of my mouth tick up. His brows pinch slightly as he follows the movement.

He crosses his arms making his tactical vest creak. "Does that-"

Gods, you have no idea.

He flashes a roguish smile as he says, "Noted."

"Inmate 2460, fall in line for showers, now!" Nova yells from the stalls and I begin to walk a little faster.

"Not with her though. She kinda scares me," I say and he chuckles as he matches my stride.

"Nova?"

"Have you ever seen her drink her coffee?"

"Yes."

"She doesn't even blow on it. She just drinks it. Boiling hot. Like a fucking sadist."

Kieran laughs out loud and the sound spreads like sparkling static across my skin making it constrict as shivers trill down my back. We walk into the shower stalls, and I turn to the benches where Nova is waiting.

"Let's go, Inmate. I don't got all day."

I salute Nova with two fingers and begin undressing, noticing that Kieran is standing at the shower stalls with his back turned.

I start removing my jumpsuit and taking the braid out of my hair while my mind wanders to what Kieran told me.

"...I heard you yesterday..."

I have no idea how it's possible. I've never heard of humans being able to mind-speak. I've heard of some claiming they did, but they ended up being snake-oil salesman charlatans, but Kieran didn't seem like the type to do that.

I place my dirty jumpsuit and underwear in the laundry bin and grab soap and a towel. Walking to my normal stall, I turn on the faucet and let the cold water splash over me.

I close my eyes and let my mind shift from shield…to blade.

It's quiet as I listen through the strange static of mental frequency. Not quite like the snaps and crackles of a radio, but like gentle static or rainfall…it's constant, smooth, relaxing even. I tune into Kieran's specific channel, and it doesn't take long. I feel it before I can hear it. It's warm and low, like thunder during a summer storm, it makes my hair stand up as I tune into him and as I peer into his mind, there's a very clear and distinct wall of ice.

Is that a shield?

I place my hand on the surface of the ice surrounding his mind and there's an ominous crack right beneath where my hand is placed. It continues to fracture under my palm until there's an obvious fissure and I can see through to the other side. It's dark though. I squint as I look harder until an enormous glowing yellow eye pops up and I jump while I fall back.

What the hell?

…Rhiannon?… His voice is all around me, swirling over my skin like warm mist.

Kieran?

…How are you here?…

How are you doing this?

…You need to leave. It isn't safe for you here…

Why?

But before I can ask further, a sickening pull from my belly button yanks me from his subconscious and I'm back in the shower stall, washing my hair and I double over, swallowing back my bile.

The pieces begin sliding together, connecting slowly as I notice him leaning on the stall entrance/exit door watching me. There are a few other astrals showering or drying off as I straighten back up and finish my shower.

How long have you been able to hear me?

He's quiet for a moment but then the soft velvet of his deep voice licks over my skin. *…Not until recently…*

How?

…I'm not sure…

The ice wall though. How did he have a shield like that? How did he know?

…My best friend was a dragon in the war. He was a blade. He showed me how to shield to keep other dragons out…

Where is he now?

There's another pointed pause before he says directly *…Dead…*

Gods.

It still didn't explain how he could hear me, though. A thread of suspicion winds its way up my neck.

"Time's up inmates, let's go!" Nova shouts.

I towel off and grab my new clothing pile, dress and file out for work duty. Kieran is somewhere in the back of the line with the other inmates as I walk with Eilidh.

Eilidh watches me as we make our way to the greenhouses.

"You okay?" She asks quietly.

"No talking!" Nova yells from the front of the line. Eilidh exhales, exasperated.

I'm okay. But I'm not sure if that's true and even though we haven't been keeping much from each other, I'm not sure if I'm ready to tell her about this just yet.

Not yet.

Eilidh and I walk back from the rec hall and I'm sore as hell. She decided I needed to start incorporating more weightlifting and high intensity interval training to my "exercise regimen." As if I had one of those. So, I feel like I'm walking on noodles for legs after doing about a thousand squat jumps and deadlifts, that was only after the eighteen-hour run on the synthetic track.

I'm clearly over-exaggerating, but it sure as hell felt like that with how my body feels right now. I have no idea how her tiny body can do all of that. She was practically running circles around me.

Jo opens the door to our cell, and we file in. She shuts the door after us and five minutes later, there's the high-pitched whine of feedback over the intercom. Everyone on the block groans. I cover my ears and grit my teeth as the sound suddenly shuts off and the sound of the Warden's deep voice thunders over the speakers.

"Inmates of cell block three," He booms. "This is yar Warden."

My blood freezes as Eilidh and I turn to peer through the bars of our cell down at the Warden and a petite female astral that looks young but with astrals, looks can be deceiving. She could be twenty-two or two-hundred and two and you'd never know the difference. She has long curly black hair and tanned skin with sleek almond shaped brown eyes. She's on her knees with one of her hands strapped to a large wooden block. Nova, Jo, Bruce, Harvey, Ryker, and Gunnar are all standing guard watching the block as the Warden addresses the inmates. Kieran stands behind the Warden with the same stoney expression he wore the last time there was a spectacle like this. My eyes stay on Kieran as the Warden continues.

"It seems my last message went unheard," he begins, "which is a shame for poor 'ol...oh was' ya name again love?"

The astral female begins to say something.

"Speak up, poppet. No one can hear ya!"

"Sabeer," She says, but the Warden interrupts her.

"No one can hear ya girl. SPEAK UP!"

"SABEER!" She wails, tears streaming down her face.

...Don't watch... Kieran's voice echoes through my head but before I can heed his warning and close my eyes the Warden swings a large mallet down, hard on Sabeer's hand. The grotesque sound of crunching bone and squelching flesh makes my stomach turn as Sabeer screams in pain, the sound ricocheting off the walls. The Warden isn't done, he pounds the mallet into her hand two, three, four more times, demolishing the delicate bones and ligaments of Sabeer's hand into a mound of blood and flesh. Eilidh rests her head on the bars and reaches out to put her hand on my shoulder.

Her mind is quiet for once. I can't blame her.

Kieran.

I reach out to him, watching his granite expression remain on the back of the Warden's head as he hardly moves a single muscle. The only movement I catch from him are his sharp tracking eyes, which for the briefest moment, flick up to me.

My heart stops for a split second.

...I hate him... He says in a low, growling whisper. *...I hate this place...*

I blink as I hear his voice ripple through my brain in real time.

...You don't belong here, none of you do. This place is fucking sick...

Tears begin to stream down my cheeks, and I bat them away as Sabeer continues to wail in agony on the wooden block.

Did she try to escape?

...She said 'no' to him. So, he's making a spectacle of her 'disrespect.'...

The Warden pulls out his cell phone and sends off a text.

"Anything else ya'd like to say, love? Or what was it…?" He puts his ear down to her as she sobs, and she veers away from his proximity. "What was that then?"

Sabeer stays quiet as he waits for her to respond.

"That's a good girl. Ya see, this is a lesson for all of ya that think it's alright to speak up. This is NOT a FUCKING DEMOCRACY." His carefully slicked back mohawk falls forward in disarray. "Ya do not HAVE RIGHTS HERE. Ya'r peasants, and I am yar KING. Yar GOD and ya will all do as I say when I say it, or ya will end up like this Mute trash."

While the Warden speaks, a man in a long white lab coat walks up behind Sabeer. Harvey and Ryker unlock her from the block and drag her off after the man. Every astral watches in deafening silence as they disappear down the long hallway.

"Who are they?" Eilidh whispers beside me, her eyes stuck on the place that Sabeer was dragged off.

"I don't know. They started showing up not long ago."

"Where are they taking her?"

"I don't know." I inhale a shuddering breath. "But when an astral leaves with them, they don't come back."

She turns to look at me, brows pulled tight and eyes flaring gold. "What do you mean?"

"I mean we never see them again after they're taken."

"So, they're being killed?" She guesses and I shrug.

"I mean, it stands to reason that they are, but no one knows for sure. I've tried asking the guards, but they don't know anything either. Not that they would tell me anything anyway."

I watch as the guards disperse and the Warden picks up a call on his cell phone, gesturing for Kieran to follow. His eyes flick up to me.

…Stay safe. Stay vigilant, Princess. By any means necessary…

He follows the Warden, and I lose sight of him.

A firm hand squeezes my shoulder, and I turn to Eilidh.

"I'm getting us out of this place, Rhi."

I chew my bottom lip as Kieran's words bounce around my brain.

"…By any means necessary…"

"By any means necessary," I whisper and look up to her bright sunshine eyes.

"Yeah," she says simply and smiles tentatively at me as she squeezes my shoulder again.

It's hard to fall asleep that night. I keep hearing Sabeer's cries and the sickening crunch of her hand under the mallet. I try not to toss and turn so I don't wake up Eilidh. So, I do the one thing I probably shouldn't do, because it's likely dangerous for both of us.

I can't help wanting to play Icarus and let the rays of the sun lick my heels.

I take a deep breath and close my eyes, and I whisper his name in the confines of my mind.

Kieran.

I honestly didn't expect to hear anything back. Maybe due to proximity. Maybe because I'm still in relative disbelief that he is a human and can mind-speak. But I jump as his deep sultry voice vibrates across my mind like a clap of thunder, shuttering all my cells into attention.

…Are you alright?…

I sigh. *Are you?*

…Not really…

I wish you were here.

He's quiet for a minute before he answers back.

…I wish I could hold you…

My chest aches as I bite my lower lip.

Kieran?

…Yeah?…

What's your favorite color?

He's quiet and then I hear his soft laughter reverberate through our mental connection and it's like the firelight in winter, warm, comforting, and bright. Hopeful.

…Um, black…

Is that even considered a color?

…I don't really care, I like it. What's yours?…
Red.
…I could have guessed that…
Why do you say that?
…Because Nina is red…
How do you know that?
…Your eyes…
They're blue.
…Not when Nina is there…

My chest begins to ache as Nina purrs softly in my chest. The fact that he acknowledges her by name and that she speaks to him…that they have a relationship it seems, fills me with emotions too fragile to touch. The ache is a Kieran sized hole, and it grows every day to fit him inside and I'm so…so fucking scared.

…Favorite food?…

His thought is a welcomed interruption, and I exhale as I answer. *I have a lot of favorites.*

…Okay, today's favorite then?… He says and even over the mental connection it sounds as if he's smiling.

Cheeseburgers. Today I would do anything for a decent cheeseburger.

…Yeah, I think I'm right there with you…

Favorite holiday?

…Summer solstice…

I'm a Samhain girl.

…You like to dress up?…

Every year. Fianna and I would play tricks on the townsfolk, play games and eat way too many sweets.

…My baby brother, Cillian and I had a swimming hole that we would go to every summer and on the solstice, there would be a big picnic by the lake, and it was like the day would last forever. We swam, ate, chased girls…

I didn't realize I was smiling until my cheeks start hurting. I chuckle softly and then cover my mouth as the bed shifts above me.

…You told me about Fianna, so I figure I could tell you about Cillian…

What's he like?

His warm laugh echoes through the connection and it's like an embrace that I never want to end.

...*He's mischievous, strong willed, clever, stubborn, and full of life. Girls love him...*

He sounds a lot like Fianna.

...*I think you two would get along well...*

If I wasn't trapped in prison, maybe I would have the opportunity. Right now, I absolutely hate that all those opportunities will never be afforded to me.

...*Rhiannon?...*

It takes me a second before I say, *I'm here.*

...*I'm gonna get you out of here...*

That takes me back on my heels a bit. *You are?*

...*Yes...*

How?

...*I have an idea, I just need you to be patient...*

Kieran...I-I'm kind of a package deal at this point.

...*What do you mean?...*

I'm not leaving without Eilidh and Xanth.

He's quiet for several seconds that stretch into minutes. I almost think he's gone but then he says, ...*All of you then. I'll get all of you out...*

You will?

...*Give me some time. But yes, I'll get you all out...*

Suddenly, the ache in my chest explodes into a kaleidoscope of emotions and I don't know which to process first. My chin quivers and my breath shudders before the tears begin to stream down my cheeks. I cover my face with my hands as the tears fall in earnest.

Kieran?

...*I'm going to wear a costume with you on Samhain. I'm going to bob for apples with Fianna, and you're going to race Cillian to the swimming hole and make all the girls in my town jealous. Then every night before we fall asleep, I'm going to kiss you and tell you that it's real. That this is real. By any means necessary, Princess...*

By any means necessary.

Then Eilidh's head pops over the ledge of the top bunk

"What in the hells is going on down there?"

I look at her with my undoubtedly swollen red eyes and then she hops down to sit on the edge of the bed beside me. "Are you okay?"

…Tell Eilidh I say hello… Kieran says. and I blink up at her as she pushes the hair away from my face.

Good night, Major Hot Stuff. I send the thought off as I push up to sit.

I hear him groan over the connection before he's quiet.

I look up at Eilidh and take a deep breath and start from the beginning, "Well, Kieran says hello."

24
EILIDH

"So, what is it you're going back to?"

It's late night, the buzzer went off hours ago and the lights are dimmed but Rhi and I both are having trouble sleeping. It's been weeks since Xanth was taken, and I think both of us are spiraling. Our conversation has kept us from thinking too much about the empty cell next door.

Tonight, we've touched on her and my favorite colors, red and gold respectively, our favorite foods, hers tends to change with her mood, but today we agree that we both love noodles with meat sauce. And bread.

Literally any and all bread.

We're running low on topics to discuss so I shouldn't be too surprised by her question, but it stumps me all the same.

...What are you going back to?...

What am I going back to? I think to myself.

My mother has likely already started recruiting her successor, should she be killed. I've got no lover and I've done everything in my power to avoid making friends. Nowhere truly feels like home.

I suppose Pyrrh is home, my people are home, but in the quiet hours of the night when there are no missions and no advisor meetings… I have nothing.

No one.

"Pyrrh and my people, I suppose," I reply, but a gaping hole sits in my chest where love and family should reside.

Rhi side-eyes me. She's gotten pretty good at reading between the lines of my short answers and I'm not sure what to think of it.

"Right. Your people." She pauses a moment, the hum of the quiet corridor fills the space between us. I feel a gentle prodding in my mind, and I open to her.

...You have more desire to escape than just some average astral with nothing waiting for them. So, stop shoveling me more of that watered down bullshit and tell me the real reason you need out of here...

I don't answer immediately. I could tell her the truth. I wasn't told much about this mission beyond needing to relay the layout of this place to my mother. I have no idea what she plans to do with that information.

Also, Rhi is a dragon. My mother would be *furious* if I knowingly gave information to the dragons. Who knows if this is the leg up the phoenixes need in order to reclaim our half of Elysia.

All of these reasons coalesce in my mind, but I don't want to lie to Rhiannon. In the last few weeks, I've relied on her, found solace in our conversations and she helped pull me from being stuck in Xanth's mind. That didn't benefit her at all, she simply cared enough to help me.

I settle for the honesty that I *can* share instead.

I start with Amell.

Three and a half years ago, I lost someone very dear to me. One of the only people I've ever truly considered a friend. He died right in front of me and there was nothing I could do to save him. I pause, catching my breath and I will myself to keep talking. *After that, I lost myself. I drank until the sun came up, slept, and then drank some more. I spent too many nights in beds I'll never remember and tried all I could to forget the look on his face before he died.* A tear drips down from the corner of my eye as I continue, staring off into nothing as I open my dark past to someone for the first time since Amell died. *Needless to say, my... job didn't like that I was gone for so many days. Also, I publicly lost control of my life. I was... demoted. Escaping here is supposed to help me get my job back.*

Rhi is quiet for a long moment. Likely mulling over all I've just told her.

I start to think she's fallen asleep when her voice carries through my mind again.

...Thank you for sharing that with me. Talking about what makes us feel vulnerable is really fucking hard. More ways that prove how brave you are...

We sit together in the darkness, nothing but the soft snores of other inmates can be heard in the dim.

My eyelids are getting heavier, and my body begins to relax into my thin mattress, exhaustion finally taking hold, when I hear the cell block entrance gate click and whine open.

I bolt upright, every hair on my body standing on end and I hear Rhiannon shift beneath me.

"It's him. I can feel him," I whisper.

Neither of us move as we listen to the three sets of footsteps walking down the corridor. Two are sure and steady, the other sounds as if they're being half dragged across the linoleum floor.

My heart clenches when the scent of him reaches me. His spiced whiskey and fresh oak now mixed with putrid shit, sweat, bile, blood and piss. I want to scream, but I can *feel* his steady heartbeat and it relieves something deep within me. My beast lets out a series of sorrowful trills, as though she's trying to connect with his and finds a similarly beaten creature within.

My relief mixes with heartache, and I know Rhiannon is feeling something similar when I hear her sniffle quietly beneath me as she sighs and exclaims,

"Thank fuck, *finally.*"

We wait in our beds with bated breath as they near the end of the hall where Xanth's cell sits empty.

Nothing could have prepared me for what I see as he is dragged past our cell.

Two hulking guards that I've never seen before stand on either side of him, similar to the way they pulled him away from me after maiming Ryker, only now his eyes are swollen, and his head isn't hung forward in a dead slump.

The raven-colored hair that hangs long at the top of his head is matted and caked with mud and debris. His beautiful midnight ocean eyes are bloodshot, and deeply etched circles hang beneath them. His lips are chapped and cracking and there are unhealed bruises and abrasions marring his face as though he had been hit repeatedly.

The jumpsuit he's wearing must be the same one he left in. Holes and ripped fabric hang off his powerful body that's been sliced and mangled. In the torn open pieces of fabric, large, awful purple and blue bruising peek through along his ribs. There are cuts and tears in his back that have shredded the art that decorates his skin, and I cover my mouth with my hand on a gasp.

He's clearly starving. I can see it as well as feel it. They haven't been feeding him. His once controlled movements are sluggish, his body trembles all over and if the two guards didn't have hold of him, I'm not sure he'd be able to move at all. He's sliding his feet across the ground as if each step is harder than the last.

I can hardly breathe. I wait for them to open his newly replaced cell door, key in a code that likely alarms his lock. I can only imagine his cell door is now reinforced after the stunt he pulled. We all received new doors but his looks more ominous.

My ears pick up the sounds of them removing his restraints and clamping something else heavy and metal down on the ground. They don't help him to his bed. They don't ensure he can even stand before they slam the renovated cell door shut and walk down the corridor to exit.

The seconds tick by.

Then a minute.

And another.

Suddenly, I'm standing, hurling myself towards my cell door and frantically calling to Xanth.

"Are you ok?"

No response.

"You've been gone for weeks."

Fourteen days, three hours and twenty-seven minutes to be exact.

Rhiannon sidles up beside me and puts a hand on my shoulder. Nudging me to continue with a grim look on her face.

"Xanth?" I try again.

Nothing.

I lean my back against the corner of the wall and cell door, as close to him as I can manage and squeeze my fingers out of the bars and towards his cell, trying to reach him.

After several long moments, Rhiannon retreats to her bed.

…Give him time. He'll come around…

I don't respond and wait until she's snoring before I try to reach him with my mind.

Thank you. For coming for me that day. I say, biting back a sob.

At first, I don't think he will respond but his breathing hasn't deepened with sleep yet, so I know he's still awake. He shifts in his bed and then finally, *finally*, he speaks directly to my mind.

...I'll always come fer ye...

I cry myself to sleep.

When the morning buzzer rings, my body is sore, and my neck is stiff.

Turns out sleeping on the floor isn't great for your body.

We brush quickly and fix our beds. Well, I fix my bed. Rhiannon leaves hers in disarray as usual. The guards come to take us to the showers, and I look over my shoulder to catch a glimpse of Xanth but Bruce, the guard who collected us this morning, shouts, "Eyes forward, Breather whore!"

The guards have been far more liberal with their use of the term *whore* for me ever since the night with Ryker. I suppose, in a way, I deserve it.

We make it to the showers, but I hesitate by the door. Taking my time as I wait for Xanth to join us. I encourage Rhiannon to shower without me and move at an obnoxiously slow pace while undressing so that I can give him a moment longer to get here.

He finally walks through the tiled door divider and his eyes meet mine.

He already looks slightly better. The dark circles under his eyes have receded a bit with the sleep he must have gotten last night. Some of the stark red veins in his eyes have disappeared as well but something hollow now resides in his gaze.

What has me moving towards him more quickly is the iron mask clamped firmly over his perfect mouth and cutting into the sides of his chiseled face.

He allows me to approach, but I see his body tense as I get closer. I cautiously reach out for his hand, and he lets me take hold and pull him towards the benches to undress.

I slowly unclasp the top few buttons on his jumpsuit, keeping my eyes trained on his for any sign of him wanting me to stop. He doesn't move; his eyes never stray from mine.

I pause when I get to the buttons along his hips. If I continue, he'll be bared to me. I won't dare make him feel like I'm using his fragile state of his to take anything from him that he wouldn't freely give.

I audibly gulp and he watches my throat. Once his eyes move back up to mine, he nods in silent consent.

The next button pops open, and his jumpsuit begins to slide down. I work two more and before I can get to another his clothes drop from his body entirely.

My eyes never move from his face. He is a sight to behold, but I want him to see me. To know I am here and not with any intention other than to help him.

I'm not sure that any female has ever given him this: something without expecting anything in return.

My hands move to the top of his briefs, and I tug them down his muscular thighs. It truly is an extreme effort not to allow the feel of him to cloud my mind, but I manage.

Guiding him by the hand, I lead him to a shower head tucked in a corner, shielding him from the other inmates. I grab the bar soap and begin to lather it over his chest. My eyes finally lower from his and my heartbeat stutters as I take in each of his cuts and bruises up close. They are way worse than I thought. I glance over the gashes, tears, contusions, welts and lesions.

This is severe physical trauma.

They tortured him.

He watches me wash him. Every stroke and slide of my hands makes him twitch and grunt in pain. I work as gently as I can, but his wounds are too extensive to avoid.

I finish with his chest, and I use my hands to spin him so that I can clean his back. I lather the soap again and rinse all the grime from his olive skin. I carefully wash and scrub his back, rear and legs until the water runs clear.

When I reach for his head to wash his hair, he drops to his knees for me. Something unreadable, something I'm too afraid to name, resides in his eyes as he looks at me. Like this, we're nearly eye level but he stares at me as though I hung the stars, and I can't control my racing heart. He leans into my palm, and I stroke the side of his face with trembling hands.

Moving up to his hair, I relish in the feel of my fingers stroking through his onyx strands. I work out each of the knots and mats, some taking longer than others.

I step closer to rinse out the soap. His eyes linger on my breasts, and his breathing deepens but he makes no move to touch me.

I can feel the slick between my thighs, but I continue my ministrations, ignoring the desire coursing through me under his heated stare. I scrub at his scalp, making sure to scrub along the shorn parts of his head on the back and sides. Once I'm confident all the soap is out, I ring his hair and help him stand.

He continues looking down at me as I take the soap and use it to clean my own body now. My shoulders, my breasts, down the plains of my stomach and between my thighs to my aching core. His eyes never leave me.

The guards holler the last call for breakfast, so I quickly wash and rinse my hair. Wrapping a towel around Xanth and then myself, we both slip on our clean jumpsuits, brush our hair and make our way to the chow hall.

The crowd has mostly died down, but I still choose a seat beside him.

Our breakfast is solemn and quiet, but I relish it all the same.

The day continues with work for me in the laundry room again and Xanth is off to his job duty for the day. It's around midday when I finally see him again.

He's standing near the weights, working to lift them up off the ground and his arms strain in a way they haven't before.

Without prompting, I move behind his head to spot him as he lifts another, his arms shaking with the effort.

His eyes open and that hollowness is still there, but so is something I didn't expect to see. Anger.

"Back the fuck off, Twitcher whore." He doesn't raise his voice, there's no threat or venom as he says the words, but they sting all the same.

"W-what?" My brow pinches and my brain struggles to catch up with this shift in demeanor. This morning, he allowed me near him. To touch and wash him and there was no sign of this hatred, yet here he is again, pushing me away.

"I said, back off." He racks the barbell and stands, wiping the sweat from his forehead with a towel and moving away from me.

"Wait, stop." My voice is firm, but a slight shake is there that I wish wasn't.

He turns back to me, his eyes a touch softer but it's only a moment before they're back to the hardened disgust I'm used to.

"Let me make this crystal fucking clear, Twitch." He moves a step closer but no further and my disbelief deepens. "I want nothing te do with ye. I have and always will hate ye. Yer fuckin kin took the only female I'll ever love, and I will *never* forgive ye fer that. Yer vile. And if that doesn't convince ye te stay away from me, maybe this will." He steps forward once more and lowers his head. "I wouldn't fuck ye if ye were the last female on this godsforsaken planet. I'd rather *die* than fuck the likes of ye." He straightens and takes a step back and my stomach drops. "I should have let that poor fuck have his way with ye. Maybe he'd have killed ye. Then I wouldn't have te dirty mah own hands with it."

With that, he turns on his heel and leaves.

I don't know why I thought things had changed. It was silly of me to assume that because he had broken out of his cell that it was some sort of breakthrough, but his hatred of my kind runs too deep.

"Yer kin took the only female I'll ever love."

A phantom pain lances through my chest and I look around to see a few astrals who had stopped to watch, most likely hoping for a real fight.

Too bad for them, I have no fight left for Xanth. It's time for me to face the truth.

He will always hate me.

"I can't believe that asshole!" Rhiannon throws her hands in the air and glares at the wall between us and Xanth. I know she said that aloud simply because she wanted him to hear, and I adore her all the more for it.

After dinner, I came back to the cell and Rhi followed. I think she could tell that something was off. Unfortunately, Xanth was already in his cell brooding when we got there.

I appreciate the enthusiasm. I say back to her, steering her back to our silent conversation.

...If he wasn't already a mess, I'd kick his worthless ass...

I think I'd rather just pretend he doesn't exist at all. It's an impossible task. I can feel him the moment he walks into a room and the smell of him calls to something ancient buried deep within me, but I can try.

...No, fuck that! He's being a dick!...

Trust me, I agree with you, but there isn't anything I can do about it. I've tried to befriend him. He wants nothing to do with me. He told me as much with even more colorful language.

...Friends? No, friendship isn't what he really wants from you and he's being a real fuckwit about it...

I don't like her tone, or what she's insinuating.

Absolutely not. If he can't even stand the sight of me, what in the hells makes you think he wants more than friendship? He told me he'd rather die than fuck me, Rhi. It seems pretty clear to me that I'm not on his 'to-do' list.

Not that I want to be.

...Yeah, about that... Rhiannon hesitates, and I take a deep breath in preparation for whatever it is she's about to say. *...He may not have much of a choice in* not *wanting more from you...*

The confusion must be clear on my face because she continues.

...You both are clearly exhibiting signs of the mating bond...

I damn near fall off the bed.

What in the hells are you talking about? Xanth is not *my mate!*

…Eili, think about it… Every time she uses that nickname, I have to breathe through the thought of Amell's voice saying it.

Consider it thought about. Now, consider it a non-issue. He and I are not mates, besides, even if we were, which we are not, *there is still the option of ignoring the bond or even breaking it altogether.*

I know this because my mother always talked about breaking her bond. She told me it was the smartest decision she'd ever made and that only the strongest of leaders would choose their kingdom over love.

Ironically, she lost both.

Now all she can do is stand in what once was her throne room and dole out orders for missions to those who remained in Pyrrh with her. Without her heart, love or compassion. Breaking her bond left her hollow and heartless.

Rhiannon is quiet for a while, and I begin to think she's dropped the subject when she finally speaks again.

…He's an absolute shitcan, but Xanth isn't a bad guy…

I have no doubt that he is loyal to those who he considers worthy of his loyalty. I respond blandly.

…Breaking the bond is extreme, not to mention painful. *He doesn't deserve it. He may just need a little more time to come around. It's hard letting go of something you've held on to since childhood. He has his own demons to fight. Please, don't shut him out just yet…*

I sigh. *I appreciate the advice, however, he asked me to stay away and that's what I plan to do. Bond or no bond.*

I refuse to believe the Gods would be so cruel as to pair me with someone who loathes me so completely that they would rather die than be with me. Not after a love as sweet as Amell's had been ripped from me so soon.

They wouldn't purposely cause me more heartache and grief.

Would they?

25
XANTH

I keep waiting for the buzzing outside the metal box to start.

The first night back, I fell asleep quickly, my body and mind too exhausted to do anything else. Last night, however, my mind kept playing tricks on me. I'd close my eyes and still smell the dank cage they put me in. I'd roll over and the rattle of the bed posts sounded too much like the rattle of the chains that held my arms up for hours.

Or maybe it was an entire day. Who the fuck knows.

Despite my lack of sleep, I'm jittery and restless. My body is sore and aching, but I plan to push it tonight at the gym. Hopefully that'll help me sleep.

Today's job is in the parts factory. It's not my favorite place to spend the day but I get to lift heavy things into the furnace, and the fire always feels good against my skin, so I can't complain. I'm also able to stick to the back and the guards don't bother me for the most part which only makes me enjoy the job more.

After breakfast, we file into the massive room that's more warehouse than standard room. Large metal pipes line the ceiling, moving belts and tall metallic machines are scattered throughout and a maze of stations that fill the cold space.

We're broken up into groups; a rabbit astral, three dragons and a ferret astral are on parts and pieces. Rhiannon, the twins and one of the deer astrals I fucked –I think her name is Dawn?– are sent to assembly. Lastly, I'm paired off with Cadmyr, Lumara and none other than the fucking phoenix are put on the furnaces.

Fuck.

I've been doing everything I can to avoid her. Something about the way she looks at me, like she's staring straight through to my soul instead of the carefully curated image I've perfected over hundreds of years, burns through my reservations of her kind.

I lose myself in her.

Far too easily, she's able to shake my foundation and it's only with immense effort that I'm able to pull away from her before I do something I can never come back from.

Like trying to kill a guard for touching her.

Gods, the way she sat with her arm outstretched the night I returned. The smell of her, like the mountains after the first rainfall of spring.

She's *intoxicating*.

The next day she washed me, and I don't know what came over me. Her touch felt like a balm against the wounds that the guards, scabs, beady eyed man and the Warden inflicted. She didn't miss a single injury, and I could feel them stitching back together beneath her touch. I leaned into her palms while I sat on my knees before her and even Azure calmed. Her skin glistened with droplets of water that cascaded down her beautifully supple skin and I felt safe.

I felt safe with my enemy.

Once I came to my senses later that day, I was able to push her away again. Back behind the bars of my hatred and thoughts of my mother resurfaced, strengthening my resolve.

She is the enemy.

We make our way towards the back of the large room and start flicking on the massive furnaces. I begin to stoke a fire to life beneath one of them and the others move to do the same. Lumara struggles getting hers to light, the flame not catching and her frustration mounting, so I help her. Without all of us working on melting this material, it'll take all day to get through the mountain of scrap metal sitting off to the side of our workstation.

I bend and reach for the hatch where the fire burns and I feel Lumara move closer. Looking up at her from my crouch, I notice her eyes moving from my shoulders to my chest and thighs, down my legs and back up again.

One of her brows quirks in invitation, her eyelids hooded as she whispers in a sultry hiss "You've been missed, Blue."

From the corner of my eye, I see Eilidh stiffen, but she shakes it off quickly and moves to grab her first scrap, her fire burning brightly within the combustion chamber of her furnace.

A small, ridiculous part of me puffs up with pride at her ability to handle the fire and heavy machinery with such finesse.

I stomp that part of me down and toe it into the dirt of my subconscious.

I eye Lumara, who's unbuttoned a few of her top buttons so a small amount of her chest can be seen. She doesn't have much for tits, but she presses her arms together in an effort to give me a glimpse of her subpar cleavage.

I close my eyes briefly and see Eilidh, her exquisite breasts near eye level with me and soaked from the shower. They're large enough to fill my hands and I can't shake the thought of what it would feel like to learn the shape of them with my tongue. Her dusty pink nipples would peak and my mouth waters with the image of taking one between my teeth and biting until she whimpers and then licking and sucking until she begged for more.

I open my eyes again and Lumara has moved another step closer, pressing her body into mine.

Eilidh is a phoenix. Her kind killed my mother. I can never forgive her. I wont ever forgive her.

I can hear Eilidh lean over to ask Cadmyr something but Lumara's grating voice makes it impossible for me to hear what she says.

"You know," Lumara traces her index finger over the top button of my jumpsuit. "I've always wondered what it's like to have you inside of me. I've heard the rumors of your... endowment." Her entire chest is against me now and she's worked her way down to the third button of my jumpsuit. "How many piercings is it again? Seven? Eight?" She pops another. "Actually, don't tell me. Let me count myself."

I watch Eilidh and Cadmyr stand up and move towards the scrap pile together and my beast roars in my chest. He's rattling, swinging his broad tail in agitation.

Mine. Azure growls.

I almost step away. I almost go to her and try to undo the damage I've caused. I almost knock the shit out of one of my closest friends for walking away with what is mine and I almost give in to the feeling within me that demands I take her. To show the world that she belongs to me.

She's. Not. Ours. I stand my ground in the face of my dragon, and he bares his teeth at me. Letting out a roar that has my jaw ticking and a slight tremble I can't contain shudders through me.

"Mmm…" Lumara purrs. "You like that, do you?" Another button comes undone as I close the door in my mind to my dragon for the first time in all our centuries together. I grit my teeth and do the only thing I know will numb the chaos swirling in my chest.

I grab Lumara by the back of her neck and bring her thin mouth to mine. The kiss is hard and chaste, gripping her long black hair in my fist. I yank her backwards and crowd her into a corner of the workstation that's not visible to the guards.

Flipping her around, I slap her nonexistent ass. "Get these fucking clothes out of mah way." It's harsh. A demand to move faster so I don't have a chance to think too hard about what the fuck I'm doing. There's no passion, no softness and every time I touch her, I feel bile rise in my throat.

It's just another piece of ass. I've done this thousands of times with thousands of different astrals. I can do this. It doesn't matter. Eilidh doesn't matter.

She quickly undoes her top so it can slide down over her shoulders and down her legs. I turn us both around so that I'm facing the furnaces, noticing that Eilidh and Cadmyr are walking back towards their stations and she's laughing at something he said.

Fucker.

Perfect. Let her see. Let her hate me.

I shove Lumara's underwear off to the side and unbutton my clothes so that I can pull out my length and slam into her, brutally hard without any prep.

To Lumara's credit, she takes it with a wince and a soft cry as I rut into her from behind. Bent over the table, she clings to the edges for stability and soon enough the pained sound turns to pleasured moans.

Eilidh's eyes shoot to mine, and I can physically feel her recoil. Excruciating pain radiates through my chest that's not my own.

It's hers.

Hers.

I slow my next thrust and Lumara writhes beneath me, breathing in short huffs and pushing herself back onto my cock but my eyes are glued to Eilidh's as she inhales sharply. Her delicate hands come up to cover her mouth with a quiet sob that cracks every wall I've built up around my heart and mind to keep her out.

She spins on the ball of her foot and runs full speed out of our workstation and towards the door. Dread creeps down my spine and spreads throughout my entire body.

"Eilidh!" I shout after her, but she's already rounded the corner towards the guards. "*FUCK!*"

I pull my already softening length out of Lumara, and she whines in protest. "No, don't stop!" Wiggling herself towards me again.

"Shut the fuck up!" I yell. Every nerve ending stands on end, my blood calling to Eilidh, needing to find her.

"Dude…" Cadmyr eyes me cautiously. "*What* are you doing?"

"I don't fuckin know." I'm fumbling to clasp my buttons and Cadmyr moves in to help me. He's suspiciously quiet for a moment and as the last button closes, he grabs my arms, holding me steady.

"We all know what this is, Blue. The only ones who don't believe it are you and her. Figure your shit out or you'll lose her, if you haven't already." His sandy eyes bore into mine. "And if you don't want her, someone else will."

His words ignite a fire within me. With a final nod, I'm running. Jumping over tables and skidding across the floor. My muscles scream with disuse, but I don't stop until I'm at the end of the large factory and face to face with the guards.

"I need to use the restroom," I pant. "It's an emergency."

Harvey looks me up and down. "Sounds like a personal problem."

I grind my teeth together. I need to get to her and every moment this fuck keeps me, the further she gets away from me.

"Please." The word is acrid on my tongue as I say it aloud, but at this point I'll beg if I have to. I just need to find Eilidh.

He huffs a laugh and stands aside. "Five minutes, Breather."

I race out the door and down the hall towards the bathrooms. I search every stall but don't find her.

Where the fuck did she go?

I peek out the bathroom door. No guards are standing nearby so I make a run for the closet and swing it open to find nothing more than a mop and a leaky sink.

Eilidh? I project to her. Seeking out the familiar channel of her mind, but I meet a wall of white flame that's never been there before. I brush my mental hands against the fire, but it burns, and I wince at the blaze. She's blocked me out completely.

Who the fuck taught her to shield?

I check every closet and door I can as I make my way back to the parts factory. My heart races and I can feel my dragon beating against the door I closed on him. Slowly lowering my defenses, I open our mental pathway, and he bursts forth, furious and fuming. He pins me, roaring in my face with spittle flying from between his massive jaws and I let him.

I deserve it.

I lost her.

26
KIERAN

"*All of you then. I'll get all of you out...*"

My promise keeps coming back like a boomerang, clipping my mind with each iteration like an uppercut. It makes my stomach twist the more I hear it, stacking itself onto the mountain of promises and proclamations that I have yet to fulfill.

But I'm still shouldering it. My knees still haven't buckled as I carry on with what I must accomplish. Not yet anyway.

It just means that I'll have to get creative to get three high profile inmates out rather than one.

And I will get them out, somehow.

I just need time to plan, coordinate a strategy, and figure out how I'm going to work with two other potentially unruly dragons that I've only interacted with a handful of times. The blue male dragon being the definite wild card of the bunch.

I'm rifling through financial plans I've just received from Bernice Yim of Atlas United for the new helipad that she's planning on constructing on the flattest section on the island, which inevitably is a section of rock between the North-East arms of the facility. Many of the guards that live in the apartments on those arms will have to invest in some noise-cancelling headsets for the next few months while construction takes place. Myself included.

I pop the last piece of my toast in my mouth as I organize the documents in my hands, including the maps Cain requested. I reach his office door which is cracked open. I tap a few knocks and push it open.

The smell hits me before anything else.

Sweat and the stink of exertion. Spit and sulfur from lit matches. Cain's back is to me as he stands before a large open armoire filled with magazine clippings, and printed pictures of the Vice President, Annalise Arden. She's shrouded in candlelight and what looks like fresh cut spring flowers.

Cain's pants are hanging at his knees, his hairy bare ass clenches as he pumps his cock vigorously, grunting in effort as his free hand touches one of the images of Annalise's red lips.

As soon as I enter the room, he slams shut the doors and scrambles to pull up his pants.

"Shit," I mutter as I step out of the door but he's already roaring my name.

Too late.

"Get the fuck in here, you nosy prick!"

Fuck. Calm. 71, 89, 8... "Forgive me sir your door was-"

"How much did you see, Halsey?"

90, 82, 71, 89... "Only your back sir, nothing else." *Also, your shrine.*

"Filthy fucking liar. What did ye see?"

8, 90, 82... "Your back and light, that's it, Sir." *Plus, you making mincemeat of your dick to pictures of Annalise Arden.* His face is purple with rage and strain, the strip of hair that he uses far too much gel on is rumpled and stuck to his large forehead, glinting with perspiration.

"You report any of this to anyone Halsey and I will ruin ye, understand?"

Sure you will, fucking asshole. "Understood, Sir."

"Report to the Breather Block and SolCon for the next few days, for interrupting. Consider yourself lucky I don't fire you, eh?" He says, swiping back his hair and straightening his shirt.

Please fire me, you stupid piece of shit. I inhale slowly while I keep my face and body neutral. *71, 89, 8...*

"What the fuck is it then?"

I step forward and hand him the paperwork on his desk.

"Oh right," he says, pushing the papers aside, pursuing each one quickly before he takes a seat in his black office chair. "The 'helicopter' pad." He announces each syllable in a mocking tone. "Right then, off ya fuck."

"I thought I needed to be seated in for the call with Ms. Yim and the other-"

"I don't give a fuck what ya want, Halsey. Get the fuck outta my office before I change my mind and fire ya anyway."

I hesitate for a moment, something inside of me shifting dangerously. A darkness and violence that I keep well beneath my conscious mind. The part of me that I reserve for war and battle, for the times when all available methods of diplomacy have been exhausted and what remains can only be resolved with fists, steel, teeth, and blood. It bristles and taps its talons on the surface of my subconscious. But I shove it down in time. "Yes, Sir." I say, my voice low as I turn to walk out.

"Haaaaalsey," Cain croons and I stop to look at him over my shoulder. "Are ya forgetting something, boy?"

Fuck. This. Guy. I turn and salute him. He smiles maliciously and adjusts his belt. "That's better. Now fuck off."

71, 89, 8, 90, 82...71, 89, 8, 90, 82... I turn and shut the door and seethe as I walk back to my office, punching a hole clean through the wall.

I press my key card to the black screen and the door to my apartment clicks open. I'm out of breath from a particularly hard run and weight training session. I shut the door and head to the sink to fill a glass of water. Thick drops of sweat drip off my elbows and nose as I gulp down the water from the glass.

I down three more glasses before I head to the shower to rinse off. Dressed in joggers and a T-shirt, I pad over to my desk and flip open my laptop to begin punching in my credentials when a notification sounds from one of the desk drawers. I open it to the black burner phone I keep in a hidden compartment.

The notification is a message:

> Unknown Number: You're gonna want to see this.

No one has this number apart from very specific contacts and if they are sending me information, it is probably something important. Every message is end to end encrypted and anything received is destroyed after twenty-four hours unless it's saved elsewhere.

I inhale and open the link.

It's a recording. So far, it's showing a woman in a red business suit and nude pumps as a very familiar deep voice says, "I want you to take off your clothes and show me how much of a slut you are for me."

Fuck, is that…?

So far it doesn't show him or her head, just her chest down but when she starts speaking…

"I like how your dick feels in my mouth."

No fucking way. I've heard her voice probably a hundred times, maybe even thousands over the past several years she's been in office. I would know that voice anywhere. She throws her expensive red suit on the floor and now she's wearing nothing but a black bra and panties.

"I like feeling your cum on my face, and when it drips down my legs while I'm shopping for groceries." She removes her undergarments and steps closer to the camera. Her dark pink nipples and taut flat stomach are in clear view as she moves into the male just beyond the frame.

"I like tasting myself on your tongue after you've fucked me with it." She begins to remove her heels when the male interjects.

"No. Leave those on." The male is still out of frame, but the voice of President Luthor Montgomery is unmistakable now. He slowly bends her over the desk and her pretty, red painted mouth and flushed pink cheeks are on full display, making it absolutely unquestionable that this is Annalise Arden leaning naked over the desk of President Montgomery.

Holy shit. This is volatile ammunition and exactly what I need as the pieces begin to click neatly together in my mind. I lower the volume of Annalise getting railed into the desk as I think.

I type back:

> Me: Good work.

I download the video to an encrypted network attached storage device and place the NAS in a safe, lock it with my fingerprint and press my knuckles into my temples.

…Kieran…

Rhiannon's voice feels like a cool breeze in the heat of summer as it kisses my brain. My shoulders relax a bit as her sultry rasp flutters through my mind.

Princess.

…Is something going on?..

Why? What's wrong?

She sighs.

…I was just sitting here and suddenly I'm hearing…I heard…

Fuck.

How do I even explain that?

I…uh…

…Are you?…

No! No, I'm not having sex with anyone. That wasn't me that you were hearing.

Gods, that makes it sound worse.

…Look I know that me being a- a vir-…

Rhiannon, stop. That was a sex tape, one that I'm gonna use to get you and your friends out of the prison.

She's quiet for a few seconds.

Then a minute.

Now I'm starting to get anxious.

What can I do to convince you?

…Let me see it…

What? The sex tape?

…Yes…

I sit up in my chair and take a deep breath. I've never done that before. Even with Daemon when he trained me to shield in the war. I don't even know if I can. But…

I can try. How do I-

…Close your eyes… She says and I do. *…You'll need to let me pass the ice shield…*

I jerk. *No.*

I hear her breathing softly, like she's close. I feel the ache in her chest at my resistance to let her in.

It's not safe, Rhiannon.

...Why don't you trust me?...

It's not that.

...Then just let me into a safe room behind the ice...

I thought about that for a minute. I feel her warm hand touch the ice shield, and it begins to falter, cracking ominously as I scramble to make a room amongst the darkness in my mind. Away from the things she cannot see, from the unforgivable shadows that will damn me from her forever. I construct my office with its oakwood floor and navy curtains, amber light from low lit lamps, rows of books and mahogany leather furniture, barricading it all with thicker, more fortified ice. Impenetrable and impossibly strong. The door to my office is where her hand breaks through the shield.

Her warm confection scent wafts into my space and I inhale deeply. Then the gentle caress of her fingers along the back of my neck. Then her lips on my cheek.

...Hello, Major Hot Stuff...

"Hello, my Princess," I say aloud and her laugh is breathy and etheric as the specter of her moves around me, like kelp along my skin in deep water. It sends shivers down my back as I see her silhouette leaning against the desk.

...Show me, Kieran...

I pull up the link on the burner phone and press play on the video. I place it on the desk where she turns and watches. The moans and grunts of the two leaders of Prism fill the quiet confines of my office like mid-level porn. The video concludes and she continues to look at the phone.

...So, that was the president and the vice president?...

"Yes," I answer.

...You're going to use that to get us out? How?...

I have an idea.

...Can I know?...

The less you know the better, Rhiannon.

She turns and I swear I see the bright cornflower blue of her irises glowing, even in her spectral form. I stop breathing as she steps closer.

...Will it be dangerous?...

Very.

She clicks her tongue as she straddles my lap and the sensation is... peculiar. It's like being saddled by a warm sparkling wind that smells of vanilla cookies, honey, and...melted sugar. I feel her lips brush against my neck as she whispers my name against my skin. I grip the arms of the chair, wishing I could place my hands on her ass, move them up her rib cage and thread my fingers through her long auburn hair. She grinds her core against my lap and my dick begins to swell with aggressive force.

"Fuck," I murmur as her breasts crowd my face. Her scent is overwhelming. Her hands cup my cheeks and slide into my hair. Now I'm so hard it hurts.

...Please be careful... She whispers, grinding herself onto my lap again and the arms of my chair groan under the pressure of my grip.

...We have plans... She whispers into my ear and runs her tongue along my neck. My hips involuntarily buck up into her and she whimpers.

But then suddenly she's gone. My eyes pop open and the sounds and smells of my office come flooding back.

I lean over onto my knees, my weeping dick leaking into the confines of my once clean pants.

I have a plan. I know how I am going to roll this out and it will flow nicely into the plans I comprised when I arrived in this shithole. Getting three high profile inmates out wasn't going to be the hardest part of this endeavor.

The thing that was scaring me...the thing that was paralyzing me beyond all else, was the mounting realization of how much Rhiannon means to me. Who *we* are. No matter how much I ignore it, no matter how often I deny the evidence laid plainly before me. At some point I'm going to have to admit it to myself and then to her.

At some point.

But not now.

Not tonight.

As I reach for my cask of whiskey, I pour way more than my usual two fingers and slug it back. I cover up all those realizations with the schemes that need to be prioritized before I act. I take another drink of the whiskey, the burn coating my throat and my raging desire as I swallow down her scent and presence. Overshadowing it with next steps and tasks as they fall into place, making a mental map of all I need to get started on in order to make this heist happen successfully.

I start by texting one of the few trusted numbers I have memorized. She messages back right away.

> Me: I need you to send a Yuletide gift to a very Bad Child.

> Her: My favorite. You got a list?

> Me: Always.

> Her: Wrap it up nicely before you load it on the sleigh.

I upload the video to a digital time locked encrypted packet and then send her the video. Once she texts back confirmation of retrieval and instructions on time and date for package arrival, I wipe the phone and destroy it.

Just like that, the first phase of my plan is complete.

I should be terrified that it could all go wrong. That I could lose more than just my job.

But…I'm not.

27
RHIANNON

"What are you doing, 2460?" Harvey yells from across the warehouse. I had stepped off to the side to connect with Kieran and got lost in him for several minutes.

"Sorry. Period cramps," I call across the warehouse. Harvey makes a disgusted face while some of the other astrals smirk or laugh.

"No one wants to hear that, Inmate. You have five minutes to make your quota."

I already met it, so suck it Harv.

I haul the last of the scrap into the furnace with Tatsu and Ryu. Meadow leans against the table picking at her nails.

"New manicure, Meadow?" I ask sweetly, hauling a particularly large piece into the flame as Ryu shuts the gate.

"Yeah, I just got this new-"

"Gods Meadow, I really don't give a shit." She scowls at me as Tatsu sniggers. "How about you make those pretty nails useful and sweep up since you couldn't be bothered with any of the hard work?" I say, shoving a broom in her chest.

"Excuse me?" She challenges, throwing the broom back at me.

Oh, hells yes. I think as I crowd her. My eyes flash red as my teeth sharpen and my chest glows orange. "Give me a reason to rip off your arms and beat your ass with them, Meadow," I say smiling, the sulfur and flames licking from my teeth as I speak. Meadow cowers back with her face twisted in both indignation and fear.

"Hey!" Harvey hollers and I drape my arm around Meadow's shoulders, feigning camaraderie as I turn to him and smile with her sour expression next to mine.

"What, Harvey? We're just talking about girly stuff! Weren't we Meds?"

"Meds?" Meadow murmurs at me.

"Play along bitch or we're both getting latrine duty."

Meadow plants a lachrymose smile on her face. "Just talking about nails and periods, Harvey. All good."

"Fucking disgusting, Mute trash. Clean up your station. It's time for dinner." Harvey turns and walks back to the entrance. I push Meadow away from me and shove the broom back on her.

"Clean it up or I'll tear your face off with my fucking teeth," I spit at her and she pales as she stands and starts sweeping the floors. "Good girl," I hiss and walk off, Tatsu and Ryu following behind.

We're walking through the warehouse, and I notice Xanth pacing the room in a frenzy, his eyes darting from the door to every corner of the warehouse floor.

You okay?

…Not now Rhi…

Ugh. Whatever. Pissy male. I keep walking and notice that Eilidh is missing. I know I saw her with us earlier when we were assigned our duty stations, she was assigned to the furnaces with Cadmyr, Lumara, and–

Where's Eilidh, Xanth?

…I said not now Rhi, I'm busy…

That silly ass motherfucker had better not have hurt her again or I am going to *literally* rip off his balls and wear them as a necklace. I reach out to Eilidh, and I'm immediately met with scorching white-hot flames.

Fuck. This can't be good

Eili? I say softly against the wall of searing hot white fire. *It's me.*

All of a sudden, the flames bank and my thoughts are granted access.

Where are you?

…Rec room…

As luck would have it, we were nearing the rec-room, and I was able to slip off and find her sitting on one of the benches flipping through a book.

"Hey," I say and she looks up at me, my heart cracks at the expression on her face.

Her eyes are dull, shadowed and swollen from crying. Her typically perfectly braided hair has strands hanging loose around her face and red blotches paint her high cheeks. She sniffles and I wonder how long she's been sitting here alone.

I sit down next to her, and she sits up so that her shoulder can rest against mine. Her movements are stunted and heavy, like she's struggling to even keep her head up.

"Rhi he...he..." Her voice sounds watery and broken.

Say it here if it's easier.

...He fucked Lumara in the warehouse...

"He did WHAT?"

...Right in front of me, Rhi. Cad had taken me to show me how to select scrap that wouldn't topple the pile and when we came back, he was balls deep in her. He made eye contact with me and didn't stop...

Everything is red.

"I'm gonna kill him," I say with absolute certainty.

"Wait." She coughs and takes my arm. "Can you just-" She takes a deep, shuddering breath. "Can you sit with me? I don't want to be alone."

I stop as I look down at her. "Of course," I say and wrap my arms around her as she continues to quietly cry. I silently plot every way I am going to murder and maim Xanth Vulcan in my mind. His immortality guarantees at least five good murders before he figures out a way to stop me from killing him again. I kiss the top of her head and smooth back her hair and start humming.

...I didn't know you could sing...

Not very well.

...Could have fooled me...

I continue to hum while I smile and stroke her hair.

...Are there words to the song?...

I smile again and begin to sing the words. I finish the song before she begins to speak again.

"What language is that?"

"They're in the old tongue. I don't even know what they mean but it always made me and Fianna peaceful when our father would sing it to us."

Eilidh adjusted her head on my shoulder, and I kissed the top of her head again. "You're okay, Pints."

She turns to look at me with a quizzical expression on her face.

"What…did you just call me?"

"Pints. For pint-sized. Because you're tiny."

She scrunches her nose at me and laughs. "Is this payback for Raisins?"

"Maybe."

She shakes her head, but a small smile tugs at the corners of her mouth.

"Listen, we have a plan. We're getting out of here and it's going to be soon. I need to go over the details with you but not here."

"Alright," she says as we both stand and begin walking after the inmates that are already in the chow hall. We both exit the rec-room, and I notice a small male rat astral standing near the entrance. One step into the hall and my eyes lock with his before he casts his eyes down and starts to walk away.

"Hi Mort," Eilidh says to him, but he doesn't respond as he turns the corner with his cart of laundry and disappears.

At dinner I sit with Eilidh and the other dragons, Xanth sits at the far end of the table, staring at Eilidh and looking thoroughly sorry for himself.

Fucking good.

He's gonna be even more sorry when I'm done with him. I finish up and squeeze Eilidh's arm.

I'll be back. I say and gesture for Xanth to follow. He gets up and reluctantly follows me to the restrooms. Nova and Jo are busy talking and whatever the subject is has them both engrossed, so they don't notice that we both head into the same bathroom.

Good.

I lock the bathroom door behind us and cross my arms over my chest.

"You have five seconds to explain yourself," I say and his eyes meet mine with a sharp edge. "I mean it, Vulcan. Five seconds and then I'm gonna wipe the floor with your sorry ass."

"I fucked up, Rhi. I made a mistake."

"A mistake?" I ask, my head cocked to the side as I take a step closer. "You think you made a *mistake* Xanth? This isn't a fucking math problem. It's not like you forgot to carry the one somewhere. You FUCKED another female in front of your MATE."

He winces as the words come out, stinging and slapping with deadly accuracy.

Good.

"I know, Rhi," he says gruffly. But it can't stand.

"Are you even sorry?"

"Of course I'm fuckin' sorry." His tone turns defensive, and it boils my blood.

I hit him with a solid right hook to his jaw, and he falters, catching himself on the sinks. He clenches his fists but doesn't make a move to defend himself, nor does he attack me.

"How about now?"

"Yes," he sputters, spitting blood onto the floor. Rage simmers in his eyes but I don't think that rage is aimed at me.

"Do you know how often I have to listen to her stifle tears at night while you *deny* her? While you push her love and friendship to the side like *trash*? When it's *you*. YOU are the one that's trash, Xanth. You are fucking *despicable*. All she's ever done was to help you. She's given you second and third and fourth chances and all you've done is *spit* in her face."

He stands up but he's slumped as if the weight of the situation is pulling him closer to the floor.

"You don't deserve Eilidh as a mate. You don't even deserve her as a *friend*. She's too good for you," I say before I backhand him hard in the other direction and he allows himself to fall onto the stalls with the force. I'm well aware that he's not putting up a fight right now. He's allowing me to kick the shit out of him, perhaps because he believes he deserves it. His dragon starts growling low as he stands up straighter, his eyes glowing bright blue and his navy scales clacking over his arms. Smoke billows from him but he doesn't make a move to attack me.

"You're a fool, Xanth Vulcan."

"You don't think I know that already?" He spits through his teeth.

"Good," I spit back getting right in his face, the sulfur and fire flaring from my lips as I bump into his lower ribs. "Because you had your chance and just like every other astral whore in this shithole, you've *fucked* it."

Blue flame spits from his teeth as he seethes back at me. Nina bellows low as red and black scales slip forward, oil-slick obsidian wings unfurl from my back.

A low rumble in my chest vibrates across the stalls as Nina's voice bellows from the depths and she speaks directly to Xanth and his dragon in the old tongue. "Know your place, Azure of the Western Guardians."

The flame in his blue eyes flickers as his dragon growls and huffs angrily but secedes. Then his dragon speaks back in the same language.

"The Phoenix is mine. He will not deny me what is mine."

Nina nods and her scales pull back, my wings tuck neatly into my skin and the flames recede into my belly. Xanth is still angry but the solemn expression that he came in with also remains.

"Fix it," I exclaim as I put my hand on his cheek and swipe over the bone. He meets my eyes as I look up at him. "I know you. This isn't you." I turn and walk to the door and unlock it. "Let go of your hatred. Your mother wouldn't want this. Show her who you really are, Xanth."

Then I push through the door and walk out.

Eilidh and I walk back to our cell after dinner. She's been quiet the entire time. Jo unlocks our door and lets us in before closing it behind us. As soon as she steps away, I start talking.

I talked to Kieran.

She looks up at me, the gold in her eyes flashes a bit brighter as she takes my hand and sits on my bed with me.

...Tell me...

A sex tape.

She balks back, her face pinched in disgust. *...Do I even want more details?...*

I laugh. *He already has it. It's of the president and the vice president.*

She laughs out loud, making her face and eyes a bit brighter. *...Oh my Gods that is gold...*

She puts her arms around me, squeezing me into her. I wrap my arms around her, holding her too, and I breathe her in. She smells like...wisping smoke from a campfire in winter, dew in the forest in autumn, early morning coffee...home.

She smells like home.

My home.

The ache in my chest surges as I hold her tighter.

She came into this place as my enemy, and I never thought we would be where we are now. I never thought I could even like her...let alone love her as deeply and as irrevocably as I do now.

Tears begin to pool and spill over my cheeks.

"Damn you for making me love you, Eilidh."

She laughs gently and sniffles. "Well damn you for making me love you back, Rhiannon."

Ciara. The thought is fleeting but it's there and Eilidh...

"Who's Ciara?"

Fuck.

I straighten up as I wipe my tears from my face. "Another name from another time." I respond and stand to walk to the rusty sink.

She sits there quietly knowing full well that I'm not telling her everything. But instead of pressing, she settles back onto her hands and crosses her legs.

"What did you and Xanth talk about in the bathroom?"

I chuckle as I splash water on my face and wipe it off with my sleeve.

"I dunno Xanth, what did we talk about," I say loud enough for him to hear me through the walls, even though I know he can hear everything we've said thus far.

"That I'm an asshole. Eilidh, will ye please talk te me?" He says back rather morosely and Eilidh ignores him as she's done all evening.

I don't blame her. She needs time.

"We had a chat," I say as I wink back at Eilidh.

She smiles at me and shakes her head. "I'm a big girl, you know? I don't need you to fight my battles."

I hold up my hands in surrender. "I know, I know." I lean against the wall. "But I needed to say my piece about his behavior."

She dips her chin to me and then stands to hop up to her bed and I crawl into my bunk as the buzzer sounds for lights out.

Eilidh?

…Hm?…

I'm sorry he hurt you like that.

She's quiet for a minute before she speaks softly into my mind.

…Me too, Rhi…

28
RHIANNON

Eilidh and I take our turns at the sink that morning before Nova arrives to open our cell door for showers. We file out just as Ryker walks up the corridor, his buckled boots clicking with each step, and stops in front of me. Since losing his arm, he's been in a shit mood, but today, his usual bitter expression is replaced by a smug smile.

"You're coming with me 2460," He orders as he fixes manacles on my wrists, an iron halter over my face and takes my arm.

"Where am I–,"

"Shut your mouth, Breather, and do as you're told." He grips my arm tight and practically throws me to start walking. I comply with a brief glance back at Eilidh whose face looks as bewildered as mine. I walk by Xanth's cell and notice he's waiting at the door, watching me and Ryker pass. His brow pinches as he steps closer to the bars.

"Where the fuck are ye taking her, Ryker?" Smoke billows from his nose and Ryker flinches beside me.

"T-talk to me like that again Breather and I will throw you back in SolCon!" He shouts as he hits the bars with his baton in a show of power. "Stupid fucking dragons," Ryker mutters loud enough for everyone to hear as we continue walking to the elevators. I didn't miss his stutter, or the way he avoided getting close to Xanth's cell door.

Is this it? Am I going to get swept up by the white coats? Am I going to figure out what they do to astrals, see where they end up? Dead, dying, or worse?

Ryker steers me to the back corridor and my heart rate begins to climb as we near the two elevators. One that leads to the rest of the prison and the other…

"Did I do something?"

"Gods, just shut the fuck up and *walk!*" Ryker shouts as he shoves me forward. He presses his badge to the black reader, and it beeps as he pushes the button to call the elevator. Each second feels like a countdown to the end. My heart rate is climbing until I feel my neck pulsing almost painfully with each wild beat. The elevator dings loudly and then the left door slides open, revealing a man in a white lab coat.

Black hair and metal rimmed glasses frame his face. He's tall, almost lanky with severe looking cheekbones and a pointed nose. His hands are tucked carefully inside his coat pockets, and he looks down at me before turning his cold eyes on Ryker. My entire body begins to tremble as he stands there surveying us for seconds that seem to drag on to years. There's faint yelling in the background. A male's voice with a thickly accented burr calling my name, but I can't be sure. My heartbeat is thrumming so loudly in my ears I can hardly hear anything at all. I swallow hard as he steps off the elevator and walks past us. My knees buckle with relief, and I nearly pass out.

The elevator dings again, the right elevator doors slide open, and Ryker shoves me forward. He presses the button for the fifth floor and steps back behind me. The silence is tense in the elevator as it jostles upward, my stomach dipping with the movement. I close my eyes and try to focus on Ryker's mind for any information. The static is loud as I tune into his mental space, clearing through the discordant sound and reaching the perimeter of his mind...and I immediately regret it.

...Why didn't I fuck this one?... Her ass is fucking perfect...Better than those skinny little deer Mute whores...Gods I'd fucking pound into that tight little ass so hard...She wouldn't walk right for a week...I bet her cunt tastes good too...

I pull out of his mind as the bile inches its way up my throat. I want to respond. I want to fight back and make Ryker feel as small as he is, but as it stands, I'm the one with more to lose right now.

So, I shut the fuck up and wait for this hellacious elevator ride to be over, all the while feeling Ryker's predatory gaze prod and grope my backside. Finally, the elevator slows, the door dings and slides open to a nice plush office. Ryker affixes a chain to my manacles and then pulls me forward like a leashed dog. We walk through rows of offices with upscale dark wood, leather furniture, and sleek decor before we reach the end office. Two large oak French doors tower in front of us and I can hear a man on the other side talking in a guttural round cockney.

No.

He knocks on the door and the man inside says, "The fuck d'ya want?"

"It's Ryker sir. I've collected the inmate you requested."

"Come in," He calls, and Ryker opens the thick doors and pulls me into the office. The decor from outside extends into this room as well except for a large armoire behind his dark wood desk and an entertainment stand off to the side. The Warden sits behind his desk, lounging back with his hands folded over his rounded but still strong looking belly. His glowing red eye whirrs and fixes on me as I enter after Ryker who quickly salutes the Warden.

I didn't see him at first, which makes sense because he's so small. But standing right behind the Warden is Mort, the small male rat astral that pushed the laundry cart from yesterday.

Everything begins to click into place.

I nearly choke on the irony of the fucking rat astral being the one to sell me out. It's almost comical. *Almost.* If it weren't for the icy dread that is now sluicing painfully through my veins as I walk through the myriad of dark fates that await me. All involving the Warden making a spectacle of me in front of the entire block in some ridiculous and potentially excruciating show of power.

I stay steady on my feet, my chin lifted as the Warden surveys me.

"Ya already know why ya'r here, don't ya?"

I dip my chin once in response as my heart thunders in my ears.

"Mort here tells me ya have plans. I would like to hear about them."

I weigh my options. I could lie, but I think that would only piss him off more depending on how much he knows. I'm heavily considering still attempting the lie when I remember what Kieran told me about the Warden's particular distaste for disrespect. *"By any means necessary."*

"He overheard me talking about escaping," I say, directly.

"Ahh, she's smart at least," the Warden says to Ryker. "And here I was ready for ya to try and deny it," he says as he leans forward onto the desk and onto his forearms. "So, the question remains, what do we do with ya?" He presses a button on the phone, holds the receiver to his ear and tells whoever is on the other line to come to his office.

Moments later, the door opens wider and Kieran steps in. My gut flips with the tiniest flicker of hope. He salutes the Warden.

"Halsey!" The Warden says jovially. Kieran surveys everyone in the room and seems completely impassive to it all. Apart from a small flicker of the eye, he doesn't acknowledge me.

"You called me, Sir?"

"Yes," he straightens at the shoulders and adjusts the large belt wrapped around his waist. "You see, this little 'Breather', as ya all call them, has been making big plans to stretch her wings and fly home."

I keep myself steady, trying not to look at Kieran as he says impassively, "Interesting."

"I was just thinking it's time for ya to stretch *yar* legs with the dolling of the punishments these days. Perhaps you should take a turn with this little pigeon and get yar sea-legs, as they say."

"I'd be honored, Sir," Kieran says and my stomach drops to the floor. It's an act. It has to be an act.

"What I was thinking, is perhaps ya shoot 'er in the kneecaps and then in the heart, let 'er bleed out a bit and then melt 'er face with the Phoenix flames." He gestures to a long horrifying weapon with a barrel the size of my head sitting off to the side of his office. "All as a demonstration of course."

"A brilliant idea, Sir," Kieran says and my entire body begins to tremble, my knees threaten to give way at the thought of being painfully and publicly executed.

"What d'ya think of that, poppet? Does that sound like a good time? No? Should have thought 'bout that before ya filled yar head with thoughts of leavin'."

My fear banks in Nina's fire as she rears up, fortifying my resolve. Weakened but not completely thwarted by the halter from letting her voice be heard.

"Of course," she says, coolly even as my body trembles. Her fiery breath courses through my veins, warming the icy dread. "Death would be an honor. Death is a mercy, and I am grateful for your benevolence in granting me such…*freedom.*"

The Warden's face grows slack at my response. In fact, all their faces mirror one another, apart from Kieran's who looks a bit… smug.

…*You brilliant beautiful dragon…* Kieran's sultry voice trickles across my brain. Nina chitters and purrs in my belly as she slips beneath, and I take a deep breath.

The Warden's lips press into a tight line, his face growing a bit more red. "Well, that is *not* the bloody point, now is it." He gruffs angrily. He turns to Kieran and says, "It's yar job to break this little bitch, understand? Ya push 'er until she is a sniveling pile of feces like this one!" He growls as he points to Mort cowering in the shadow of the armoire. "Ya tear the spirit from 'er and report back. One week, Halsey."

"Yes, Sir," Kieran replies and takes the chains from Ryker.

"-And Halsey," the Warden continues as Kieran starts for the door with me behind him. "Make sure she stays alive." His eyes glitter maliciously as he looks at me. I keep my face stony and impassive as I am being led from the Warden's office, Ryker following behind me.

Kieran leads me back to the elevators, presses the button and the doors slide open. He tugs me inside, harder than necessary, and I stumble as Ryker shoves past me and stands behind me in the corner. Kieran presses the button for the second floor, and we begin the long descent down to Solitary Confinement.

When the doors push open, it's the smell that hits me before anything else. The air is thick with the smells of piss, sweat, shit, and vomit. My eyes begin to water. It's absolutely disgusting, dark, and indescribably dank. I gag at the sheer texture of the putrid air. The tiny hairs on my arms stand on end as I listen to how quiet it is. I know there are astrals here, I can feel them, feel their agony and torment as I walk past the tight metal boxes all lined up against the hallway walls.

Kieran stops at one of the boxes and opens the door with his badge. The heavy door swings open with a creak. A single light bulb held by the cord dangles from the top of the metal box ceiling and flickers. The smell wafting from the opened door forces me to swallow the bile that creeps up my throat. Dark fluids stain the walls, and I can't tell if it's feces or blood, maybe both. He pulls me into the cell, my head lowers as I crouch to fit into the confines of the box. Kieran's hand lingers for a moment before he steps back.

I look up into his cold and ruthless eyes. My chest aches as I think of how silly I was to believe he was different. He had looked at me with heat in his eyes, spoke kinder words, his gentle strong hands ran through my hair, his breath warm on my body. But now it's sheer cruelty.

...I need you to trust me... I feel his voice vibrate across my brain gently. I jerk slightly in response, relief slowly trickling its way back, but I can't be sure what's real. It's a bandage over a bullet hole. Not enough, but he's the only hope I have of getting out of here with my life.

Okay. I volley off to him. His teal eyes are the last thing I see before he shuts the door.

I know it's been a while. Hours certainly, but it's hard to know since the light went out the moment the door closed.

My jaw aches and the manacles are cutting into my wrists. The blood trickles down to my fingers as I rest with my legs scrunched up to my chest. The tight living conditions make it impossible for me to straighten fully, and the ceiling is too low for me to stand. I felt around in the dark and found a drain in the middle of the floor for me to piss in but then I'd have to be able to pull off my jumpsuit, which is impossible with the manacles and no space to move. So, I ended up going through my jumpsuit and now sit in my soiled clothing.

My olfactory senses are starting to adjust to the unbearable smell of this place which can't be a good sign. My entire body is cramping from the lack of activity and my poor posture.

Xanth was down here for two weeks and here I am whining about day one. I chuckle to myself as I let myself slip into sleep.

I wake to the door opening and the light stings my eyes. A large masculine figure stands in the doorway, but I can't quite make-out any details.

The smell of leather and smoke sifts through the assult of stink and it's the first comfort I've felt in hours.

Kieran? I try and it brushes lovingly against the frigid wall of ice that surrounds his mind.

...Stay quiet... he pitches back to me quickly as I stumble on weak legs out of the cell. My limbs tingle from being cramped for Gods only knows how long. He unlocks the chains, removes my manacles, and unbuckles the halter on my face. The relief is instant and immeasurably good as they all fall away. Next, he hands me a hospital gown to change into. I'm shivering as I pull off my soiled wet jumpsuit and he wraps me in a blanket. It smells like fabric softener, and I pale to think of how bad I must smell in comparison. He places a white hospital bracelet around my bloody wrist as we walk down the hall. There's a wheelchair waiting at the end by the elevator.

...Get in and keep your head down... He instructs and I obey. He covers my head with the blanket, and I angle my head down to look at my feet. *...Don't look up, whatever you hear, feel, or see. Understand?...*

Yes. I respond through our mental connection, and I'm jolted forward. He pushes me into the elevator, and I feel the dipping sensation of us moving upwards. *Where are we-*

...Not yet Princess, stay shielded and stay quiet...

I do as I'm told and slam up my steel walls, waiting patiently for the feel of his thoughts as we continue in the elevator. A ding signals our arrival and then I am wheeled off the elevator. He pushes me onto a dim but open sounding corridor, and it reminds me of a mall at night. I am so unbelievably curious, but I keep my head down.

"Good even-well I suppose it's rather early morning, Sir. Anything I can help you or your guest with?" The man that is talking sounds like a concierge at a fancy hotel. His voice is aristocratic and demure. I think of the butlers back in Ignis Castle briefly and stuff the memory down into a box behind my steel walls.

"My cousin needs me to watch over her while she recovers from surgery." There's a clinking of coins and Kieran says, "if you could keep it quiet, Kev, that would mean the world."

"Of course, Sir. Anything else?"

"Just your discretion," Kieran says and he pushes past "Kev", the wheels squeaking obnoxiously on the high shine wooden floors. Then we reach a low pile carpeted hallway, and it feels like we've been walking forever when we finally stop and he badges into a door, ushering me through. He shuts the door and pulls the blanket off me. I look up and stare slack jawed at a wide-open luxury living area.

I'm glad I'm sitting down.

I look around at the shiny amenities, the plush furniture and the floor to ceiling windows which display a dark as pitch night sky with a vast ocean lapping at the cliff sides. It must be cloudy because no stars wink in the smoky blackness.

The stars. How long had it been since I'd seen the stars?

I blink and I don't realize a tear has streaked down my face. Not from sadness or any other emotion per se, but from staring wide eyed for several long minutes at the beautiful house Kieran had brought me to.

"Are you alright?" He asks quietly and I stand on shaking wobbly legs, tugging the blanket tighter around my shoulders.

I nod as I continue to stare in amazement.

The open concept room has high, vaulted ceilings with a massive sunroof built into the ceiling and windows that stretch the expanse of one wall. The decor is minimal but elegant, allowing the natural light of the outdoors to highlight the beauty of the space. Beyond the windows, the vast ocean is visible, and I imagine it shines like diamonds in the midday sun. The kitchen opens on the left with a large island at the center and three bar stools sit on the other side. To the right of the kitchen sits a cozy living space with a massive, over-stuffed pale gray sofa and a leather armchair situated around an intricately carved coffee table. A short hallway flanks the living space with a few closed doors that I imagine lead to the bedrooms.

"Rhiannon?" He continues as he places his hand gently between my shoulder blades. "Can I get you anything?"

I look back at him and his beautiful turquoise eyes shine brightly under the low, gilded light.

I swallow against my dry throat, "A shower."

"How was it?" Kieran asks as I emerge from plumes of steam.

"I don't think I've ever been this clean in my entire life." I say honestly as I tuck the fluffy white towel under my armpits. He approaches with a glass of water, and I drink it down in four audible gulps.

He sits the glass under the sink to refill it. Handing it back, I gulp it down again. When the last drop hits my tongue, I set the glass down a touch too hard on the marble counter. He shakes his head, a mirthful smile playing at his lips as he hands me a small pile of clothes.

"I wasn't sure what size you wear, so I just took a guess," He says before he steps out so that I can change. I slip on the black joggers and gray T-shirt, my wet hair curling in all directions, and becoming wilder the drier it gets.

When I step out of the bathroom, Kieran is leaning back with his arm propped on his leg on his bed, looking delicious in his dark jeans and a faded black t-shirt.

"Are you hungry?"

"Always," I say and he stands, holding his hand out to me. I take it and he leads me to the dining room where there's a turkey and salami sandwich with salted chips waiting. I sit down and begin to eat.

Fuck.

It's the best thing I've ever eaten in my whole entire life.

Kieran is watching me with an amused expression as I take large bites of the sandwich, savoring the flavors and groaning like I've never had real food before. After prison food, it sort of feels like it.

"Don't go too fast," he chuckles as he hands me a bottle of water. I take a sip and sit back, eyeing the sandwich like it's going to walk off my plate if I look away.

"Kieran?" I ask and I feel his gaze brush against my skin. I look up to meet his eyes. "What am I doing here? Where am I?"

"I couldn't leave you there," he says softly. "Not in that place."

"How is it possible though? How can I be here? Aren't there cameras and other guards?"

"I took care of it," he says with finality, as if that explained everything.

"How?"

"It's complicated, but I need you to trust that I have it all handled."

"Kieran," I say as I drop my eyes to my hands. "Implicit trust is hard earned with me. It takes more than just my romantic feelings to achieve it. You need to talk to me."

He prods his cheek with his tongue and puts his hands on his hips as his gaze drops to the floor. "The more you know, the more culpability you incur, Rhiannon. At least if we're caught, you can say I forced you."

"I would *never* say that."

"But you *could*. So that you could survive."

"I don't want to survive anymore, Kieran. I want to *live*."

With you. The fleeting thought is like a shooting star across my brain, and it stops me short. My eyes flick up to his and he's staring at me, his lips part as he exhales a soft breath.

He steps closer to me, and I hold up my hand.

"First," I say as he halts his momentum, and I continue. "First, I want you to tell me. Everything. The plan. How you got me here. What our next steps are. I need to know, Kieran."

Implicit trust comes with explicit communication.

He runs his tongue over his front teeth and nods once. He crosses his arms over his broad chest and begins.

"There's a camera in your cell at SolCon. I recorded your feed for the twenty-six hours you were down there. I took that feed and spliced it into several segments, creating a constant video stream looped it to seamlessly start over for an indefinite period of time. I pieced together your movements, so it doesn't look like you're doing the same thing over and over and give it away that it's a recording, but I needed enough material to loop it and make it believable."

I shut my mouth and blink.

That was…really fucking smart.

"And you just…know how to do all that?"

"I have a lot of very peculiar talents, Princess," he says chuckling.

"Peculiar is an interesting choice of words," I say, as I begin to meander around his apartment. I look down at the band on my wrist. There are a series of numbers and then a name. Gwyneth Haley. "So apparently, I'm your cousin Gwyneth now? Kinda gross that I wanna bone my cousin."

He laughs as I round the island towards the kitchen, dragging my fingers across the smooth marble countertops, marveling at the colorful backsplash that looks like a mural of sea glass with pops of blues, greens, and opaque whites. It reminds me of Kieran's eyes. "What other peculiarities are you hiding, *cous*?"

He laughs softly again, and I feel his gaze follow me as I peruse his grand apartment, meandering into the entertainment room and scoping out the back wall with books and trinkets lining the wall.

"I speak three different languages," he says and I nod as I touch the bindings of some of the books. "I've been to every continent on Elysia."

"Not Altas?" I ask, not looking at him while I continue my passive search for nothing in particular.

"No. Not Altas. Although I'll need to say it to keep up appearances. To me, it's always been Elysia."

Good answer. I think to myself, but it's heard all the same as his mouth twitches at the corner with the ghost of a smile.

"And for the most peculiar of the peculiarities. Why me?"

His head hitches to the side as he surveys me with his brows arched. "Why you what?"

"Why do you want to help me? Why do you want to do all this and risk your job and your life? Why do you…do you…"

Want…me? I finish in my head.

He straightens up and uncrosses his arms. He licks his lips as he takes a few steps towards me.

"Are you implying that I have a choice?"

I scoff and lean onto my hip. "Of course you have a choice! You have…all the choices. You just…chose kind of…wrong I guess."

"And why is that?" He asks, sliding his hands into his pockets as he steps closer.

"Because I'm dangerous."

"So am I."

"Because I've killed people."

"So have I."

"Because I have secrets that I can't share."

He clicks his tongue and says, "So do I."

He is so close now, crowding into me and I peer up at his tropical ocean eyes, feeling my fight begin to bleed out onto the floor. But I have one more…

"Because…I'm a powerful dragon."

"Oh Princess," he says tucking a wild curl behind my ear, "that…is my favorite part."

29
EILIDH

The inmate behind the serving counter in the chow hall this evening slops a large scoop of chili into my bowl and it splatters out onto my clothes.

I spare it a single glance and then glare back at Fawn who meets my stare with equal ire.

"Enjoy," she says, her voice dripping with sarcasm and a saccharine smile that I'd like to rip from her doll-like face.

"Fuck you, too," I deadpan and walk away. There's an audible gasp behind me, but I've lost the will to give a shit. I sit down at an empty table and keep one eye on the door as I bite into the stale bread on my tray.

I said I adore all breads, but this blasphemous thing is more rock than bread, so I don't think it counts.

Dipping it into the chili, I try another bite and stick my tongue out as the gritty texture of the chili mixes with the stale bread and creates a sludge that's hard to swallow.

"My sentiments exactly the first time I tried the chili here." Xanth drops his tray beside me, noticeably absent is his bowl of chili and instead he's grabbed a few slices of bread and loaded them with a few packets of peanut butter that are always out and available.

He takes a seat and his knee brushes against mine, sending a burst of electricity across my skin. I make an effort to move away from his touch as Cadmyr sits down along with the twins in front of us.

I've been ignoring Xanth for days now. Yet another unfortunate reality of prison is that I'm forced to be around the same group every single day and I could only hide for so long. Later that day, he found me in my cell and spent the entire night trying to talk to me. Even one of the inmates yelled at him to shut the fuck up at one point but his stubborn ass continued on anyway.

He's been blocked from my mind, but I feel him throughout the day, poking and caressing the thick walls of flame, seeking entrance that's never granted.

I say nothing and continue to bite into the vile food, using it as an excuse to remain silent while the four dragons carry on about the worst things they've ever eaten.

After a particularly revolting story from Tatsu about a snail mucus and goat cheese incident that he compared to the cheese noodles they served us the other day, I gulp down the last of my water and stand to leave.

The moment my feet hit the ground, Xanth is standing behind me, ever the persistent stalker, ready to follow wherever I go next. Since the day I ran from him after he fucked Lumara right in front of me, he hasn't let me out of his sight. He's even gone as far as requesting latrine duty when that was my assignment for the day.

No one requests latrine duty.

Ever.

I think the guards found it funny, so they agreed and handed him a mop and bucket filled with bleach water.

Every. Single. Day.

He requests to go to whichever station I'm assigned to. I even saw him paying Nova in the halls when she stared at him like he'd lost his mind after he asked to join me on lunch duty. She told him it wasn't a two-person job and so he paid her off so he could stand beside me, and we alternated placing food on all the perplexed astrals' faces.

I've gotten quite a bit of hate because of it.

The deer shifters have named me their enemy number one. A dragon I'd only seen in passing named Adalinda blew smoke in my face and asked why I needed a bodyguard when she bumped into me during a drill and Xanth shoved her into a wall so hard it cracked. The guards scoff at him but whatever Xanth is paying them with, keeps them from stopping it.

From the moment I wake up until the moment I fall asleep, all I smell, all I feel, all I see, is Xanth.

Yet I haven't given in.

I've taken his advice and distanced myself as much as I possibly can. I haven't spoken a
single word to him, I've kept up my shields and I go about my days acting as though he doesn't exist.

He can't *exist to me.*

Otherwise, I'd have to admit the crushing pain that squeezed my soul when I watched him slide inside of Lumara. Her moans still echo in my brain and play on repeat along with all the other females he's fucked since I got here. I hear them constantly. Taunting me. Teasing me. Reminding me that he has never cared about me, and I should not care about him.

That even if this inescapable draw that I feel to him *is* the mating bond, he doesn't want me. Made clear in every word he's ever spoken aloud and by his actions up until the past few days.

I won't be fooled into thinking that things have changed again.

He came out of SolCon a broken and tortured soul. I wanted to catch him as he fell. I wanted to be the one who helped him heal and talk about what his dragon had said to me during the fight with Ryker.

"...Mine..." He had growled.

Now, I'm not sure if that was real or just a figment of my imagination.

One thing I know for certain is that Xanth Vulcan will never want me.

I'm lying in my bed, thoughts spiraling out of control over 'what ifs.'

Rhiannon is still missing.

This is the second night that she hasn't been in her cell since letting me know that she was worried she could be in trouble.

Guilt rips through me.

She's been trying to get us out and in turn, she may have been caught. I've tried reaching her several times, but she feels too far for the connection to reach. I was able to reach Xanth while he was in SolCon but perhaps it was a freak accident. I can't be sure.

Whatever the case, I'm unable to reach her and it's driving me insane.

What if she's the next astral the Warden puts before us all and maims? What if the white coats have taken her and I never see her again?

Fear twists my stomach, and I work to steady my breathing.

She's fine.

She has to be fine, because if she's not…

I'm not sure what I will do.

In the last few months, she has weaseled her way into my heart and if there is a possibility of her being gone forever…

A stark reality slaps me upside the head.

Rhiannon is my friend. I love her.

Bile stings the back of my throat, and I jump from the top bunk just in time to vomit into the rusty toilet.

"Eilidh, are ye alright?" Xanth asks. I can tell by the nearness of his voice that he's pressed against the bars as close as he can get. "Do ye need m–" he pauses. "Do ye need help?"

I don't answer. Another wave of nausea washes over me, and I retch again.

How could I have let this happen?

I was supposed to learn the layout, gather intel for my mother and then return home.

Get in, get out.

Yet here I am, lying in bed and worried *literally* sick about my cellmate who I've just realized has become my friend. That doesn't even begin to touch on the fact that she is a dragon, and my mother will likely murder her the moment she sees her.

If she's not already dead.

My stomach is empty, so I dry heave into the rotting bowl and wipe sweat from my brow.

"Please, talk te me. I can feel yer panic and it's driving Az–" another pregnant pause. "My dragon, insane. He needs te know ye're ok." His hand is stretched out to reach my cell and I can see his fingers in the reflection of the metal sink above my head. "*I need te know ye're ok.*"

I slump against the wall beside the toilet, still refusing to speak. My beast keens and presses against me as tears stream down my face.

Xanth's voice is a whisper now as my eyes grow heavy. "Come back te me, Little Dove"

The next day, I'm sitting in the rec hall near the small shelf of books, avoiding Xanth who's been lifting weights while staring at me for the past hour. He makes my mouth water when he stares at me like that so I've done all I can to prevent any kind of eye contact.

I've just finished flipping through a bodice ripper when Major Haley waltzes through the door. He sets his sights on me, and I tense.

Rhiannon didn't come back last night. If anyone knows where she's been taken, it's this motherfucker.

"Where *is* she?" I growl low in my chest and dip my chin as I stand to get in his face.

Or at least his chest. The...lower part of it anyway. Why are all these assholes so tall?

One of the downsides to being five foot two is you can't really get in many people's faces. Thankfully, I've developed other intimidation tactics.

I grab hold of his balls and pull him in tightly to me when he doesn't answer right away. He jerks in response, eyes widening and I see a bob in his throat as he swallows, hard.

"I said, *where the fuck is she*?" I'm whispering between my teeth, but he grunts and turns a shade paler.

"She's safe." The words are pained as they breathe past his lips. "I have her and she is safe. That's what I came to tell you."

I release him and he exhales heavily.

"Why didn't you start with that?" I'm not immune to his looks but I couldn't care less about his kaleidoscopic eyes when my friend has been missing for over two days.

He looks around the room pointedly. "There are ears everywhere. Let's find somewhere we can talk." He takes me by the wrist and leads me out of the room into the hall where a small alcove sits hidden in plain sight. We tuck ourselves into the space and he hangs his head low to talk quietly.

"Rhiannon has been with me in my apartment. Cain ordered that she go to SolCon, so I wired the cameras and took her back to my room. She'll be back tonight, but I needed to tell you she is safe and that we've found a way."

"Found a way for what?" I ask.

"I got my hands on something. Let's just say that the Warden's obsession has been a very bad girl and flew a little too close to the sun. Balor will lose his godsdamned mind."

I nod. "You mean the sex tape? What does his meltdown have to do with me?"

He taps my nose with a calloused finger. "That, dear dragon, is how I'm going to get you all out."

I stare at him.

"What do you mean 'all of us?' Me, you and Rhi?" I pause. "And stop calling me a fucking dragon, I'm a phoenix dammit."

His eyes go wide. "M-my apologies. I guess I haven't seen one in–" he hesitates, and I note that he changes his initial thought which only makes me burn with suspicion. "I've never met a phoenix before."

My eyes narrow on him, but he doesn't crack.

"Anyway," he continues, "you, Rhiannon and Xanth will be out of here soon. I promise."

My blood runs cold.

"Xanth? He's not part of the plan."

"Rhiannon made me swear to get him out too. I need you to tell him because I'm pretty sure he'd rip my head off with the way he's been staring at us while we've been talking."

Awareness prickles my spine, and I peek around Kieran's bicep to see Xanth standing a few feet away with his fists held tight at his sides and death in the endless depths of his eyes.

"I'm not really on speaking terms with him at the moment," I say.

Not that I ever was, I suppose.

"Can I rely on you to give him the message? I just need you both to be ready. You'll know what to do when the time comes."

I hesitate for a moment and then huff. "Yeah, I can talk to him."

"Thank you." He squeezes the top of my arm and turns to leave.

Just as he takes a step, Xanth rushes him, his face an inch from Kieran's.

"I can smell the bane on ye," he seethes and I have no idea what the fuck he's talking about. "Ye can't fool me, asshole."

The two males stand at nearly the same height and it's like watching two titans battle for dominance.

"Stand down, Inmate," Kieran barks.

"Major Haley, sir," I say, breaking their deadly staring contest. "Can Xan– I mean, inmate 2465 and I be excused to a meeting room, please?"

Kieran eyes Xanth one more time, both males are still tense, but he takes the high road and backs up a step. "Right. You two, follow me." He slips into the role of guard so well that even I have trouble deciphering his true allegiance. I only hope that whatever he has with Rhiannon is strong enough to guarantee our escape.

Xanth and I fall in step behind Kieran, and I jab him with my elbow when I smell smoke wafting from him.

He looks at me, and his eyes visibly soften.

Major Haley walks us to a room with only a single table and chair.

"Interrogation room. Soundproof." He stares at me pointedly and nods, then eyes Xanth with suspicion. "You've got fifteen minutes. Make it count." Then he closes the door, and I'm left with a fuming dragon at my back.

I shift to the side and spin so that I can face him. Taking a step back, I give myself some additional room to breathe. They removed his iron mask yesterday and I can see his chiseled jaw and full lips and the glint of his piercing which only makes me sway. His scent is everywhere. It's intoxicating and my eyes keep fluttering as his warmth seeps into the cracked pieces of my chest.

He doesn't want you. I remind myself.

"We only have a few minutes, so I'll make this brief," I say. "I–"

"Are ye fuckin' him?" Xanth cuts me off. Fire dances in his blue irises like a promise of pain to anyone he deems worthy.

I rear back as though he physically struck me. "Are you fucking kidding me?"

"I asked ye a question." He steps closer to me. "Are ye fuckin' him?"

I take a breath, trying to calm myself but it doesn't work. I inhale again but the oxygen only serves as fuel to the flames, and my festering rage explodes.

I bring both of my palms up and shove him with all my strength. He staggers backwards but remains standing.

"FUCK YOU!" I scream. "How many females have you fucked since you've been here, Xanth? How many?" My fury barrels out of me and hot tears streak my face. "I bet you have no idea. You have fucked your way through half the colony of inmates in this godsforsaken prison, taken a female right in front of me while my soul cracked and yet you have the *audacity* to accuse *me* of sleeping with someone?" I grasp the chair at my side and throw it into the wall, splintering the legs. "You are an *asshole*, and I *should* fuck someone else so that I don't have to cry myself to sleep every night knowing that I almost gave myself to someone like *you*."

I'm sobbing rivers of tears, and I can feel my phoenix rising. Massive white feathered wings burst from my shoulder blades and talons jut from my fingertips as Solara works her way up my spine.

"No," I say between watery gasps. "I'm not fucking him. But I can promise you that I will find someone else, Xanth. I will deny what's between us until my last breath if I have to because you *do not* deserve me, and my love does *not* come free." My body shakes and the space where my heart beats feels void and empty.

Xanth.

Fucking Xanth.

He looks at me with wonder in his eyes. He rakes his gaze over my wings, hunger darkening his eyes and I retract my talons. As soon as they've disappeared, he's on me.

Tongues, teeth and nails digging into skin. He kisses me like it's the first time and my tears continue streaming down my face. He moves his mouth to lick them from my cheeks, and I cry even harder.

"Ye're right, Little Dove. I d'nae deserve ye." His hands are everywhere. In my hair and on my ribs. They stroke the sides of my breasts and then grip my thighs to pull me up his chest where our lips meet again, and he devours me.

He leans over the table with me tucked against his chest, laying me down. He doesn't come up for air as he presses his body on top of mine, and I feel him brush against my mind. This time, I let him in.

Our thoughts collide and I can hear him chanting.

...So fucking beautiful...So fucking...Mine...I'll spend forever proving mahself te ye...

I let out a moan that morphs and ends on a high pitch note when he grabs one side of my neck and bites down.

Hard.

Something primal springs to life within me and I grind my hips against him as he continues to bite and lick the space between my neck and shoulder, marking me.

...Ye're all I want, Little Dove...

My hips grind against him again and his face moves lower. I grip his hair and his lips skate down the center of my chest, inhaling my scent.

...So fucking good...Ye smell like the sky...

His tongue laves across the underside of my breast, and I'm lost. No thoughts other than how good he feels consume my mind. It's completely and utterly euphoric.

He sucks and scrapes his teeth against the flesh of my breast and then I feel a piercing sting as he clamps down on my nipple.

I suck in a breath, letting out a pleasured scream that has him growling.

I don't know when it happened, but my clothes are undone and his fingers begin to trace circles on the tops of my thighs, eliciting goose bumps to pebble across my skin.

The tip of his finger circles closer to my center and I'm panting through the pain of his bite.

"Please," I beg him.

That's all it takes.

He shoves two fingers inside of me and sucks my nipple deep into his mouth. My back arches off the table and I start to convulse as my pleasure catapults through my blood.

He curves his fingers inside of me and strokes a place I didn't even know existed. I begin mumbling unintelligible nonsense as he works me with his fingers, my hips rolling against his hand. His head moves lower, kissing down my stomach and licking along the line between my hips. I writhe and plead for him.

"Keep going, oh gods, yes, just like that."

"Mmmm…" He growls and it's the same mixed voice that I heard the night he went to SolCon. "Say mah name."

"Xanth," I breathe, "Gods please Xanth I need *more*."

"That's mah good girl," he purrs. "Now come fer me again, Little Dove."

His tongue circles my clit as he slides in another finger, filling me completely, and it sends me careening over the edge for the second time.

I'm moaning his name, praying to ancient gods and crying as he wrings every ounce of pleasure from my body. My thighs tremble around his head and it only encourages him to continue.

"Xanth!" I shriek, "I can't, I can't." I push at his head. He lifts his free hand and wraps it around my wrists, pinning them to my stomach.

"Ye can, and ye will," he says in a low sultry voice, gliding against that spot inside of me as my walls clench around him. "This little cunt is mine, and I want te hear ye sing."

A loud knock sounds.

Fuck!

I scramble up, but Xanth doesn't let me get far. He doesn't even allow me to fix my clothes as I spill the plan to him half naked and panting. He watches me with hooded hungry eyes as the details of Kieran's plans fall from my lips. His hands never stop roving over my naked body, like he wants to commit the feel of me to memory.

"We're leaving," I finally say after relaying everything I know to him. "Soon." I take a resolved breath. Steadying for what comes next. "Then you won't have to see me ever again." I shrug my jumpsuit back over my shoulder and cover my breasts, feeling far too exposed.

Xanth rumbles. "I d'nae want that. I want *ye*, Eilidh."

I huff a laugh, unable to find the fire that I entered this room with. "No, you don't. You are going to be free, Xan. You'll get to go home, to the *only female you've ever loved.*" I throw his words back at him. "Don't fill my head with lies."

On that final note, I slip from his arms, and the door opens. Major Haley stares at me with a knowing look and I dip my chin.

"Goodbye, Xanth," I whisper over my shoulder

"Eilidh, no, Let me exp–"

I race down the hall, filled with conflicted emotions, my body still buzzing with my release and a bruised heart.

I will not fall for this again.

I'm going home.

30
RHIANNON

I wake up with the sun in my eyes and it scares the hell out of me at first. Once situational awareness sinks in and I realize where I am…and what planet I'm on, I sink into the soft bed and let the sun continue to stain my eyes and warm my skin.

The sun. Gods, the *sun*.

It feels like life and warmth, embraces, flowers, trees, and movement. It's everything. I lay there like a lizard sunbathing and soaking in the golden light. I stretch my arms over my head and sit up.

How long was I asleep? When did I fall asleep?

The last thing I remember was Kieran having me finish the sandwich and lay down. He insisted on sleeping on the couch, which I fought hard against and won when he snuggled in beside me. He isn't here next to me this morning…but then again. I look at the nightstand on the other side of his bed where there's a clock. Flickering red digital numbers read 15:45.

Of course, his clocks would be in a 24-hour format. I do some mental math and realize it's 3:45 pm.

He's still at work.

I have some time to…I don't know. Poke around? Am I allowed to do that in his apartment?

Maybe I need to make a checklist of things I should do so I don't go crazy.

Yeah. Yeah, that makes sense.

First on the list…*holy shit I need to pee*. I make it to the toilet just in the nick of time and luxuriate on the smooth porcelain seat. No cracks, no leaks, and I'm pretty sure the seat is heated. The bidet scared the hell outta me but after I relaxed it was nice.

First item, done.

Next on the list...lunch. Wait, maybe dinner? *Should I eat before he gets home? I could make him dinner.*

That's it!

That's number two on the list.

I walk towards the kitchen and open the silver French doors to an ornate fridge.

I don't really have any expectations about what I think I'm going to find in Kieran's fridge, so when I open the doors, I take it all in with an open mind.

He has a lot of bottled water and orange juice. His vegetable drawers are full and so are the meat drawers. Like, a LOT of meat. I counted four rib eyes and four T-Bone steaks, six chicken breasts, eight racks of lamb chops, four dozen eggs, two whole racks of pork and beef spareribs and, last but not least, I giggle as I look at the lone cube of tofu that sits ironically in the corner staring at me, both of us wondering why the hell it's in his fridge in the first place.

I suppose it's a good thing there are lots of vegetables.

"Okay, so...steak. I'm gonna make him steak."

I've done this hundreds of times while camping with Fianna and our father.

This was gonna be great.

It was not great.

I couldn't figure out how to work anything and I burned the shit out of the steak. The oven got *way* too hot so the bread I tried to bake burned as well. To top it all off Kieran walked into the apartment right as the steak caught fire because the burner was on too high, and the flame lit on the oil.

"What were you trying to do?" He chuckles as he puts out the flambéed ribeye with an extinguisher.

I blow my frizzy disheveled hair out of my face and say as nonchalantly as I can muster, "I...was making you dinner." I shrug with one shoulder. "Surprise!" I say halfheartedly and he arches a brow.

"You nearly burned the place down."

"Well, I figured you'd enjoy dinner and a show."

He smiles wide and laughs, my cheeks flush red as I watch him. It was worth every stressful second to see him laugh and smile like this.

"You care if I take over on the dinner front?"

"By all means, Hot Stuff," I say, tossing the charred steak in the garbage and placing the cast iron skillet in the sink where it sizzles and spits from the intense heat.

Thirty minutes later and the doorbell rings. Kieran stands from the couch and tips the pizza delivery kid before flopping back onto the seat beside me.

"I hope you like pepperoni," he says as he offers me a paper plate and I grab two large slices.

"Do you know how long it's been since I've had pizza?" I ask while shoveling a slice in my mouth and my eyes roll back. "Where did you order this from anyway? I didn't think Prism had helicopter pizza delivery guys."

"Yeah, I suppose the pizza in the prison kitchen isn't all that good," he chuckles as he pops half a slice into his mouth. "We have a food court here on the guards' floor. There are a few pizza places that'll deliver to our rooms."

"They serve pizza in the chow hall? And you have a fucking food court up here?" I ask, my face incredulous.

"Well, the inmate pizza is... it's a...version of it." He stuffs the rest of the slice in his mouth.

I scoff and think for a second. "The flat bread thing? With the red sauce? That's supposed to be pizza?"

He nods and then we both start laughing.

"Gods, you know it's bad when they can't get something like pizza right," I say laughing while I stuff in another bite.

Kieran looks down at my bare legs and then back up to me. "So did you not want to wear pants today or?"

"Is wearing pants a rule in your apartment?"

He wipes his mouth with a napkin and swallows. "On the contrary, I much prefer this."

I smile as I realize he must not know *how* bare I really am under his T-shirt.

He walks over to a long cabinet and presses on the door, popping it open. He steps into a hidden compartment and returns with a bottle. "So, it's been a while since you had pizza. But how long has it been since you've had this?"

I exaggerate fainting. "Oh gods, wine? Too long!"

"Figured as much," he says as he pulls down two long stem crystal wine glasses and then pours in the bright cranberry red wine. "Don't know how you feel about Pinot Noir, but-"

"I'm sure I'll love it," I reply, even though I really don't know the difference. I just know there are many versions of red and white wine and they all kind of taste the same, to my mother's shame and chagrin. I think she hoped her eldest daughter would be well versed in viticulture, but I wanted to hunt deer and punch things a lot more than gossip and sip wine while holding court.

Kieran hands me the glass and I take a healthy sip. By healthy, I mean I throw it back like a shot and he sputters as he chokes on a laugh.

"Shit Rhiannon."

"What? Isn't that how you're supposed to drink it?"

He wipes his mouth and laughs out, "Well it's certainly 'a' way to drink it. You won't be getting the most out of the experience drinking it like that though."

"An experience?" I say quizzically, offering my cup for a refill. He obliges and fills the bottom of the glass as I hop up on the counter and cross my legs. "Okay, Major Hot Stuff. Show me 'the experience' of drinking wine."

His eyes flit over my legs briefly before he leans against the counter and begins vigorously swirling the wine in his glass. "First you swirl it, like this."

I copy him, making a tornado of cranberry red in the belly of my glass. "What does this do, exactly?" I ask as I try not to get too aggressive and spill it everywhere.

"It opens up the wine."

"Didn't you do that already?"

He bobs his head smiling, "Fair point. What this does is allows the wine to breathe, and lets some of the alcohol vapor dissipate, allowing air pockets into the wine to bring out different flavors."

I keep swirling my wine with him until he stops. "Next step is to check its legs."

My lips purse as I watch him look at the sides of his glass. Without looking back at me he begins to explain, "Legs are what's created after you aerate. The drops run down the sides of the glass and if the wine is more tannic or viscous, it'll look like little red legs."

"Hm," I say as I look at my glass up against the light. "I think my wine might be disabled."

"What?" He asks as his eyes flit up to me looking into my glass.

"It doesn't have legs."

He smiles and pinches the bridge of his nose. "That was…so bad."

"What? I thought it was clever." I shrug and then put the glass to my lips, but he stops me.

"We aren't done yet, Princess," he says, his tone low and sultry with a hint of edge that has my thighs tightening. My eyes flash as warmth begins to bloom in my limbs.

"I didn't realize there were so many steps," I say as he continues to watch me. He puts the glass over his nose and inhales. My brows pinch and he gestures for me to copy, so I do…even though it looks ridiculous.

"What do you smell?"

I smell the wine, and I find that it smells like, "Wine. Red wine."

He smiles wide and laughs in that way that makes my insides turn to mush.

"Well, you're not wrong, but look for specific features," he explains and sniffs his wine again. "For instance, I smell pepper and bing cherry."

"Huh." I look back at my glass and inhale again. "Okay, *maybe* pepper."

"Now try the wine. But sip it and swirl it around your mouth, coat your tongue with it."

I nibble on my lip as I watch him sip the wine before swirling it in his mouth. Nina purrs in my belly as I imagine other parts of my body he could taste like that. His eyes flit up to mine as I put the glass to my lips and sip, swirling the wine in my mouth, letting it sluice over my tongue.

The pepper is there and the tart cherry, but also something else. My eyes stay closed as I try to picture it in my mind.

"What do you taste?"

"I can't think of the word but…"

…*Show me…* He pushes gently into my mind and it's like a physical touch that makes me gasp, the warmth in my limbs flashes with light and my cheeks surge with color.

I picture a hot summer day, after the sun has baked the pavement all afternoon, the heat hovers in thick waves as dark gunmetal gray storm clouds blanket the sky, granting a respite from the scorching rays. The clouds open, releasing thick drops of rain. They hit the pavement and turn to steam. The scent of each drop wafts in the air, pluming in a cloud of rich scent as the rain falls in earnest.

Kieran's sigh is shuttered and seductive. "Petrichor."

I open my eyes, and his glorious teal eyes watch me as he licks the wine from his lips.

I uncross my legs. "I want to try something," I exclaim softly, straightening up on the kitchen counter.

"Okay." He straightens a bit too. I take another sip of the wine and set down the glass. I pull him over to me as I part my knees and situate him between them.

"Take a sip of your wine," I say in quiet demand as I keep my eyes locked on his. He complies and takes a sip from his glass, swirling it in his mouth. "Swallow," I say softly and I watch his throat bob. I run my fingers down his jaw and press my thumb over his bottom lip, pulling it down and he opens for me. I lean in and run my tongue over his teeth.

The groan he emits is guttural and predatory, as he grips my thighs and pulls me towards him so that my bare sex is pressed against his hips. He leans into me, covering my mouth with his but I pull back.

"Now wait a second," I interject, and he growls as I press my hips into his. "I thought we were tasting."

"You want me to-"

"No, I'm the one learning here. I learned what the wine tastes like by itself, but I want to taste," I say as I lick over his lips again and he chases my mouth but stay just out of reach, teasing, "what it tastes like on you."

His eyes darken as he grabs his glass and takes another swirling sip. After he swallows, I grab his neck and press my mouth to his, swiping my tongue over his.

Warm spices, fresh cut wood, wild tart blueberries, freshwater springs after the snow melts, the smell of rain and the static of lighting before it strikes.

His fingers press into my thighs as I flood the images and descriptions of his taste into his brain.

He breaks our kiss and presses his forehead to mine. "I like your way better."

I laugh and wrap my legs around his waist as he lifts me off the counter by my ass, his fingers caressing the bare skin underneath.

"You aren't-"

"Take me to bed, Kieran," I demand as I grind into his hips while his big hands grip my backside, and he walks with me through the door to his bedroom.

He lays me on my back as he slowly lifts the oversized T-shirt up over my hips, exhaling when the fabric brushes over my stomach and skims the bottom of my breasts. Once the cotton has brushed over my nipples, he leans down and grazes his teeth on the underside of my left breast, swiping his tongue over the abused flesh, laving over my tightly constricted nipple and I arch into his mouth. His kisses travel down each of my ribs, the flat plane of my stomach, the valley of flesh between my hips until his warm mouth presses onto my mound. I grip the sheets in my fists as his tongue dips into my core and I exhale, crying out as he swipes over my aching swollen clit. His hands skate up my sides and gently massage my breasts and I start to pant.

"You know what you taste like, Princess?" His voice vibrates along my sensitive slick sex, and I whimper at the sensation.

I shake my head, not daring to look down at the heated gaze that I feel burning through me as he watches me from below, knowing I'll crash as soon as I look.

"You," he mutters low and then flicks his tongue over my clit as I move my hips down, trying to catch more of his mouth. "Taste like dark chocolate, and when I dream of flying." He starts as he teases my entrance. "Like cold water in summer, and the rush of falling."

He threads his fingers into mine and I grip them tight like they are the anchor holding me to reality as he mercilessly swipes his tongue over my clit until the sweat is beading on my back and brow.

"Kieran, I'm-" I pant as I open my eyes and see his turquoise eyes burning over the mound of my core and I come undone as my entire body contracts and I fly apart. His fingers grip mine as I cry out, arching my back as he continues to lave over my drenched sex. My awareness scatters and comes back together again. I sit up and grab his face in my hands, pulling him to my mouth. The tang of my climax still fresh on his slick mouth as I unbuckle his belt.

He toils through each exhaustive button on his shirt. I pull down his trousers to reveal his black boxer-briefs and marvel at his substantial erection. I dip my fingers into his waistband and gently glide them down until his cock springs free. I look up at his parted mouth and glowing ocean eyes as I grasp his length, stroke down his velvet skin and lick over the sensitive crown.

He threads his fingers through my hair, massaging my scalp as I take him all the way to the back of my throat, his hips jerking slightly as I salivate and constrict around his throbbing member. I pull back and look up at him again. His features are dark and heated, strained like he held back from bucking into me. The teal glow of his irises are shadowed, reminding me of dark storm clouds over the ocean until his eyes flutter closed. His head lolls back as I jut my tongue out flicking over his root, my eyes watering as I gag. I begin pulling back and let the tips of my teeth ghost over his sensitive skin.

"Fuck," he hisses as his eyes fly back open to look down at me and they look…different. A light-yellow halo peeks out from the stained-glass mosaic of blue/green. Before I can marvel further, he picks me up and throws me to the center of the bed. He stands at the edge, watching me like a wolf moving in for the kill.

Gods, I want it. I want him to devour me. Tear me apart piece by piece. Tear into my skin and drink from me until I fade into nothing.

I lean back onto my forearms and slowly open my legs, displaying my cunt like a swollen succulent prize. A dark and fervent invitation for my predator to take.

And take.

And take.

He exhales a low growl and crawls over me, until his body hovers over mine, his hard length a breath away from my core. His lips glide over my jaw and then finds my mouth, thrusting his tongue inside and I hold him there, intertwining my tongue with his and I arch my hips, feeling his cock slide along my wet sex. We both moan and whine at the sensation. He lowers his hips to press into mine and I hold my breath.

"Are you sure?" He asks softly. The honesty and concern in his voice nearly breaks me in two. Despite his raging desire, his most basic instincts practically devouring his mind and body, he still yields to my consent.

As if I would deny him. As if I would ever want anything else. As if being completely destroyed by this male wasn't the one thing I never realized I always wanted.

"Yes, I'm sure," I say clearly, as I reach down, grasping his thick cock and lining him up with my entrance. His jaw clenches as he watches me closely.

"Tell me to stop if it's too much." His voice skitters across my skin and my flesh beads as it constricts in response.

Then he slowly presses, his crown breaching my entrances and the stretch…

Fuck. FUCK. I suck my lips in as I inhale a sharp breath and he stills, his eyes never leaving mine.

I exhale, letting the intense pinch and pressure wane. I gently kiss his mouth and say, "Keep going."

"Are you-"

"Yes," I interject with certainty.

"I don't want to hurt you," he says, his eyes now filled with concern.

I pull him close to me and whisper over his mouth as I look into those beautiful, worried eyes, "But I *want* you to. Keep going," I say as I open my legs wider and his chest rumbles in a low growl. He advances further and the sharp pinch and pressure surges up my spine making me gasp. I squeeze my eyes shut.

"Rhiannon," he whispers gently, wiping my hair from my forehead.

Nina growls low and slithers up my spine, spitting flames through my body and heating my blood further. I begin to move my hips, circling them so that he slides gently along my walls. The sharp pain begins to dull, and it's…good. *Really* good. I sigh as the pleasure begins to build with the pinch and pressure of his invading cock.

"Keep…keep going Kieran," I whine as I thread my fingers through his hair and he dips his mouth to mine, pressing his chest against me as he gently strokes further inside. The pinch builds but the movement of my hips mixes the pain with delicious pleasure.

"More," I beg softly, and he slides a little more, kissing down my jaw, and nuzzling his face into my neck.

"F-fuck," he utters so low and quiet I barely hear. My mind begins to spin, and I feel his mind spinning in time with mine. He pushes in further and I mewl softly as he nears sheathing his entire length. I continue to move my hips, the slide building upon something remarkable.

"M-more, Kieran, please…p-please." I continue to implore him, panting as the mounting pressure begins to unravel the tapestry of everything that I am, unweaving all I know until I'm a mess of color and thread. He slides his hips forward and bottoms out into me and I cry out, tensing my legs at his flanks. He meets my eyes, a silent but pointed check in and I nod. He kisses my lips and pulls away to kiss my neck, inhaling sharply and the cool air is stark against the heat between our bodies.

"Gods, Rhiannon. The way you feel-" he starts as he retracts back a tiny bit and then presses in again. The sensation is still sharp but it's waning and becoming impossibly good the more I move my hips. "You're so-"

"I'm so?" I breathe as his hands reach down to squeeze my waist.

"Tight," he exhales and it sounds almost exasperated as I run my heels down his low back until they flex on his tight ass.

"Does it hurt? Am I-"

"Fuck no, Rhiannon," he says clearly. He pulls back and slides in again, the pinch and pressure less this time. "It's incredible. I'm never coming back from this."

He grazes his teeth over my neck as I circle my hips, a sparkling heat, electric and bright, begins to mount and build at the base of my spine, and as I move, it begins to crackle its way up my back.

"I-I need to-" he sputters as he continues to move slowly, rhythmically, toiling to keep the pain from creeping back.

But I want him unhinged. Wild. Unleashed. I want that sun that hid behind the ocean of his eyes to blaze and burn everything to the ground in a flurry of righteous magnificence.

"Do it," I say arching my hips up to him, my legs splaying wide, I reach my arms overhead and grip the sheets.

"I don't want to hurt you." His breath is warm as it brushes against the shell of my ear, making me shiver.

Nina hisses low in my chest, the heat flares as sulfur and fire licks at my throat. "Fuck me like I know you want to, my wild hearted male."

His head lifts to peer down at me, and that corona of yellow is devouring the ocean of teal, slowly creeping its way to the center where his pupils are blown wide. He's panting and I swear his canines have sharpened as an animalistic growl rips from his chest. He grabs a fistful of my hair and pulls it back as his hips snap hard into mine and *fuck*.

FUCK.

It's sharp and electric as it catapults me forward and I moan with his increased pace. His tongue laves over my collar bone as his canines cut into my skin. His thrusts are merciless as they drive harder and faster into me. I'm sighing and groaning, and I can hear Nina baying in my chest.

It's so good. Fuck, it's too good. One of his hands roots my hip in place on the bed as the other holds my head back by my hair and the slide of his cock inside of me is tearing me apart in the best way.

"Mine," an otherworldly voice snarls from his throat as he fucks me with reckless abandon.

The words have me hurtling to an edge I've never been to, leaning over a chasm where the void is dark and everlasting. He's pulling me, tugging me over.

"Fuck, oh fuck," I cry as he pistons into my aching core.

"Mine," he repeats and the muscles in my body begin to flutter as he pulls my knees back, opening me wide to him and my eyes pop open as I am suddenly thrust over the edge while he drives into me.

I scream his name as he fucks me through my free-fall. I dig my fingers into the skin of his back, and he groans even louder, his hips jerking as his cock pulses. My skin burns where he clamps his teeth down over my shoulder as he roars and spills out his release, the warmth of it fills me and as he continues to push into me, it overflows.

His movements slow and our chests expand out of sync as our skin slides together. His face is still on my neck, and I press my mouth to his ear. I feel Nina purr at the back of my throat as we both whisper. "You…are *mine*. All mine. My Wild Heart. My Kieran." My chest burns like a brand as the words fall from my lips, like paint strokes of flame covering my skin.

He groans and presses up onto his forearms so he's looking at me with waning gold around the turquoise waters of his eyes.

"I'm yours, Rhiannon," he says in a rasping voice that has my walls clenching around his still sheathed cock. His eyes flutter as he groans at the sensation. He continues in that lower, more primal sounding voice. "And you, Rhiannon…*are mine*."

My mother told me a lot of things growing up. She explained a lot of the etiquette around being a lady in an ancient court of dragons. The responsibility of carrying yourself with dignity, honor, and respect. Wearing clothing that matched your station and speaking properly. To always, *always* be thinking one step ahead of everyone else. To be cunning, strategic, unyielding, and ruthless in our tac.

It would have been nice of her to mention what it's like for a female to lose her maidenhead.

Because fuck. *Fuuuck.*

I wake up and I have a second heartbeat between my legs. Kieran snakes his arms around my waist and pulls me to his bare chest, he takes a deep breath and the rush of it displaces my hair.

His voice is gravelly with sleep as he speaks. "How bad is it?"

I smile as I put my hand over his and thread my fingers through his. "Well, my pussy has a pulse. So, there's that."

"I'm so sorry," he says, and he pulls me closer to his chest where I turn to face him.

He takes my breath away with how beautiful he is as the sun hits his soft bronzed skin and untamed copper hair. His glorious springtime eyes shine like two Mediterranean stars as they flit back and forth between mine. He pushes my curls out of my face and tucks them behind my ear.

"Dragons heal fast," I say, nudging his nose with mine. "By breakfast, I'll be right as rain."

It's a stretch, but remarkably I could already feel the ache receding as I wrap my leg around his hip feeling his morning erection press against the sensitive flesh of my abused core.

"At this rate, just give me OJ and I'll be ready for more," I whisper, nipping his lips.

"Princess," he rasps as he brushes his fingertips along my arm then cups my cheek. "I don't want to push it."

I smile gently at him. "If this is all I get with you, Kieran... I don't want to wait. Soon I'll have to go back. Back to that cell, the abuse, and the fear." His brow gently pulls together as he surveys my face with pained concern. "I know this is a gift. An overshot of unbelievable luck, my wildest, most extraordinary wish come true," I whisper and I drop my eyes to his chest, playing with the sparse copper hair there. "But the balance is coming and when the pendulum swings the other way, I need to be ready."

"We," he says, running his thumb over my lip.

...Mine... His voice growls into my skull.

I smile warmly at him, and he pulls me to his mouth and kisses me softly. The ache between my legs dissipates as the slickness begins to build.

"Are you hungry?" He asks.

"I'm always hungry," I respond and his lips stretch into one of his smiles that makes my heart stutter out of rhythm.

"Good. I'll make you a breakfast worthy of this swing of the pendulum," He chuckles and sits up, pulling a T-shirt on and a pair of gray sweatpants from the floor and yanking them up over his hips.

"Whatever happened to the 'no pants' rule?" I say as I stretch out my arms overhead and he laughs as he makes his way to the bathroom and brings me a glass of water. Only just now realizing how thirsty I am, I drink it down in three swallows.

"Do you drink everything like you've been trapped in a desert for days?"

I arc a brow at him, smiling playfully.

He sucks his teeth and says, "Noted." I hand him back the glass as he walks out of the room and heads into the kitchen.

I sit up on the side of the bed and stand. I had pulled on one of his T-shirts before I fell asleep last night and it looks like a dress on me as I make my way to the toilet. After I finish, I head to the sink and smell something odd while I'm washing my hands. Cloyingly sweet, like syrup, or opium. It's faint, but it's like walking through exhaled smoke, earthy and unmistakable in its presence. I follow the smell to the drawer closest to the counter. I slide it open and find a small pharmacy bottle full of pills. The smell is overwhelming as I open it. These had to be the random sweet smell I recognized from Kieran before. I pull up my steel walls, willing the fortification and strength of those walls to keep my thoughts behind them.

But it isn't enough.

I feel him...constantly. His train of thought is like radio static in the background, his emotions like breath in my lungs...which would only really mean one thing.

But it's impossible.

He's human.

At least, mostly human. Most humans I know don't have glowing yellow eyes or impossibly sharp teeth, or abnormally robust strength that rivals other astrals. Maybe these pills are what gives him the edge? Maybe they make him more than human?

"Everything okay?"

I jump out of my skin. "Shit!" I yell and drop the bottle of pills on the counter. Kieran is leaning against the doorframe of the bathroom. "How...is it that you're six foot forever and are somehow still that sneaky?"

He smiles mischievously and waggles his eyebrows. "What did you find there, Snoopy?"

"I...am not...okay maybe I am snooping a little bit, but these?" I say picking up the bottle of pills and holding them up. "I recognized this smell from when I first met you."

His smile falters a bit as his eyes flick to the bottle of pills. "Huh. I didn't know you could smell it."

I shrug. "Maybe I'm just weird," I say passively. "Or something."

He rests his head on the door frame, his gaze steady on me as I place the pills back in the drawer.

"You aren't keeping anything from me, are you?"

"I am keeping *a lot* of things from you Rhiannon," he says baldly. "But it's not because I want to hide it from you. I would tell you everything if I could, but the secrets I have...they aren't safe for you to know."

I meet his eyes, imploring and achingly beautiful. At least he wasn't denying that he had secrets. I have them too, so I can't be too angry with him for that.

"Are these pills a part of those secrets?" I ask. He nods gently. "What can you tell me then Kieran? What can I know about...about my-my-,"

"Mate?" He finishes for me, and I balk back.

I shake my head and scoff inappropriately. "No that-that's not possible. Astrals and humans don't mate."

"On the contrary I think they do," he says as he crosses his arms over his chest.

"They do not," I counter defiantly. "It doesn't happen. It will never happen."

He clicks his tongue and nods. He begins walking forward and crowds into my space. I hold my ground as I stare up at his eyes.

"Close your eyes, Rhiannon."

"Why?" I argue and he dips his face low, brushing his lips over mine and my resolve bends.

"Please?"

"You're fighting dirty," I say and he closes his eyes instead.

"Nina." His voice is different, it's still sultry and low, but it's that otherworldly quality to it that has me shuddering. Nina immediately rears up, her fire flaring through my limbs and my chest glows as the scales clack forward and my back aches where my wings beg to spring free.

She slithers forward, hissing as she says, "My wild hearted male." My eyes grow wide as I realize what he's doing.

He can call my dragon.

He can summon Nina.

Only I can do that. Only me and…and…

"Your mate," he finishes my thought, and my eyes snap up to him.

"N-no," I say as the fire in my limbs cools and Nina coils back down my spine. Huffing in frustration. "There would be a mark. If we were mates there would be a mating mark a-and-"

Before I can finish, Kieran turns to his left side and lifts his shirt. A long black dragon with sweeping black wings soars over the ladder of his ribs with its snout chasing after a round bright moon.

"Didn't have this yesterday," he states pragmatically and I blanch, but he wasn't done. "Have you seen your chest?"

My eyes blow wide because no. No, I haven't.

I stretched out the crew neck of his undershirt and there, at the center of my chest, is a full moon and the black nose of a dragon just underneath it. Its leathery black wings splayed wide under my breasts.

I swallow hard and breath, "N-no. No that's not-"

His head tilts to the side as he says, "Why not?"

"Because-" my chin quivers and I push past him and walk over to the bed, balling my fists.

"I don't understand," he replies, his voice low.

"Because I will live for hundreds...thousands of years. Tell me Kieran," I say as I turn to face him. "How long is the average human lifespan? Eight maybe nine decades? Ten if they have good genes?"

He drops his head to look at the floor as he slides his hands into the pockets of his sweats.

"Rhiannon."

"And I've already missed at least three decades of your life so far, so I get to have twenty or thirty more of your prime before you begin to wither."

His face tightens, his jaw flexing as his eyes slide up to meet mine.

"And if it's true, Kieran, if you are my mate, I would gladly see you to the bitter end. Relish every single day that I get with you. But you have to understand how losing you in a few fleeting years would ruin me. I would be a shell, a husk, a pale specter of what I once was when you were alive."

"I'm not going anywhere, Rhiannon. I'm right here."

"For now," I say with finality, and I didn't realize I had started crying, but the tears unshed from my eyes flow freely, dripping off my chin. The weight of it sits heavy on my chest as realization cracks my ribs.

My time with him is limited.

"So...so I will accept it. I accept the bond because it is-" I take an unsteady breath as I try to find my strength, but I feel Nina chitter in my chest, the sensation tearing me apart the more I let the reality of it sink in. "-a fucking miracle. But I can't help thinking about how I only get you for...for-"

He takes me in his arms and holds me to his chest, kisses the top of my head as I begin to sob.

"Rhiannon," he whispers as he breathes deeply into my hair. "Rhiannon I-"

"I know. I'm sorry. I'm just...selfish."

"No, Rhiannon I..." He kisses my cheeks and then finds my mouth, pressing his full lips into mine, now wet with tears. He walks me back to the bed and I crawl back letting him move over top of me. He kisses me deeply now, pulling whimpers from my mouth with each swipe of his tongue. I open my legs and let him press his body close to mine, I scoot back farther on the bed, and he follows me as I pull the T-shirt off.

I flip our position and straddle his hips. I grind my still aching core against his growing erection in his sweats. He inches them down as he lays flat on his back, and swipes his big, callused hands over my thighs, hooking his thumbs in the crest of my hips as I rub my wet core against his thick shaft.

I grasp his cock in my hand and center myself over his tip and begin to inch myself down. The pinch is less this time as I slide down, my head lolling back as he groans.

When I'm completely seated, his fingers flex to squeeze my skin and I begin to move, rolling my hips, feeling that delicious slide of his cock rocketing pleasure up my back. I begin to move faster, bouncing on his dick as he sits up to kiss the dragon too between my breasts and I hold his head to me as I continue to move.

He laves over each of my nipples as the pleasure builds, and Nina begins to rise again, snarling and snapping her way to the surface as I near that edge.

"Let me see her," he growls, and I open my eyes to see the golden glow has returned. "Nina," he growls as I lean over the precipice, the pressure and fire building in my hips as she rises to meet our lover.

Our mate.

"My...Wild Heart," Nina hisses as the orange glow flares in my chest, the sulfur and flame wisps from my teeth and the black and red scales slip from my skin. My back aches as my wings begin to unfurl. Sharp talons gleam gold with bony prominences as they spread wide. My hands grip his hair as my orgasm rises.

"K-Kieran," I whimper. "I-"

He says something in the old language in that dark mysterious voice that makes my toes curl. Nina roars loudly and I fly off the edge.

"Our mate. Our mate," Nina roars as my body contracts and falls apart in his arms. "Mate."

He growls low and grazes his teeth over my neck as he pulses and spills into me.

"My Rhiannon. My Nina." His voice rasps as I milk every drop from him, my wings folding around us in an oil slick obsidian and gold embrace.

"Kieran," I pant as I cup his face in my hands. "W-what was it that you said? In the old language?"

He exhales and opens his eyes, the flash of gold still shining in his bright turquoise eyes.

"I said," he whispers and wraps his arms around me, pulling me closer to him. "I love you."

31
KIERAN

Growing up, my mother loved to watch romance movies. She wouldn't let me stay while they were on, but I'd sit in the doorway and watch through the crack of the door anyway.

I never really understood the hype. It was always the same premise: two people fall in love during some varying degree of unique circumstances; they fall apart and eventually find their way back together again. It was predictable, but most of all, it was unbelievable.

No one behaved like that in real life. Not even my parents that I knew loved each other more than anything. Maybe it was the drama of it all. The poignant longing and insatiable lust between the two people that was so addictive. Perhaps it was the idea of having a love that would surpass notions of permanence that made it so desirable, knowing that no matter what, the love you share with someone else would be everlasting.

I've always thought it was bullshit.

But now…as I look down at my watch for the eightieth time in the last fifteen minutes, my legs bouncing beneath my desk, my fingers fidgeting with the only pen I haven't broken yet out of sheer stir-crazy anticipation, I realize I've fallen into the drama of those movies more perfectly than I care to admit.

I suppose the saving grace of this whirlwind romantic interlude with Rhiannon is that it is far from perfect.

It's messy and chaotic. We have secrets that we can't share out of fear for the other. We're both shrouded in shadows that could very well be what drives us apart but for now…

For now.

My entire being is addicted. Waiting with ravenous impatience every minute of my shift to run back to my apartment and take her to bed. Or on my couch, the dining room table, the kitchen island, or against any of the walls. My entire place is smeared with our collective sweat. If I was in my right mind, I would probably be grossed out.

Yet all I can think about is my next fix...

And I need it soon.

...Almost done?...

Then she does that. Her luscious voice constantly skating across my brain to tease my senses to attention. She bulldozed my focus before but now nothing else seems to really matter and it's as terrifying as it is compelling.

Five minutes, Princess.

She whines. *Whines* like a puppy over our mental connection and my cock strains in my pants. I adjust myself as the second hand of my watch seems to slow and my legs bounce harder.

...I need you, Kieran. I can't take it anymore...

I grit my teeth as the minute hand drags lazily to the next. I can almost hear time laughing in my face.

...Do you know how unsatisfying it is to use my hands now? They feel nothing like yours...

Gods. Fucking. Dammit. The secondhand crawls even more slowly to the next mark.

...Or your tongue. Gods your tongue, Kieran. I'm thinking about it right now as I fuck my fingers...

My dick is painfully hard now, standing at full attention. I don't know how I'm going to walk out of here without the entire office seeing how fucking turned on I am.

I growl her name over our mental connection as I clench my fingers into a fist.

...Oh Gods, yes do that again. Fuck, I'm so close Kieran...

Don't you fucking dare get yourself off before I get home, Princess.

...I've gotten myself off at least ten times since you left for work...

I sigh in exasperated frustration. I am going to tear her apart as soon as I walk through the front door of my apartment. That is to say if I don't keel over from torturously painful arousal first.

...Kieran... She whimpers and I look down at my watch just as the

minute hand slides to 5:00 pm and I'm already up and walking out the door of my office.

"Major Haley!" A kind but aristocratic voice calls from behind me as I call the elevator.

Fuck, what now?

"Sorry to bother, but I just wanted to ask how your cousin is doing?"

Now? At five? "Better." I lie. *I don't fucking care, Kev just let me go home.*

"Wonderful news. My mother underwent the same type of surgery last year and it was a tough turn around. But I'm glad your cousin is doing better."

Ugh. "I'll be sure to send her your well wishes."

"Absolutely. And if you need anything, let me know."

"Sure thing. Thanks, Kev," I say smiling, all while keeping most of my back to him, which I know probably looks psychotic, but I wasn't about to reveal my driving predicament. The elevator door dings, and I walk through as he waves goodbye.

The rest of my power walk home is a blur as I round the corner to the Northeast arm of guards' quarters and jog the last few steps as I near my apartment. I open the door and there she is, standing ten feet from the door…wearing absolutely nothing.

The door shuts behind me and all is still apart from the riot of lust that rages between her and I.

Her eyes are already glowing red, the black and red scales peppering her flesh, and those silky opalescent black wings with bright shining gold bones…*fuck*. I start unbuttoning my shirt and belt as her wings completely unfurl, blocking out the waning sunlight in an ominous shadow.

"Wild Heart," Nina hisses through Rhiannon's lush, parted mouth.

I don't know what it is about hearing them both, but it opens a chasm so deep within me, ancient, wild and forbidden. It takes over with such unwavering force that every cell of my body answers like an autonomic nerve response. Even if I had a choice, I would choose this. Every time. Until I die.

She flaps her wings and she's airborne, her feet only a foot or so off the floor, the wind they create displaces my hair as I peel off my pants. I run for her, and she cants back, her wings beating harder as she gains altitude, but I catch her calf and yank her down.

She laughs but doesn't fight as I pull her body closer and push her naked body against the windows, her wings splaying behind her as her ass presses up against the glass. Her legs vise around my waist and she weaves her fingers through my hair.

"Tell me, Princess," I breathe in her ear as I pull her hips down, the head of my cock seated at her entrance and she squirms, letting her head drop back onto the window as she sighs. "What were you thinking about while you made yourself cum ten times today." My fingers bruise her skin as I clutch the bony crests of her hips and push her down, sheathing my cock inch by inch inside of her tight warm cunt.

Her fingers flex in my hair, gripping it tight as she squeezes her eyes shut, rolling her hips in eager anticipation. "I-I thought of-" She pants as more of me impales her. "Oh Gods, Kieran." She yells as I press her all the way down to meet my hips. She locks her ankles around my waist as I grip the mound of her ass, retract and then push all the way back in.

Fuck. It's everything. Everything. All my strength goes into not pounding into her.

"You. I thought of you," she sighs as she tightens and squeezes her thighs.

"I think you can do better than that," I growl as I peel her away from the window and lay her on the dining room table. Her chest begins to glow sunset orange and flames flicker from her teeth as she props herself up on her elbows.

"Does my mate like dirty talk?"

I grab her jaw and bite her lips. "I *love* your filthy, smart-ass mouth."

She moans as I slide back into her and then her dirty mouth begins speaking.

"I thought about how wet you make me. How good your tongue feels between my legs."

I drag my teeth along her neck, right over the soft heady spaces that make me dizzy where her scent lingers. "Keep going," I mutter against her skin as I continue to move, my thrusts slow and steady.

"I got myself off thinking about your tongue and your fingers inside me," she whimpers as she bucks her hips up to meet the snap of mine.

"B-but it's your cock that's ruined me," she continues, her panting becoming frantic as her walls begin to flutter as she nears her climax. "I came the hardest...when I th-thought about being...f-fucked by your massive dick."

Her back arches as she screams, and her cunt seizes my cock tight. I'm in an all-out frenzy as I fuck her through her orgasm, mine a breath away as the pressure mounts in my balls and I groan as I finally explode, following her over into the abyss.

"When?" She asks softly.

I sigh as I pull her in closer to my chest.

"In a few hours," I reply against the skin of her shoulder.

She's quiet as I feel her heart beating in a slow and steady rhythm. It's soothing. Something I've grown to cherish in the few days that she's been here. Feeling her breath and her body shift closer as she sleeps. Hearing the low hum of Nina's purr as I touch her bare skin.

We both knew that her returning to her cell was coming.

I knew that it was going to be hard.

However, there were variables that I didn't account for that make this entire thing way more challenging. Which vastly understates the magnitude of how desperately I do not want her to leave.

"How are we going to do this now, Kieran?"

I exhale a breath I didn't realize I was holding, and it ruffles her wild, curly hair. Another thing I've grown incredibly fond of is her riotous mess of curls that seem to mimic her personality. Untethered, unyielding, tenacious, and devastatingly beautiful.

"It's only for a little while longer. And then when you, Eilidh and Xanth are out, we can go somewhere and just...be."

How being together will even be possible is yet to be seen, entirely dependent on what will manifest once Cain is finally taken care of, but if everything works out the way I'm planning, this will *not* be the last time she and I get to have time like this.

She turns to face me, her cerulean-blue eyes glowing bright as they flick back and forth between mine. "What about my family?" She shifts a little more, pulling herself up to be at eye level with me. "What about *your* family?"

More unaccounted-for variables. More locked away shadows that cannot be revealed. Not yet. *Not yet.*

71, 89, 8, 90, 82. Calm.

Her brow pinches and I realize that the ice wall may be Rhiannon proof now and I squeeze my eyes shut, fortifying the parts of my memories that cannot come to light.

"Why do you say those numbers?"

"They calm me down."

"What do they-"

I can't tell you.

She blinks and sits up.

"Kieran," she begins, wrapping her arms around her knees. I sit up next to her and even though she's much more petite than I am, her overall essence takes up significantly more space and I want to bask in it like the summer sun. "I don't want to pry. Your secrets are yours but as your *mate?* I feel like I don't even truly know you. I know absolutely nothing aside from your job and that you have a brother."

I hate that she's right. But it's too soon, and all I can do is shake my head. She folds her legs and places her hands in her lap.

...Implicit trust comes with-...

-explicit communication, I know. I finish for her.

"I want to trust you."

"But you can't?"

"I do...mostly."

I nod and decide to pivot. "I gave Eilidh an update a few days ago. She knows you're safe."

"Thank you," she says, taking a deep breath. "I feel bad she's been stuck down there while I've been having the time of my life up here."

"I think she'd rather not be privy to our ongoing activities."

She bobs her head and smirks. "Yeah, I think that would gross her out a bit. But then again, she does like to surprise me."

I laugh and the color rises to her cheeks. I run my index finger down her face, and she looks at me. Godsdamn, her eyes could kill me if they wanted to.

"I wish she could see this though." Rhiannon gestures to the sliver of sunlight that crests the water in the distance. "Feel the sun. She needs it so desperately."

I chew my lip and then say, "I'll make sure she gets to the sun, Princess. I promise."

"What if the plan doesn't work?"

I turn to face her. "It's going to work."

"But-"

"Rhiannon, I can't tell you everything. But this plan? I know in my gut that it's going to work. I'm sorry that I can't give you much more than that, but I-"

"Yes, yes, I can trust you," she sighs and gets up, peeling one of my T-shirts off her naked body and I absolutely *hate* that.

"Rhiannon," I call to her as she passes through the doorway into the kitchen. She slows and turns her face in profile to me. "I love you."

She twists to look at me, the corners of her mouth gently curved in a playful smile that doesn't touch her eyes. "I know you do, Major Hot Stuff."

It's the middle of the night when I wheel her back to the 3rd floor block with the manacles and halter back in place. She braided her hair back and I already can't stand it. She's back in her black jumpsuit and shrouded in a blanket.

I made sure to bring her back during the change of guard shift so that the others would be preoccupied while I said goodbye for now and there wouldn't be any questions.

When we reach her cell, Eilidh is already waiting at the door. Her eyes look dull and swollen, the dark purple swipes beneath her eyes are a familiar mark of the nights she's invariably tossed and turned in worry and a pang of guilt wrenches through my gut.

I refuse to let it last. These past few days were a gift I won't soon forget.

The other dragon, Xanth, is also at his door gripping the bars like he would rip them from the frame again, given the chance. His face is drawn with worry and anger and that pang rips through me once again.

"Rhi?" He rasps, reaching for her and she takes his hand. "You alright?"

Rhiannon looks up at him and nods. Her attention moves to Eilidh and tears well before they fall from her friend's dark golden eyes.

I unlock the manacles but leave the halter on. "I have to…until-"

…*I understand*… Rhiannon's voice whispers across my mind as her eyes meet mine briefly. I open the cell door and Rhiannon steps through to Eilidh's waiting embrace. Eilidh clutches her head and kisses the side of her face over the stupid halter.

"Did ye hurt 'er?" Xanth growls from the neighboring cell. My eyes slide to meet his and my lips curl in a sneer.

"She's my mate you fucking asshole." The whisper is low and venomous, received like a slap to the face as the blue dragon male stares at me in wide eyed bewilderment.

"Are ye fuckin' serious, Rhi?"

I scoff and shake my head. Rhiannon looks back at me as Eilidh releases her from her embrace, staring daggers at me.

I'll be back.

Rhiannon nods at me but her eyes look distant, and I hate it.

I hate this.

I grip the bars to her cell.

"Rhiannon."

"Thank you for bringing me back, Major Haley," she says and walks back to her bunk to sit. Eilidh is watching me from the corner, her eyes shadowed.

"Why does she smell different?"

"She smells like that because they-"

"SHUT...the fuck up 2459," I bark and Xanth seethes as he white knuckles the bars.

Eilidh's chin lifts as she surveys me closely. She leans into the bars and rests her head between the gaps.

"It's true then?" She whispers so quietly that it's barely heard over the snores of the other inmates and the constant drips of water along the block.

I dip my chin to her, and she sniffs.

"Good," she says shortly.

"And why's that?" I ask quietly.

She tilts her head and smiles softly. "Because now I know you have something to lose."

> Her: Santa has taken to the skies.

I read the text message two more times before I send back a reply.

> Me: Is there rough weather over the mountains?

Her response is immediate.

> Her: Clear skies and no wind. Perfect for flying.

I relax into my seat.

> Me: See you at New Years.

I wipe the phone and break it in half. I put on my running clothes and head to the track to wait out the final moments before all hell breaks loose.

32
BALOR

"Indeed, Warden. The president and I are very impressed with your method of cleaning up the Mute vermin and we would love a tour of your facilities. I've already got my assistant working on media contacts for full coverage of our visit." Her velveteen voice purrs in my ear, and I wipe the sweat from my brow.

"Y-yes, Vice President Arden. It'd be an honor to have ya– I mean, to host ya and the President in our facility." I suck in the barrel of my belly and flick my gaze to the sapphire men's bone corset hanging in my armoire.

I'll need te dress for the occasion.

"Wonderful!" She chirps, and I nearly blow the load I've been sitting on for the duration of this phone call. "We have a press conference tomorrow morning and after President Montgomery finishes his speech we will fly out. I can't wait to use the newly installed helicopter pad."

"I'll be sure to make myself available to escort ya from the landing pads, m'lady." I unzip the front of my pants and fist my aching cock.

"It's been a pleasure, Warden. We will see you tomorrow." The phone line goes dead, and I tug, hard, on my erection.

"No, m'lady, the pleasure is all mine," I say to the empty room before spilling out onto the photo I have of her perfect, pouty red lips.

"Sir." Ryker stands in the doorway, saluting with the wrong fucking arm because he lost his right one to one of the filthy Mutes in the Breather Block.

Fucking idiot only thinks with his dick, now he has to yank his cock with his left arm like a sad stranger.

"The fuck d'ya want, Ryker?" I palm my gel and slick my hair back into place. One more hour of this shit before I can go back to my room and prepare for Annalise's visit tomorrow. I should probably tell Halsey we're expecting company, but I don't want the dim-witted fuck to be anywhere near her when she arrives. I'll already have to find a way to get President Mech-gomery out of the way for a while so I can confess my feelings for her. I don't want another asshole to have to deal with.

"Evening reports for the Breather Block, Sir. No major events occurred during dayshift. One shank found beneath a mattress was confiscated, and the inmate is now in SolCon where he'll rot for the next week."

Dear fuck do I have to do everything around this place?

"Solitary confinement isn't enough. Send 'em' to floor one."

Ryker smirks. "Yes, Sir."

But instead of going off and taking care of it, he stands there gawking at me like an idiot. "Now, Ryker?" I tap my pen against the oak desk.

"Sir?"

Irritation flashes hot in my blood. "Get the FUCK OUTTA MY OFFICE." I bellow and Ryker does an about face before hustling out the door.

Finally, peace and quiet.

A ding sounds from my computer, alerting me of a new email.

I tab over to my inbox. It's likely travel arrangements from Annalise's assistant for tomorrow's visit so I don't think twice as I click on the new email from a private sender and open the attachment.

Annalise Arden stands in a skin-tight red business suit and nude pumps in front of the camera. Her face isn't showing but I recognize the outfit and her perfect tight body immediately. This was the day she swore into office. I watched the replays of that speech she gave at least twenty times and came a dozen more to the way her breasts pushed together when she raised her arm and repeated her oath.

"I want you to take your clothes off and show me how much of a slut you are for me." A male voice comes from behind the camera and a roaring starts in my ears.

"I like how your dick feels in my mouth," Annalise purrs.

The roaring in my ears grows but it doesn't stop my cock from stiffening as I watch the woman who stars in all of my fantasies peel the suit from her body and toss it on the floor like it didn't cost two times my monthly pay. Her black lace bra and matching panties are on display and my rage fuses with lust as she continues.

"I like feeling your cum on my face, and when it drips down my legs while I'm shopping for groceries." She unhooks her bra, her perky tits bouncing at their release. Next, she drops her panties and my pants tent while a reddening madness crawls up my neck and face.

"I like tasting myself on your tongue after you've fucked me with it." She reaches for one of her heels but the man on the other side of the camera stops her.

"No. Leave those on. Bend over the desk, Vice President." He bends her over a large desk, the presidential desk, and her gorgeous face comes into view along with the perfect angle to see her tits bounce as he slaps her heart shaped ass.

My cock jerks and cum slides down the front of my leg. I tighten my fists and slam them both on my desk, splitting a crack down the center.

President Montgomery leans down behind Annalise and licks the cunt I've wanted to taste for years. He bites down on the ass that's held my attention like a moth drawn to a flame.

"NO!" I holler to the empty room. I yell at the recording as though it'll stop what I'm seeing from happening.

I slide open the hidden compartment of my desk and finger the pistol I have sitting there beside an image of the President.

"Tell me how much you want my cock, Vice President," the prick asks.

"Please, I want your cock." She presses her ass back towards him with want and something in my chest fissures.

She begs him. The sound of her pleading sending me right over the edge of sanity.

The boredom lacing his voice has me gritting my teeth. "Well, since you ask so sweetly, how can I resist?" His pants drop to the floor and then he's inside of her.

I watch as the love of my life is railed into the desk of the president and my good eye starts to twitch.

Once.

Twice.

My fingers dig into my desk at the same time as Annalise's do and I let out a guttural scream as she comes all over the president's metal enhanced dick.

All I see is red.

33
XANTH

"Today's top story: The Presidential Address. Happening in mere moments, we've got Carol on scene reporting live." The newscast host with a plastic smile and dead eyes looks into the camera and presses a finger to his ear. "Carol? How are things going over there at the capitol?"

The screen switches to a woman in a blue blazer and bouncing blonde curls.

"Thanks, Richard! We've got an excellent view here in the front row to witness President Montgomery deliver his address. He's expected to discuss the rise in Rebellion attacks as well as provide an update on our deployed troops that have been fighting to expand our borders by neutralizing Mute communities. All of Altas will be watching this morning, Richard."

My fist tightens around my fork, still piled with a bite of eggs.

Fucking 'Mute communities'? Those are our lands. Our homes. Gods-damn human pieces of shit.

Ryu and Tatsu are sitting on either side of me, picking at the over-cooked breakfast. The chow hall is fairly quiet today. Everyone has an open ear to the TV as reports of Rebellion attacks in Prism have become more frequent lately. Just last night, a group of assumed Rebels broke into a human government officials home, shot them, and strung them from the rafters for relatives to find later. It is brutal and violent, but I've never been one for sympathy.

Good riddance.

The screen pans back to the man in the news station studio. "We're all waiting with bated breath, Carol."

A hush stretches over the crowd outside the capital.

In a whispered tone, Carol talks into the camera. "Here he is, viewers, President Luthor Montgomery, son of the late President Mavin Montgomery, and grandson of the founder of our proud country himself, Altas Montgomery."

I grind my teeth.

He did not find this land. Astrals were here for thousands of years before the human vermin invaded. This is Elysia. Not Altas.

The camera pans to the president, a tall, sharply dressed man with alligator skin shoes and an Armani suit. His watch likely costs more than the entirety of a low-income citizen's annual salary. The metal accents of his neck enhancement gleam in the morning sun. His patented red tinted glasses cover his eyes, and his slicked back white hair reflects the flash of hundreds of cameras.

A woman, Vice President Arden, climbs the short steps behind him and stands to the side as he takes the podium. Her cherry red lips pop against her cropped black hair, all black suit with a knee length pencil skirt and shining black Louboutin's.

The microphone blares feedback into the crowd and the staff standing near the stage cringe back.

"Good morning, People of Altas," he starts. "I know you've all come with questions that I intend to hear and answer, but first, I'd like to start by saying thank you–" He turns and gestures for the Vice President to join him. "Vice President Annalise Arden, has been working tireless hours to launch the next phase of our sterilization campaign and deserves a round of applause."

The crowd applauds and the President's hand slips behind Annalise, swiping over her low back before he pulls her in close to his side. Her lips are only a breath away from his.

"Such an inspiration," he whispers to her but the microphone on his lapel broadcasts the private moment to everyone in the crowd and all that listen in at home.

He drops his face down to her neck and her cheeks flush, but he only grazes her with his nose before releasing her and she takes a few unsteady steps back from him.

Luthor clears his throat. "Now, as I was–"

A shot goes off.

For a fraction of a second, the crowd is silent. As if the world is shocked into silence as to what happened for all to see. Every being in the chow hall stops as well. No loud clatter of dishes or low mumbling chatter. Everything is completely still.

A trickle of blood drips in a steady stream from the center of the President's forehead.

One beat.

Then two.

Annalise Arden screams a blood curdling shriek as Luthor Montgomery slumps against the podium, dead. Blood flows down the front over the Crest of Altas, like an omen.

No one moves as the camera pans to a burly man standing with a golden pistol still held aloft, wisps of smoke still streaming from the barrel.

He's breathing heavily through the live feed and when he drops his weapon, my eyes nearly bulge from my head as I realize who he is. One hand lifts to slick back his hair and the other slides into his pocket to pull out a metallic blue and silver pill. He drops the pill onto his tongue and swallows.

Venom.

I'd recognize that pill anywhere. I deal it to assassins. Hells, *I've* used it to kill people. Where the fuck did he get his hands on Venom? It's an underground drug that is almost never seen in Prism…

Realization hits me like a tank.

My belongings when I was arrested. I had two pills on me when they confiscated my things. Motherfucker.

The man's eyes roll, one whirring and spinning out of control in a mechanical panic. He falters, his eyes locked on Annalise, and he shouts.

"I loved ya! I've always loved ya. If I can't have ya, neither can he."

The man falls to the ground and another beat passes before three massive bots flood the stage, sending a dozen bullets into the dead man on the floor.

Balor Cain, the Warden of Ironsgate Penitentiary, has just assassinated the President.

Pandemonium broke out in the chow hall the moment the live feed ended, and I was able to slip out of the hall unnoticed.

Eilidh, where are you? I project to her, but I'm met by a wall of white fire. I always do now.

I close my eyes and feel for her. Her heartbeat calls to mine, humming in a rhythm only I can hear, and I follow the tympany of her body into the rec hall where more panic rages. I don't see her immediately, but I can sense her in the riot of inmates fighting to escape now that the Warden is dead. Guards are beating inmates into submission with batons and electric prods.

My eyes frantically dart around the room and then...

There.

She's tucked herself beneath one of the game tables covered with a white cloth.

I run to her, winding my way through astrals and humans all yelling and fighting for dominance. I reach the table and slide beneath the cloth, grabbing her before she can run and pulling her onto my lap.

"Don't. Not yet." I press my body into hers and she squirms. Despite the pandemonium, my body responds to her proximity. Her heady scent floods my system and everything else falls away. "Keep doing that, Little Dove, and we won't be leaving any time soon."

Her body stills and her golden gaze bores into mine. A small line forms between her brows, and I want to kiss it.

"What the fuck are you doing here?" She snaps.

"I told ye, I'll always come fer ye."

Her eyes blow wide, and she shakes her head. "Don't say things like that to me," she whispers.

I smooth out her silver hair that's escaped her braid and press my forehead to hers.

"I'm sorry, Eilidh. I'm sorry fer everything."

Her breath catches and while the mob outside reaches a fever pitch, all I can hear is her heartbeat thumping wildly in her chest.

"D-don't. You don't mean it." She tries to pull away, but I squeeze her tighter.

"I've never apologized fer a godsdamn thing in mah life. I've never felt truly sorry fer a single thing I've done, and I've done mah fair share of fucked up shit, Little Dove, but I'll apologize te ye a thousand times if it means ye'll stay." I swipe a calloused thumb over the dusty pink bow of her bottom lip, and she inhales sharply. "I'll regret that moment in the parts warehouse fer the rest of mah days." I breathe in deeply, allowing her rain kissed scent to pull me under her spell. "There's no one else, Eilidh. There's no one at home fer me other than mah Paps. The woman I loved was mah Mum and she died a long time ago." My chest constricts as I stare up into the eyes of a Phoenix. My sworn enemy that flipped my world on its head with her incredible fire, her big, beautiful eyes and this fucking line between her brows that I know only appears when she's angry, thinking hard or when she's about to come.

My cock twitches at the last thought and she whimpers softly.

Fuck.

I shift to adjust the way my back presses against the table leg, pulling her into my lap further to keep us hidden beneath the linen and her hips roll against my length. My groan mixes with her soft moan.

That's all the encouragement I need.

I grip her face and slam my mouth to hers.

Electric fire tears through my veins. The need to feel her, to have her closer, to *consume* her is unbearable. Like a drug I can't get enough of.

Her tongue swirls around mine and I'm undone. Azure rears his head, and I push him back, fighting my own battle amidst another that rages around us outside the confines of our secret space.

"X-Xanth!" Eilidh shouts when I clamp my teeth down on her neck, making her bleed as she seeks her pleasure through our clothes, grinding and bouncing on my impossibly hard cock.

"Shhh, Little Dove," I whisper to her. "I'll murder anyone who hears the sounds ye make fer me. So, unless ye want te take responsibility fer the lives of every godsdamn astral and human in this room right now, I suggest ye stay quiet fer me."

I pop a button on the lower half of her jumpsuit and slip my hand inside. Moving her underwear to the side, my fingers glide through her slick cunt and I growl.

Her head falls back, and my mouth finds the center of her throat. Sucking and kissing while my fingers thrum against her clit.

"I-I'm going to… X-Xanth… I'm going to…" One hand covers her mouth as a low moan escapes, her fingers digging into my bicep with the other. I glide three fingers inside of her and her mouth drops in a silent scream. The hand over her mouth slides down over her neck and chest, kneading her breast and the sight has me transfixed.

"Good girl," I praise. "Good *fucking* girl."

I swirl my fingers around her clit again, but my Little Dove surprises me. She peppers soft kisses down my neck and chest. Fumbling with the buttons at the bottom of my jumpsuit, she snaps two open and pulls my length free. Her knees tuck under her between my legs and she looks up at me with shining eyes that I wish to drown in. Without a word, her mouth pops open with an audible smack and she sinks down to wrap her perfect fucking lips around the head of my cock.

I hiss as my fingers clench in her hair, and it emboldens her as her tongue runs circles around my tip in the same way she worked my tongue.

"F-fuck-k."

A smile tugs at her lips as her eyes flutter up to look at me, and I grow impossibly harder in her luscious mouth. She looks fucking incredible with my dick between her lips and my inked hands running through her opalescent hair. Her mouth opens wide as her tongue hangs out, but she keeps her eyes on mine as she sinks back down over my length. This time, her bottom lip brushes against each of the piercings that run along the underside of my cock.

It's fucking erotic.

One, two, three piercings in and her cheeks start to fill with me. Four, five, and I can feel the back of her throat work against my head, my chest thundering at the feel of her. Six, seven, and this is where I know a female's limit is. I've never had anyone get further than seven and I move to pull from her lips so she can sink over me again, but her hands grab my hips, and her fingernails dig into my skin.

I hope they leave marks.

Her eyes are still fixed on me, I run my fingers through her hair and stare back at her, panting and waiting for her next move.

Eight.

My fucking heart stops as my brain short-circuits, malfunctioning in a frenzy of pleasure. My vision blurs and I don't dare breathe.

Nine.

Her eyes begin to water, and I can feel her throat constricting around my cock. *So fucking tight.*

She pushes down and her lips touch the base of my dick when I lose all control. An animalistic roar bursts from me as her cheeks hollow, and she sucks me all the way down again. Her head bobs, pulling the soul from my body with her plush lips and I'm squirming. My legs fight for purchase on the floor, my hands push and pull her hair as I fuck her face and she takes all of me, deep in her throat.

My mate. My fucking mate.

I can feel my release building, tightening steadily in my balls but I don't want to. Not yet. I want to stay like this, buried in her throat and moaning like a fledgling forever.

Her hands grip my hips tighter and her tongue reverses, the underside wrapping around my cock and it's too much. The new sensation has me completely unraveled, pumping into her throat as I finally spill into her.

"Fuckin' hells." My voice is raspy and spent. "Where'd ye learn that?" I think for a moment. "Actually, don't tell me. I'll fucking kill whoever taught ye how te do that."

She laughs lightly and the sound is a balm on my aching chest.

"D'nae leave, Eilidh. Please," I beg after the moment has passed, knowing soon we will have to leave the safe haven of this tablecloth.

"You can mark me off your list now." Her eyes grow distant, and I can physically feel her pulling away from me without moving an inch. I grip her wrist but she just stares, pulling away all the same. "You've finally had a piece so you can move on, now that you've fucked me out of your system."

"Who in the hells said I wanted te fuck ye out of mah system?"

"It's what you do, Xanth. You never fuck anyone twice. Now you can leave here without any beds unturned." She slips from beneath the cloth, and I crawl out behind her.

"Eilidh–"

"No, Xanth. The things you've said to me, the things you've done, I can never forgive you." Her eyes turn watery and my heart cracks. "The Warden is dead and we'll be leaving soon. It's over. It's all over." She backs up and a group of dragons fist fighting step in front of us.

I push past them and shove my way through the crowd, needing to get to her, needing to fix this.

But she's already gone.

34
RHIANNON

The prison is in an outright freefall after the televised assassination of President Montgomery. It's not pandemonium due to the outrage of his death, but out of the realization that Warden Cain was the one who fired the shot and then publicly offed himself with Venom right after. Which was supposed to be some grand gesture of love for Annalise Arden.

In my opinion, it was ridiculous and overly grandiose.

Also, Romeo and Juliet want their plot twist back, Balor Cain.

On top of it all, Annalise Arden didn't look too broken up about the Warden's suicide "admission of love" because she was too busy trying to idiotically revive Luthor Montgomery who had been gone the second the bullet went through his skull, which was as sad as it was pathetic.

It was clear that there was something more between the two leaders of the Human Republic, if the way they interacted at the beginning of the Address was any indication. At the very least, they were clearly fucking – as seen in the video I was shown – but watching Annalise scramble fruitlessly trying to put parts of him back together; stuffing bits of his brain matter that scattered on the podium back inside the hole in his skull and apply pressure was just…

Awful.

And pitiful.

But I can't help the burning slice of sympathy that rips through my chest as I watch her scream and struggle, pleading to the human's 'God' who's clearly not listening. I swallow hard against the sudden tightness in my throat.

If the tables were turned, I would be doing the same thing, and the realization makes me nauseous. I would be that woeful mess, trying to find a way to make sense of the sudden events that eviscerated my heart. To beg and plead to Gods that don't care to make it not so.

As far as I know, humans can't have mates. It's not a part of their DNA. They made up their own clever version with "soulmates", a watered-down version of the unyielding love astrals find in their one true mate. It is simply not the same.

A mate is something ancient amongst astrals that is as magical as it is inexplicable. It's one of the strongest bonds that we know of, connecting astrals on such an intrinsic level that it surpasses much of our understanding of the laws of nature. It is undeniably and irrevocably transforming. A symbiosis of both beings' power, strength, healing, and magic that benefits and bolsters both astrals, depending on the strength of their bond which will last the entirety of their lives. Some even purport that the bond transcends time and space, and the pair forever are searching for each other in every lifetime thereafter.

And when a mate dies…

There is no other option for the one doomed to remain.

So, as I watch Annalise shout for help, for someone to save him even though it's utterly pointless, I find myself blinking back tears at the thought of me on my knees, upon a stage, being watched by tens of thousands of onlookers, and how I would be just as doleful and nonsensical. Wild-eyed, irrationally trying to bring him back, while part of my soul is ripped from my body. Torn from me with such abject permanence that coping with it isn't even an option. At least that's how it feels as the pain cleaves my chest in two at the very thought of losing Kieran.

My mate.

And I don't understand it.

He's… impossibly human. At least I think so. I don't know anymore, and he refuses to tell me anything. So, I stand with my arms clenched at my sides by the bathrooms, as I watch the madness unfold around me. Astrals and guards hack and maim each other as Nina scrapes her talons down the inner wall of my ribs to join the fray when Kieran's voice rips through my brain like a warning shot.

...Don't engage. Don't attack the guards. Hide. Go to your cell and stay there...

I scoff each time he blares his warning through my mind and yet I feel my muscles lock, holding me hostage against what I *want* to do.

What I *want* is to fight, let my rage and aggression out on Bruce, Ryker, and Harvey for all the abuse and objectification. I want to tear into them and make them feel what it's like to hurt and feel unequivocally small.

But somehow, it still wouldn't be enough.

...Rhiannon, talk to me...

Nah.

This stupid fucking halter on my face dampens my power but it doesn't silence it. Nina bellows in my mind, her flames flaring in my blood as I decide to still hold agency despite the bond with my mate holding tension like a rope to keep me out of the fight.

When Kieran wants to talk, I'll listen.

But for now...

I may not be able to spit flames in this godsforsaken halter, but the fire courses through my blood, reinforcing my body with Nina's power and I step into the battle to unleash my fury. My scales slip from my skin and my talons sharpen along my nails as I lock my gaze on Bruce, who's using a cattle prod to shock Ryu as Tatsu screams for his brother while being held back by Gunnar. Bruce's gaze is so focused on Ryu's seizing body that he doesn't see me approach and I snatch the cattle prod from him, breaking it in half across my thigh in one swift motion. Bruce's eyes widen in shock as he reaches for his baton. I step into him and dodge the first swing of the weapon. Countering, I swipe my talons across his meaty thigh. Blood sprays from the deep gashes on his leg and he buckles and screams as he falls to the ground.

He rears back and swings his baton again. I'm able to catch it mid strike with my forearm, the vibration sending shockwaves of pain up my arm, but my adrenaline and Nina's fire mutes the sensation as I clasp my hand around Bruce's throat. His eyes widen and his face turns a bright shade of red while he struggles to breathe. He drops the baton and grasps my arm, but I dig my talons into one of his wrists and he chokes on a scream. Nina roars her delight as fire streaks up my spine, the sulfur waning at the back of my throat from the halter.

Bruce's plump face turns purple as I continue to squeeze his neck, constricting his airway so that he sputters and fights for air. His eyes blown wide with terror, he struggles to take a breath.

"Remember this, you insignificant mortal prick," Nina and I purr, pulling his face close to ours, digging our talons into Bruce's other arm so that he can't grab for his throat. "I *am* the death that creeps at your back. Always watching, always waiting."

Bruce's eyes bulge as he gasps, his face shifting into a grotesque mask of mottled purple and blue before he finally goes limp. I throw his heavy slack form to the ground, noting the color returning to his face as he lays, still breathing, on the linoleum. Gunnar still has a hold of Tatsu who's screaming and struggling, trying to reach his brother who's still twitching from the electricity that coursed through his body moments before. My eyes meet Gunnar's pale face, his mouth slack with shock at what he just witnessed.

"Release him or die, little boy," Nina and I growl in unison. Gunnar releases Tatsu who immediately runs to Ryu, clamoring to his knees at his brother's side.

Tatsu shakes Ryu's shoulders and screams his name as I continue to stare at Gunnar who looks like he hasn't decided what to do next.

I decide for him.

"You-" I point at Gunnar who's holding his ground despite the fear that flickers across his bright blue eyes. I lock onto those eyes and find that thread that connects me to his mind. I feel it, sizzling, strong, and bright silver. I grasp hold of it and sink into his consciousness like a dagger piercing flesh. He drops to his knees and his teeth grind as I sink further into his brain. "Where does your allegiance stand, human child?"

"I-I..." He struggles against my hold, but a fleeting thought pulls to the forefront of his mind.

"Show me," I prod. Providing him an opportunity to come to me instead.

"I don't agree with the torture. I don't agree with any of this. I want to be part of the solution, not an accessory to murder and the destruction of an

entire civilization." His jaw flexes and his mouth goes tight as his thought tumbles forward.

"Good boy," I purr. "That makes this easier."

He nods his head as he flexes his jaw, straining against the mental blade I have against his mind.

"Say it out loud." The demand is a hiss that runs through my teeth as Nina and I continue to speak as one. "Say it!"

"I will not harm the astrals," Gunnar grunts, the muscles along his jaw undulating as he yields.

"Such a good boy," Nina and I croon as I retract the blade from his pliant brain, and he breathes as I take his face in my hands.

"Y-you-" Gunnar starts, panting to catch his breath. "-you didn't have to do that. I would have…I would have said it anyway."

I cup his cheek with my hand and trace the tip of my thumb along his cheekbone, bending to line up my gaze with his. "Then help us, Rookie."

I turn away from Gunnar towards Tatsu who's started chest compressions on Ryu. I run over and palpate for Ryu's pulse. It's weak and thready. Gunnar walks over and kneels at Ryu's head, causing Tatsu to bare his teeth at him.

He is not the enemy right now. I project to Tatsu as green scales clack over his skin and a bright green light flares at his chest.

…He held me back while my brother-…

"The continuous electricity from the cattle prod likely kicked his heart into a lethal arrhythmia. We have to shock it back into a normal rhythm or he's gonna die," Gunnar says and both Tatsu and I look at him with varying shades of bewilderment.

"I trained to be a medic." Gunnar shrugged as his left hand prods Ryu's chest like he's searching for something. "There aren't any AED's nearby so…"

Gunnar hauls back his right arm and his fist comes down hard on Ryu's chest, right over the area he prodded moments ago.

"What the fuck are you-" Tatsu roars, his voice shifting to that of his beast as green flames lick from his teeth, but I interject.

"Wait, Tatsu." I grasp his shoulder as Gunnar hauls back again and lands another hard blow to Ryu's chest. Ryu still doesn't move, and panic is starting to creep up my neck. Gunnar clasps both of his fists together, interweaving his fingers before he emits another, more powerful blow to the same spot on Ryu's chest and he jerks into consciousness, his eyes wide as he gasps.

"Ryu!" Tatsu screams as he grasps his brother's face. I look back up to Gunnar who's breathless and sitting back on his knees.

"Get him to the infirmary," I order and Gunnar nods, helping Ryu to his feet by slinging his arm over his shoulder, Tatsu on the other side.

I watch them depart and see that the fighting has expanded from the chow hall, spilling into the corridors. I notice Lumara peeking out from the corner of the hall, avoiding Orsa and Calysta, two female bear shifters squaring off against two of the guards wielding batons and cattle prods. I charge over, Nina roaring in my chest as I continue to hear Kieran's voice echo in my mind to stop.

I don't listen.

I shove one of the guards hard into the wall and he drops his baton. The other hits my side with his weapon and I buckle at the impact. Calysta takes a swipe with her Grizzly claws at the guard, but he parries and shocks her with the cattle prod. She screams and falls to the ground. I grab the baton on the ground and hit the guard attacking Calysta hard across the face. I hit him again with an uppercut to his jaw which forces him back, knocking him into the tables and benches as he hits the ground.

Suddenly, a horrific burning pain sears through my back as I'm hit with a cattle prod from behind. I fall to my knees screaming through a tight jaw as all my muscles lock and my teeth clamp together. My back arches unnaturally as the shock courses through my body.

A resounding pop fills the air and the shock stops abruptly. I'm panting as my limbs involuntarily twitch and look up to see Kieran standing in the entrance of the chow hall holding up a pistol, smoke wisping from the barrel. Calysta and Orsa turn and run out of the chow hall as the two unconscious guards lay motionless on the floor.

Bruce falls to his knees as the cattle prod clatters to the floor, blood leaking from the gaping hole at the top of his head from a single gunshot wound. He falls, his heavy body hitting the floor with a wet splat, dead.

I look over at Lumara, staring wide-eyed as her back remains plastered to the wall. Running footsteps approach, Kieran's proximity like a warm comforting liniment as he nears. His big hands cup my face and his teal eyes lock onto mine, wide and anxious.

"Rhiannon." His voice is shaky and terrified as he says my name. "Are you alright?"

I nod clearing my throat. His thumbs swipe over my cheekbones as his eyes continue to search my face. He looks up to Lumara and barks. "1538, I need you to take this inmate to the infirmary." Lumara swallows wide eyed and nods as she steps forward and places my arm around her shoulder.

Why aren't you-

...Reinforcements are arriving. I have to get this place under control...

You have *to?*

Kieran swallows as I meet his eyes, worry still flickers there as Lumara stands with me on her shoulder.

Come with me...please Kieran.

...I can't...

My brow pinches as the corners of my mouth pull down.

...I'll come and find you soon...

I nod and he cups my face gently, his calloused thumb running over my mouth before he turns and runs out of the exit. Lumara watches our interaction closely and is quiet for a few moments as she begins walking with me, my limbs still trembling with each step. Nina shudders in my gut as we stumble forward.

"So," Lumara begins, and I don't know why I'm glad she's talking. Perhaps so that it can take my mind off the pain in my body and the ache in my chest as my mate runs further away from me.

Why the fuck is he leaving me like this?

"You and Major Haley, the hot redhead with all the secrets, huh?

My gaze slides up to Lumara. "What are you talking about?"

"It's a bit obvious," she scoffs as she continues to support my weight as I falter a few steps. "His scent is *all* over you."

Shit. "He was just touching me, so clearly his scent is going to be-"

"Nice try, but you and I both know that's not the case."

Double shit. "You have a point somewhere here, Lumara?"

She smirks and adjusts my arms around her shoulder. We round the corner to the infirmary which is swarming with varying degrees of injured astrals. Bips are flitting about hurriedly trying to attend to each one. "My *point*," she snarks, "is that you smell like him which means he won't be able to keep covering with the masking pills."

My stomach drops. "The what?"

"Masking pills. The ones he takes to hide what he is."

My insides feel like they fall right out my ass as I stare dumbfounded at Lumara.

"You know what those are, right?" Lumara asks as she stares back at my clearly nonplussed expression.

I am getting a fucking idea. "Care to share?"

Her face is so self-satisfied that I want to slap her, but as it stands, she kind of has me in a bit of a chokehold at the moment.

"Well, it depends on the type of herb he uses, but it masks his scent and his DNA from other beings. He uses it to be human."

"So, you're saying Ki-Major Haley isn't human?"

She chuckles as she shakes her head. "Your boyfriend is so far from human, I'm surprised you haven't picked up on it. I guess the Bane he uses is potent."

"Bane?"

"Do you know anything?" she laughs. "Aren't you friends with a dragon mafia lord?"

Bitch.

She helps me to an open seat since all the gurneys are occupied with wailing astrals.

"Can you just get to the point, Lumara?" I sneer as she unwraps my arm from her shoulder. A Bip wheels up and begins its spiel, but I interrupt to continue my conversation. "Tell me what you know," I say forcefully and she steps back, her mouth pursed. I dial back my force and bank into a level of vulnerability that makes me wildly uncomfortable. "Please."

She crosses her arms, taking another step back. My heart starts to hurry its beat as she nears the door.

"Lumara," I say, the desperation in my voice almost makes me gag.

She places her hand on the doorframe, her eyes still surveying me. She takes a breath and says, "Bane is taken to mask a very old group of astrals that are supposed to be extinct. They are the oldest species apart from the phoenixes and dragons. They're incredibly elusive and most of us thought they were destroyed during The Great Clash. They allied with the phoenixes, and we all know what happened to them."

My heart is practically bruising the inside of my rib cage as it flings itself wildly against my chest, and my skin begins to itch as creeping anticipation prickles along the surface, marching its way up my spine.

"Still no clue?" Lumara quirks a brow and I nearly growl as she continues to dangle the information in front of my face, taunting my ignorance like a cat batting at its prey.

"What...is he, Lumara?" I whisper, my voice low and dangerous, hardly flinching as the Med-bot starts an IV in my arm and connects me to a bag of fluids.

Lumara smiles and looks down the hall before looking back to me. For a fraction of a second, I think she's going to keep it to herself, leaving me breathless and in the dark.

"What's in it for me, Dragon?" She asks darkly, her eyes shining with malice.

Nina growls and chuffs in my chest as my talons threaten to pierce through the tips of my fingers. "How about I let you leave here...*alive*."

Lumara pales and swallows, taking another step back.

Fuck. "Wait. I'll-," *I'll what? What?!* "I'll owe you a...a favor."

She halts her retreat and crosses her arms across her chest, her head tilts to the side as she thinks. "A favor I can call in at any point I want?"

I swallow, suppressing another growl, every cell in my blood screams no, and yet...

"Yes."

Her lips curve into a satisfied smile as she parts her lips and slowly mouths the word without making a sound.

"Werewolf."

TO BE CONTINUED...

ACKNOWLEDGMENTS

Whew! What a wild ride that was.

When we first started story boarding this idea, neither of us could have predicted the twists and turns this story was going to take. The characters began speaking and acting for themselves and the journey they've taken us on has been a beautiful one. Our hope is that you love them just as much as we do! Along the way there have been people who have lifted us up and supported our efforts that we couldn't have done this without.

We'd like to start by thanking our partners. Without their love and support this dream of publishing would not have been possible. Between long nights writing and editing, to the hours long video calls between the two of us as we giggled and pulled our hair through this, D and P have been our biggest cheerleaders. We love you both to the ends of the Earth and beyond.

Next, we'd like to thank Jesse Bell and Brenda Armstrong for their help in making this book what it is today! The two of you took a chance on us and the story we had to tell as new authors and we couldn't be more grateful for the energy and love you poured into this. Not just to read and offer feedback, but truly and unequivocally love the story and are both excited to read more. It has truly buoyed our confidence, and we cherish you both.

And finally, to our readers; THANK YOU for reading Survive! This book has been the catalyst to an incredible friendship between the two of us and every single person who chooses to pick up and read our book is another candle lit in honor of the love and effort we've poured into this series. Thank you, thank you, thank you. We can't wait to see where this journey takes us, and we are so glad that you are along for the ride.

Now get ready…because we've only just begun.

HUNGRY FOR MORE? CHECK OUT OUR WEBSITES AND SIGN UP FOR OUR NEWSLETTERS TO STAY UP TO DATE ON WHAT WE GET UP TO NEXT!

bsteffensbooks.com | lesellsbooks.com

www.ingramcontent.com/pod-product-compliance
Lightning Source LLC
LaVergne TN
LVHW011928070526
838202LV00054B/4534